IONA
A Space Station Olympus
Novel

S. L. Wideman

Other books by the Author:

Space Station Olympus series:
Iona
Kore (coming in 2016)

Non-series books:
Verucca Victorious (coming in 2015)

To my family, who believed in me.

In loving memory of Laurie A. Wideman

PART ONE

Wife of Eros

Preface

By the time the Zyspadaden came to them, humans were about to lose their third Earth. Plagued with war and disease, the planet was being torn apart. Needed minerals had long since vanished and the air burned. The Zyspadaden made an offer to the humans: We will save you in exchange for life. They built a few hundred space stations, all of them long and lean, with many levels that housed cities going on for miles. Unlimited air and water, and an energy supply known only to the Zyspadaden sustained life for eons while the humans searched for a new planet to inhabit.

But Mankind was in disagreement as to how the new colony would be set up. Torn between various religions and ruling ideals, a space station was set aside for the members of each theology. When they left Earth Three, each went their own way. Space Stations *Olympus, Nirvana, Aaru, Shangri-La,* and many others named for the various beliefs they now encapsulated fled among the stars in search of a new planet. The humans settled into their new lives as part of their ship.

Slowly, so slowly no one knows when it first happened, life changed. With no planet found and contact between the various Space stations lost, the culture and life on-board started to change. The human hosts given to the Zyspadaden as payment for the rescue assumed the roles of the gods of their space station. As time passed in endless space, the humans forgot about living on a planet. The Zyspadaden lost their identities and became, body and soul, the deities they pretended to be until neither the humans nor the Zyspadaden could remember not living on a station under the rule of their respective deities.

Chapter 01

When Aphrodite deemed one worthy of her magnificent presence, her visits were always filled with fanfare. Eros felt his blood pressure rise when the door to his private home crashed open and the Goddess of Love and Beauty swept inside. Behind her glided her retinue of the Seasons, Graces, various admirers and servants, followed by a small army of chubby cherubs tossing rose petals on Eros' once pristine marble floors.

Aphrodite embodied her title. Her pale blonde hair always styled in a controlled mess; half up in an elaborate braid and half tumbling down over her ivory shoulders. Her make-up expertly applied to highlight her bedroom eyes and kissable lips. Her sensuous body draped in sheer material that could just barely qualify as a dress, the fabric clinging to her curves in a way that made Eros uncomfortable when he was around his mother.

"To what do I owe this honor?" Eros asked, not looking up from the new dart gun in his hands. He turned the gun over before shaking his head and handing it back to Hephaestus. The grotesque God of the Forge handed him another model.

Aphrodite heaved a great sigh as she threw herself onto a couch. Her body artfully arranged to be seductive and in distress, one dainty hand held limply to her forehead. "Oh, it's awful! My temples are empty and my devotees have abandoned me! I am ruined!"

"You're exaggerating, Mother." Eros clicked the safety off the next gun and took a practice shot, aiming at a board across the room. Once the gold dart struck the target, it vanished from sight. Eros gave a low hum and handed the gun back.

"I am not exaggerating! I've been everywhere on this station; from Cypress to Athens, Sparta to the island levels of Naxos. My coffers are empty." Aphrodite moaned loudly. "I've been replaced by a human!"

Eros sighed, not wanting to put up with his mother's paranoid delusions this day. "Who is it this time, Mother? Some farmer's daughter who got a love letter instead of you? Another devotee of Artemis whom you think has slighted you?" He turned back to Hephaestus, picking up a third gun. "That last one felt too heavy. I need these to be more discreet."

"This new host of yours does have smaller hands," Hephaestus said carefully, his words slightly slurred by his deformed lips. The ugliest of all the gods, his twisted body misshaped from birth. He made it strong from long hours in the forge, creating weapons and trinkets for the other gods. However, nothing Hephaestus did or created could fix his body or heal the twisted leg he kept in a brace.

"Are you two listening to me? My problems are more important than Eros' little dart gun!"

"Of course we're listening, Mother. You think another human has replaced you."

"Not just any human," moaned Aphrodite as the three Graces fanned her. "This is the big one! They are flocking through the levels to just to get a glimpse of her. They ignore me when I walk by, but push each other out of the way if they think she is near. People were throwing jewels to her that should have been meant for me! I'm ruined, Eros! Ruined!"

Eros set the gun on the table and massaged his temples. "This is the same speech you gave about Galata of Athens last month. And of Iris of Corinth the month before that. Not to mention Achlys of Aegae and Dadora of Pagasae. All lovely ladies who gathered a small amount of attention whom you saw as rivals."

"This is different! People are really leaving me this time! They call this one the Aphrodite-in-the-flesh." She peered at him from over the side of the couch. "You have to do something, Eros. Help your dear mother."

"Leave it be," Hephaestus advised before Eros could say anything. "This will all end soon enough. She's a human, Aphrodite. They age and grow fat. No matter what she looks like now, she will wither with time and lose her youth and beauty, unlike you who will remain as lovely as you are now. People will forget her soon enough."

The attendants gasped in horror at his words, and Hephaestus quickly realized his error. Though his words were meant as a compliment, the Goddess of Love and Beauty did not hear it that way. Aphrodite bolted off the couch, glaring at him. "You think she's beautiful!"

Eros backed away from them, leaving Hephaestus to fish himself out of danger. Though he hadn't said that, Aphrodite latched onto one word. When she was in one of her moods, it was best to be extra careful so as to not anger her further.

"Aphrodite, honey, I don't know this girl," Hephaestus stammered, trying to defuse the situation.

"You think she's beautiful! You think she's more beautiful then I! I, the Goddess of Love and Beauty! I, the personification of Desire! No mortal will ever be more beautiful then I!"

Hephaestus shook his head, holding his hands up in a gesture of peace. He was used to her outbursts. "Of course not, darling. I would never think any human could hope to hold a candle to your magnificence. The humans can only dream of how beautiful and special you really are, and never know the truth of the reality."

"It doesn't matter. You called her beautiful." Aphrodite pouted as her attendants shot reproachful glares at Hephaestus. Eros knew that his mother's devotees and faithful attendants felt it was a sin for one as lovely as Aphrodite to be married to one as ugly as Hephaestus. Already predisposition to hate him, there was nothing the God of the Forge could do to make things right.

"Everyone loves her more than me," whimpered Aphrodite. "No one thinks of me. I'm going to wake up some morning and find myself alone and that mortal in my place."

"Never, Lady Aphrodite," simpered one of the Seasons. "No one could ever replace you."

Eros loaded the dart gun, checking to see if it was smooth enough. "She's just a human, Mother. Why not make her one of your attendants? You can replace that one there," he said, pointing randomly at one of the Graces. "Isn't she getting a little long in the tooth?"

The Graces gasped and huddled around their offended sister. Eros knew he just landed next to Hephaestus on their least favorite person list. Not that it mattered to him. A few sweet words and a couple of gifts and he'll be back in their good graces in no time. At the absolute worst, their ire with him would last a week.

"I do not want her!" Aphrodite stamped one dainty foot in anger. "I want her gone! I want her to suffer!"

Eros shook his head and went back to the guns. As he examined one, he heard his mother give a happy little gasp that made his heart turn cold. "Whatever it is, Mother, the answer is no." Eros dared not look up, concentrating on the gun harder than he should. "This human is your problem."

Aphrodite's delicate ivory hands curled around his shoulders. He felt her lean in and swallowed hard as her breasts pressed against his back, her hands playing with his wings. Her sweet perfume made him feel light-headed and, for a moment, he wondered why he was saying no.

"All I want is for you to do what you do best," she whispered. "Just do this one teensy-weensy favor and I'll be just so delighted."

Eros' hands shook as he tried to resist her. This was how she got every other god in Olympus to do what she wanted. It didn't matter that he was her son, he was male, nothing more than a pawn in whatever scheme she was plotting.

"Mother," he started, hearing the weakness in his voice. He cleared his throat and tried again. "Mother, the answer is no."

"You don't know what I need." Her breath tickled his ear.

"Still no," he said shakily.

"It's so simple," she pressed. "All you have to do is go to the Arcadia levels, to the city of Tiryns, and make this trouble-maker pay. One little love dart should do the trick."

"That doesn't sound so bad," Eros said, relenting to his mother's powers. "What's her name?"

"Iona Demarchis of Tiryns. Just look for the largest gathering of the simple-minded morons and you'll find her in the thick of them."

"Well, I suppose," Eros started and then gasped as cold water was thrown on his face. He blinked as if waking from a dream to see Hephaestus placing an empty glass on the table. He pushed the wet locks of his curly brown hair out of his blue eyes.

"My hand slipped," Hephaestus said with a shrug.

Able to think clearly, Eros pulled himself from his mother's grip. "All you want is for me to make this girl fall in love," he asked suspiciously.

"Yes! Just one little itty-bitty dart and she'll fall in love with a man of my choosing; someone lowly and ugly, fitting for an interloper like her."

"That's not how the darts work, and you know it,"

Hephaestus said. He held out his glass to a patiently waiting figure in the shadows. Once his glass was refilled, he continued, "Eros can only cause feelings of love, lust and desire in the target. However, the object of said feelings must be near-by."

"I have a few candidates in mind. I can see to it that they are near by when Eros shoots her."

"Who?"

The goddess smiled. "I will see to it that the most loathsome and foul men are in her path after the dart strikes. It would serve her right to spend the rest of her life shackled in love with some lowly commoner, forced to muck out a living. Her looks will fade and she'll be a haggard crone before she hits thirty!" Aphrodite turned to her husband, her smile becoming sinister. "Or, I could have Eros kidnap her and bring her to your forge before pricking her. You'd like that, husband; a devoted little wife to slave away next to you in that hot forge."

"I'm not going to do it. My darts are not for your amusement. They are for the serious business of love. I can't just go down among the levels every time you get jealous."

"Serious business," Aphrodite scoffed. "Tell that to Apollo! He's still steamed over that whole Daphne affair."

"That…That…" Eros struggled. Saying he was young and it was a dare from Hermes wouldn't help his case.

"Or, how about that little Hyacinths ordeal? I'm sure Zephyrus would love to hear about your involvement in that. Do you think he'll remain your loyal servant when he learns the part you played in his lover's death?"

"You wouldn't," Eros whispered.

"Try me."

Eros looked down at the guns and darts. He didn't want his friend to ever find out his shameful secret. Aphrodite was cruel enough to go to Zephyrus and tell him everything; from the dart that helped Zephyrus find the courage to approach Hyacinths, to the accidental reveal to Apollo, to the jealous homicide. He couldn't risk it.

However, looking over at Hephaestus, Eros found his courage. Zephyrus would understand that Eros meant well, and he was the one shielding him from Apollo's wrath. He couldn't let his mother blackmail him now. If he did, she'd never stop.

"Go ahead," Eros said, standing up straighter. "I'm not helping you."

Aphrodite's triumphant smile faded. At first, she looked angry and Eros started to worry that she'd scream or throw a fit. Suddenly, her mood shifted and she pouted. "You don't love me anymore," she whined, tears glistening in her crystal blue eyes. "You care more about that human harlot than you do your own mother."

"By Zeus, you got her going," Hephaestus moaned as Aphrodite wailed. The Seasons, Graces, and various attendants rallied around her while the chubby cherubs dumped a basket of rose petals on Eros' head in disgust.

Eros glared at Hephaestus, brushing off the petals. "I thought you wanted me to stand up to her."

"My own son has pushed me away," Aphrodite sobbed into the hem of her dress. "I have been stabbed cruelly in the heart! Betrayer! Backstabber! All I have did for him was give him life and love him. I raised him up to be a god, gave him statues in my temples, and how does he repay his own flesh and blood? He stabs me though the heart. Oh! Look how I bleed!" She held out her pristine hands to her attendants before collapsing once more in sobs.

"Mother, really," said Eros helplessly. She could have threatened him, yelled at him or promised him the world and he would have the strength to hold his ground. But tears were his only weakness. He sighed, looking over to Hephaestus, who himself looked ready to surrender.

"Betrayed for a human," wailed Aphrodite. Her shoulders shook as she cried, each watery sob cutting deep into Eros' heart. "Oh, woe is me! I might as well just lay here and waste away. I have nothing left to live for."

"Mother, get up off the floor." Eros sighed, rubbing the bridge of his nose. "Fine, you win. I'll go to Tiryns and use a dart on this girl. Will that make you happy?"

She jumped up, brushing the dirt from her dress. There was no evidence of her sobbing on her beautiful face, leaving Eros to wonder if it was all a ploy. "I'm ecstatic, my son," she said sweetly. She stroked a soft hand over his cheek. "I'll go gather my little army of worthy suitors. You'll have an hour to find Iona Demarchis and shoot her before I release them. Ta-ta!"

With that, the Goddess of Love and Beauty swept from his

home in a whirlwind of perfume and petals. The Seasons, Graces, and attendants swarmed around Eros, each giving him a kiss before they followed their goddess. The cherubs with their ever-present petal-tossing were the last to leave.

"You don't have to do it, you know," Hephaestus said.

"Well, you weren't much help. Besides, it'll keep her out of my hair for a while."

"After centuries of dealing with that woman's mood swings, I've learned to just let her ride it out. She would have run out of steam eventually and probably forgotten all about asking you in a week or two."

Eros shook his head. Hephaestus might be able to escape Aphrodite's wrath, but he was too close to his mother for her to just forget any slight. "I'll take three of this model," he said, holding up one of the dart guns. "First chance you get, of course." He scooped up the gun and a few extra packs of darts.

"First chance I get might be in a while," Hephaestus said, cleaning up the table. "Artemis wants a new bow and Hermes needs some extra cameras for his newest reality show idea. For a messenger god, he certainly likes to branch out beyond the news. Not to mention Hades asked for a special gift for Persephone. It's their anniversary." There was a wistful sound to his voice when he spoke of Hades and Persephone. Though Hades, dread God of the Underworld, was hated and not mentioned by the mortals, his marriage was far better than that of Hephaestus and Aphrodite.

"Really? Hades? Way to go, Father. That is an honor. I didn't think that creepy uncle of mine ever talked to anyone in Olympus."

"You don't have to call me Father. You know you're not really my child."

Eros shrugged. "You're Mother's husband and you've always been there for me, more than Ares has. In fact, you've tried to be there for all of us. You were there when I first opened my eyes. You were the one who held Anteros' hand when his last lover died. Even if some of my brothers cling to that arrogant bastard, I will never acknowledge Ares as my father. You, Hephaestus, are the only father I have."

"Thank you," Hephaestus muttered, ducking his misshapen head. The pride he felt from Eros' words could easily be seen on his ugly features.

"Hopefully, this will be the last time she asks me to abuse my gifts. How many more times can she come crying to me about this or that mortal? I swear, she has a new 'enemy' every week. Surely this station isn't producing so many beauties that the humans can't remember the glory of Aphrodite."

"And if it is?"

Eros laughed. "I'd spend more time down in the levels than up here."

"Your mother is an envious and vain woman. If anyone so much as looks at another woman in her presence, she feels slighted. Or worships another goddess. Let's not forget that whole Hippolat fiasco, and all that poor boy did was worship Artemis. This girl never stood a chance."

"I was afraid of that," Eros said. "What's her name again? All I remember is that she's in the Arcadia region, in Tiryns." His mind still fuzzy from Aphrodite using her powers on him.

"Iona Demarchis of Tiryns. I'm surprised it took Aphrodite this long to come to you. She's been complaining about this girl for nearly a month now."

"Mother must have been out making some other mortal's life miserable," Eros said. He waved good-bye to Hephaestus and turned to leave. On his way out the door, he paused by the lone figure in the shadows. "Clean the place up before I get back. It's a disgrace." Then he left for the PortMat to take him to the populated levels.

Hephaestus finished packing the guns and started to limp to the door. He, too, paused by the figure. With a sad lopsided smile, he said, "It was nice seeing you, Psyche."

"It's always a pleasure to have you in my husband's home."

Chapter 02

The Arcadia region of the populated levels of the Space Station *Olympus* housed the hardiest residents. While Tiryns was a pleasant city level, the capital level of Arcadia was Sparta, and it ruled with an iron fist. The towns and cities paid homage to the warlike culture, supplying the best military academies in the station. Statues of Ares, the patron god, stood at nearly every street and crossroads. At the lifts of the Arcadia levels, engravings of Ares and his warrior children glared out at the travelers.

Inside the city of Tiryns was a section devoted to temples and worship. Eros appeared in the back of Aphrodite's temple, his legs shaky from the PortMat's instantaneous travel. As a god, he was in tune with the whole of Space Station *Olympus* and felt the hum of the engines beneath his feet and the call of mother space just beyond the thin metal layer of the walls. It was always more pronounced after PortMat travel when, for that moment, he is at once in both his human and natural forms. Cautiously, he made his way out to the alley between the temples and entered the city.

Tugging his cloak over his wings, he started his search for Iona Demarchis. It wasn't as hard as he feared. His mother's complaint that the people regarded this woman as Aphrodite-in-the-flesh rang true. All he needed to do was find the crowds and there she was.

Merchants packed the streets; selling locks of the girl's hair, scraps of torn clothing, and relics she may or may not touched were hawked from colorful booths, store fronts, and street corners. Lockets with her picture sold on nearly every corner as good luck charms and bards sang ballads of Lady Iona's beauty and kindness. The people of Tiryns were pleased to have a real goddess walking among them. Billboards around him flashed advertisements selling goods for temple sacrifices, clothes, and something called Nico's Trojan Horse Tours, along with announcements about this new Aphrodite-in-the-Flesh.

The crowd was too thick for Eros to get a clear shot with his dart. He stayed back, following the throng of people. He knew that he'd get to her at the temple if all else failed. No matter what, he planned on finishing this mission before the next day.

"Would you like to buy a locket, young man? It's guaranteed to attract the eye of Lady Iona," one vender said, grabbing Eros' arm. "All the men who bought my lockets have had the pleasure of meeting her."

Skeptical, Eros picked up a locket. "Really," he said, opening the locket. "How does it work?" On one side of the locket was a basic prayer to Aphrodite, and on the other held a simple portrait of Iona Demarchis.

While the vender rattled on about how fortunate his lockets have made various men, Eros stared at the portrait. It was hard to tell anything about her beyond a mountain of frizzy hair.

"Say, buddy, listen," the vender said, "you buy that locket, and I'll give you the temple discount. After all, I'm all about helping out a fellow Cupid."

Eros looked up. "What?"

"Your wings. You must be high up on the devotee list to actually get body modifications. I heard only those allowed to live in the upper levels were allowed to mimic the gods." The vender pointed to the feathery wings on Eros' shoulders poking through his cape.

"Oh, yeah, I've been a devotee all my life."

"What brings you down here? Surely, you must see the beauty of Aphrodite every day."

Eros took a quick look around before leaning in close to the vendor. "I'm here because this Lady Iona has caught favor with Aphrodite," he lied. "I'm sure you know how this goes. The goddess is interested, so we take a look. Just keep it to yourself, okay."

The vendor nodded and winked. "Won't tell a soul," he whispered, but Eros knew the man would tell anyone who'd listen that he met someone from the upper levels. Possibly even tell about his mission, and Eros prayed to whichever member of his family was listening that no one believed the old man. Once Aphrodite's revenge was complete, it would be clear what kind of "favor" she gained from the goddess.

"You know," the old man said, turning from Eros to dig through a desk, "I had the pleasure of meeting the lady Iona." He pulled out a stack of photographs. "Here, see. This is the first time I met her."

Eros took the picture. In it, he saw a trio of young girls. One, the oldest, posed with her arms wide and took up the most room, wearing an eye-gougingly bright pink dress. Directly behind her, in a slightly less bright pink dress, was another girl who mimicked her pose. Behind them stood a girl with red hair in a green dress, gazing shyly at the camera. A tall man stood behind them, one hand possessively on the redhead's little shoulder.

"Which one is she?"

The man pointed to the redhead. "That's the lady Iona. The one in front is her eldest sister, Philomena. She's a celebrated singer now. The one in the middle is Errita. I hear she's made a name for herself as a weaver. About as good as Athena, they say."

"Better not let Athena hear that," Eros muttered. "And, I take it, that's their father in the back?"

"Hmm? Oh, no, that's Kelmis. Poor fellow. He was betrothed to young Iona. She was just three days away from her eighteenth birthday and they could wed, and he drops dead of a heart attack. She goes into mourning and stays away from everyone for nearly two years before we see her again. She must have loved him. Anyway, she used to walk around in all black with a veil. One day, she's out of the mourning gear. Got a picture of that. Much better than the ones I used for the lockets."

He shoved another picture into Eros' hands. This one was much clearer. He felt like laughing. This was the girl that these people believed to be Aphrodite? Her reddish-brown hair frizzed untamed around her heart-shaped face. Her green eyes were too wide and her lips were too thin. She gazed as shyly at the camera then as she had done as a child, too afraid of her own shadow. This was not the confident woman his mother brought to mind. No wonder Aphrodite was furious.

"Tell you what. I'll give you the locket, as a gift. But I need my pictures back."

Eros smiled, handing the photos back to the man. "Thank you. I'll be sure to announce your generosity when I return home."

With a picture of his target, Eros made his way toward the crowd. Still stuck on the fringes, he could only hear the people shouting to Iona Demarchis, calling her by his mother's name.

"Please, Aphrodite, bless my newborn so she may attract a good husband!"

"Aphrodite, I am in love with this man. Make him love me back!"

"Take these flowers as a sign of my devotion to you, Aphrodite!"

As Eros got closer, he could just make out the crowd thrusting babies at the woman in hopes of her blessing them, or trinkets of their affections. It was no wonder that the real Aphrodite was angry. Even if this girl refused, the crowd pushed their favors on her. Soon, her arms filled with jewelry, flowers and silk scarves.

She continued to make her way to Aphrodite's Temple, and Eros wished he just waited there for her. He pushed his way through the crowd, needing to catch up to his target. Once she entered the temple, he could sneak up on her and finish this tasteless business and go back to his simple life.

On the steps of the temple, the crowd stopped as two groups fought over who had the right to escort her inside. Using the moment of confusion, Eros shoved his way closer to his target. He could hear the argument between the gathering devotees of his brothers, the Cupids, and the devotees of Ares.

"We have devoted our lives to emulate those of the Cupids, sons of Aphrodite," declared a man with a lovely set of fake butterfly wings, a devotee to Eros' brother Anteros. "As such, we belong to the temple of Aphrodite, and should be the ones to escort her inside."

"A son is not the same as a lover," a cold voice said from the middle of the burly Ares devotees. Eros felt his heart freeze as he recognized the voice. Phobos, his brother and favored of Ares, stepped out to fight. Ares must be aware of Aphrodite's anger against Iona to send his son, the God of Fear.

Rushing forward, Eros felt the effects of Phobos' presence in the crowd. People murmured, backing away from the two groups that surrounded Iona. Fear pounded in Eros and he knew that he had to get to her before Phobos ruined everything.

Throwing off his cloak, he took his place at Iona's side. Phobos' bright eyes widened before anger clouded them. Phobos, and his twin Deimos, did not get along with the Cupids. The feeling was mutual.

"Seeing as how Lady Iona is entering Aphrodite's temple, we will escort her," Eros said, his eyes locked on Phobos. Of everyone there, it was only his brother he needed to convince to step down. "It's Aphrodite's will, after all."

"It's Ares' will that we escort her inside," Phobos snarled.

"Really, I can walk in on my own," Iona said, shifting the armload of trinkets to keep them from falling. "This isn't necessary."

"Yes, it is," Eros insisted. "Aphrodite herself wants you to receive the treatment of the gods, and that means a full escort. The devotees of her sons will suffice, for they represent love and desire."

"Flowery little prick," Phobos growled. "What she needs is a strong escort to keep undesirables away. This is why Ares, himself, sent me."

"Ares has no authority in Aphrodite's temple," Eros said. "The Cupids will escort her inside."

"Ares has authority in all of Tiryns, and that includes the temples!"

"The steps are just behind me. I can walk up them alone," Iona said. "I've done it before. Really."

Eros leaned close to his brother and whispered, "How do you think Mother will react when she finds out that her perfect plan – that she came to me on – was ruined because of Father?"

"She'll be glad that the little harlot was dealt with. I have the strength to take care of this mess. What are you going to do? Prance through the flowers until she gags?"

"Mother sent me down personally, and I'm not leaving until Iona Demarchis is in love with one of the men of Mother's choosing. If that means shooting you, then so be it."

"You haven't got the guts, brother."

Eros' hand went to his gun. "Want to bet? I'll have you so in love that you'll spend your days picking flowers, playing 'loves me, loves me not' for hours."

Phobos growled as he weighed his options. Eros was close enough to shoot him before he got his own gun out. "Fine, you have today only to keep Mother happy. After that, I'm handling this my way and no little dart will stop me."

"Thank you."

"Don't thank me, Eros. If this blows up in my face, you will be one dead god."

Eros turned back to Iona, smiling triumphantly. His smile slipped as he saw her elbowing her way through the Cupid devotees.

He quickly made his way by her side, stopping her.

"My lady, we will be escorting you this evening," he said gallantly.

She frowned, clearly not impressed. "I can walk in all by myself. I've done it before. What is wrong with you people today?"

"It's Aphrodite's will."

"But I can walk by myself."

Eros repeated in a slower tone, just in case she didn't hear him before. "It's Aphrodite's will."

"Very well," Iona said, dumping the trinkets in Eros' arms. "Let's hurry this up. I have other things I need to do today."

Not worrying about the few trinkets that fell as he walked, Eros followed her inside. The other devotees trailed behind him, smug that they won the battle of wills against the devotees of Ares. Phobos watched them leave, thick beefy arms crossed over his broad chest. When one of the Cupid devotees made some insolent move, Phobos growled and sent the little pansy running.

Eros took one more look out into the crowd and noticed that a small throng of men joined them. This must be the group sent by Aphrodite, for they were the hairiest, filthiest, and most slovonly group of men Eros ever had the misfortune to lay his eyes on. He knew his time was limited and quickly followed Iona. It was time to finish this.

Once inside, a priestess came up to greet them. "Lady Iona, we are so thrilled you have graced us with your presence once more. I took the liberty of preparing a private back room for your prayers, just as you like."

"Thank you," Iona said. She started to the back rooms, and Eros followed her.

"Not you, young man. Only Lady Iona may enter the back room."

"He is carrying my offerings," Iona said.

Eros flexed his wings. "I am of the favored. Do you think that Lady Aphrodite would be angry if a favored of her beloved son entered her sanctuary? I am as much a servant, if not more, than you."

Though the front rooms were where the rich prayed and ceremonies to Aphrodite were performed, some of the people enjoyed private back rooms to escape the everyday lavish displays of worship. The room was spacious with a large, dominating statue of Aphrodite at the back wall. Couches and piles of pillows lined the walls and fountains with mischievous cherubs dotted the room. Incense hung heavy in the air, designed to promote a loving atmosphere.

"I will check back on you later," the priestess said. She eyed Eros and sniffed. "Don't make a mess."

Iona blushed, looking over at Eros, as for the first time. Her too-wide green eyes raked over his body. He smirked, sure that she liked what she saw. What woman wouldn't? He was tall with tan skin pulled over taunt muscles. He was fitting to be the young God of Love.

"That won't be necessary," Iona said, turning away from Eros. "He won't be staying with me."

Eros was stunned by her words. He was the God of Love! The perfect example of manhood and lust, and she just refused him! Not that he'd touch her. She was certainly no prize. Besides her frizzy hair and wide-eyed stare, her hips were too big for her to be a beauty. She would be better suited as some field-born fertility goddess, like Demeter or Flora. Plus, she was at least in her mid-twenties, quickly moving toward old maid status.

Once more, Eros flexed his wings. "I am a high devotee. Why shouldn't I stay?"

"Because I prefer to do my prayers and offerings in private. You'll only bother me." She turned to the priestess. "I will send him out once we have set up these offerings."

"The priestess nodded and started to speak, but a thudding from the front of the temple distracted her. "I will check on that. You," she pointed at Eros, "do not annoy Lady Iona. When she tells you to leave, you do so."

"Yes ma'am," lied Eros.

After the priestess left, Eros dropped the offerings at the base of his mother's statue. He pretended to leave, watching Iona the whole time. She was too busy arranging the offerings to notice that he was still in the room. Hiding behind a pillar, he loaded his gun.

Chapter 03

"Oh, Mighty Aphrodite," Iona implored, her arms spread up to the statue, "look down on this most lowly servant. In your wisdom, you granted me a slimmest taste of your beauty. I beg that you do not look too harshly on those who mistake this humble girl as your gracious vessel."

Eros rolled his eyes. With words like that, how could his mother still think she was a threat? He eased himself around the pillar and aimed the gun. The thudding at the front of the temple continued, and Eros could hear angry voices now in the mix. Aphrodite's suitors were getting restless, and he needed to make sure Iona was pricked before the first one made it this far.

"Accept these offerings, great Aphrodite, and hear the prayers of your servants," Iona continued as Eros aimed for her back.

Eros fired; the dart silently launched from the barrel. It should have been an easy hit, her back clearly in his sights. Just as the dart was about to pierce her skin, she moved to pick up an offering. The dart sailed past her and struck the wall.

He ducked back behind the pillar, hearing her sudden gasp of surprise. Did she see the dart? Did she notice that it vanished? Did it hit her at all? Just a scratch, he prayed. That was all that was needed. Just one tiny scratch.

"Who's there? Show yourself!"

Eros cursed, checking from behind the pillar. She wasn't looking at him, but she was looking for him. She circled a pillar not far from him. Waiting until she was out of sight, he ducked behind a fountain. He quickly reloaded his gun, knowing he would have to be more careful.

Peering around again, she was gone. Cautiously, he made his way to the last place he saw her. He knew she was still in the room, but it was hard to hear for soft footsteps with the loud fountains next to his ear.

Holding the gun ready, he slowly moved through the prayer room. He stayed crouched as he looked for Iona. Somehow, she managed to vanish. Not so much as her shadow could be seen.

"Don't move." Iona's voice came from slightly behind him and he felt the cold steel of a dagger at his throat. He hadn't realized she was armed, and that was a mistake.

"Put your hands up where I can see them. Don't make any sudden moves, or else." She pressed the dagger more firmly against his throat to let him know what the 'or else' could be. Obviously, the dart missed.

Slowly, he held his hands up. He took his finger off the trigger, not wanting to give her an excuse to harm him. He knew Aphrodite would want the girl dead if he went home with so much as a nick, but why risk getting hurt in the first place?

She cautiously walked around him, keeping the dagger at his neck. When she was standing in front of him, she took the gun from him. "Just what do you think you were doing? Who sent you?"

"It's really not what it looks like," Eros protested. He felt the dagger at his throat tremble. She was either too scared or too eager to use her weapon. Either way, he needed to disarm her.

Acting fast, he pushed her dagger hand away from him and grabbed his gun. There was a brief struggle and she was stronger than he thought. The gun pointed down as she dropped her dagger to grab at it with both hands. He managed to pull the gun away from her and push her away from him at the same time. He won!

His victory was short-lived. Even as he pulled the gun closer to himself, he felt a sharp pain in his leg. He looked down in time to see the dart vanish.

"How did you do that," Iona asked. "The dart that hit the statue vanished, as well."

Eros could merely stutter. His tongue felt too thick as the love potion coursed through his veins. He was on fire, burning for the vision of loveliness in front of him.

How could he have ever thought she was unworthy of the praise as Aphrodite? She made his mother look like a slob. Her red-brown hair, far from the frizzy mess he first assumed, was piled lazily up in a bun that made him think of afternoon lovemaking and just tumbling out of bed. His hands twitched to push aside the curls from around her heart-shaped face and out of her beautiful green eyes. He could spend days staring into those soulful eyes, the color of spring and new life.

He looked over her body. It was too perfect. Those lovely

wide hips were perfect for bearing a child, and he had an urge to produce many babies with her. She was worthy of the title of a love goddess.

Her tongue darted out and moistened her kissable lips. He was transfixed by them, watching as she spoke. He couldn't hear a single word. She was a goddess and he was unworthy of her.

"Hey! I asked you how you did that," she demanded, finally breaking through his stupor. Dumbly, he held up his gun as if that explained everything. She looked at it, then tilted her head as she looked past him to his wings.

"Do I want to know how a high devotee of Eros got his hands on a dart gun?" She sighed. "Look, from now on, leave the shooting to the real Eros. You could have hurt someone! And that still doesn't explain how you got disappearing darts. If you stole them, I do not want anything to do with this. I do not mess in the affairs of the gods."

"I would never hurt you. Not in a million years."

"And the darts?"

Eros tried to look embarrassed. He couldn't tell her the truth. "I, uh, stole them. I wanted to be like my idol so much that I took two darts. And when I saw you, I wanted to be with you."

Iona did not look impressed. "Before or after you shot yourself?"

"What?"

"Did you want to be with me before or after you shot yourself?

Eros knew there was only one answer to that, and it was a lie. "Before. Absolutely, before."

"How long does that dart last?"

"Maybe a few hours?" A lifetime.

She turned from him, walking back to the statue. "You can leave. I don't need another love-sick man in my life. I'm telling you what I've told the last twenty guys who thought to ambush me in the temples: I'm not interested." She turned back to him and added, "And leave the real shooting to the real Eros!"

Before he could answer, there was an explosion of noise outside. The voices of an army of men echoed through temple as Aphrodite's suitors called out for Iona. Frightened, Iona backed up to a column, her eyes on the door. Eros put a protective arm around her.

"What was that," Iona asked, her eyes wide.

Eros shrugged, pulling her closer to him. "I'm not sure. You wait here and I'll go look."

Iona grabbed his arm. "No, don't go out there! It sounds like we're under attack." She flinched as her name rang out through the temple. They were getting closer. "Please, don't leave me alone."

The doors to the private room opened and the priestess came running in. Her clothes were torn and bloodied along the hem. Dirt smudged her face and her eyes held a look of wild panic. Running up to Eros and Iona, she grabbed Iona's arm, nearly pulling her from Eros' grip.

"Lady Iona, we have a problem outside." The priestess' voice high with panic. "The devotees of Ares and the Cupids are fighting a new group of men that just showed up. They are claiming that you are betrothed to them by order of Aphrodite. They are tearing the temple apart to find you!"

Iona shook her head. "I'm promised to no one."

"So, you have no man in your life," Eros asked, the idea filling him with joy.

"No," Iona said. "Sadly, I was betrothed, but he died a few years ago. There is no one now."

"There are a lot of men claiming otherwise," the priestess said as there was another loud crash outside the room.

Eros cursed under his breath. He just knew that Aphrodite wouldn't leave well-enough alone. Damn his paranoid mother! She didn't just promise Iona to a single loathsome man, but to an army of them. She worked them up into a frenzy and set them upon the temple. Now, not only would he have to hear about her precious temple being destroyed, but it they found Iona now, they'd tear her apart.

"Stall them," Eros demanded as he pulled Iona back to him. "I'll get her to safety."

"Who will get me to safety?" The priestess cried as Eros took Iona to the back of the room. "What about my safety!"

Eros ignored the priestess, finding the maintenance entrance behind the statue. He pulled Iona along the hallway towards the back of the temple. He knew there was a way out from there, either by going over to Ares' temple or using the PortMat. Any way he could, he'd get her to safety.

He opened the grate. "Go through this," he said. "You should be able to wait in Ares' temple until you can safely slip away home."

"Not with the way that crowd is," came Phobos' voice. The God of Fear stepped out of the shadows. It irked Eros that his brother knew his actions before he could perform them. Phobos' bright eyes raked over Iona's form and her trembling made his lips curl up in what might pass for a smile.

"Who are you," Iona asked.

"No one you need to know," Eros said, watching his brother warily. "How bad is it out there?"

"Bad enough that they'd spot her the second she left the temple," Phobos said, examining his nails. "They might even camp out overnight just to make sure she doesn't sneak by them."

Iona looked over at Eros. "I can wait until dark, but I can't stay hidden forever."

Phobos smiled. "Well, you can always get an escort to take you home. Someone who can fight off the crazy hoard of suitors."

"And who do you suggest we use as an escort," Eros asked.

"Certainly not you, brother dear. You're not a fighter. Those men would tear you apart."

"Then, who do you suggest takes me home," Iona asked.

"A loyal soldier of Ares."

Eros pushed Iona behind him, acting as a shield. "No," he declared. "I won't let you near her."

"Then she'll die," Phobos said idly.

Eros sighed. He didn't trust his brother with Iona. Protecting her should be his job. However, how could he protect her from the horde of men searching for her? Phobos was right, he was not a fighter.

Turning to Iona, he said, "Wait here. I need to talk to my brother for a moment." Eros and Phobos moved away from Iona until they were just out of earshot.

"What do you think you're doing," Phobos asked. "Mother wants this girl to fall prey to one of those men, and you're helping her escape?"

"Mother wants her to fall in love and spend the rest of her life scraping a living in a hovel," Eros said. "If she dies now, then that won't happen."

Phobos chuckled, shaking his head. "You really think that her death will annoy Mother? That's most likely why there is an army of them out there instead of just one lucky man. You, dear brother, are going to be in trouble when she finds out this girl is still alive and not in a million pieces."

"I can deal with Mother," Eros said. "Now, about getting Iona safely home?"

Phobos laughed out right, causing Iona to look over at them. "You are something else," he said. "What do I get for helping you?"

"What do you want?"

"It doesn't work that way. What I want, you can't give me."

"I have connections. Unlike you, I'm actually known."

"Don't push your luck. Her life is in my hands."

Looking down, Eros said, "You're right. What can I offer you to ensure that Iona makes it home safely?"

"I've got my eye on someone," Phobos said. "Mother wouldn't approve, so maybe you can push things along."

"With Mother or your interest?"

"Both."

"Yeah, sure. I'll help you out, as long as Iona makes it home in one piece. She gets so much as a scratch on her, and I'll make sure that this crush of yours hates you forever."

"You're a little too much into this whole thing," Phobos said.

"The name of your target, Brother?"

Phobos smiled. "A devotee of Demeter named Odessa. You'll know her by her lovely dark skin and three scars down her face."

Eros quirked one eyebrow. "Scars? Wouldn't the future wife of a god need to be perfect?"

"She is perfect to me." Phobos glanced over at Iona. "So, do we have a deal, or do I leave your precious mortal to her fate?"

"We have a deal."

They walked back to where Iona was nervously pacing. The noises of the crowd were getting closer and she was visibly scared.

"You will go with my brother," Eros said. "He'll get you home safely."

"Are you sure? What if they find me?"

"Don't worry, babe," Phobos said. "No one is safer then I."

"You'll be safe," Eros promised. "You both should get going. I'll lead them away from this room."

"Wait! What's your name," Iona asked.

"No time," Eros said. He turned and ran, knowing that if he looked back his will would break. It was hard enough leaving Iona's side, but knowing he placed her into Phobos' hands was tearing him apart. He ran from the room, waiting until he was far enough away and made enough racket to draw the crowd of suitors as far from the woman he loved as he could.

Chapter 04

"You can't keep yourself locked in the garden forever!"

Iona sighed, trying her hardest to ignore her mother. It had been six months since her escape from the temple, and her life had only gotten worse. She thought that there was nothing harder than being mistaken for a goddess, but now she knew better. In these six months, Iona's life became a whirlwind of suitors, failed marriage attempts, and embarrassment of being known as the bad luck bride.

"I won't be here forever, Mother," Iona said, picking a dry leaf from one of her plants. "Just until this silliness stops."

"It is not silliness," Hedyla said as she sat next to her daughter. Almost on cue, they could hear music down in the front of the house as one of Iona's suitors serenaded them with a song he wrote. His painfully tone-deaf singing grated on the women's ears. "Okay, maybe it's a bit silly, but this is serious business. You're my only child who is not married. Look at your elder sisters! Philomena is happily married and living a life of luxury on Level 24 in Thebes, and Errita has a thriving business with her husband and is talking about wanting kids. You, on the other hand, are just wasting away here, all alone."

Iona smiled. "I'm not alone. I have you and Father."

Hedyla rolled her eyes. "You should want a husband, Iona. You are a stunning girl. So pretty, in fact, that even Aphrodite competed with you. And, yet, you are the only one we can't marry off to save our lives."

"Don't talk like that." Iona picked up her watering can and tossed the remaining water over the edge of the roof garden. Looking down at her now wet suitor, she called out, "I'm not taking requests today! Try again tomorrow!"

"That's rather cold. You won't have suitors knocking on the doors forever. Just pick one and get married. Stringing them along for six months is just cruel."

"I did pick. I picked ten different men and was stood up at the altar ten different times in the past six months! They all found someone the moment I said yes to their proposal."

"I'm sure one or two got cold feet. It's not every day they get to marry a woman reputed for being Aphrodite-in-the-flesh. It must have intimidated a few."

"I wish you wouldn't call me that. And it wasn't cold feet. I was left humiliated while they found love with kitchen maids or strangers on the street."

"I'm sure that was just an exaggeration." Hedyla plucked a flower from a near-by bush and twirled the stem between her fingers. "Are you sure it's them who are at fault? Maybe you're just setting your sights too high and none of these men can match what you want."

"My sights are just fine. My sights weren't what caused them to leave me stranded." Iona reached into a basket by her feet and scattered crumbs in the flowerbeds. "I don't care who I marry, but I want to marry someone whom I know loves me. I want our eyes to meet and the whole world to melt away. I want to know that I encompass his every thought, fill his every dream, and be the very air he breathes. I want the love I've seen you and Father share."

"Your father and I are different. I wasn't putting off marriage or looking for perfection. Your father and I met at Hera's temple when I worked there. It was love at first sight."

"And that's what I want. Love at first sight."

"I think you should just settle on marriage and worry about love later," her mother said. "Too bad Kelmis died. He would have made a wonderful husband for you."

Iona sighed. She knew the stories of her betrothed, of how he saved her father's life in a war game and the two became fast friends and business partners. Her father owned a large wool-dyeing farm on the outskirts of Tiryns, and his business partner, Kelmis, hinted that a marriage merger would solidify their dealings and help the image of the company. She was three-days old when her parents decided she'd marry a man her father's age. He was a nice man who showered her with gifts growing up, and she always knew that she was expected to marry him. But, she wondered if she ever loved him, or the idea of Kelmis that she had been fed as an infant. Now, free to choose her own husband, she wanted a man her age and not one her father's.

"I have no doubt Kelmis would have been a perfect husband," she said. "I do miss him, Mother." She had been the dutiful daughter and mourned the death of her betrothed. She had been a nervous wreck as her eighteenth birthday approached and felt so guilty at the relief that first flooded her when she heard Kelmis had suddenly died. She mourned longer than necessary until her mother forced her to remove the black veil. Her first day out without it, some creepy shopkeeper snapped her picture. After that, she started to attract unwanted attention. A man following here or offering to help her there had exploded into people thinking she was Aphrodite. Iona longed to hide once more behind the mourning veil.

A movement in the flowerbed distracted Hedyla and she frowned. "Oh, honey, don't do that. Your flowers will be infested."

Iona looked down. Crawling through the flowerbed, carrying off the crumbs, were little blue half-human creatures. The top half was that of a man, and the bottom half was a giant ant, and they measured roughly one inch in length. Little antenna poked out of the tops of their heads.

"The Aneriams help my garden," Iona said, sprinkling more crumbs for the little blue creatures. "They make sure there are no insects to ruin the flowers and I give them treats for that."

"You'll be overrun by those pests if you keep feeding them," Hedyla huffed.

Iona shrugged. "They are the reason why my garden thrives."

"You are the reason, Iona, not the Aneriams. They are just mindless little creatures, not gardeners. You are out here nearly every day, hiding from your suitors and tending to your flowers. You hardly go out to the temples anymore. Really, I rue the day our family fell into favor with Flora and received permission to grow real flowers. The mechanical flowers never get infested."

"I have no need to go out. My suitors come here for me."

"And the temples?"

"The crowds have gotten to be too much. I'm tired of the fighting and the pushing and having people trying to pull me apart. Even the merchants suffer from the crowds. It's just safer if I stay away for a while."

Hedyla sighed. "You're not staying here. You're going to visit your sisters."

Iona looked up at her mother. "What? When was that decided?"

"Last night. Your father got his papers to travel to Delphi. While he's gone, I don't want you moping around here. You're going to go see your sisters, and when you come back, we'll have news."

"What kind of news?"

"We need to know why all your suitors suddenly find someone else. You should have been married years ago. That match with your father's business partner was perfect. Too bad he died, he would have been a great husband for you."

"Maybe I can remain single. Or be a devotee at a temple. I've been talking to the priestesses for Flora. I'm gifted in the garden, and working with flowers would bring me happiness. Our family was once blessed by Flora, and I have experience working with real flowers." Family legend told of how Iona's great-grandfather received favor with Flora by creating a beautiful flower, one that still holds a place in Flora's private gardens. As a reward, the Demarchis family was gifted with real flower seeds, a luxury that was only found in the godly levels of Space Station *Olympus*.

Hedyla gave her a sad smile. "Sweetie, only girls who can't get a husband become devotees. You can easily get a husband. You don't need to lock yourself away in a temple."

"You were a devotee. You lived in Hera's temple for nearly five years before you met Father."

"I never thought I'd find love," Hedyla explained. "I had been dumped at the altar and there were no suitors waiting in the wings. My parents thought that I'd never get married. You can find a husband."

"Apparently I can't," Iona said bitterly. She was twenty-seven and single. All her friends married years ago. The mentality of Space Station *Olympus* was to marry early. Few women remained single, and most of those who did often worked in temples. Iona knew her options were limited.

"We'll find you someone. Who do you see yourself with?"

Iona looked down. There was one person she wanted, but she never learned his name. When she made her escape from the temple six months ago, there was a man who helped her: a devotee of Eros. She couldn't stop thinking about him. Each time he crossed her mind, she felt light-headed. She was almost certain he was the one leaving little gifts in her room.

But, he pricked himself with a stolen love dart, and she feared the power of it worn off. The little trinkets she sometimes found on her window sill could just be from any one of her here-today-gone-tomorrow admirers.

"No one," she murmured, not wanting to talk about her desires.

"Your father and I got your papers for you to travel to Thebes and visit Philomena. You also have a pass to see Errita. It should take your father a month to see the Oracle, so take your time with your sisters."

"I don't have much of a choice, do I?"

"No."

Iona sighed and stood, wiping her hands on her skirt. "All right, I'll go pack. They are expecting me, right? Philomena doesn't handle surprises well."

That much was true. When they introduced Philomena to her husband, the surprise of it caused her to rage for three days. She was happily married now, but the first meeting was disastrous.

"They're expecting you. I've made sure Philomena had enough notice."

Iona shook her head. "How long have you been planning this, Mother?"

"For two months now, ever since that last time you were left at the altar. We're just worried about you, Iona. It's not healthy for you to stay cooped up in this garden all day."

Iona gave her mom a kiss on the cheek. "All you needed to do was ask," she said and went down to her room. She knew they worried about her. Their neighbors whispering she was cursed, the strange circumstances of her suitors becoming suspicious; it wasn't normal.

As she packed, she turned on her viewscreen to hear the latest news from the station. Down in the island levels, Naxos was half-submerged under water. A bit of space debris struck the outer shell of the space station and the best of the maintenance crews were risking their lives to fix the hole. There was a dour prediction of the people on the Minor Gods level could be sucked into space unless the blessings of Hephaestus were made. On the brighter side, there was a huge wedding in Thebes for some councilman that Iona never heard about. With half an ear, Iona listened to the story on the wedding. She started to smile as the entertainment was announced and Philomena was the spotlighted singer.

She packed away some of the gifts mysteriously left in her room. Simple things like jewelry and perfumes, things her sisters might not question her having. Any time her mother noticed her with a new necklace or could tell she was wearing new perfume, Iona always said it was from an unknown admirer. As she was packing these away, a glitter by her bedroom window caught her eyes. Making her way over, she noticed a necklace hanging from the top sill.

"Thank you," she said softly. "My family is sending me to Thebes, so I'll be gone for a while." She looked out the window, but saw no one. She hoped her mysterious admirer heard her and that he was the winged man from the temple.

When she was done packing, her father came in to get her. "Ready?" he asked softly. Her father was a quiet family man, but ruthless as a business man.

"I'm ready," she said. Her father took her to the Lifts and handed her the packet of traveling papers. "These will get you to Thebes and Corinth, only."

"Thank you, Father," Iona said. She hugged her father and watched as he got on the Lifts for the godly levels. He was surrounded by pilgrims and devotees, eager to walk in the presence of the gods. She had to wait for the next Lift up to Level 24.

Taking a deep breath, she tried to stop the fast beating of her heart. It would be her first time outside of Tiryns. Iona never visited her sisters before, preferring the quiet life at home. She never saw any of the space station beyond her home.

The Lift doors opened and the travelers stepped forward, papers in hand. With one last glance back to Tiryns, Iona wondered if she'd ever see the devotee of Eros again.

Chapter 05

"I bet you don't have that kind of entertainment in Tiryns," said Philomena as she led Iona out of the theater. Philomena was in her element as they navigated the busy streets, crowded by the throngs of admirers. With a flourish of her pen, a quick smile, and a witty word, Philomena charmed her audience and gently pushed forward for home.

"Well…" Iona started, but her brother-in-law, Zotikos, interrupted her.

"The theaters of Thebes are among the best in all of the station. Sometimes, the gods themselves take time out of their busy day to come and watch a show," Zotikos said with pride. "I swear, I've seen Apollo in the audience during some of Philomena's concerts."

"That is fascinating, Lord Zotikos," Iona said.

"You don't have to call me Lord. We're family."

Iona smiled as she stepped closer to her brother-in-law to give the sea of fans an easier chance to talk to Philomena. "I know. I will try to remember that from now on." In truth, she wasn't sure what her sister saw in Zotikos. He was a nice guy, but not Philomena's type. All her life, her sister was attracted to young men from wealthy families. Zotikos was older than their father and rich, being the second - or third - cousin of the king of Thebes, but he had no chance to ascend to the throne. Iona worried that her sister married Zotikos only because of his status.

However, in the past two days with Philomena, she saw a new side to the marriage. Philomena seemed to truly care for Zotikos. A longing filled Iona as she watched her sister and brother-in-law laugh and cuddle in the garden or hold hands after a visit to the theater. As old as Zotikos was, he made Philomena extremely happy, and that was all that Iona cared about.

Making her way out of the cluster of fans, Philomena rejoined them. "Oh, look," she said, pointing to the holographic upcoming events poster. "They're showing a comedy next week starring Orestes. I'd love to go see that. His shows are always so ingenious."

"Anything my darling wishes," Zotikos said. He held her hand as they left the theater and the throng of admirers. Their presence made Iona feel better. She was a little nervous to have so many people pressing close to her.

"I just love comedies," Philomena said, huddling closer to her husband. "They make me forget my troubles."

"What troubles do you have, my love," asked Zotikos.

Philomena looked over at Iona, a small smile on her face. "Well, not my troubles, actually. I am worried about Iona. After all, I have Mother and Father calling me all the time to talk about how she can't find a husband."

Iona laughed. "I was wondering how long it would take before you started in on my marriage woes. It only took you a few days to crack."

"That was my doing," Zotikos said. "I know that it's a sensitive subject for you and I wanted your visit to be pleasant. I told her to let you get settled first and not pounce the moment you walked through the door."

"And I'm sure the visit has been pleasant," Philomena said. "But now, we need to talk about your real reason to visit before you leave."

"Are you sending me to Errita," Iona asked. "I thought I was staying a little longer. Father will be in Delphi for at least a month."

Zotikos looked shocked. "What? No, you're here for as long as you want. My home is your home, Iona."

"I just thought…I mean, I thought you were signaling for me to leave."

"No, little sister, but I wouldn't be doing my job if I didn't talk to you about it. Zotikos and I want you to stay as long as you need."

Iona sighed. "I know it's a problem. Mother and Father think it's the end of the world that I'm not married. I don't see much of a problem with it. It's not like women can't make it without a man."

"Marriage is your best bet," Philomena said. "You don't have the skills to support yourself."

"I have skills."

"No you don't. Now, take me, for example. Even if I didn't marry Zotikos, I could support myself as a singer. Errita made herself a thriving business independent of her husband. What skill do you have besides looking pretty?"

Iona looked down. "I can be a gardener. I have been thinking of working in the temples of Flora."

"Temple work is for women who either swear off men or can't find a husband," Zotikos said. "You're too pretty to waste away. Why not try to find a husband here in Thebes. We have much heartier men here than in Tiryns."

"We'll see," Iona promised. She had no desire to be humiliated again by another suitor who promised her the sun and moon, and ran off with another woman. She didn't tell them that she had already done more than just thinking about serving Flora. She talked to the priestesses in the temple and planned on officially joining once her family visits were over. Just after her arrival with Philomena, she got the call that they were looking over her application.

They exited the main city limits and entered the section with the fanciest homes. Zotikos lived on the end of the street, surrounded by the crème de la crème of society. They were near his home when a man came rushing around the corner and crashed into Iona. She gasped as she hit the ground, the wind knocked out of her. He lay across her, getting up far too slow for Iona's taste as she struggled to remember how to breathe.

"I'm so sorry! I didn't see you there," the man exclaimed as he finally got up. He reached down to help Iona up.

"You clod," Philomena snapped. "What were you're going! You could have hurt my sister!"

"I'm really sorry. I'm late getting home, and I was just not watching where I was going. It's all my fault," he said. He turned to see Philomena standing there, and his jaw dropped. "You're Philomena Arcius, the singer! I'm such a huge fan."

This seemed to calm Philomena's anger towards him. "Why, yes I am," she said, batting her eyelashes. "It's always good to meet a fan."

The man clenched her hand in a hearty shake. "I am Hyrieus Leonidis. I have recordings of all your songs and seen nearly all your concerts. Your picture adorns my walls. I moved to Thebes just to be closer to you. It must be fate to meet you."

Philomena blushed and giggled. She was obviously flattered, but Iona was worried. She experienced the same kind of obsessed fans back home, and they were the ones who scared her.

"I am so sorry for knocking down your companion," Hyrieus continued. "Please, forgive me."

"You are forgiven," Philomena said graciously. "I think you just knocked the wind out of my sister. You are all right, aren't you Iona?"

Iona forced a smile on her face. "I'm fine. No harm done."

Hyrieus' eyes widened again. He gasped and pointed at Iona, and she knew what that meant. Her peaceful visit was ruined.

"You're Lady Iona! The Aphrodite-in-the-flesh from Tiryns!"

Iona took a step back, the forced smile to stay on her face. "I don't go by that name anymore. You must be behind the times. A few days ago, it was announced that there was a new Aphrodite-in-the-flesh; a girl named Ameranth in Naxos. Or was it Ismene of Nemea?"

Hyrieus smiled. "You will always be the real Aphrodite-in-the-flesh. I had the honor of seeing you a few months ago. You are true beauty."

"I am not special. I look nothing like the statues of Aphrodite. I am neither slender nor blonde nor beautiful. I am a humble gardener."

Philomena huffed. "I look more like the statues of Aphrodite than Iona."

"Your family must be blessed," Hyrieus proclaimed, "to have so many lovely daughters. Please, Lady Iona, allow me to visit you while you are in Thebes. It would be an honor to behold your company at least once."

"We would be honored if you visited," Philomena said, her hand over Iona's mouth to stop her protests. "She is staying at my home. Why don't you come over tomorrow for lunch?"

"I would be honored." He left after getting Philomena's address.

"Dear, I don't feel comfortable with you inviting strange men to my home," Zotikos said.

"He's a fan," Philomena said. "Besides, he's coming to see Iona. I think I just did what Mother and Father haven't been able to do; get Iona a husband."

"I wouldn't hold my breath," Iona said softly. With a sigh

she followed Philomena and Zotikos back to their home.

Iona's worst fears came reality the next day. Philomena's home was descended upon by admirers and worshippers. She could no longer leave the house without some man offering her gifts or reciting poetry to her supposed beauty. Iona did not believe they could have found her so lovely when there were reports on several new Aphrodites-in-the-Flesh in Naxos, Nemea, and Crete. She was dethroned, and glad of it.

She found herself in a self-exile in Philomena's rooftop garden, praying that the throng of admirers would dwindle down. Each day, fewer came to the house, but it was still too many for her to bear. At first, Philomena tolerated the visitors, but when more than one came to see Iona, she grew angry. By the time two weeks passed, Philomena was ready to kick Iona out of the house.

"It's not my fault," Iona protested, weeding out a flowerbed. "If I had my way, none of them would be here to see me. I just want to be left alone."

"You have a funny way of showing that," Philomena sneered. "How many young men did you turn away today? Yesterday? The day before? How many more will you decide to deny the *joys* of your company?

"I really wish they would just leave me alone. I didn't want for any of this to happen. It's more of a curse than it is a blessing."

Philomena crossed her arms. "And these people really think you are Aphrodite? You don't even look like her statues! I'd be a better match! They should be worshiping me!"

Iona stood up, wiping her hands off on her skirt. "I don't even know how this happened. It was just, one day I'm me, and the next everyone believes I'm Aphrodite. I think it was some strange mix-up."

"I'll say it was."

"Lady Iona?" One of Philomena's house servants timidly came up to them. With her eyes downcast, she said, "There is a call for you."

"Who is it?" asked Iona.

"I do not know, but it sounded urgent."

"Is it a suitor? Because, if it is, you have my permision to just hang up on them."

"No, Lady Iona. I do not believe this is a suitor. It is a

woman."

Iona went downstairs and picked up the line. She was surprised to find out that it was from the priestess of the Temple of Flora.

"I'm so glad you called," Iona said. "I was meaning to contact you. It looks like it may be a little longer than I thought before I'd be home."

"Actually, that was why I was contacting you," the priestess said. "Given the attention you attract, we have decided to deny your application. We do not need the crazed followers that the more popular gods attract. We are a small and proud temple, and we would like to stay that way."

"But," Iona protested, "things are starting to calm down. By the time I get home, I will no longer have these people after me. I can be as anonymous as you need."

"I'm sorry, Lady Demarchis, but our mind is made up."

"Please! All I ever wanted was to work in a garden. Please, reconsider," Iona pleaded. "My ancestor was blessed by Flora for helping her on a task. I have lived my whole life caring for real flowers. It should be my destiny to garden."

The priestess once again said she was sorry and hung up. Iona stood there, staring at nothing as her words sunk in. She was not going to be a devotee to Flora and work in a garden for the rest of her life. She was doomed to live the life her parents expected of her; to marry or forever shame her family name.

"Oh, Iona, I'm so sorry," Philomena simpered. "I guess they denied you at that little temple you were thinking of joining?"

Yes, they denied me," Iona whispered. "I guess, if it comes down to it, I can always join Aphrodite's temple."

"Don't bother. I have a better idea."

"Oh? What?"

Philomena smiled. "Tomorrow, Zotikos is having a dear friend of his join us for dinner. He's a senator and sometimes teaches at the Academy; a respected man. He heard about you and wants to meet you."

"I don't know. After everything that has happened, I don't think I can handle that."

"There is no saying no, Iona. He's coming and you will dress nicely and greet him. There will be no more moping about my garden, playing in dirt and feeding those disgusting Aneriams. Zeus knows I'll have a hard time getting rid of them once you're gone."

Iona sighed. "I have no choice in this matter, do I?"

"No," Philomena said as she left. "Who knows, he might be the one."

Chapter 06

"This is a joke right?"

Iona couldn't believe her eyes. Philomena said that one of Zotikos' friends was visiting for dinner, but the man who was seated with her brother-in-law could not be the suitor for her hand. The man in the dining room was older than Zotikos with only a few hairs clinging stubbornly to his pink scalp. Not the kind of man Iona pictured herself with.

"What's wrong with Lord Antinous? He's a prominent man in Thebes, and you should be thankful that he's got his sights on you," Philomena said as she pulled Iona's hair back in an elaborate braid. "There, I think that should do it."

"That man has at least one foot in the grave. I don't have to worry about him running off with some chamber maid. I have to worry about him dying before dessert."

"Just give him a chance. He fancies you."

"Fancies me? He can barely see me! His eyesight failed him years ago."

"Oh, hush. Mother raised you better than that. Now come on, let's not keep the men waiting." Philomena took Iona's arm and led her into the dining room.

Downhearted, Iona sat next to the old man. Lord Antinous beamed at her, stroking her hand with one that felt like parchment paper. On the other side of him was his nursing staff, who made sure his life didn't extinguish too soon.

"I have heard how lovely you are," Antinous said, his voice wavering with age. "I am very pleased to notice that the rumors do not do you justice."

"They must not have been good rumors, then," Iona said. "I'm really no one special."

"You are special to me," Antinous said.

Philomena smiled as she pulled apart her honey bread. "Isn't that sweet," she said. "You two make a wonderful couple."

One of the nursing staff reached over and took Antinous' plate. He cut the food so finely that it was nearly a paste. Another of the staff moved closer to the old man and fed him.

"Why don't you help him," Philomena whispered to Iona. "You'll be doing that a lot as his wife."

Iona frowned. "We haven't even talked about an engagement. It's a bit early to talk marriage."

"No long wait for marriage with me," Antinous said. "I won't be long in this world, so I prefer to do everything as quickly as possible. We can be married tonight, my love."

"Not tonight sir," said one of his nursing staff. "You have an important meeting in an hour and a half with Lord Galen about the import tax from Sparta. Not to mention breakfast with King Nikkos."

"Oh, my," breathed Philomena, "the king? How wonderful. Are the two of you close?"

"Very close. We are related on my mother's side of the family," Antinous said and Philomena kicked Iona under the table. This was, in Philomena's opinion, a match made on Olympus.

"We can have an afternoon wedding," Zotikos said. "We have permission from Iona's parents to marry her off if a suitor could be found."

"You got what?" Iona couldn't believe what she was hearing.

"Don't make a scene," Philomena said. "Mother and Father want to find you a good husband. What better husband than one who has connections to a king?"

Antinous' papery hand crept under the table and was on to her thigh. That made her shudder, but everyone's eyes were on her. She forced herself to smile graciously, but she knew there was no way she could even pretend to marry this man. She pushed her food along her plate, trying to ignore the hand while Philomena planned the wedding.

Pushing herself away from the table, she quickly stood. "If you'll excuse me, I need some fresh air."

"Something wrong, my dear," wheezed Antinous.

Lying, she said, "I just feel a little overwhelmed. All this talk of weddings has gone to my head. A walk in the garden will help clear my mind."

"Would you like company," asked Antinous. "I can have my staff wheel me out along with you."

"No need," Iona said. "I just need some fresh air and time to digest all of this. Finally getting married … It's a dream come true."

She left briskly from the room, heading up to the roof garden.

She felt dirty, allowing that old man to paw at her. If she was forced to go ahead with this wedding, she would wither away. Iona was a flower in a small pot. Only proper love, or a chance to be a gardener, would cause her to bloom. Antinous was a weed, poised to choke the life out of her.

Sitting by one of the far flower beds, she sighed. Several of the Aneriams scurried out to surround her. She let them crawl over her lap and chocked back a smile as one small Aneriam held out a crumb for her.

"Well, thank you," she said, taking the crumb. The Aneriam smiled and hurried back to join the others.

"I can't marry," she said, looking down at the small blue beasts. "Especially not him."

"If you're not careful, it would be him," said a soft, male voice behind her. She stood and turned, her heart beating faster as she saw the same devotee to Eros that she met in the temple.

"How did you get here," she asked.

He flexed his wings and smiled. "Maybe I flew?"

"Don't joke," Iona said. "You shouldn't be here."

"Do you want me to leave?"

She shook her head. That was the last thing she wanted. She wanted him to stay. She wanted him to be with her forever. She had never seen a man as beautiful as he. He saved her life and never left her mind.

A smug smile crossed his face. "I didn't think so," he said, moving closer to her. Iona's breath caught in her throat as he reached out and gently stroked a hand down her cheek. "That old fop isn't what a lady such as yourself needs."

"What is it I need?" she whispered, moving closer to him. She reached out, running a hand over his wings. Even though she knew they had to be fake, she felt him shiver under her touch.

"You need a strong, young man," he said. His arm snaked around her waist and pulled her closer until she was pressed against his lean body. He kissed her neck and murmured, "You need a man who will appreciate you and give you the freedoms you deserve."

"Who are you," she asked. "I never got to thank you for saving my life."

"I was worried about you," he said, not answering her first question. "When you left the temple, I was so worried you'd never make it home. I visited you for days after that, just watching and making sure you were unharmed." He smiled, his lips against her soft neck. "You're wearing the perfume I left for you."

Iona's heart beat so fast she thought she would faint. He had been the one leaving those little gifts for her. She knew she should have been worried about him sneaking into her room to leave the gifts, or sneaking into Philomena's home, but she was just overjoyed that it was him.

"You came for me," she said. "You came here for me."

"I couldn't stay away," he said before kissing her. The garden, her upcoming wedding, everything vanished under his soft lips and passionate embrace. In that moment, Iona made up her mind. This man was the only one for her.

If only she knew his name.

"Who are you," she breathed as soon as she could pull away from him. "No one could tell me who you are. I tried asking the other devotees, but none remembered seeing you before that day. I even looked for your brother, the one you had escort me home. Neither of you exist."

"High devotees," he explained. "We are directly under the gods themselves."

"You were really sent by Aphrodite that day?"

"Yes."

"To protect me?"

"Yes."

Iona smiled. That would be perfect. A king was as good as a mortal husband as she could get, but this was better! Her family couldn't deny this marriage if she went to them with it. He was just under the gods, better than a mortal.

"Does that make you so happy? If I knew being sent by a goddess to your side could make you smile like that, I'd beg for her to send me every day."

"That's not what made me so happy," Iona admitted. "I was just thinking of my future."

"And?"

"And thinking that I'd like you to be in my future."

He smiled down at her. "How do I figure in your future?"

Embarrassed, she looked away. "You'll laugh if I tell you. It's just a silly dream anyway. Right now, my sister and her husband are plotting my nuptials."

"I can stop that," he promised. "I stopped all your other suitors."

"How could you do that?"

He lifted the gun at his side and gave it a shake. He smiled at her, his silence telling her everything.

"I thought we agreed that you'd leave the real shooting to the real Eros," Iona said. It did make sense, though. How her suitors suddenly found a new love after getting too close to her, how she was always alone despite being confused as Aphrodite. She had someone filching darts from Eros on her side.

He smiled sadly. "Iona, darling, who do you think I am," he asked.

Before she could answer, she heard Philomena calling her name. Startled, she realized that her sister was coming up to the garden. She couldn't be caught with him! Not just yet. She was not ready to tell Philomena about her mystery man until she got a marriage proposal from him.

"My sister is coming," she whispered. "You have to go. For now, please. We'll see each other again, I promise you."

"We will see each other," he said. "Tomorrow. Meet me at the clearing of the South Woods, at the pond they say Artemis bathes in every new moon."

"Iona? Who are you talking to? I hear voices." Philomena was closer and Iona knew that she would see them soon.

"Tomorrow, at Artemis' pond," Iona whispered. "I'll be there."

He pulled her close for one last kiss. It was bliss. Every nerve in her body was on fire and she longed to burn with him. The world melted away under his touch and nothing mattered as long as he was with her.

She groaned as he pulled away from her. They were both breathing heavily and the parting of ways was the hardest she ever gone through. He smiled at her before jumping off the building. His wings spread, gently lowering him to the ground. Soon, the shadows of the night swallowed him and she was alone. Just the warm tingling on her lips told her that he was real.

"There you are, Iona," Philomena said. She pulled Iona back and out of her happy daze. "Come on, Lord Antinous is about to leave. Come and say good-bye."

"Sure," Iona said softly. She allowed Philomena to lead her down from the roof.

"Iona? Why is your lipstick smeared?"

Chapter 07

The South Forest of Thebes spread south from of the city and wrapped up to the eastern wall. None of it was real, though legends said it once was. Mechanical replicas built by Hephaestus replaced all animal life, making the Pool of Artemis a picturesque spot. Animatronic squirrels and mechanical deer frolicked in predictable patterns as birds sang from the fake, plastic trees and clockwork flowers opened and closed on a timer.

Iona straightened the shawl around her head as she peered around the pool. Every little noise caused her to jump; a fish splashing in the pool or a falling twig scared her.

Looking around, Iona was surprised to see a small patch of flowers. Drawn to them, she knelt down and touched the petals. She smiled, feeling the soft velvet of real flowers. Under the blossoms, a little line of Aneriams meandered around as the blue insect-men worked.

"Well, how surprising is that," Iona breathed. "A little bit of life in the middle of a tin forest."

"I hadn't realized I'd have competition when I suggested this place."

Iona turned to see her mysterious date standing behind her. He had a blanket over one shoulder and a small basket clutched in his hands, and she could smell the food inside. Until that moment, she hadn't realized she was hungry.

"I was worried you wouldn't show up," she said, standing. "After all, I don't have the best record with men."

"Only because I've kept you from mistakenly marrying the wrong man," he said, setting the basket down. "You can thank me at any time."

"If I had proof it was really you, I'd thank you," Iona said. "What did you bring?"

"Just your favorite foods," he said, spreading the blanket. He opened the basket and pulled out a container. Opening it, she gasped at the sight of candied nuts.

"How did you know?"

He smiled, running a hand through his brown hair. "I've been watching you for a while, Iona. I know a lot about you."

"Should I be worried that you've been stalking me?"

"When you say it like that, it sounds so dark," he said. "No, not stalking. I just wanted to make sure you weren't hurt by the foolish decisions of your family."

"That still sounds chancy. I am not sure if I feel safe knowing that you know more about me than I know about you."

"All that I know is common knowledge. I did not have to spy on you to find out your favorite foods. All your suitors know this knowledge."

Iona sat down next to him. "I got a message from Lord Antinous this morning. It seems that he fell madly in love with a street urchin on his way home last night, and was married at first light this morning."

"I told you I'd handle it," he said, tapping his gun.

"I don't suppose I'll learn your name now," Iona asked, dismissing his claim to have caused Antinous to fall in love. For all she knew, he was still under the sway of that blasted dart he shot himself with at the temple.

"I am Amor Myloneous, son of Penia the priestess."

Iona frowned, looking closer at him. "Is that your real name?" There was just something that seemed off about it. It could be how he hesitated before telling her who he was, or the way his eyes shifted away from her.

"I've been called many names," he said. "I was born Amor Myloneous, but I gave up that name when I entered the services of Eros. I'm not even supposed to really be here with you, or protecting you. If anyone knew who I really was, it would only bring you pain. For now, just call me Amor."

"Very well," she said, pausing before stressing, "Amor."

"I promise, I will tell you everything as soon as I am able."

Iona frowned, crossing her arms. "I'll hold you to that promise," she said. "If I never get it out of you, than I shall haunt you in the depths of Hades until you tell me."

Amor smiled. "I shall remember that." Turning the conversation to safer ground, he asked, "What were you staring at when I arrived?"

"Flowers," Iona said. "Real flowers. There is a little camp of Aneriams tending them and everything."

"You know what real flowers look like?"

Iona looked down at her lap. "Yes. My many-times great-grandmother was a servant of Flora. The goddess gifted my family with a few seeds for our roof garden. The garden at my home has real flowers, though only a few." She sighed, looking over at the small patch of flowers. "If things don't improve, we might have to get rid of them."

"Improve how?"

"My parents don't know this, but I've heard them talking, and I've heard Philomena talking as well. Some of Father's business partners are pulling away, believing we are cursed. This whole 'not marrying' business has a few people a little on edge."

"Try spinning it into a positive light," Amor said. "Maybe, tell them that you are infused with the power of Aphrodite, and that you are the factor that has led so many men to their true loves."

Iona smiled. "We never thought about it like that. I'll try that next time."

"So, you were telling me about real flowers?"

"Yes. I love to garden," Iona said. As they ate, she told him stories about her life and her dreams of being a gardener. Amor told her a few stories of his childhood and what it was like to serve the gods. He was a bit guarded, and Iona was nearly positive he was holding back on her, but she found that she didn't care. She enjoyed his company and what few minor details he wasn't telling her weren't all that important.

After the picnic, Amor jumped up and pulled Iona to her feet. "Come on, let's go for a swim."

"What? Here," Iona protested. "I don't have anything to wear."

"I don't mind."

She crossed her arms. "I mind. I am not undressing for you."

He only grinned and pulled off his tunic. She gave a small squeak and covered her eyes. Though she admired him and wanted him, she was too embarrassed to openly gawk at him. The only time she ever seen a naked male was the statues in the temples.

She heard him laugh and then there was a splash. Cautiously, she peaked through her fingers and saw him in the pond. The water was clear enough for her to just barely make out the undergarments he wore. With a sigh of relief, she dropped her hands.

"I take it," he said, "that your reluctance to swim means you are naked under your clothes?" He leered at her hopefully.

"I am not," she protested. "I am exceedingly proper under my clothes, but I won't let you see."

He smiled and flipped over to float on his back. "Actually, I'm glad you won't join me," he said. "I'd hate to think that others might see you."

"And what does that mean?"

He pointed up to the ceiling. "Apollo watches everything. The chance of him watching his sister's sacred pond is highly unlikely, but very little is missed by him. That's why I usually watched you at night. Artemis is less likely to care about what I am up to, but Apollo is too nosy for his own good."

Iona shivered, looking up. All she could see was the simulated blue sky, but now she felt like she was being watched. She took a step back in the shadows of the trees.

She watched Amor as he floated around the pond. "Aren't your wings going to get ruined," she asked.

"Nope. They are of exceptionally high grade. It's almost as if they are a part of me."

"When did you get your operation done?"

Amor ducked under the water. When he came back up, he looked thoughtful. "About five years ago, I guess. It's odd, but I feel like I've always had wings."

"Did it hurt?"

"I don't remember." Amor dipped beneath the water again. This time, when he surfaced, Iona crept closer to the water's edge. She was still under the shadows of the trees, but close enough that she could almost touch the edge of the pond.

"I hope I'm not coming on too strong," Amor said, swimming over to her, "but I really am falling in love with you. I need to know if you feel the same way."

"I feel the same way," Iona said. "I know I shouldn't, I don't know you."

"And yet, I see the pain in your face. What is wrong, my dear?"

"I'm just scared," Iona said. She plucked a silk flower from a near-by bush and twirled it between her fingers. "We have only really known each other for a short time, but I want to spend the rest of my life with you. I'm scared that you'll leave me or that the Oracle will tell my father of another for me to marry and I'll never see you again."

Amor frowned. "What was that about the Oracle?"

"My father left to speak with the Oracle about a week ago to find out why I am having a hard time finding a husband."

"This is great!" Amor pushed himself out of the water and took her hand. "I can fix this!"

Iona didn't look hopeful. "How? I don't think even as a devotee to Eros will get you the status needed to convince one of Apollo's mystics to give the answer we want."

"I can think of something. Apollo is extremely predictable," Amor said. "I promise you, Iona, we will be married and it will be with the blessing of the gods."

"I want to believe you, Amor. I really do."

Amor leaned in and kissed her quickly. "Have faith in me, Iona. I'd battle Hades for you and move all of Olympus. I will not rest until you are my bride."

Iona smiled. "You're so sweet."

"Iona! What are you doing out here!" Philomena's shrill voice startled the two lovers. Iona looked up to see her older sister at the far edge of the clearing, hands on hips. It was only then that she noticed that the skylights were starting to dim as the night simulation began. It was later than she thought.

"Oh, Hera! I didn't know it was so late! I'm sorry Philomena," Iona said, standing up. She heard a splash and realized that Amor retreated back into the pond.

"We've been so worried about you! You left this morning and no one has seen or heard from you since! We had no idea where you had gone or if you were all right," Philomena snapped. "You're just lucky that a merchant friend of Zotikos' saw you walking into the woods or we would never have known where to start!"

"I'm so sorry, Philomena. Amor and I got talking and I must have lost track of time."

"Who is Amor?"

Amor climbed out of the pond, reaching for his clothes. "I am Amor Myloneous, son of Penia the priestess," he said. "And I know who you are, Lady Philomena. I've heard you sing on occasion."

At the sight of Amor's body, Philomena's features softened. Even in the slowly darkening forest, Iona could see the glint in her sister's eyes as she took in every muscled inch of the young man. Philomena was not as interested in temple politics as Iona, so she was unsure if Philomena knew the significance of the wings.

"Well, hello there Amor," Philomena said sweetly. "That is such a lovely name, and incredibly fitting for one as handsome as you. How did you meet my baby sister? She never mentioned you before."

"We met at the temple of Aphrodite," Iona said, moving slightly to stand between her sister and Amor. "He saved my life."

"You have my deepest thanks," Philomena purred. "Any friend of Iona's is a friend of mine. Do stop by my home any time you like, and I do mean any time."

"I will keep that in mind," Amor said.

Philomena smiled and motioned for Iona to join her. "We should get going. I was so worried about my baby sister. Everyone will be pleased to hear that she was safe in the company of such a wonderful young man."

"Will I see you again," Iona asked, turning to Amor.

"Of course," he said, taking her hand. He kissed the back of her hand lightly, his lips a brief breathe across her skin, but she felt the heat all the way to her heart. "I will wait for you here tomorrow."

"I'll be here," she whispered. "Nothing will stop me."

He smiled and released her. She slowly walked to her sister, who quickly grabbed her arm and pulled her along. Iona kept looking back to see Amor watching her go until she could see him no more. Had she been paying attention to Philomena, she would have noticed that her sister had a lot of questions about Amor. Things like, did he prefer blondes and what was his favorite food? All that Iona could think of was that she was finally in love.

For the next week, Iona and Amor met every chance they could. She even got a chance to witness Amor using the love darts on her behalf. While walking in the market just outside of Thebes, a young man decided that she was beautiful. The excitement of her once being an Aphrodite-in-the-flesh died down now that Amaranth of Naxos was being hailed as the goddess. Iona was just a normal woman once more, but there were still men who found her appealing.

"I am sorry," she told the young man, "but I am not free. I have a man I adore."

"And he lets you walk around without him?" The young man moved to block her once more. "How irresponsible of him. Why, just anyone can swoop in and take you."

Before Iona could answer him, Amor chose that time to swoop in. However, he did not take her. Instead, he put his arm around the boy's shoulders and turned him away from Iona. "You are right," Amor said. "Now, what a lovely lady like her needs is a flower. You can't be taken seriously if you don't present a flower to the woman of your dreams."

Amor pushed him toward a burly female flower vender. Iona's eyes widened as she saw him stab the boy in the back with a dart. Before the dart could vanish, the young man was staring deeply in the eyes of the handsome woman with the flowers. Amor chuckled as he led Iona away.

"You didn't have to do that," she said. "He would have found someone new by dinner time on his own."

"No sense in taking chances," Amor said as he took her to dinner.

Iona's week of bliss came to an end when Zotikos and Philomena cornered her in her room one night. She was getting ready to go out with Amor, he promised her a night of star-gazing. When her sister and brother-in-law entered her room, she thought things were going all right. Then Philomena crossed her arms and Zotikos shut the door.

"Iona, I'm worried about you," Zotikos said. "We are all extremely worried about you."

"Why are you worried," Iona asked, comparing two sets of earrings. "Philomena, which one looks better?"

"The aquamarine ones," Philomena said. "And, Iona, you can't go out on this date."

"Why can't I? I've finally found someone who hasn't vanished on me. This is what you and Mom and Dad have wanted."

"This Amor isn't who he says he is," Zotikos said. "I had some of my friends look into him."

Iona set the jewelry down. "And what does that mean? What did they find out?" She turned to face her brother-in-law, a little afraid of what he discovered. She knew that Amor wasn't truthful about his name, but if he was a high devotee, he might not be allowed to tell his real name. She accepted that.

"There was a man named Amor Myloneous who served Eros, but he died five years ago. He was sent up to the godly levels, but his body was soon sent back down. You can visit his grave in Corinth when you see Errita."

"Are you sure about the body part," Iona said. "Amor did tell me he serves in the godly levels. Obviously they can't tell their real names."

"He is using the name of a dead man," Zotikos said. "He has not been honest with you."

Iona slowly stood, facing him. "And is that all? Just a false name? So far, everything else sounds about right. He's been honest about his occupation and he did have a real name."

Zotikos shook his head. "I found out that there has been an imposter in the Cupids. According to the Soldiers of Ares, someone has been pretending to be a follower of Eros, if not Eros himself."

"That's not Amor," Iona protested.

"I think it is," Zotikos said. "Iona, you're like a sister to me. When I married Philomena, I took you and Errita into my heart as well. Your well-being means a lot to me."

"I know that," Iona said, "but you are wrong about Amor. And, I've been watching the news. If someone is pretending to be a god, we would have heard about it."

"Not if the gods want to keep it quiet," Philomena said. She reached over and picked up a necklace. Modeling it in the mirror, she said, "Where did you get this? I've never seen gems shaped like little flowers before."

"Amor gave it to me," Iona said. "He knows that flowers are important to me.

Philomena rolled her eyes. "You and flowers," she muttered.

"The point I'm trying to make," Zotikos said, taking the flower necklace from Philomena, "is that he's not who he says is."

"He loves me," Iona said. "You and Philomena have tried to set me up with men that don't truly care about me, but see me as a prize. Amor really loves me. Those who work for the gods must leave their old lives behind."

Zotikos ran a hand through his thinning hair. "I don't think it's healthy for you to fixate on this man. The gods themselves have a habit of using mortal women. I don't want to see you tossed aside by this man."

"He's not going to toss me aside." Iona finished putting her jewelry on and started to leave. "You'll see, he's the one."

Zotikos grabbed her arm. "You're not going out of this house," he said.

"What's that supposed to mean?"

"You're under house-arrest," Philomena said. She snatched up some of Iona's perfume and sprayed it on her wrist. "Tomorrow, you're going down to Corinth to stay with Errita. Until then, you're not leaving this house. No more Amor."

"You can't do that to me!" Iona pulled her arm free from Zotikos' grip. "You have no right!"

"I have every right! You're in my house, under my rules," Zotikos said. "This fake suitor is only stringing you along, and I will not allow that to happen."

"Amor loves me," Iona cried. "Philomena, tell him! You know that Amor loves me!"

Philomena sighed. "He *says* he loves you, Iona, but who can really tell. I know many of the younger girls who perform are plagued by false suitors who say they love them, but when the question of commitment comes up, they run away. All the girls believe as you do. The best thing is for you to enter in a marriage supported by your family."

"But –" Iona started. Zotikos interrupted her, "But nothing. As the man of this house, I decide these matters. I've informed Theron of this Amor fellow, so don't get any ideas of sneaking off while you're at his home."

Iona felt hot tears sting her eyes. "You can't do this," she repeated.

"We can and we have," Philomena said. "It's for your own protection." She walked over to the window and closed the wooden shutters. Iona's heart nearly stopped as Philomena locked them and tucked the key in her pocket. "I suggest you start packing. We leave in the morning."

Chapter 08

Errita and Theron lived in a relatively modest home on the outskirts of Corinth. When Iona first saw it, she had a hard time imagining that a much sought-after seamstress and station-famous athlete lived in just a two-story building with the fake garden on top, but it was comfortable for the two of them, and one room set off to the side for the bundle of joy that Errita prayed for.

"What do you think of this dress?" Errita asked, holding up the garment she was weaving. "It's for the Temple of Aphrodite. I really like how I have the goddess looking down from the bodice, and I'm going to embroider lovers along the bottom hem."

"Hmm? Oh, yes, wonderful," Iona muttered, not bothering to look up from the window. For a week, her visit had been a virtual imprisonment. Forewarned by Zotikos, Iona was not allowed to travel from the home without an escort. Not that she thought there was much of a chance of Amor finding her, she hadn't had the chance to leave him a note.

"Sister, you're not looking," Errita chastised. "You're still thinking about *him*."

"I can't help it," Iona said. "You understand what it's like to be in love. When Theron courted you, you couldn't concentrate on even the simplest stitches."

"You know that you can't see this Amor fellow again," Errita said, moving the dress to the next section she would work on. "Why can't you just forget him? Theron knows some wonderful men who would make a good husband for you. No old senators like Philomena wants you to marry. Strong, young, healthy men, many who are the children of the gods."

"What if I don't want to marry any of them? You and Philomena had some say in your marriages. I want a say in mine."

Errita didn't answer as she worked on the dress. Iona sat in the silence, waiting. Finally, she stood and walked over to where Errita was working. Looking at the dress, she could see her sister's vision.

"It looks nice," she said. "You know that you always do such wonderful work. Why do you need me to tell you that?"

"I like to hear it, that's why." Errita set her work aside and stood. "Some of Theron's friends are coming to dinner tomorrow."

"I'm really not in the mood," Iona protested.

Errita sniffed. "You're not hiding yourself away like you did with Mom and Dad, or tried to do with Philomena."

Iona sighed, looking out the window. When either of her sisters made up their minds about something, not even Zeus himself could persuade them to change. If Errita wanted a dinner with guests tomorrow night, then a dinner and guests she would have.

"I'm going for a walk," Iona said. "I really need some fresh air."

"Why not go up to the roof garden for fresh air," Errita asked.

"Your flowers aren't real," Iona said. "I'm going to go get my shawl and leave. I don't care if you really must have someone escort me around, but they better be ready when I am."

Iona left her sister and got ready. She wanted to contact Philomena and ask if Amor ever stopped by her house, but she was a little scared. If he had, would Philomena actually tell him where Iona was staying? She doubted it. Philomena sometimes kept secrets, liking the power it gave her. It took her three days to tell Iona that she knew that her betrothed died. For years, Iona did the respectable thing and mourned the death of Kelmis, as both her betrothed and as a friend of her father's. Her only memories of him were like those of a doting uncle who often gave her little trinkets and a pat on the head. Now, with Amor, she knew the love she felt for the ghost of Kelmis was but a pale imitation of the real thing she felt for her mysterious lover.

Pulling her shawl around her head, she left the house. At her heels was one of Errita's servants. He was her shadow on nearly all her outings. She knew that everything she did, he'd report back to her sister and brother-in-law.

As she entered the city, she smiled. There was a small market happening and the streets were crowded. With luck, she could lose her guard for a few moments. Iona headed deep into the heart of the market, but the servant stayed at her back.

Iona stopped as she drew near the temple of Aphrodite. This one had statues of Eros and his brothers outside it, and they caught her eye. Walking up the steps, she drew near the statue of Eros in wonder. She recognized the curly hair and beautiful facial features. Though in stone, she could imagine warm skin under her hands.

"Amor," she breathed, looking at the replica of her beloved.

"Excuse me," came a female's voice by her side, "but what did you say?" Iona turned to see a woman in black standing next to her. Her shawl was pulled far back and her graying hair fell over her sad blue eyes.

"I'm sorry," Iona said. "I didn't say anything."

The woman frowned. "Oh, I must be hearing things. I had hoped … I guess I'm wrong." The woman moved past Iona, staring at the statue. As Iona turned to leave, the woman said, "The gods play such cruel jokes on us. I never thought that they could be so mean."

"What do you mean?"

"I had a son once. He followed my footsteps in devotion to Aphrodite and became a loyal devotee to Eros," the woman said. She sniffled, reaching a hand out to touch the statue of Eros. "When he was called by the gods, it was the happiest day of our lives."

"Your son stays in the godly levels," Iona asked. She felt a prickle of knowledge in the back of her mind. If she was right, this was an amazing coincidence.

The woman shook her head. "He did stay there, and they said he died there. We buried a body, but I was never allowed to view it. After that, the new statues came down. My son, my lovely son," she said and stifled her sobs, "they made the statues to look like him."

"What was your son's name?"

"Amor. Amor Myloneous, most faithful and beloved of Eros."

Iona gasped, turning to look fully at the woman. Here was her proof that Amor existed, that his story was true. Surely a mother could know whether her son is dead or alive.

"You're not sure that the body buried was your son's," Iona asked slowly.

"They had him wrapped in linen when they brought him down. I asked to see him, to say my good-byes, but they said it was best if I didn't disturb him. I never saw his body."

"What if it wasn't your son they brought down," Iona said.

The woman sighed. "I've told myself that so many nights. My son was taken from me. My position in the temple destroyed. I am all that you see now; a pathetic beggar."

Iona reached out to the woman, but was pulled away. A strong hand dragged her deeper into the temple, and though she tried to see who was holding her, her captor's hood was up. Iona heard her sister's servant call after her, but the mysterious person swiftly pulled her through a door and slammed it shut. The servant must not have seen where they went, because Iona heard him walk past the door, calling for her. Once the servant passed, the figure pushed Iona up against the wall.

"Are you out of your mind? Do you know what you are about to do?"

"You're hurting me," Iona said, tugging on her arm. "Let me go!"

The man pushed back his hood to reveal Amor. His brown eyes flashed angrily, but he loosened his grip on her arm. "Don't ever talk to that woman, Iona. Your life could depend on it."

"Wasn't that your mother?"

Amor smiled sadly. "Once upon a time, yes, but she can't know I'm still alive. As far as the whole station is concerned, Amor Myloneous is dead. You are the only person who knows me by that name."

"What else should I call you," Iona asked.

The sadness deepened in his smile and eyes. "Oh, Iona," he whispered, "when you learn the truth, you'll wonder how you never made the connection. You're so close." He patted the statue of Eros. "You can almost reach out and touch the answer."

"What if I make a connection, but it's too strange to believe?"

"Don't tell me what you think just yet," he said, placing a finger on her lips. "Let's leave the big reveal for later."

"As you wish," Iona said. "How did you find me? I wasn't able to leave you a note when I was whisked away from Philomena's home."

"I knew you had another sister. It was just a little investigation to figure out where you went," Amor said. He pulled Iona closer to him and kissed her until the world tilted under her feet and she forgot all about the sad woman still staring at the statues. "Nothing would stop me from finding you, my love."

He took her hand and pulled his hood back over his head.

"Come on, we can't talk here. I know where we can be safe." He led her through the back of the temple. He was right, it wasn't safe. Iona was worried that her escort would find her and then Errita would know that Amor found her. She did not want to be shipped off home or back to Philomena's now that she and Amor were together. She trusted him to take her to where they could talk privately and he did not disappoint her. He led her out of the temple and out of the city until they came to the far wall of the level.

"We can't go any further," Iona said. "There is nothing beyond that wall but space."

"Not quite," Amor said. He touched the wall and there was a click. A panel slid open and Iona braced herself for the pull of space. When nothing happened, she peered into the darkness of the new open. She couldn't see anything in the gloom, but she heard the clanks and sighs of moving machinery.

"Follow me," Amor said and took her hand. She whimpered as he led her into the darkness.

Chapter 09

There was no light in the tunnels between the known walls of the land and the mysterious working of the space station. Iona had no idea how Amor knew where he was going. He stopped and she heard another click. This time, a door opened to a large windowed hallway that ran all along the outer edge of the station.

"Oh, wow," she breathed, staring out into space. There were so many stars, far more than she ever imagined. Below the space station was a rust-red planet. Iona stood on her toes to peer down at the planet, fascinated by the clouds swirling in the atmosphere. Behind her, in the wall that connected to the living levels, were machines that regulated the air, gravity and temperature.

"Welcome to the maintenance hall," Amor said. "This is where the magic of the gods comes to life."

"What do you mean?"

"Space Station *Olympus* wouldn't exist if it weren't for these machines. The gods make sure they continue to run so you humans can live," Amor said. "Well, actually, Hephaestus runs these machines, but the others like to think it's a group effort."

"We shouldn't be back here," Iona said. "What if we get caught?"

"Don't worry," Amor said softly. He kissed her hand. "I had to talk to you in private, and this was the best place I could think of. No one will find us here."

He pulled her closer to the windows. If she stared out long enough, she could forget that there was a ground beneath her feet and feel like she was floating among the thousands of stars. She pressed her hands on the cold glass, amazed by the beauty before her.

"It's so beautiful out there," Amor said. "After I first started serving Eros, I would come out to these halls to be alone. He said they were his favorite places to go and think, and they became mine. The rare beauty of space is one of the many realities that the gods can't replicate. We try so hard, but there is no substitution for the real thing."

"You brought me out here to talk about space?"

"No. Just like space, you've never known the true splendor of love. All those grubby men with their false promises and greedy eyes – that's not love. They are a pale imitation of the real thing. You were meant for the real thing, true love. You were meant for the beauty of space."

Iona felt her heart stop beating as fear gripped her. "You're not saying good-bye, are you?"

"What? No! Iona, I'm saying that you are not meant to know that false love that your family is pushing you toward. You are meant for the real thing. For me." He took her hands and kissed her fingers. "I will be your perfect love."

"That's what I want," Iona confessed. "My family won't listen to me because you've been listed as dead. They think that you're this impostor Zotikos heard about."

"What impostor?"

"Zotikos heard from some soldiers of Ares that someone was impersonating Eros. They think it's you and that you mean to just use me and toss me aside."

Amor shook his head. "I can promise you, I am no impostor. I think I know who started that rumor, and I will deal with him."

"How can I convince my family, though? They won't listen to me."

"But they will listen to the gods."

Iona looked confused. "Well, of course we will listen to the gods' will, but I doubt Zeus himself will come down to champion my cause."

"Would you settle for the word of Apollo?" Amor gave her a big smile. "When you told me that your father was seeing the Oracle, it gave me an idea. The Oracle will announce that you are to be my bride, and your family will know that it is meant to be."

"Stop joking! I can believe that you stole the darts of Eros, but not that you know what the Oracle will say. Stop doing this, Amor. Don't get my hopes up that we will have a future."

"I do not lie, Iona. The Oracle will announce that we will be wed."

"Nothing would make me happier, Amor, but you can't promise what just can't be controlled."

Amor pulled her closer to him. "From this day on, Iona, I will give you the beauty of space. You are my true sun, moon and stars. Everything between us will be real. No more lights to simulate the night sky."

"You'll be my reality, too," Iona promised. "You will be my real flowers and true garden. Not the fake imitations that everyone else plants." She leaned in closer to him, kissing him softly. This was a wonderful dream. Every time she thought that the Fates conspired against her to keep her from love, Amor pulled her through. Already, she could picture her wedding and how happy she would be living with him for the rest of her life.

"Hey! You two don't belong here!"

Iona pulled back to see a dark-skinned woman walking up to them. She wore a gold-colored jumpsuit with a stylized 'H' over her left breast and a metallic cap over her curly black hair and carried a large tool case. Her eyes were slanted with golden make-up painted in exotic swirls, highlighting the loveliness of her face.

"It's okay, we're allowed here," Amor said. He flicked the cloak back to show his wings. "I have permission."

"No one is allowed back here," the woman snapped. "I don't care who you worship, this is a restricted section." The woman turned to the wall and pulled open a small panel.

"There's no need to tattle on us," Amor said, but it was too late. She pulled a lever in the panel and the alarm sounded. Amor cursed and grabbed Iona's hand. They ran down the hallway and he pulled her sideways into a corridor. As the door closed, she heard soldiers running by.

"We can't stop here," Amor said. He led her through the labyrinth of hallways, hiding behind doors when their pursuers got too close.

When darting into a workroom, they were confronted by the ugliest man Iona ever seen. His body looked twisted and lumpy, his muscles bunched and piled up on his body like modeling clay. His right leg was in a brace and it hurt Iona to look at it, the foot twisted at a 180 degree angle.

"Hephaestus," Amor gasped. "What are you doing here?"

"I work here," Hephaestus said. "What are you doing here?"

"I just wanted to show Iona the stars. We weren't doing anything."

Hephaestus looked over at Iona. She tried to hide behind Amor, but he could still see her. His craggy, misshapen face softened.

"This is Iona?"

"Yes, I'm Iona Demarchis. Pleased to meet you," Iona said softly. "Amor was only showing me the stars. I've never seen anything so wonderful."

Hephaestus looked over at Amor. "You do know the trouble it will cause if she's caught here." Though he didn't say anymore, Iona had a feeling there was something she missed.

"Please," Amor said, "don't tell anyone we were here. I mean anyone. Please, Hephaestus. I'll owe you one."

Hephaestus nodded. "What you're doing is dangerous. If this adventure were discovered, I can't take sides. You know that. I'll protect you the best I can, but there is a limit to what I can do." He smiled. "And you don't owe me anything. Call it a free favor."

"Thank you," Amor breathed. He took Iona's hand and smiled. "We'll be more careful from now on."

"I'll have someone escort you back to Corinth," Hephaestus said. He tapped a button on the wall and, a few minutes later, the woman in the gold jumpsuit walked in.

"I see you found the intruders, Lord Hephaestus," she said. "What shall I do with them?"

"Escort them back to Corinth, Neoma," Hephaestus said.

Neoma looked as if she swallowed something disgusting. "My lord, they are trespassing. And that one," she added, pointing to Amor, "worships *her*."

"Aphrodite is my legal wife. And Er-...um, Amor is like a son to me. They are welcomed in my domain anytime they wish to view the stars. Is that understood, Neoma?"

"Yes, my lord."

She motioned for them to follow her, even though her look of disgust never changed. Iona moved to leave, but Amor stayed for a moment longer. Before he left, Amor shook hands with Hephaestus.

"Was that really Hephaestus, God of Mechanics," Iona asked, trailing behind Neoma.

"Yes, that was Lord Hephaestus."

"No one in my family is going to believe this."

Neoma stopped and turned to Iona. "You will not tell anyone about meeting Lord Hephaestus or of this place. You pathetic mortals aren't even supposed to know about these halls. You should have been executed! Lord Hephaestus showed you mercy."

"Ease up," Amor said. "Iona won't tell anyone. She's trustworthy."

"As if I'd believe the word of your kind," Neoma sniffed. She turned sharply and walked briskly to the exit, forcing Iona and Amor to run to keep up with her. She opened the doors between the maintenance halls and the living levels. In a few short steps, Iona found herself outside the city of Corinth by the wall.

"Remember, you can't tell anyone about what you've seen," Neoma said before shutting the door. The panel blended in perfectly with the rest of the wall. Though Iona just traveled through it, she never would have known a door was hidden in the wall.

Looking back at Amor, she realized that the lights were starting to dim as night approached. Her family would be worried about her.

"I should get home," Iona said. "I had a wonderful time, Amor. I will meet you here tomorrow."

Amor took her hands in his. "I will count the seconds," he promised. She expected him to sweep her up in one of his breath-stealing, world-tilting kisses, but he merely winked and ran off. A little disappointed, she walked back to Errita's home.

Entering the modest home, she found her brother-in-law, Theron, and Errita waiting for her. Her mind raced with what she could tell them and still keep the secrets of what really happened. She would never tell them she met with Amor, or that she had the honor of meeting Hephaestus. But what could she tell them that they'd believe?

"Where have you been," Errita demanded. "We were worried sick about you! We sent Achimedes out to watch over you, and you somehow managed to give him the slip! We had no idea where you were or if you were safe!"

"I wanted to be alone for a while," Iona said. "I'm a big girl, Errita. I went shopping and stayed near the temples. Oh, Errita, the Temple of Aphrodite has the most amazing statues. I could stare at them all day."

"We were trying to find you all day! Achimedes said someone kidnapped you at the temple! Where were you?"

"What's going on?" Iona caught the tremor in her sister's voice.

"I got a call from Mother," Errita said. "Father contacted her. He was accepted in to see the Oracle. He should be home in a few days with the message. We're leaving for Mom and Dad's."

Iona felt her heart sink. If they left tomorrow, it would be another time she left Amor without word. "What time?"

"In a few days. Theron has a charity event tomorrow afternoon and I am still working on an important robe."

"Philomena and her husband will be joining us as well," Theron said. "I expect them to arrive in the morning, so no more running around unescorted. Zotikos was firm about the dangers of that Amor fellow."

The next day, Iona was careful as she left the house. She was mindful of the time as she wandered from shop to shop. It took her a few tries to slip past her guard, but she finally lost him as he flirted with a pretty maid in a local restaurant. Iona made her way to the Temple of Aphrodite to meet with Amor to tell him the good news and promise to see him in Tiryns.

"I will show up a few days after your father tells you the news," Amor said, kissing her neck. "I can't wait to see the look on their faces when you marry me."

"I can't wait either," Iona said. "That day won't come fast enough."

"Until then, my love, take this gift and think of me." Amor slipped a ring on her finger. She gasped, looking at the unique design. Arrows and flowers entwined in a form that was as special as his love for her.

"Oh, Amor, it's beautiful," she breathed. "I'll never take it off."

"I asked Hephaestus to make it for you. It will only fit your finger."

"He was able to make this in just one night?"

Amor smiled. "I asked him for it the day I met you. I just feel that now is the right time to give it to you."

She left him with high expectations. In just a few days, she and Amor would be officially engaged. She had Amor's word that the Oracle would name him as her husband, and she believed him. He knew Hephaestus, and lived near the gods. She had a feeling he was far more than what he said he was, and that made her victory all the sweeter.

Two days later, she and her sisters left for her parents' home. Her spirits were high and she couldn't wait to see her parents.

Chapter 10

Returning to her parent's home was bittersweet. Iona knew that this was the last time she would enter as an unmarried daughter. The next time she visited her parents, she would be a wife. Soon, she would be told that Amor is her betrothed and they would quickly be married.

"I'm going to freshen up," Iona said, walking up to her old room. She wanted to look her best when she got the news. She also wanted to compose herself and pretend to be surprised when they named her one true love.

Humming under her breath, she changed into her favorite purple dress and put on some of the jewelry that Amor gifted her. With a smile, she admired the ring from Amor. She could picture herself placing the wedding band next to the gold arrow-and-roses band.

She took a moment to straighten her veil before walking downstairs. She made plans to visit the Temple of Aphrodite that night to give thanks for this wonderful day.

The scene that greeted her in the living room was not one of jubilation. Hedyla was muffling her sobs in her veil while Philomena and Errita comforted her. Metasis, her father, was in grave conversation with Zotikos and Theron. Iona felt a flash of anger as she observed the reactions of her family. Obviously, her parents decided to not wait for her to come down before telling everyone else the Oracle's words. She couldn't help but wonder what horrible lies her parents were told about Amor.

"It's not that bad," Iona said. "I know the Oracle came as a shock, but he's a really nice man. Mother, you'd like him if you gave him a chance."

At this, Hedyla sobbed harder. Her sisters' faces were blank, not giving away what they thought.

"You've met this monster," Metasis gasped.

"He's not a monster," Iona said. "He's nice and he loves me. You can't believe what you've heard, Father. I know him."

"He's a serpent," Zotikos snapped. "Iona, I don't think you understand what has been happening. The Oracle told your father why your suitors have mysteriously left you."

"Yes, I know," Iona said. "I know all about that. He told me."

"You know he's a serpent," Metasis asked horrified.

"No, he's not a serpent. Father, Amor is a nice man. He's a devotee of Eros and I love him."

There was silence in the room. Zotikos gave a low, nervous chuckle.

"Who is Amor," asked Metasis.

Iona frowned. "Amor Myloneous. The man the Oracle said is to be my husband."

Metasis shook his head. "Honey, the Oracle didn't name any man. It named the serpent that circles the station from space."

"A serpent?"

"A winged serpent," Theron added. "One that eats the tender flesh of maidens." Theron looked down as Hedyla gave another wail.

"I don't understand," Iona said. "Am I to be a bride or a snack?"

"Maybe both," Zotikos said. "This serpent has chosen you, so no mortal man can claim you. Believe me, Iona, I would have preferred Amor over this fate."

Iona shook her head. "No, this isn't possible. Amor promised me!"

"Men say things that they don't mean," Errita said. "He lied, Iona. There was no way he could predict what the Oracle would say."

"You don't understand," Iona protested. "Amor was the real thing. He knows the gods! I've seen it! He wouldn't have promised me if he wasn't telling the truth."

"No one can truly know the gods," Theron said. "I'm the son of Apollo, and I don't know my father. None of us can know the gods."

Iona shook her head. "You don't understand. I believed him. We're meant to be together."

Metasis pulled his daughter to him. "I'm so sorry, Iona. We have no choice in this. It's the will of the gods."

"I've never even heard of a serpent circling the station," Iona said. "How can I be betrothed to something that I've never even knew existed."

"I've never heard of it either," Metasis said, "but if the gods say it's there, then I believe them."

Iona could not remember seeing a massive serpent when Amor took her to see the stars. She could remember the dead planet under them, but not a serpent. "I don't think there is a serpent out there," she declared. "Maybe you heard wrong, Father."

"Believe me, Iona, I heard right. I even begged the Oracle to give me some hope," Metasis said. "There is nothing more for us to do. We have been ordered to take you to the Temple of Aphrodite for purification. Tomorrow, you will be dressed for your wedding and brought to the eastern airlock, number 135, and ejected out to your husband."

"That will kill me!"

"Your wedding is also your funeral," Hedyla sobbed. "Oh, my poor daughter. You're too young to die."

"What if I refuse? I defy the gods! I won't let you send me into space!"

Metasis sighed. "We have no choice. If you are not delivered to the airlock tomorrow, than we are cursed."

"Isn't it also a curse to sacrifice your own daughter? How many of our heroes have suffered the wrath of the gods for killing their own children?" Iona looked around the room. "Why won't any of you help me? Why are you so ready to let me die?"

Philomena stood. "How can you say that? Listen to Mother, her heart is breaking. None of us want you to die."

"Then help me! Don't just deliver me to my death!"

"And have our lives cursed? If we give you to your husband, only one person must suffer. If we keep you, we all suffer," Philomena said.

Hedyla stood up, angrily. "That's not why we're doing this. Of course we'll suffer if we deliver Iona. I will mourn her for the rest of my life, but we cannot defy the gods. We have no choice."

Iona slowly sank to the floor as she realized that she would have no help. Her parents resigned themselves to her fate, while her sisters would rather sacrifice her than give up their good lives. She was going to die.

"How long do I have to live," she asked softly.

"Just twenty-four hours," Metasis said. "The wedding won't wait much longer. We are under orders. The guards will be here soon to pick you up."

Iona stood and squared her shoulders. She could see the hope in her father's eyes that she accepted her fate. It would be so easy for her to just give in. However, her heart would not forget Amor. He would arrive in a few days. If she could just wait it out until he came for her, they could run away. He knew Hephaestus, and she hoped that the God of the Forge would take pity on them. Surely a god can speak on her behalf in this matter.

"I'm sorry," Iona said. "I can't do this." She turned and ran for the door. Theron easily caught her, tossing her over his shoulder.

"Let me go! Theron, don't do this! I thought I was like a little sister to you!" Iona kicked and punched Theron as he carried her up to her room. He ignored her pleas and tossed her on the bed.

"I'm sorry," he whispered, "but we must fulfill the will of the gods. No matter how horrible the sacrifice, they will not abandon us. You'll see, Iona. Your sacrifice will bring greatness on our family, and we will always honor you."

"And what greatness will you claim for the murder of your sister-in-law?"

"If we do this, Errita will finally be blessed with a child. I can't risk that. If it's a girl, we'll name her after you."

"I hope she's barren," Iona spat. For a second, Theron looked horrified before he shut the door. She heard him lock it and walk away. She was trapped, forced to wait for the guards to come and take her away.

"Oh, Amor," she cried, covering her face with her hands. "I didn't want it to end this way." She felt the sobs rise from her chest and explode as she wailed. She curled up on her bed, crying so hard that her body shook. Every time she started to calm down, she thought about Amor and started to cry again.

She gasped as she heard voices downstairs. The guards had arrived. Choking back her sobs, Iona realized that her time run out.

"I can't let it end this way," she whispered. She ran to her window and looked down. Vines grew along the wall, but she wasn't sure if they could hold her weight. It was a long drop to the ground, one that could break bones in her body if she landed wrong.

Hearing the footsteps coming up the stairs, she made up her mind. She'd rather try to escape than just wait for them to find her. Swinging herself over the edge of her window, she grabbed the vines and started to climb down. She made it only about two feet before the vines broke and she fell. Iona couldn't stop the shriek that ripped from her lips as she plummeted to the ground. As she landed, the wind was knocked from her lungs.

For a moment, she lay there, unable to breathe. Panicked, she wondered if she'd ever be able to breathe again, or if this was how she'd die. When she drew her first breath, the air never tasted so sweet. She was surprised that no one came out to investigate the noise she made. Not wanting to waste her good luck, she slowly started to stand.

"Oh," she moaned as she put her weight on her left leg. Sharp pains shot up her left leg and it hurt to breathe too deeply. Limping slightly, she moved to the wall to look at her leg. She didn't see any bones sticking out, which made her feel slightly better.

"My, my, it looks like you twisted your ankle," came a smooth voice to her right. Iona looked up to see the same soldier of Ares who helped her many months ago when she first met Amor. His bright eyes pinned her to the wall and she found herself trembling with fear. "Possibly even broken it. That must hurt."

"Are you the one they sent to take me to the Temple of Aphrodite," Iona asked, her voice wavering.

The man nodded. "Be a good girl, Iona Demarchis, and don't fight this."

Iona slowly moved along the wall, limping whenever she put her left foot down. "You helped me once before," she said. "Help me now. I can't marry a serpent. I love Amor."

For a second, the man blinked. He stared at her as if she grown another head before a grin split his face. He started to laugh; a slow, rolling chuckle that gained momentum into a deep belly laugh.

"You," he gasped, holding his sides, "you want me to save you?" Tears ran down his face from his laughter. Iona failed to see the humor in her request.

"Why are you laughing? I thought you and Amor were friends."

"Friends? I hate him! Always grabbing at Mother's skirts, too scared to ever fight back," he said. He raised his voice to mimic a woman's and simpered, "Mother, Phobos hurt me. Mother, Phobos is being mean to me. Whaah!"

"Amor doesn't sound like that," Iona snapped. Then she

paused. "Wait! Who did you just say you were?"

"The makings of your nightmare," the man said. He grabbed her and threw her over his shoulder before bringing her inside. Iona groaned as she was flipped upside down and his hard shoulder dug into her stomach. She was almost positive he called himself Phobos, the same name as the son of Ares and God of Fear.

"I found her," Phobos said. "She was trying to escape through the window."

Hedyla gasped. "Iona, are you all right?"

"Oh, I'm just doing great," Iona said. "My ankle hurts, I can barely breathe, and you're planning on feeding me to flying serpent, but I'm doing just fine."

"Don't be flippant," Zotikos said. "None of us are happy with this decision."

"You're feeding me to a serpent!" Iona tried to wiggle off Phobos' boney shoulder, wincing as he pressed painfully in her stomach. "If you were really unhappy over this, you'd help me escape."

Zotikos looked much older than he was, the despair naked on his face. He opened his mouth to talk, but Philomena stopped him. "Iona, I will not allow my husband be cursed because you finally got your wish. You will be married; something you've always wanted."

"I never wanted this," Iona protested. "I wanted a quiet life in the Temple of Flora! I never even wanted to be married!"

"That's enough," Phobos said. He walked out of the house with Iona still on his shoulder. He dumped her on the bottom of his carriage and they left.

Iona couldn't stop sobbing the whole ride to the temple. It was only when Phobos pulled her up and whispered, "Pull yourself together. Don't let them see you cry," did she stop.

He dragged her to a back room and shoved her inside. "I'll be back tomorrow to escort you to the airlock," he said. "Get some sleep. Your bridal maids will be here at sun rise."

"Bridal maids or funeral attendants?"

"Whatever." The door slammed shut and Iona sank to the floor in despair.

Chapter 11

Iona barely slept that night. She lay awake in her bed, listening to every small sound. She prayed that it was Amor coming to her rescue. Each time, she was disappointed as it was only a guard or a servant checking up on her. In small spurts, she managed to get some sleep that night.

Her last meal was breakfast. She glumly pushed bits of fresh fruit around on the plate, too depressed to eat. Amor had not come to save her. She was unsure if he even knew her fate. What if he showed up some time after this farce to find her dead?

"Oh, wedding jitters," asked Philomena as she entered the room. "When I married Zotikos, I was too nervous to eat. You remember that, don't you? I nearly fainted at his feet."

"It's not wedding jitters," Iona said, shoving a strawberry ruthlessly through a sea of honey and juices.

"You're still not hung up on who you're marrying, are you? Maybe the serpent is nice? Have you ever thought of that?"

"I want Amor."

Philomena sniffed. "Well, I wanted a handsome, young husband, but we can't be choosy. Zotikos turned out to be a great guy. Give your husband a chance."

"This isn't the same thing," Iona protested. "Your wedding wasn't doubling as your funeral!"

"Nothing can be done," Philomena insisted. "Come and look at your dress. Mother and I spent all night picking it out. She and Errita will be here later, after the ceremonies."

Iona stood up, wincing as she put pressure on her hurt ankle. "Something can be done," she said. "There still is time. You can help me get out of here. I can ask for sanctuary in the Temple of Flora or a Temple of Hephaestus. I can proclaim my virginity to the gods and live in a temple. Anything would be better than being fed to a serpent!"

"I don't think so," Philomena said. "Stop being silly."

"Please, Philomena, help me!" Iona grabbed her sister's arm. "You can't just feed me to a serpent! Why would you do this?"

Philomena gave her a cold look. Iona took a step back,

suddenly scared of her sister. "Why am I doing this? You mean, besides that it is the will of the gods?"

"I'm your sister," Iona said weakly. "Why won't you even consider saving me?"

"If you marry that serpent, then Theron has been promised a child within five years. Would you deny Errita the joys of motherhood? You leave and abandon this marriage, and she could be barren for the rest of her life. You know how much she and Theron want children. By Hera, you are the most selfish person I've ever met."

"What were you promised, Philomena? I know you wouldn't be so eager for my marriage if you weren't getting something out of this. What did the gods promise you?"

"I was promised a more lucrative career. Zotikos had some money from his position and connections, but it's been my singing that has given us our lifestyle. Your marriage means a better life for me," Philomena spat. "And who do you think will take care of our parents in their old age? Not Errita, I can tell you that. I hoped it would be you, but with you out of the picture it will fall on me. So the better my career and position, the better our parents will live during their twilight years."

"What of me," Iona asked.

Philomena shrugged. "You could wind up the best of all of us, living as the wife to a rich monster. Though how a winged serpent could see you from space is beyond me."

Iona's heart sank. Just because she hadn't seen any serpent didn't mean there hadn't been one lurking in the inky blackness of space. "I think I know when it saw me," she whispered.

Philomena unpacked the wedding dress. "Oh, do tell."

"Amor took me away from the living area of the levels once. He showed me the stars." Iona smiled at the memory. "It was so beautiful, Philomena. Real stars and space that just went on forever. It's like smelling real flowers when all you know are the fake ones."

"I prefer fake flowers," Philomena said. "You don't get those nasty blue pests in your garden beds."

Realizing she would get no help from her sister, Iona finally inspected her wedding dress. The deep amethyst purple dress was one of her favorites. If she had to meet her death, this was a nice dress to it in. Philomena brought some of her jewelry, and Iona had a sinking suspicion that her sisters already divided her possessions among them as she noted that only the cheapest of her jewelry had been brought. Iona was thankful she was still wearing Amor's ring and that it wouldn't fall into her sisters' hands.

Soon, her mother and Errita entered the room, followed by servants and a large copper tub. Silently, Iona allowed her family to bathe her and slather perfumes on her body. The fact that many of the funeral rites and wedding rites were so similar was not lost on Iona. When she was dressed and decked with jewels, she was escorted into the main part of the temple. Wisely, the servants stayed by her side so she could not escape.

Iona was placed on a dais. Several of her old suitors came up with gifts that they laid on the ground or on the edge of the dais. They offered words of congratulations and left to mourn her fate. Many of them praised her still as Aphrodite, repeating how they found their one true loves after meeting Iona. She heard them talking about how the serpent was really Hephaestus, but Iona knew better. Hephaestus was too kind to allow her to be shot out into space. Amor was not among the suitors and she could not see him at all in the crowds.

The feast lasted for several hours, but she was not allowed to eat. The dead, she was told, do not eat. Iona's only job was to sit there and look pretty. Words were said in her honor and everyone around her had a good time. She felt it was disrespectful for everyone to be laughing and drinking when she was about to die. Though not allowed to eat, she was able to sneak a few morsels to try and calm her grumbling stomach.

Finally, the time came. She planned on jumping off her dais and running once they were out of the city. She could find her way back to the maintenance halls and hide with Hephaestus. She would do anything to get out of this unholy marriage.

With fear, she watched as Phobos walked up to her with a cup in his hands. He knelt in front of her and held out the cup. She could smell something sweeter than wine and honey.

"Take your last drink," he ordered.

"And if I refuse," she whispered, not wanting everyone to overhear her.

He moved back slightly and reached into his pocket. When he brought his hand back, she could see a syringe filled with a light green liquid. "Either you do this the easy way, or the hard way. Don't make this worse on your family than it already is. Imagine how traumatic it will be for them if I have to wrestle you to the ground, break a few of your bones, and drive this needle into you."

"The easy way," Iona said, taking the cup. "Have you spoken to Amor?"

"Drink first, and then I'll answer."

"Answer first, and then I'll drink."

Phobos smiled. "I can just hold you down and shove this needle into your veins and you'll never get your answer," he said. He grasped her hurt ankle and squeezed, a reminder that she would be no match for him.

Iona drank the contents of the cup. When she was done, she set the cup down and glared at him. She silently demanded that he tell her what she wanted to know.

"I have decided," Phobos said, "that I like you. Not romantically, so don't get any ideas. However, I think I approve of you, and I don't believe I've ever said that in all of my life."

"And about Amor?"

"I don't approve of him at all."

"I meant," Iona started, but had to stop as the world blurred in and out of focus. She blinked before continuing, "I meant, did you talk to him?"

"You won't die tonight," Phobos said. "Not if everything goes to plan." The world swam out of focus again and when Iona opened her eyes, she realized her head slumped forward.

She tried to ask him what he had done to her, but her tongue was too heavy. Phobos reached out and picked her up. He carried her over to a funeral platform and gently laid her on top. Her family came over to arrange the flowers and to see to it that her body was in the right position. Her father and Theron lifted the platform up and the funeral march began.

From her prone position, it was hard for Iona to see any of the people following the platform. She could hear them, though. Hundreds of mourners wailed about her dying so young. Flowers and jewelry was thrown up on the platform. Iona wished she weren't drugged so she could shield herself after a necklace landed on her face.

After what seemed like an eternity, they arrived at Airlock

135. She could hear them opening the airlock before she was brought inside. Phobos lifted her from the platform and laid her out on an altar.

"Be brave, Iona," her father said. "We love you."

"My first daughter will be named after you," Theron promised. "And we will tell her how brave and beautiful you were."

"We will never forget you," said Zotikos. All three left her as she bitterly thought of how easy that was. Just dump her in the airlock and go. They weren't the ones waiting for death.

Phobos' head leaned into her view. "Whatever you do, don't move," he advised. "This may be unpleasant, but if you move, you will die. Stay here, and you will live."

He tilted her head to the side so she could watch the airlock doors. Just beyond those metal slabs was the vast vacuum of space. She heard Phobos leave and then there was silence. This time, when the world blurred, it was from her tears.

Time slowly ticked by. Iona could hear the mechanical sounds deep in the station and thought of Hephaestus. The ugly god had been so nice to her, and she never got a chance to repay him. Was the airlock operated by Hephaestus? Maybe she had a chance. He'd never open the doors if he knew she was in there.

Her limbs started to tingle as the tranquilizer wore off. She was able to lift her head a bit, but not enough for her to get off the altar. She tried to call for help, but her voice was still paralyzed.

As she lifted her head again, seeing if she could get more of her body up, she heard a loud, metallic bang. Iona looked around the airlock the best she could for the source. Seeing nothing, she rested her head down. It must have just been part of the space station.

Then the noise came again. This time, she heard a grinding sound after it. Lifting her head, she saw the gears on the airlock door slowly moving. Her heart beat faster as she realized that the doors were going to open.

Click. Click. Click.

Slowly – extremely slow – the gears on the door moved. Iona watched in horror as the gears clicked slowly, taking their sweet time in opening. Beyond it lay the vacuum of space and her death. Despite what Phobos promised, she was sure she'd die.

The gears finished their clicking and there was a grinding as the doors inched open. Iona closed her eyes, too scared to see her death. The darkness behind her eyelids became a brilliant red as light flashed through the airlock. She heard a loud whoosh of air and held her breath. A single tear slid down her cheek as she waited for death.

When her father looked in the airlock, the doors were closing and Iona was nowhere to be seen.

Chapter 12

"Lady Iona? Lady Iona, are you all right? Take a deep breath. You can breathe here."

Iona was only vaguely aware of the kind voice. She squeezed her eyes shut, worried that it was a trick. She could still see in her mind's eye the airlock doors starting to open and feel the force of the air being sucked into space. She held her breath, waiting for the airless space to crush her lungs.

"Please, open your eyes. I promise you're all right."

Unable to hold her breath any longer, Iona gasped. Sweet air filled her lungs ... then another ... and another. Once it registered in her frazzled mind that the voice was right and she was alive, she started to cry. Phobos must have told Amor about the wedding and he saved her! She had not been swept into space as she had feared!

A soft hand gripped her shoulder. She opened her eyes, expecting to see Amor. Instead, she found herself facing a young man with curly light brown hair and a short beard. Behind him, she could see a console with blinking lights.

"Who are you?"

"You can call me Zephyrus. I'm your escort to your new home and grateful servant of your husband."

Iona frowned slightly. She heard the name Zephyrus before, but could not remember where. Still clinging to the vain hope that her prayers been answered, she asked, "Are you Amor's servant?"

Zephyrus looked confused. "No. Amor isn't the name of my master." He smiled gently at her. "Lady Iona, you already know the name of your husband. The Oracle told your family. That's why you're here."

Iona's heart sank as she realized what Zephyrus said. She hadn't been saved. She was in the lair of the winged serpent. Blinking back tears, she muttered, "I guess it was too much to hope that Phobos talked to Amor."

"But, it's because of Phobos I knew to bring you here," Zephyrus said. "My master is away on business, and we did not know your wedding would be so soon. If it hadn't been for Phobos, you would not have survived."

Iona burst bitterly into tears, curling up on the small table. For a short while, Zephyrus allowed her to cry before reaching out and gently helping her to sit up. She wiped the tears from her eyes. She would mourn her losses later.

"Do not be so sad, Lady Iona," Zephyrus said. He sounded confused, unsure of why she was crying. "My master is kind man and you will be well taken care of in his home."

"I miss my family," Iona lied.

"I am sorry. Nothing can be done about that. They are not allowed here."

"They would not want to come here," Iona said bitterly, "knowing what I married."

Cautiously, Zephyrus asked, "What did you marry?"

"A monster. None of this was my wish. I am just a stupid pawn."

Zephyrus placed a cloak around her shoulders. "Come. I think everything will be explained when we get you home." He helped her across the room, allowing her to lean on him and pamper her hurt ankle. Outside the door was not the grand home she been dreading, but a long street lined with exquisite mansions and modest temples. Zephyrus hurried her along, pulling whenever she tried to stop to read the names over the temples.

"Hebe? Eileithyia? Who are these temples dedicated to? I don't believe I've ever heard of these gods."

"They are no one for you to worry about," Zephyrus said, hurrying her along. However, the more Iona thought about it, the more she was sure she heard of some of the gods. She had the strangest feeling that she was expected as they passed a temple with three women sitting by the doors. The way they watched her made her feel nervous. Further down the road, a trio of men with wings waved as she passed.

"Now, I'm sure I know who they are," Iona said. "I've seen them somewhere." She was nearly positive they looked like the other Cupids, the brothers of the god Eros.

"No you don't," Zephyrus said and pulled her down the street. Her husband's house sat at the end of the long street, and it was the only one without a temple. The marble walls were a light cream and rose color, and far grander than any home from Iona's wildest dreams. Frolicking cherubs adorned every room that Iona could see. Most of it was tastefully decorated, but she did see one tacky painting on velvet over a fireplace. Reading the inscription under it, she murmured, "Congratulations, Narcissuses."

"Come, there is something your husband wanted you to see," Zephyrus said. He brought her to the back of the house and into the most gorgeous garden Iona ever seen. The scent of so many flowers was thick in the air, and Iona could see a small line of Aneriams marching under some of the foliage. She doubted even the temples of Flora had gardens this beautiful.

"This is magnificent," Iona breathed. "I have never seen so many flowers before."

"My Master created this when he learned you enjoyed gardening. He had to promise some favors to get real flowers."

Iona knelt down to smell a bright red flower. "These are so lovely," she said. "I've only seen fakes of this kind. I never knew they smelled so sweet."

"That one is called a rose." A cold voice stated from behind Iona, causing her to turn guiltily. She felt as if she had been caught where she was not wanted. The woman behind her was tall and regal, with dark hair and a chiton that shimmered all the colors of the rainbow when she moved. "You must be the Lady Iona."

"I am. Who are you?"

The woman smiled, but it did not reach her dark eyes. She slowly circled Iona, measuring her worth. "You may call me Lethia. I am the stewardess of this house, and your personal maid. Anything you need, you tell me. I will see to it that your stay here is pleasant."

"Did you help set up the garden," Iona asked.

"I did," Lethia replied. She reached down to pet the petals of the rose. "Your husband was adamant that this garden meets your approval. He worried over it for days."

"Thank you," Iona said. "This garden is more than I could have hoped for." Iona wondered how this serpent known all this. Could a mere glance through a window reveal so much about her? How could he have created all of this in two days' time? Once more, she wondered if her husband was really a serpent.

Lethia nodded. "Your husband wanted the best for you. When I married, my husband created a similar gift. He found out that I enjoyed painting, and he made me a room in our house for me to paint to my heart's content."

"That sounds so lovely. Do you still paint?"

"No," Lethia said coldly. "I haven't touched my paints since my husband died."

Feeling awkward, Iona asked, "When will I meet my husband?"

"He is expected to return tonight," Lethia said. "There are some rules that you must follow, Lady Iona. Failure to do so will result in a painful death."

"A painful death," Zephyrus scoffed. "Really? Is that necessary? You're going to frighten her."

Lethia turned her cold eyes to Zephyrus. "It is necessary. I merely tell her this for her own protection. You should know this."

"You still don't have to be so dramatic, *Lethia*," Zephyrus said. The way he said her name reminded Iona of how Amor introduced himself.

"What are the rules," Iona asked.

"You can't leave this house or the gardens. You must never go down the street. Your husband's protection doesn't extend past the front door, and you will find that not everyone here is as friendly as we."

"What else?"

"You cannot contact your family. As far as they are concerned, you are dead." Lethia smiled slightly. "Trust me, it is for the best."

Iona blinked as tears suddenly blinded her vision. It wasn't to be expected. She knew her family thought she was dead. She had a funeral, after all. However, it was hard to think she couldn't correct them, to let them know she was alright after all.

"I can't ever talk to them," she asked, her voice squeaking. Zephyrus put his arm around her, giving her shoulder a squeeze.

"You are dead, Lady Iona," Lethia said. "When your father looked back in the airlock, he saw the doors closing and you gone. To them, you are dead."

"I don't feel dead. This isn't Hades. Why can't I tell them I'm still alive."

Lethia took a deep breath. She gave Iona an annoyed look before saying, "Your old life is over. You are no longer Lady Iona Demarchis of Tiryns. You are the wife of the master of this house, and will have no contact with the mortals you used to know."

Zephyrus bent down and whispered in Iona's ear, "You can't have contact with your family, but I am under no obligation."

"All right," Iona said. "I accept your rule."

Lethia frowned. "What did he say to you?"

"I told her that it would be all right," Zephyrus lied. "You should know that, Lethia." Again, he stressed her name. Lethia flinched slightly and her haughty demeanor slipped. Iona could see sadness under her icy glare before her mask was put back in place.

"Lastly," Lethia said, "you must not ever attempt to look at your husband. He is busy during the day and will come home at night. You will have all your lamps extinguished by that time and you will not attempt to sneak a peek at him."

"Oh, really now! That's just stupid," Zephyrus exclaimed. "How can you even make that a rule?"

"Why am I not allowed to see him," Iona protested. "I am his wife. I should be allowed to see my own husband."

"It's for your own protection," Lethia said.

Iona looked up at Zephyrus, but he shrugged. "I think it's a silly rule," he said. "I mean, the two of you -"

"It's for her protection," Lethia interrupted. Zephyrus turned to look at the woman. They had a silent battle of wills that consisted of mouthed words and pointed glares. Finally, Zephyrus relented. With a sigh, he turned from Lethia and pretended to find a flower interesting.

"Is it because he's a serpent," Iona asked. "Is that why I'm not allowed to see him?"

Zephyrus made a choking sound and Lethia smiled. "A serpent," she said. "Ah, yes. That's why you can't see him. In the dark, he can take a human form, but if you dare to gaze on him, he will transform back into his natural state."

"Lethia, really," Zephyrus protested.

"She deserves to be warned," Lethia said. Zephyrus grabbed her and pulled her back into the garden. Iona could hear them whispering, but not what was being said. Finally, a grumpy Zephyrus returned.

"Despite my not wishing to upset you, Lady Iona," he said, "Lethia does have a point on your being warned. The final rule is the most important one."

"So, I will never be allowed to see my husband, see my

family, or leave this house," Iona asked. When Lethia nodded, she sighed. "All right, I'll abide by your rules."

Lethia gave her a cold, triumphant smile. "Good. Now, Lady Iona, if you will follow me. I will show you around your new home. Zephyrus, you are dismissed."

"I think I'll tag along," Zephyrus said. By his tone, Iona knew that he didn't trust Lethia, and she was starting to not trust the woman either.

"Someone should go and tell the Master that his bride has arrived," Lethia said.

"Fine," Zephyrus growled. "But this is the last time, Lethia. Lady Iona is my mistress now, not you. This is the last time you'll ever boss me around."

Lethia took Iona by the arm. "That's just fine by me," she said. "Come, Lady Iona. There is much to see."

Chapter 13

Eros stormed into the Apollo command center of Olympus. The command center was the eyes and brain of Space Station *Olympus*. Zeus may be the supreme god and ruler, but Apollo was the true power behind the throne. He knew everyone's dirty little secrets and nothing got past his greedy sun cameras. On every level, Apollo had several cameras hidden in the ceilings, statues and various everyday objects to capture the lives of the mortals below him. Eros knew he kept cameras throughout Olympus to spy on his fellow gods, as well.

"Apollo, we need to talk," Eros announced.

Apollo didn't acknowledge him. Instead, he leaned down over a minion, staring intently at one of the thousands of video screens.

"Zoom in on camera fifteen-dash-seven-C," he said. "Yes, that one. A little closer, over the lake."

"Yes Lord Apollo," the minion said in a hollow voice. Eros tapped his foot as the picture on the image on the screen became larger.

"Oh, nice. Twins," Apollo purred. "Make a copy of this tape and send it to my rooms. And find out their names."

"Yes Lord Apollo."

"Are you quite done, or are you going to spend the rest of the afternoon oogling girls as they bathe," Eros snapped.

Apollo moved to another minion and whispered in his ear. Eros could not stand by and be ignored any longer. He moved towards the notorious womanizer. He went here for answers, and he would not leave until he got them.

"Apollo, we had a deal! You betrayed me," Eros snapped. He grabbed the sun god and forced him to face him. Apollo's bright eyes narrowed as he brushed off Eros.

"I did not betray you. I fulfilled our bargain. You got your little human and Aphrodite is none the wiser."

"Had Phobus not warned me, she would have been swept out into space," Eros spat. "What possessed you to pull such a stunt!"

"Do you or do you not have that lovely little plaything in

your house," Apollo asked in a bored tone. It was then that Eros noticed the screen that the minion was staring in to. His home as Psyche led Iona around the rooms. She made it safely to his home, and he knew that he should be glad.

"Why a winged serpent? Why put her through a mock funeral? What is your game, Apollo?"

Apollo leaned coolly back against the monitor as he studied Eros. "Call it payback for all your little stunts," he said. "Take your pick: Daphne, Zephyrus, Coronis or any of the others." He turned back to the console, watching as Psyche left Iona in a bathing chamber. "You have your little human, so I suggest you start thinking really hard about how you'll pay me."

On the screen, Iona started to take off her funeral dress. "Don't watch her while she's bathing," Eros snapped as he realized what was about to happen.

Apollo shrugged and motioned for the operator to change the channel. It now showed a cozy scene in the Fates home as the three women knitted and talked by the fireplace. Eros breathed a sigh of relief to know that, for now, Apollo would not be spying on his bride.

"Don't forget about paying me back," Apollo advised. "It would be a real shame if Aphrodite were to learn of sweet Iona's whereabouts. At the moment, your mother is still out for this human's blood. I'm sure that she'll calm down in a few months, but it's best to hide her until then." The screen flickered back to Iona. She relaxed in a tub, her long red-brown hair floating around her nude body, barely covering her from Apollo's hungry view.

"Apollo, stop watching her," Eros demanded.

The sun god turned to look at the monitor with a smile. "She is quite lovely for a human. I'm sure she'd amuse me for a week or so."

Eros saw red. He lunged at Apollo, striking him across the face with his fist. Apollo staggered back, taken by surprise. Before he could fight back, Eros grabbed the front of his tunic and punched again. All Eros cared about was the sound of his fist connecting with Apollo's face. It took five of the sun god's minions to pull him away.

"I will kill you if you touch her!" Eros tried to lunge again, but the minions held him down.

Apollo wiped the blood off his face. Eros could see that he broke the sun god's nose and was pleased to know that he had marred Apollo's beauty. When Apollo faced him, his face was red with rage. His eyes flashed with the promise of murder.

"You won't do a thing," he sneered, pulling himself back up. He rubbed his jaw before continuing, "You forget your place, Eros. Look around! I am one of the major twelve gods of Olympus. I have a whole level dedicated just to my worship and temples on every single occupied level. There are feast days in my honor and statues to my greatness.

"What do you have? One home on a level set aside for the temples of the forgotten gods. No real temple or worship to speak of. Any worship for you has to go through your mommy. You don't even receive offerings. You're forgotten, a nobody. I can do anything I want! I am a god!"

Eros clenched his fists, the desire to strike Apollo rising in him. He knew he should pick his battles more carefully, but the arrogant sun god angered him.

But he was right. Eros was nearly a non-entity, seen only as the son of his mother. His brothers had been forgotten except for the faithful Cupids who continued to worship them. He needed Apollo's silence to keep Aphrodite from finding Iona, and to do so, he would have to humble himself for the sun god.

Eros started to kneel, but the minions still held him up. Apollo nodded and they let him go and he knelt on the ground. He kept his head low and said, "Forgive me, Lord Apollo. I did not mean to overstep my bounds. I am appreciative of your help." The words burned in his throat.

"Just groveling won't win my forgiveness," Apollo said. "I demand some kind of repayment."

"If it is in my power, Lord Apollo, then name it."

Apollo tapped his chin as gazed back at the screens. Eros tensed up, scared that the sun god would ask for the one thing Eros could not give. Finally, Apollo reached over and changed the scene on the screen to reflect two blonde twin girls laughing as they shopped. "I want them," Apollo said. "You will use those damned darts of yours and make them mine."

"For how long," Eros asked.

"Forever."

Eros frowned. He knew that Apollo would grow tired of them and toss them aside. No woman, mortal or otherwise, ever sated him for long. Looking up at the arrogant deity, Eros sighed. "As you command, Lord Apollo."

Apollo smiled. "Very good, Eros. That wasn't so bad, now was it? Just remember with whom you are dealing and everything will work out."

Eros stood and left. One minion stopped him at the door to tell him where to find the twins. He quickly did his duty and left the distasteful scene of the twins suddenly deciding to travel to be servants at the Temple of the Delphi. It wouldn't be forever, but just long enough so that Apollo wouldn't notice when they woke up their lustful stupor and left him. All he wanted was to get home and be with his wife. He had a feeling that Apollo would be watching and wished that he could stop him. Apollo loved to watch everyone. It was his one true power.

Once Eros walked through the door, he was greeted by Psyche. This woman had been his old host's wife, and she hoped that he would honor that bond. It just couldn't be. When his old host died after the transference, so did the love that he felt for Psyche. In respect for his old host, he had not tossed her out on the street. That should have been enough.

"Your little wife is waiting for you in your room," Psyche said. Her voice was tight and she looked as if she smelled something unpleasant. "I told her the rules of the house."

"What rules? I never left any instructions for rules."

"The same rules I followed when I came here," Psyche said. "She will not wander out of the safety of the house and she will not contact her family. Also, your identity is safe."

"And your identity? Does she know who you are?"

"No. I told her my name was Lethia. As far as she's concerned, I'm her maidservant."

"What kind of stupid name is Lethia? Where did you come up with that?" Eros sighed and dropped his darts and gun on the table. "Are you sure it's wise to have her follow the same rules my old host had you follow? It never did you two any good."

"It must be this way," Psyche said. "She is convinced that if she looks at you, you will turn into a serpent and eat her."

"She believes what? What possessed you to encourage that?"

Psyche smiled sadly, some of the tightness draining from her face. "It has to be this way. You know this, Eros. Deep down, you know that this must all happen like this or you will lose her."

"And if I decide to tell her the truth? She can be trusted."

"You can try," Psyche said. She ran a hand up Eros' arm. "My husband made my first nights here memorable. Do the same for Iona. Give her some happy memories."

Eros pushed Psyche away from him. She was lovely, his old host would not marry someone unworthy of being named Psyche, but she was not what he wanted. He could remember what his old host felt and the times he spent with Psyche. But, his old host was dead. He would never be that Eros ever again. The sooner he got rid of Psyche, the better.

"Don't ever touch me," he said and walked away. As much as he detested her, there was a spark in Psyche that Iona was missing. Something soul-deep, but he couldn't put his finger on it. He stalked down the halls to his room. It was dark, lit only by a single candle that barely cast any light beyond his doorway. Iona was in his bed, her back to the door. He could tell she was awake by the way she jumped when he entered, but she was extremely conscious of the rules.

He blew out the candle and undressed. Sliding under the covers, he pulled his wife closer to him. He kissed the back of her neck, hoping she would turn in his arms and kiss him back. Instead, she stiffened and refused to move. He could almost smell her fear and it broke his heart.

"What's wrong," he asked softly. "You are my wife. Why would you pull away?"

"I'm scared," she whispered. "I lost everything today. I had no time to prepare myself for my wedding or for the fright of nearly being pulled into space."

"There is nothing to fear here," he said. "I will always protect you."

"My family thinks I'm dead. So does the man I loved. I feel so alone."

Eros kissed he shoulder. "You have me."

Iona took a deep breath and burst into tears. Each sob was an arrow through Eros' heart. He wanted to tell her the truth, to turn her around to face him. Once she saw that her husband was Amor, she would be happy again. However, his arms felt like lead when he tried to turn her to face him.

Clearing his throat, he started to tell her the truth. The second he tried to verbalize the truth, his traitorous tongue betrayed him.

"I will give you space tonight, my wife. I love you, Iona, and I always have. I know you were in love with another man, but he is not here. I am, and you are mine."

Chapter 14

Iona stretched lazily as the imitation sunlight streamed through the open bedroom windows. A light breeze lifted the sheer curtains, causing them to flutter over her body. She rolled over in the bed, one hand reaching to the spot where her husband had lain, but all she found was a warm, empty place. He left before she woke. Like a bolt of lightning, the previous day's events came back to her. Iona curled up on the bed, staring at the indent her husband left behind. She betrayed Amor! She dared to let another man hold her.

It was just…he sounded so much like Amor. In the dark, she could pretend it was he who held her, he who comforted her. She knew it wasn't, but the fantasy was preferred to her reality. While he slept, she explored his body in the dark. He felt like a fine man, but he was not human. She touched the feathery soft wings on his back and she was sure her hands skimmed over rough scaly skin on occasion. Without light, it was impossible to tell what he truly looked like, and the meager impressions she was able to obtain were not enough to put her fears to rest.

"Lady Iona, are you awake?" Lethia entered her room with a pile of clothes in her arms. If she noticed the tears in Iona's eyes, she ignored them. "The bathing chamber is ready for you, should you wish to use it this morning. I have breakfast set up in the gardens and a list of what you will need to know about running this household."

"Thank you," Iona said, wiping the last of her tears away. "That is very kind of you."

Lethia placed the clothes on the end of the bed. "It is my job," she said coldly and left.

Iona quickly bathed and dressed. Her husband must have known that purple was her favorite color for her new clothes were in every shade she ever imagined. The chiton started as the lightest lilac and ended in a hue of regal violet. Jewelry of silver and amethyst were left for her to adorn herself with, along with a new ring. A simple note attached let her know that this was her wedding ring and her husband would be honored if she wore it. Iona could not bring herself to take off Amor's ring, but she could not ignore the request of her husband. After transferring Amor's ring to her right hand and her wedding band to the left, she left to have breakfast in the gardens.

The table set up in the gardens was covered with all of Iona's favorite foods. There was too much for her to eat it alone. Trembling slightly at what this would mean, she asked, "Will my husband be joining me for breakfast?"

"No," Lethia said. "He's gone for the day and won't be back until nightfall. It is his custom to stay away during daylight hours."

"How can I eat all this food?"

"Just eat what you want. Do not worry about any leftovers. The cooks were a little overzealous about your arrival. I'm sure this won't happen again."

Iona sighed, knowing most the food would go to waste. She tried to eat more than she normally would, but as amazing as the meal tasted, she saw there were several untouched delicacies left when she was done. To her amazement, the leftovers vanished and the plates were cleared by an invisible force. She could feel unseen people rushing by her, cleaning up. Whispers could be heard on the wind and Iona strained to listen to what they were saying. She was sure she heard her name spoken.

When the table was cleared, Iona met with Lethia to learn about the running of her husband's house. Since he was hardly home, there wasn't much for Iona to do. Her unseen servants knew their jobs well and Lethia was more than able to keep the house active. All Iona had to do was meet with Lethia in the morning and agree to what had to be done that day. If she so desired, Iona could have the final say in any shopping that would be done, but she could not leave the house to oversee it.

That afternoon, Iona went back to the gardens. She found a lovely spot to sit near the back where she discovered a fountain. She ate her lunch there and fed crumbs to the Aneriams and was fully bored. She would have loved to do some gardening, but she wasn't sure if she was allowed to or if the gardening was done by the unseen servants.

"Lady Iona, how are you this morning?" Iona looked up as Zephyrus found her. His cheerful face helped chase away her boredom. "How did you sleep last night?"

"I slept well," Iona said, "but I am bored to tears. There is nothing for me to do here. Lethia has this place running like a well-oiled machine. I am utterly useless."

"I'm sure if you asked her, she'll find something to occupy your time," Zephyrus said as he sat next to her. "I remember when she first came here. She'd spend hours painting pictures for her husband. The old stewardess of the house ran the home with the same efficiency that Lethia now runs this home. Like you, Lethia didn't have much to do until the old stewardess retired."

"How long has Lethia been here," Iona asked. "She doesn't look that much older than me."

Zephyrus looked down and Iona heard him mutter a curse. She had the feeling he hadn't meant to let it slip that Lethia was older than she looked. Iona thought that maybe she was the daughter of a minor deity, blessed with immortality. If that were the case, Iona would be old before Lethia ever retired.

"At any rate," Iona said, hoping to change the subject from Lethia's age, "I get the feeling she doesn't like me very much."

Zephyrus scratched his ankle. "Yeah, well, she has her reasons. Don't worry though. She won't dare give you wrong advice just to spite you. Not if she wants to stay in this house."

"What are her reasons? She just met me."

"Lethia…she was in love with your husband. After her husband died five years ago, she thought that the master of this house would take her to be his wife. She waited and waited for him, but he fell in love with you instead. It's hard for her to watch a man she wanted marry another woman."

"She can have him! I don't love him! I love Amor! I want only Amor Myloneous."

"Amor Myloneous?" Zephyrus sounded surprised. He looked over at Iona and burst out laughing.

"What? What is so funny?"

"I'll tell you later," Zephyrus said. "Though, if I were you, I'd forget about this Amor and give your husband a chance. He's a good man, Lady Iona."

"How can I give him a chance? I am not even allowed to see him and the only time we have together, I'm sleeping. I know nothing about him."

Zephryus quickly looked around the garden. Lowering his voice, he said, "I'm going to tell you a bit about your husband. I can't reveal his identity, but I can tell you a little bit about his personality. There are powerful people hunting you, and your marriage is the only thing keeping you safe. He's the only thing keeping me safe, as well."

"What do you mean?"

"I angered Apollo. This happened about three years ago, and I've been hiding under your husband's wings ever since. I know Apollo knows I'm here, but he cannot harm me while I am in service to your husband." Zephryus pointed up to the ceiling where the lights blazed to mimic day. "He's probably watching us now. Always shut your windows at night when you change, Lady Iona. You never know when he'll be spying on you."

"What did you do to anger Apollo," Iona asked. Though, if Apollo could see her, that meant she was not off Space Station *Olympus* and her husband was not a space serpent. That also meant that there was a chance that Amor might find a way to rescue her.

"Three years ago, I fell in love. His name was Hyacinths and he was an athlete. Devoted to Apollo and about as handsome. For a while, we met in secret and it was my own personal heaven. We kept our love a secret for fear that his career would end if anyone ever knew. I was just a lowly Wind and had no protection to offer him. I don't even really have a home. We were happy and I was working hard to prepare a place for us."

"How does Apollo fit in all of this," Iona asked. "He's a womanizer. He doesn't chase men." Though, even as she said it, she knew of two stories where Apollo found comfort in the company of men. Neither story ended well, and she had a feeling she knew how Zephyrus' story would end.

"Hyacinths was beautiful, even for a man. He was like your husband, breathtaking in his beauty. Apollo saw us together and started watching us. He must have come to desire my Hyacinths and wooed him. How could I compete with a god?"

"What happened?"

"Apollo and Hyacinths started meeting in a meadow. Hyacinths told me that they played games and practiced for his upcoming events, but I did not believe him. Consumed with jealousy, I followed them one day. Apollo must have known I was there, that's all I can believe. He told Hyacinths to strip down and he did the same. My lovely Hyacinths even volunteered to help that bronzed Lothario. My heart broke to see the loving looks he gave

Apollo.

"Then Apollo suggested they play discus. Apollo would throw and Hyacinths fetched it, much like a dog. My lover was panting after that no good sun god and I knew in my heart that Apollo would never love him like I did. He was just using Hyacinths for his own gain. Once he was done, he'd toss my sweet Hyacinths aside like trash and I'd be the one left to pick up the pieces. I wanted to spare him that pain. I had to act or forever watch my lover mourn after Apollo's spurned affections."

"Did you confront Apollo," asked Iona fearfully.

"I wish I had," Zephyrus said bitterly. "No, I got angry at what I was witnessing and decided to get even. When Apollo threw the discus, I got to it first. I threw it back, aiming at Apollo. I had hoped it would strike him and then I'd grab Hyacinths and run. Instead, something went wrong." Zephyrus took a deep breath, steadying himself. "The discus struck Hyacinths in the head. When I saw this, I ran. Apollo was the one who held him as he died. Apollo was the one whom my lover gazed at in his moment of need. In my darkest nightmares, it's Apollo who hears Hyacinths' declaration of love after I ran like a coward. Your husband gave me sanctuary after Apollo learned I was the one who tossed the discus back."

"I am sorry to hear that," Iona said. "It was an accident. You didn't mean for Hyacinths to be hurt."

"No, but I did want to hurt Apollo. That in itself is a crime."

Iona patted Zephyrus' leg. She had the nagging suspicion she heard that story before. It was so familiar to her that she suspected the ending before Zephyrus told her. It also made him seem familiar to her. She just wished she could remember.

"You've been living here for three years, then," Iona asked.

Zephyrus nodded. "Apollo is not an especially forgiving god. He never forgets a grudge. If your husband hadn't protected me, I'd be dead by now."

Iona sighed. She threw a few more crumbs to some wandering Aneriams as she thought over Zephyrus' story. Her husband might not be such a bad guy if he helped Zephyrus. She could try to give him a change, but where would that leave Amor? She loved him and she was sure that he would not abandon her. Did she really want to give up on him?

"Lady Iona? You mentioned loving this Amor Myloneous

and that is keeping you from loving your husband, right?"

"I wouldn't say that my love for Amor is the only thing keeping me from my husband," Iona said.

"What else can there be?"

"Is he really a serpent?"

Zephyrus gave another fugitive glance around the garden. He leaned closer to Iona and whispered, "I'm supposed to tell you that he is, but that's a lie. I can't tell you more than that. To reveal his identity would mean death for us both."

Iona nodded. "Then I shall not ask you again."

"As for this Amor that you love," Zephyrus said, "I can try and find out what he is doing now. All you have to do is give your husband a chance. Do we have a deal?"

"I will give him a chance, but I am not going to fall in love with him."

Zephyrus smiled. "I will wager that before the year is out, you will love your husband more than you love Amor." He held out his hand.

"And I will wager that no man will ever be near my heart as Amor," Iona said as she shook his hand.

She intended to honor her word and give her husband a chance. Zephyrus painted such a glowing picture of him that she felt like she owed it to him to get to know her husband. Friends were all Iona felt that they could be. Once Amor found out where she was, he'd come for her and she'd gladly be with him. She stayed awake that night, waiting for her husband to enter their bedchamber. Her heart beat faster when she heard the door open and the candle blown out. For a second, she caught his shadow on the wall and he looked monstrous. How could he be the handsome and kind master that Zephyrus knew?

"Are you awake my love?" His voice sounded so like Amor's that it brought tears to her eyes. She swallowed to keep from crying. Tonight, she would be brave and talk to her husband.

"I'm awake," she said. She felt the bed dip as he got beneath the covers. As last night, he pulled her closer to him and wrapped his arms around her. She couldn't stop herself from tensing up, fearful that he would continue.

"How was your day," he asked. His breath was warm against her ear and she could smell roses.

"It was good, but rather boring," she said. "I spent most of it sitting in the garden. With your permission, I'd like a small portion of it to call my own. I miss gardening."

"The entire garden is yours to command. You may plant whatever your heart desires or change what I have planted. I want you to be happy."

"Thank you," she said. "I wanted to make sure I had your permission before I did anything. You did such a wonderful job with the gardens, there's not much for me to do."

"It's your garden my love." He kissed her shoulder, but pulled back slightly when she tensed at his touch. "Everything I have is yours. I am your humble servant."

"Speaking of servants, I spoke with Zephyrus today," Iona said.

Her husband laughed. "He's not a servant, per say. He's a friend."

"He told me about how you helped him," she said. This time, it was her husband who tensed. Iona wondered if that story was supposed to be a secret, or if there was something else he was worried that Zephyrus had let slip.

"What did he tell you?" His voice was cautious, almost scared.

"Just that he fell in love with a beautiful young man and Apollo also desired him. He told me about accidentally causing his lover's death and how you've kindly protected him."

She felt her husband breathe a sigh of relief and relax behind her. "Oh, yes. That's what happened. Zephyrus is an old friend and when I found out he was in trouble, I offered my help."

"There is something more to that story, though," Iona said and felt her husband tense again. She knew she was right. If she could remember why Zephyrus' story was so familiar to her, maybe she could figure out who her mysterious husband was. She was certain he wasn't a serpent.

"There is nothing more to what happened," her husband insisted. "Go to sleep, Iona. Don't worry yourself with things that aren't there."

For a moment, Iona was silent. She wanted to ask him about Lethia. Did he know about his stewardess' infatuation with him? Were they ever lovers before he claimed Iona? Iona wondered if she was strong enough to hear the answers.

"Hmm, what's this?" Her husband's hand found Amor's ring. "This isn't the wedding band I placed with your jewelry."

"It was a parting gift," Iona said. "Your ring is on the other hand." She took his fingers and placed them on the wedding band. He quickly moved his hand back to Amor's ring.

"Did a man give you this ring?"

Iona hesitated. She already told him that she was in love with another man, but she wasn't sure how jealous he would be if she continued to wear his ring. Softly, she said, "Yes."

"Did you love this man?"

"With all my heart."

She closed her eyes, expecting him to be angry. She waited for his response as he traced the arrow design over and over again. When he moved, she held her breath, thinking he was going to kill her. Instead, he turned over in bed and moved to the far side so that his wings barely touched her body.

"I don't want to lie to you," Iona said softly. "I told you only the truth."

"I know," he said. The pain in his voice surprised her. She barely knew him and she felt as if she had just torn his heart out.

"I can take it off if you wish." She made the offer, even though it was not what she wished.

She scooted over the bed so that she could hold him. It was difficult with his wings, but she managed. She could imagine she was holding Amor.

"No," he said softly. "Keep the ring on for as long as you wish. Take it off when you have come to love me."

"I don't know when that will be."

He brought the hand with the wedding band to his lips and placed a kiss on her finger. "I can wait forever if I must."

For the second time that day, Iona made a vow to try and get to know her husband. She placed her head on his shoulder and fell asleep, dreaming that she was married to Amor.

Chapter 15

For the next few days, Iona found a simple pattern to her married life. She spent the greater part of her day in the gardens after her morning meetings with Lethia. Anything she wanted, she was allowed to have. To amuse herself, she worked on cross-breeding the flowers and documenting the comings and goings of the Aneriams.

Her nights belonged to her husband. He never offered to tell her his name so she took to calling him 'Beloved'. They would lie in bed for hours, just talking about their day. Slowly, she came to know more about him; that he liked theater, detested Apollo, and wished he could live on the upper levels of Space Station *Olympus*. She told him about her dreams to be a gardener and how she wanted to have children someday. She told him of Kelmis and how she didn't really mourn him, but mourned only to please her family, and how guilty she still felt about it. He told her to not worry, that if Kelmis loved her, then he'd want her to be happy. She rarely mentioned Amor, but he was always on her mind.

Before long, his visits became more amorous. At first, she pushed him away when his touch lingered for too long. She was surprised when she realized she pushed him away less and leaned into his caresses more.

The night they consummated their marriage was filled with the sweetest of love-making. Afterward, her husband held her as she cried, thinking of poor Amor.

"I'm sure he'd understand," her husband whispered as he kissed away her tears. "You're a married woman. He could not possibly expect me to allow you to remain chaste."

"I can't help it," she whimpered. "I think I still love him."

"And me? Do you think you love me?"

Iona buried her head in the crook of his neck. "Aphrodite help me, but I know I'm falling in love with you," she said. "Every night I look forward to talking to you. Every day I long for you. Amor is less and less on my mind, but I still feel as if I've betrayed him."

He tilted her head up and kissed her forehead. "Then it's settled," he declared. "You think you still love him, but you know you love me. This Amor fellow will have to give up on you. You are my wife, Iona, and I will not let you go so easily."

"What if Amor comes to rescue me?"

Cautiously, he asked, "Do you want to be rescued?"

Iona sighed, lightly tracing circles on his chest. "I don't know, beloved. Sometimes I think I want to, but only so I can see my family again."

"When you fantasize about being rescued, is it forever? Or do you eventually dream of coming back?"

"I used to dream of it being forever, but lately it has been that I come back," she said. Her words pleased her husband and he kissed her deeply. She soon forgot about their conversation as his lips wandered down her neck and she lost herself in pleasure.

The next morning, Lethia was waiting for her in the gardens. The stewardess appeared colder and angrier than normal. With an icy voice, she informed Iona that some of the unseen servants were gone and that Iona must now take on more responsibility with the household.

"Where did they go," Iona asked. "What made them leave?"

"You did," Lethia said. When Iona started to protest, Lethia continued, "You are now fully becoming the mistress of this house. These things happen in cycles. Once you prove you can run the house on your own, they will return. This has happened before, so don't worry about it."

"When has this happened before?"

"With the master's last wife. The night he lay claim to her, the servants started their departure. When she proved to be capable to run the house, they returned." Lethia's tone told Iona that she knew what transpired between herself and her husband that night. Iona blushed.

"What do you mean, his last wife?" Even as she asked, she remembered Zephyrus mentioning it once, that after the death of her husband's first wife, Lethia believed she would be the mistress of the house.

Lethia's smile grew colder. "You are not the first, you know. He's been married before."

"What happened to her?"

"She's gone and forgotten."

Lethia took hold of Iona and started her new training. The

household chores were draining. It wasn't as if Iona were lazy, she always did her fair share of work when she lived with her parents. However, Lethia's rules were far more rigorous than any that Iona ever encountered. The clothes had to be washed and hung a certain way with particular articles of clothing never touching, the floors polished in a diagonal pattern and never crisscrossed nor straight, and the windows had to be opened and closed at specific times.

"I can understand all the other rules," Iona said as she closed the shutters in the back of the home, "but I don't' understand the windows."

"Apollo can see through the windows," Lethia said coldly. "You and Zephyrus are fugitives here, kept safe only by my master's good will. We do not need that peeping sun god to see you."

"But, Zephyrus told me that Apollo already knows he's here," Iona said.

"He does, but that doesn't mean we should allow him to spy on us." Lethia latched the windows and started out of the room. "Besides, you are the one we are most interested in protecting."

"And what is my crime? I was betrothed against my will and forced to leave my family. I'm the one being held hostage here. I've done nothing wrong. I've followed the wills of the gods my whole life."

"You think you've done no crime," Lethia scoffed. "It takes tremendously little to offend the gods. Small things like the wrong offerings, stumbling over the words of a prayer, wearing the wrong color to a temple...all of these things are crimes if the gods are not in a good mood." Lethia turned to look at Iona and said pointedly, "Being mistaken for a goddess is a crime, as well."

Iona gasped, "But that wasn't my fault. A lot of girls are called Aphrodite-in-the-flesh, not just me. And I always gave her anything given to me in her name."

Lethia shrugged. "Life isn't fair. You do know what happened to the other poor girls who were mistaken for Aphrodite, don't you?" Iona shook her head. "Some were taken to be Aphrodite's new attendants, some were married off to men that the goddess picked, and others were killed."

Iona looked down. "I was nearly married off. If Amor hadn't helped me, I would have been married to someone I despised by now."

"Are you sure," Lethia asked. "Are you sure that marriage was what the goddess intended all along?" She smirked and left Iona to ponder what she learned.

In the gardens, Iona thought over everything that Lethia had told her. All her life, she venerated the gods and now the one she came to venerate the most was angry with her. She had no powers, no special skills and no protection.

Was that what drew her husband to her? Did he only love her because she needed his protection?

"Lady Iona, what's wrong?" Zephyrus sat next her. She hadn't heard him enter the gardens. In her time in her new home, she came to counting on the young wind god as a friend. He was, as far as gods went, powerless. With no temple and no real worshipers, his name was praised during spring, but only as a footnote to more powerful gods.

"It's nothing," Iona said, not wanting to burden him with her doubts.

"You look so sad. Was it Lethia? Did she say or do something to upset you," Zephyrus asked. "You shouldn't let her get to you, Lady Iona. Lethia is a bitter woman."

"What? Oh, no, it's not Lethia. She's been really kind to me and has been showing how to run the house. I'd be lost without her."

"Then what has made you so sad?"

Iona looked down. She knew Zephyrus adored her husband, so she didn't want to let him know that she was starting to doubt his reasons for wanting her. Instead, she said the first thing that came to her mind. "I miss my family, that's all. I just realized that yesterday was my mom's birthday, and I wasn't there to see her. I just wish I could see them and let them know that I'm all right."

"You know that's against the rules," Zephyrus said. "No contact with your old life."

"I know," Iona sighed. "Are you sure there's no way to get a message to them? They don't even have to know it's from me."

"There may be a way," Zephyrus said softly. "If your husband approves, I might be allowed to take a message to them."

Iona's eyes lit up with delight. "Oh, could you! That would be wonderful!" Hearing that she might have a way of telling her family she was all right made her miss them more.

Zephyrus nodded. "Only if your husband allows it," he said.

"Thank you," Iona said. She hugged her friend, feeling happy once more. "Oh, what have you found out about Amor?"

"Not much," Zephyrus said. "He's a hard man to track down."

"You learned nothing?"

Zephyrus opened his mouth to say something, but a rustling in the bushes made him pause. Iona felt her heart drop as Lethia stepped out, her eyes glittering maliciously. How much had she heard?

"If you are so interested in seeing your family," she said, "I'm surprised that Zephyrus hasn't told you how to view them without breaking the rules."

"What do you mean," Iona asked.

"Lady Iona wants to get a message to them, not just see them," Zephyrus said. "There is a difference."

"Let her do this without breaking the rules," Lethia said. "Then she can decide if she wants to risk the wrath of our master."

"How can I see my family?"

"The answer is in the fountain," Lethia said, pointing to the structure Iona was sitting on. "Speak the name of the person you wish to see and, if it is permissible, the image will form in the water."

Iona turned and said, "I wish to see Metasis and Hedyla Demarchis of Tiryns." The water in the fountain glowed and a picture formed. At first, Iona was glad to see her parents, but her joy vanished as she realized they were crying. Her mother was sitting on the couch with one of her old dresses in her lap while her father sat next to her, gazing at a picture.

"They are still mourning me," Iona whispered. "How selfish I've been! Here I am, happy and well with my husband, and they still think I'm dead. I had forgotten all about that."

"It can't be helped," Lethia said. "As far as they are concerned, you are dead. If you are wise, you'll leave it at that and just be content to gaze at them from here." With that, she left.

Iona turned to Zephyrus with tears in her eyes. "We have to get a message to them. I can't bear to think that they are so sad when I've been so happy."

"I will talk to your husband tonight," Zephyrus promised.

Iona nodded, but she wasn't going to leave it just up to

Zephyrus. That night, she waited her husband. She heard him enter the house and the low murmur of voices as he spoke to his servants. She winced as she heard him cry out, "What do you mean you showed her the fountain!" Iona cowered under the covers, wondering if she'd have the strength to ask her husband for the favor she wanted. When he entered their bedchamber and crawled under the covers, she could feel that he was shaking with rage.

Cautiously, she said, "Beloved, there is something I want to ask you."

"I know," he spat. "You want to see your family. That traitorous she-snake had no right to show you how to work that fountain."

"Please, Beloved," Iona begged. "I just want to get a message to them. I can stay here and we can send Zephyrus. I just can't bear the thought of them mourning me."

"Iona, I can't do that. As long as the rest of the station believes you're dead, you are safe. If I send out a message to your family, then it will become known you are alive and you will be killed."

"Why would I be killed? If you're talking about the whole mess with me being mistaken for Aphrodite, that's blown over by now. Another girl was named Aphrodite-in-the-flesh long before we married."

"You mean Amaranth of Nox?"

"Yes. I'm sure I've been forgotten by now. Aphrodite will have no reason to hate me."

Her husband sighed. "Iona, darling, that girl is dead. Aphrodite had Poseidon flood Nox and declare that the floods would continue unless she was sacrificed. It happened right after our wedding. And Aphrodite has a long memory. If she finds out you're still alive, she will go back to trying to making your life miserable."

"But I am married to you."

"Never underestimate a goddess," her husband said. "Let your family mourn. It's what's keeping you safe. Aphrodite believes you dead, far from her wrath and no longer a problem. If she were to find out you were alive, she'd believe you were plotting against her. Believe me, she believes everyone is plotting against her."

"We can send a message and not let them know it's from me," Iona said. "Please, Beloved. Let me do something to put their minds at ease."

Her husband sighed. "Iona, I can't," he said. Then, he added, "I can bring your sister's here, but only this once," in a strangled voice. Even in the dark of the room, she saw him slap a hand over his mouth. She had the impression he hadn't meant to say that.

"Can you," she asked. "Would you really do that for me?"

"I'd brave Hades for you," her husband said. He groaned and gathered her up in his arms. "And yes, I can bring your sisters here. Only this once, and only if you promise to do as I say with no questions."

Iona smiled and kissed him. "I am yours to command," she said, showering every inch of his face and neck with soft kisses. "I obey your every whim."

"I wish," her husband grumped. "All right, here are my demands. First, you can't tell them the names of my servants. Zephryus and Lethia will help, but don't mention their names. Pretend that they don't exist. Secondly, you can't tell them about me. As far as your family is concerned, I am nothing more than a monster."

"But, it would put their minds at ease if they knew how well you've cared for me," Iona protested.

"Thirdly," her husband continued, ignoring her, "you must never, ever ask for them to visit again. This is a one-time only deal. Understand, Iona?"

"Yes, Beloved. I promise."

Chapter 16

A week later, Iona waited nervously for her sisters to arrive. Her husband warned her again that night of her promise. In great detail he explained that she was in danger and failure to follow his rules could lead to death. If Aphrodite ever found out where she was, they would all be in trouble.

"But I still don't understand why she'd hate me," Iona protested. "There must be another girl who has taken the name of Aphrodite-in-the-flesh by now. I'm nobody."

"I don't know," her husband confessed. "For some reason, Aphrodite is fixated on you. I would have thought that she'd move on by now, but she continues to come back to you. She won't be satisfied until you are truly dead."

Iona wished she knew how to appease Aphrodite's anger. She thought she did nothing wrong by never accepting the title of Aphrodite-in-the-flesh and by giving all the offerings shoved in her arms to the goddess. Was that her mistake? Did Aphrodite believe that Iona thought herself on par with the goddess' priestesses? Would it have been better for her if she ignored the offerings or passed them off on to an official representative of Aphrodite?

She was brought out of her worries by Zephyrus calling out that he returned. As he walked in the gardens, she could see her sisters behind him. Though Iona had no idea the connection of Zephyrus or Lethia to her husband's identity, she would keep them from her sisters.

Philomena entered the gardens first. She was clothed in a dark blue dress with a dramatic mourning veil over her head. Iona couldn't help but smile when she saw that her sister enthusiastically threw herself into the part of the grieving sister. No matter how much Philomena truly missed Iona, it was no match for how much of a role she could play.

Errita was next, wrapped in one of Iona's dresses that was too big for her and dabbing at tears in the corner of her eyes.

"Iona! It is you," Philomena exclaimed as she rushed forward to hug her youngest sister. "When this man said he could bring us to see you, we were skeptical."

Iona smiled widely and hugged her sister back. "Welcome to my home," she said. "I've missed you both. It can get rather lonely here."

"How lonely can you possibly be," Errita asked, sniffling into the hem of the dress. "All around you are rich temples and homes that dwarf Philomena's immodest mansion. You must have some exciting new friends."

Iona shook her head. "I'm not allowed out of the house. The gardens are my only freedom."

Philomena and Errita shared a look. Iona felt a chill go down her spine, knowing what that meant. Her sisters had knowledge of something and they would only reveal that in their own sweet time. She was sure that it was something to do with her mysterious husband.

"Well, you have a nice enough place," Philomena said. "Though, I haven't seen a single servant."

"My master has only a modest amount of help. Lady Iona currently runs the entire house and has done so particularly well," Zephyrus said. "She has proven her worth for a house of this size and the meager amount of staff on hand."

"Where are they, then," Philomena asked. There was a strange challenging tone to her voice as she glared at Zephyrus. "Why don't you call them out, Iona?"

Iona stammered as she tried to think of what to say. The unseen servants left now that she learned how to manage the house to Lethia's specifications. She hadn't thought of what she'd do when her sisters visited.

"My servants...I, uh, I..." Iona stumbled over her words before Lethia entered the gardens. As regally as if she were announcing the arrival of a queen, Lethia told them that lunch was about to be served Iona watched amazed as lovely girls and handsome men came out of the house and set up the table and chairs.

"These are your servants," Errita gasped.

"They are," Lethia said. "We are proud to serve Lady Iona."

"This is just amazing," Errita said. Iona nodded and tried to not look too shocked as the servants left. Only Lethia remained to serve them the food. One of the servants, a strangely familiar young man with beautiful purple butterfly wings that looked gorgeous next to his dark skin and dyed purple hair, brought out the food and placed it on the table for the women. He winked at Iona before he left.

"Well, shall we eat," Iona asked. "We have so much to catch up on."

"Married life certainly agrees with you," Philomena commented. "To think, we were worried about you. How foolish that seems now."

"Worried, nothing!" snapped Errita. "I thought I lost my baby sister forever."

Philomena sniffed. "I thought the same thing," she said. "After all, I was the one who was home when Father came running in telling us the airlock opened and you were nowhere to be found. Zotikos and I set up a memorial in our garden."

"Theron and I send daily prayers at the temples in your honor," said Errita. "I'm glad they've been answered, seeing how healthy you are."

"You didn't have to do any of that," said Iona, embarrassed. "As you can see, I'm doing quite well."

"And eating like a horse," Philomena said. She was eying the massive amounts of food on the table. Iona, used to the overabundance and enthusiasm of her unseen servants hadn't given it a second thought. But, seeing the plates of meat and fruits, surrounded by bowls of vegetables and bottles of wine made all feel far too rich for her humble background. A few plates of expensive sweets were also set on one end of the table.

"They always go a little overboard," Iona said. "I think having guests excited them. I don't normally have this much set out."

"I've never seen such a banquet," Errita said. "What is it your husband does?"

"I don't know," Iona said before trying to change the subject. "How are mom and dad? Are they well?"

Errita took a large plate and piled it high with roasted duck, a vegetable mixture and sweet rolls. "They are fine. They miss you, of course, and blame themselves for your demise. I'm sure it would please them to know that you're not dead, just living in the lap of luxury."

"Yes, Iona. Why haven't you tried to contact us before now," Philomena asked as her hand hovered between picking a crisp roast duck or succulent fish. She finally chose a bit of each.

"I wanted to contact you all before now," Iona said. "I am under strict rules here. My husband did not want me to contact anyone from my old life. It had something to do with protecting me."

"I am curious," Philomena said, "as to what this serpent husband of yours looks like? He is obviously keeping you locked up for his own evil purposes. And this food? How do you know he's not trying to fatten you up for the slaughter?"

Iona caught Zephyrus watching from the edge of the garden. She almost expected him to be angry to hear her sisters talk of his master like that, but he looked amused. Taking his cue, Iona decided to not take offense to her sister's horrifying suggestions.

"My husband is a caring man," Iona said truthfully. "He is also diligent in his work. He leaves during the day and comes home at night. Other than that, I cannot tell you anything else."

"Because you don't know anything else," Errita pressed.

"Because I am under oath to not reveal anything else," Iona said. She looked back at Zephyrus for approval on her words and missed the calculating glint in her sisters' eyes.

"He is a serpent, isn't he," asked Errita.

Zephyrus stepped forward and said, "My master can take human form, but only for his wife under the cover of darkness."

Philomena looked scandalized at this juicy tidbit of knowledge. "What is it like sleeping with a man who can become a snake?"

Iona blushed. "I would rather not say."

Her sisters seemed to accept that, but Iona could see the curiosity in them. She was careful to keep the conversation away from her husband while they ate. Nervous, and knowing that Zephyrus and Lethia were listening in, Iona decided to keep the visit short. She hoped that if she proved to be obedient enough, her husband would allow more visits.

As lunch ended, Iona asked the one question she was terrified to hear the answer to. Taking a deep breath, she said, "Philomena, has anyone seen or heard from Amor since I've been gone?" She heard Zephyrus make a noise deep in his throat, but she ignored him. He told her nothing, and she needed to know if he was still planning on rescuing her. Especially now that she was unsure if she still wanted to be rescued.

Philomena's eyes widened and she placed a hand to her

breast dramatically. "Oh," she moaned. "I was hoping you wouldn't mention him. I just simply didn't want to tell you."

"Tell me what?"

"It's too awful. Can you ever forgive me?"

Iona frowned. "Forgive you for what?" Sometimes talking to Philomena was talking to a stubborn brick wall. Getting any information would be hard until you asked in just the right way.

"After you left and the news of your demise spread, Amor came to visit me. He was just distraught over your death. We all were." Philomena sighed and looked enormously guilty. She played with her dress as she said, "He started visiting me and we'd talk about you. I don't know how it happened, but we started talking less about you and more about me."

Iona felt sick as she was sure she knew where this was going. She clung to the small hope that she was wrong. "Philomena, what happened?" *Please,* her mind pleaded, *please by all that is holy, by all the gods in Olympus, that Amor was so distraught over my leaving that he hung himself. Please may that be the ending of Philomena's tale of woe. Please, may it not be...*

"One day, during one of his visits, we kissed," Philomena said. "Well, he kissed me, to be precise. He said that he found me to be the most captivating woman in all of the station. I knew it was wrong, but I couldn't stop myself. We've been lovers for a while now."

Zephyrus made a choking noise, but it was lost in Errita's outraged shriek. "What! We all knew that Iona was in love with Amor. How could you!"

"I'm sorry, it just happened," Philomena said. "Please, Iona, forgive me. He was so insistent and dreadfully sweet."

Iona felt her heart break. That was the solution she dreaded. She was not sure whom she was angrier with: Philomena for saying yes to Amor's advances, or Amor for making them. She almost expected it. She knew that Philomena found Amor attractive, and what her sister wanted, her sister got. She did not want to think of her eldest sister actively pursuing the man she loved. She had to believe Philomena's account.

"I guess I didn't mean that much to him," Iona said, her voice wavering as she tried to fight back the tears. "The next time you see him, Philomena, don't tell him I'm still alive."

"You're not going to do anything stupid, are you," Errita asked.

Iona shook her head. "Not unless you consider staying with my husband and leaving my old life behind stupid."

"That's a good thing," Philomena said. "After all, Amor hasn't asked about you and has even expressed how fortunate it is that you died. I think he was just having some fun with you."

Iona twisted Amor's ring around her finger. She was shaking and could feel the sting of tears that threatened to fall. "I'm sorry," she said, "but I must cut our lunch short. I'm not feeling well. You'll be escorted back down. It was lovely to see you all again."

"I suppose time does fly when you're having fun," Errita said, finishing her wine. "We must do this again. Maybe you and your husband can come down for a visit?"

"I wish we could, but I promised my husband this would be the last time I asked to see my family."

"A promise to a monster needn't be honored," Errita sniffed.

"He's not so bad," Iona said. "At least he's loyal."

Philomena gave a grunt. "Are you sure he's loyal? After all, he leaves you all day long. What if he has another family, other girls stashed away in grand homes who think they are the only ones?"

"And that concludes the lunch," Zephyrus said, moving between the sisters and Iona. "Let's go, times wasting. You'll want to be back before dark."

"Maybe he doesn't have girls all over the place," Errita said, "but he is a monster."

"He's not a monster," Iona said.

"Then what is he?"

Iona did not have time to answer. Zephyrus took her sisters away and left her alone in the garden. She put her head down on the table and cried. Only the sound of plates clinking broke into her depression and she looked up to see the mysterious servants clearing off the table. One, the familiar young man with butterfly wings attached to his back, sat next to her. Without a word, he offered her comfort and she cried on his shoulder.

"Do not despair," he whispered. "Everything will turn out all right."

Zephyrus, for his part, led the sisters back to the PortMat at the end of the lavish street. He sent them home to the Temple of

Aphrodite in Tiryns. On an impulse, he turned on the temple's monitor to keep an eye on them. He did not trust Iona's sisters any more then he would trust Apollo. He watched the sisters look around the temple and make their way toward the entrance. He kept the cameras on them and heard everything they said.

Once on familiar ground in the temple, Errita turned angrily to Philomena. Hands on hips, she declared, "What was all that about? Since when have you been seeing Amor? Doesn't loyalty mean anything to you?"

"What are you so angry about," Philomena huffed. "Is it because I'm sleeping with a man other than my husband? What a hypocrite you are, Errita. I know you've had lovers whenever Theron is gone."

"I thought we agreed to tell the other when Amor showed up. How could you keep that a secret?"

"Ah, so that's why you're upset," Philomena said and headed toward the exit. "That was just a story. I haven't been able to find Amor any more than you have."

"Then why did you say you two were lovers?"

"Isn't it obvious? Iona is just being greedy. Did you see her home? She's married to someone of divine parenting and she's hiding it. All those excuses about not knowing what her husband really was? She's lying to us. I got a good look at those servants, and I'd swear some were actually minor gods. Who else but Iona would find a way to get everything and deny us it all?"

"She did have a lot," Errita agreed. "I had to work for my wealth, as did you. It just falls in her lap. It always has."

"She's playing dumb," Philomena said. She mimicked Iona's voice, "Oh, he's not a monster. I don't know what he is, but he's not a monster."

Errita laughed. "Not a monster? I wanted to call her a liar. She knows her husband isn't human. If he's not a monster, he's a god. She is just toying with us, rubbing her good wealth in our faces. After all we've done for her, this is how she repays us!"

"I suggest we get our revenge," Philomena said. "We'll continue to look for Amor and you see if Theron can't use his divine contacts to find out who married Iona. Once we know who it is, we can find a way to tear them apart. She'll learn to not treat us like dirt."

They left the temple, plotting their sister's downfall. Jealous of what she posessed, they would ruin everything. Deep in their hearts, they each planned on being the one to take Iona's place among the gods. Philomena hoped the husband would be Apollo and she could woo him with her singing while Errita set her prayers on Zeus. Neither one noticed the cameras turning to watch them as they left.

Zephyrus turned off the monitor, feeling sick after what he just witnessed. He jumped up and quickly punched in the coordinates for Olympus. He needed to find Eros and fast.

Chapter 17

The official dwelling of Aphrodite on Olympus was not the mirror-covered love den that most would assume. It was not dominated by pink lace or feminine frills like her various temples throughout Space Station *Olympus*. This home was tastefully decorated in neutral colors and dark wood furniture.

Eros always assumed it was because of Ares, God of War and all things macho. As his mother's lover, Ares spent most of his time in Aphrodite's private home, and things like lace cozies and pink flowers would have given him hives. It was no secret on Space Station *Olympus* that Ares and Aphrodite were lovers, but they all pretended it was.

At that moment, Aphrodite's beautiful lips were pulled down in an ugly frown a she glared at her oldest son. Eros stood patiently waiting until his esteemed mother finally decided he was worthy enough to learn why she demanded to see him. The silence lengthened and Aphrodite's anger grew.

Taking a risk, Eros broke the silence. "Was there something you wanted, Mother?"

"Don't you 'mother' me," Aphrodite exploded. "You know exactly what you did!"

Eros managed to keep a calm exterior, but he felt the cold fingers of fear grip his heart. Did his mother found out about Iona? Did Apollo make good on his threat and expose his wife's hiding place? If so, then of a certain sun god who was going to need a new host body.

"What do you mean," he asked innocently.

"I sent you to cause that little whore from Tiryns to fall in love with the loathsome male of my choice. I recently took a trip down there to see your handiwork, and do you know what I found?"

"I'm occupied most of my day, Mother, and haven't returned to Tiryns since your little errand, so no. I don't know what you found."

Aphrodite stomped over to her son and jabbed him hard in the chest with one well-manicured finger. "I found out that she supposedly married a winged serpent after *not* falling in love with any of the men I sent her way."

"I fail to see how that's a problem," Eros said, taking a step away from his mother. He brushed the spot where she touched him. "She's married to a monster. So what if it's not a human monster?"

"Don't get cheeky with your mother, boy," Ares snapped as he walked into the room. He pulled a war helmet off, shaking out the wild strands of his black hair. There was a thud as he dropped his helmet on a table. "I checked, and there are no winged serpents in Space Station *Olympus*."

"Maybe you heard wrong?"

"I'm a god. I'm never wrong," Ares said. He plopped his bulky frame down on one of Aphrodite's dainty couches. "Besides, her whole family is convinced it was a winged serpent. They put her in an airlock and were done with her. They've mourned her ever since."

Eros shook his head. This was confusing him. "Then why are you two upset? If they put her in an airlock, she's dead. Who cares what she met in space, your problem is solved."

"The problem isn't solved! There's a PortMat in that airlock! What if she's still on Space Station *Olympus*," Aphrodite cried. "What if she's plotting against me as we speak? I can just see it now. That pathetic little mortal and whoever helped her, sitting in the dark and planning my downfall. They couldn't destroy me through my temples. What if they try to destroy my body?" Aphrodite gasped at the horrific thought. "What if they force me to take an ugly host!"

"She's mortal," Eros said bored. It was obvious his mother had no idea he was holding Iona. His secret was safe for now. "She won't know how to use a PortMat."

"Maybe her lover did," Aphrodite said. "What was his name? Arnold? Amos? Something like that."

"She got sucked into space," Eros repeated. "Really, Mother, you're worrying over nothing."

"Amor! That was the name," Aphrodite said triumphantly. "It was Amor Myloneous. I knew it was something that sounded familiar."

"Wait? Who?" Ares suddenly looked interested. Eros felt his heart sink again. Aphrodite might be easy to fool, but not Ares. He had an annoying habit of remembering anything that could get someone in trouble. If someone mentioned the name yesterday, he would have had no idea who it was, but since it was something that would cause a fight today, he would remember.

"I don't know," Aphrodite said. She sat down on a couch next to Ares, dramatically draping herself across his burly armor-clad chest. Ares looked uncomfortable to have such affection displayed in front of Eros. "Up until her sudden marriage, she was sneaking off to see some guy. Amor, son of Penia or Peony or something along those lines. All I know about him was that he was handsome and belonged to the Cupids. Maybe you should find out which of your little devotees is harboring that thorn in my side." That last was for Eros.

"Wasn't Amor, son of Penia, the name of the mortal you took as host," asked Ares. He fixed one dark eye on Eros while Aphrodite, slightly tired of the conversation, started kissing his neck.

"Um, Amor is a very common name in the Cupids," Eros said. "You know, like Jason or Ajax."

"No, no," Ares said, a wicked grin spreading across his face. He pushed Aphrodite aside, far more interested in getting Eros in trouble. "I'm positive that this is the same Amor."

Sighing, Aphrodite turned back to her son. She would have to get rid of him before Ares would allow her to wrap him in her charms. "Is that true," she asked.

"I don't know," Eros lied. "There are several Amors in the Cupids. It's possible I picked one, but I can't remember. Who cares what a short-lived human's name is, anyway? All that matters is that I'm Eros now, not what's-his-name."

"It does seem strange that the name given as this mortal woman's lover is the same as the name of your host," Ares said.

"Oh, leave it," Aphrodite ordered. "I'm actually not interested in who her lover is. I can easily sway any male to my whims. I'm more worried about where she is. Find me that girl!"

"How about I continue your search," Eros offered. "You shouldn't have to worry about such a trifling matter, Mother. It will give you wrinkles."

"Wrinkles!" Aphrodite ran from the room in terror, her hands to her face to feel for the first sign of imperfection. Eros smiled and turned to leave. He was stopped as Ares grabbed his arm. His strong grip would leave bruises by morning.

"Your mother may not care who Amor really is, but I do. She

wants this Iona of Tiryns to suffer, and I will see to it that this mortal begs for the sweet relief of death. Not only her, but anyone helping her."

"Let go," Eros said coldly. He added, "Father," because he knew it would cause Ares to back off.

Ares frowned and let go of Eros' arm. He looked around the room for any devices of Hephaestus' that might be listening in. "I'm not your father," he said loudly. "Everyone knows Hephaestus is your father. Aphrodite and I are just friends. No siree, no love-making going on here. Just friends."

"Yeah, sure. Whatever you say," Eros said as he walked away. He knew why Ares and Aphrodite wanted to keep their continued affairs a secret. It wasn't that Hephaestus was a violent man, but he was a smart man. Whenever he found his wife and Ares together, he set a trap to teach them a humiliating lesson. A physical attack wouldn't phase Ares, but to have all the gods laugh at him wounded his pride.

Eros treasured those memories.

He made his way toward the PortMat room for this wing of the Olympus housing level. He wanted to get back to his loving wife and see how she viewed her sisters' visit. He knew he should talk to Zephyrus and Psyche, and that they would tell him the unbiased truth. As much as he loved Iona, her loyalty to her family made her blind to their faults.

"Eros! There you are!" Zephyrus came out of the PortMat room and waved. "I was just about to come looking for you."

Eros smiled. "How did the visit go?"

"Not so good," Zephyrus said. He started the PortMat controls. "It probably went well for Iona, but her sisters are the vilest pair of spiders I've ever met. They know she's lying about her husband, and they suspect that you're a god."

"Did she say anything?"

"She tried not to, but the more secretive she was, the more suspicious they became. It was not a good idea, Eros." The beam of light appeared and the two men entered it. Instantly, they were transported down to the minor gods' level. "I think they are planning something."

"I can handle anything that they can come up with," Eros said.

"There is just one more thing," Zephyrus said. "The elder sister, Philomena, has convinced Iona that Amor is now her lover."

Eros made a choking noise. "As if I'd touch that venomous harpy! Iona didn't believe her, did she?"

"I think she did."

Eros cursed and made his way to his home. He had to smooth things over with Iona. Or, the thought suddenly, this could be a good thing. If Iona no longer loved Amor, she was free to fall in love with him. He would not have to fight with himself for her affections. He might have some explaining to do when she found out his identity, but he could worry about that when the time came.

As he entered his home, he was surprised by his younger brother, Anteros, leaving. Anteros, like Eros, was one of Aphrodite's sons that oversaw the aspects of love. Eros was the god of fertility, desire and sexual needs while Anteros was the god of requited love. The last two brothers were Himeros of unrequited love and Pothos of yearning.

"Anteros, how are you," Eros asked as he hugged his brother. "What brings you to my home?"

"Psyche asked me to help with the lunch party," Anteros said. "It was nice meeting your new wife."

"I'm tremendously blessed."

"You always were," Anteros said. He looked behind him, back in the home, before pulling Eros closer. "Listen, brother, I'm worried about you. I would have come over even if Psyche hadn't invited me."

"What is there to be worried about? I'm doing great."

Anteros sighed. "It's this whole Iona thing. You have to be careful. I don't want to see you get hurt."

"Nothing will happen," Eros said. "You worry over nothing."

Anteros quickly looked around and pulled Eros into the home. Keeping his voice low, he said, "If all of us on this level know about Iona, then it's a sure bet some of those uppity gods know about her as well. Pieces are in play, Eros. We will keep our silence while we act our parts, but the story feels like it is changing."

"What are you talking about?"

Anteros looked at him closely. "We all play our parts, brother. You, the big gods, the humans – each time we take a new host body we must enact the play. Think about it." Anteros gave another look around the house. "Each time you change hosts and a new Eros is born, what happens? You fall in love with a human girl, you hide her away and marry her. She becomes your Psyche."

"That is ridiculous," Eros protested. "I only find a new wife because with a new host's eyes I see the mistakes I've made. This Psyche is a cold-hearted old hag and I only let her stay out of respect for my old host. She's nothing like my Iona, who is kind and loving and warm."

Anteros sighed, shaking his head. "You change hosts too often," he said. "If you were more like me or Pothos, and didn't have to change every century or so, you would see the pattern in the lives of the big gods."

"On that note," Eros said as he pushed Anteros toward the door, "this is where you leave. Thanks for visiting and I promise to come by and see you and my brothers soon. However, I have a lovely wife who needs me." Anteros and some of the minor gods were conspiracy nuts. He heard the whole 'pattern to life' story several times, almost as often as he changed hosts. It was so sad what being forgotten did to his brothers.

Eros met up with Psyche just beyond the foyer. He was sure she heard his conversation by the cold light in her eyes. He didn't care. He planned on finding a way to let her go once he made his marriage with Iona official. In a crisp voice, Psyche informed him of how the lunch went and that Iona was distraught.

"Anteros helped her into her bed," Psyche said. "I did not hear what he told her, but it helped her calm down a bit. She fell asleep after a while."

"Thank you, Psyche," Eros said. He started to make his way to her room when Psyche called out to him.

"What ever became of my predecessor?"

"Your what?"

"The girl who was Psyche before me. What happened to her?"

Eros shrugged. "I think she left and got married or something."

Psyche frowned and walked away. Eros quickly pushed the question from his mind and entered his room. His loving wife was huddled under the blankets, whimpering in her sleep from her earlier crying. Tears dried on her cheeks and he reached out to gently trace the paths of her pain. He got ready for bed and slid in next to her. In her sleep, she turned to his warmth and curled up against him.

Eros lay there, gently stroking his wife's hair. He needed to figure out his next move. Now that she had a taste of seeing her family again, she would ask for it over and over. He knew this, just as he knew he would say yes. There was something in the back of his mind, a next step, but it eluded him. It was probably just more of Anteros' conspiracy babble.

He ran a hand down her arm, fingers gently grazing her skin. When he reached her hand, he noticed something was wrong. He looked down. He was holding her right hand. After a quick check, he found his wedding ring on her left hand. But nothing on her right hand.

Amor's ring was gone.

Chapter 18

A few weeks after her sister's visited, Iona started to wake up feeling sick. Her husband, ever attentive to her needs, asked her ever night how she felt. He offered to bring a healer to the house and get her anything she could need.

"Maybe it's nothing," Iona said. "I think I'm getting better."

Either her husband didn't believe her, or Lethia was more in tune with Iona's needs than she thought, but a month after she got sick, Lethia brought over a special midwife. The healer called herself Eileithyia after the goddess of childbirth. She looked the way Iona would have imagined a midwife; plump and matronly with a gaze like steel.

"Well, I suppose congratulations are in order," Eileithyia said after examining Iona.

"What congratulations," asked Iona.

Eileithyia started to pack her bag. "Over the child, of course. Why else would you call for me?"

Iona paused for a moment. "What child? I can't be pregnant! That's not possible."

"Given the way you and your husband act every night, I'm surprised it took this long for you conceive," Lethia said coldly.

Iona blushed. She had not realized that Lethia was aware of her private time with her husband. Either they were loud, or the house maid listened in at the door every night. "But, what if I don't know how to raise a child? What if my husband doesn't want a baby? What if I mess up?"

"Don't worry about a thing," Eileithyia said, patting Iona on the arm. "You'll do fine. All first time mothers worry."

"Everything will be fine," Lethia said. "I'll make sure she does all right."

That didn't make Iona feel better. The thought of cold, impersonal Lethia caring for her at her most vulnerable filled her with dread. She would rather have Zephyrus or her husband with her. Anyone but Lethia.

That night, she told her husband the news. He got excited and hugged her close, kissing her over and over again. "Our child will be a god," he promised, his hand lying on her still flat stomach. "He – or she – will sit next to the gods of Olympus."

"You really think so," Iona asked. "You really think our child will be a god?"

"Iona, love, I know this. You'll see."

At his words, Iona felt another desire rise in her. "My love, when will I be able to see you? We've been married for months now, and I still don't know what you look like."

"Does that bother you?"

"Yes. When I didn't think I'd ever love you, it didn't bother me at all. But now, when I am in love with you and happy to be your wife, I want to know who I am in love with."

"What if I am ugly? What if you see me and are repulsed by my ugliness?"

Iona smiled. "You are not ugly," she said. "I have felt every part of your body, and my fingers know you are not ugly."

Her husband was silent. Finally, he said, "As soon as it's safe, I will show you who I am. Just know this, my sweet wife, I am a man who is madly in love with you and will do anything to keep you happy."

Iona believed him. He told her to find any room in the house she wanted for the nursery. Lethia offered her help, but Iona wanted to do it alone. The cold stewardess followed her around anyway, commenting on every room and persuading Iona from choosing anything.

"Too drafty."

"Too small."

"Too dark."

"Too bright."

"All right, fine!" Iona turned to Lethia after having gone through every room in the house. "Where would you put the nursery?"

Lethia gave her a tight smile. "Follow me." She took Iona to a pale blue room just off the master bedroom. Iona had never seen the room before, but it was already set up like a nursery. A pitiful long-forgotten crib sat covered with cobwebs in one corner and dusty toys littered the floor in another corner. A rocking chair sat between the two corners, looking forlorn with no mother to sit in it.

"Whose room was this," Iona asked.

"This was going to be my son's room," Lethia said. "Once, long ago, I was expecting my first child with my husband."

"I didn't know you had children."

Lethia looked down. When she did answer, her voice was icy. "I have no children."

"Oh," Iona whispered. "I am sorry."

"Ancient history. This room needs to be a nursery, so why not make it yours."

Iona nodded. "This room would be perfect. Are you sure you don't mind? If I have a girl, I would have to make some changes."

"Feel free," Lethia said. "I look forward to seeing new life in this room. I'll leave you to your work, Lady Iona."

Left alone, Iona took stock of the room. The old toys would have to go, and she wanted to repaint it to something more neutral. She didn't know if she was going to have a boy or a girl, and felt it would be a disaster if her girl had a blue room. Also, she wanted a cute covered crib and not the rotting hunk of wood that currently occupied the room.

Iona threw herself into changing the room. For a few weeks, after the morning sickness abated, she would go in and clean the room from top to bottom. She wanted to throw out the old furniture and toys, but thought Lethia would want them. She held on to the room for gods' only knew how long. After carefully packing the toys and furniture, she allowed Lethia to decide if she wanted to throw them out.

"How will I get new furniture for the baby's room," Iona asked her husband once she cleared out the room. "And I need new paints for the wall."

"Have you asked Lethia," her husband suggested. She could tell his mind wasn't on her nursery problems as he nibbled and kissed the skin of her neck and shoulder.

"I'm a little scared to ask her," Iona admitted. "I just packed away the last reminder of the child she lost. I'm invading the last memories she has of a happier life."

Her husband made a snorting noise behind her. "She'll get over it. Lethia has a daughter, one that did use that nursery. They just haven't talked to each other in years."

When Iona talked to Lethia the next day, the cold woman was oddly happy to help. She bought the right kind of crib that Iona desired and helped her pick out a neutral, but cheery shade of yellow for the walls. Iona thought she saw a smile creeping in the corners of Lethia's mouth a few times as they painted the room. As the new nursery took shape, Iona started to feel as if she and Lethia might actually become friends.

The days and weeks passed and her stomach slowly pushed out. The more she filled the nursery with toys and books, the more often her thoughts turned to the family she left behind. Her sisters were childless and she knew that her mother wanted grandchildren. When she thought of the advice her mother would give her, she felt an overwhelming wave of sadness. Iona's promise to her husband prevented her from ever hearing that advice, or seeing how happy her mother would be holding her first grandchild.

As the sadness grew to be all consuming, she begged her husband to allow her to see her family once more. At first, he said no, but when she started to cry, he relented. The rules were the same: no talking about her husband or mentioning the names of his servants.

Zephyrus brought her message to her sisters, announcing her pregnancy and inviting them to visit with her. Her sisters wrote back at once and Zephyrus told an overjoyed Iona that her sisters would arrive the next day.

Chapter 19

"Oh merciful Hera," Philomena gasped as she came into the house and saw Iona. "You are really pregnant!"

Iona laughed, running her hands over her rounder stomach. It was nothing more than just the barest of bumps, but she was proud of it. "This is nothing," she said with a smile. "I am only three months pregnant. The midwife has told me that I will get much bigger."

"How did this happen," asked Errita.

Iona blushed. "Well, we are married," she said slowly. "These things do happen."

With that, Errita burst into tears. "These things do not just happen," she sobbed. "Theron and I have been trying for years to have a child! We've tried over and over and over! We tried everything; sacrifices to Hera, prayers to the gods, changes in our diets and habits. We even went to the Oracle to find out what more we needed to do to have a child. We even sent you here on the promise that the gods would bless us! Do you see a baby in my arms, Iona? Where is my baby?"

"I'm sorry," Iona said, taking a step back. "I didn't realize that you two had gone through so much."

"Really, Errita," Philomena said, "it's not Iona's fault she got pregnant before you did."

"I'm never going to have children," Errita wailed. She flung herself on a couch, her body shaking with her sobs. In between her moans and gasps for breath, she said, "Theron injured himself and we can't have relations any more. He's in too much pain!"

"What happened," Iona asked. She knelt by the couch, wanting to comfort her sister. The joy of her pregnancy was forgotten.

After Errita calmed down, she said, "He left to compete in some games in Athens for the Naxos Floods relief fund. There was an accident and his leg was crushed by a falling beam. His career is over. He'll never be able to play again. We are suffering and the collectors have decided to call our debts. We're losing our house!"

Iona took Errita's hand. "I'll do what I can to help," she

promised. "I can't do much, but I'll do whatever I can."

"She's not the only one with problems," Philomena said. "Zotikos is deathly ill. It's not as dramatic as a sports accident, but I'm in danger of losing my husband to death. He's old and it takes him longer and longer to recover from even a simple cold. He dies and I can lose my house. My career in the theater won't last forever. Someday, they'll realize that I'm not the young, vivacious woman they first hired and kick me out for some prettier, younger model. What will I do then?"

Iona looked down, guilty that she shoved her happiness in their faces. She had no idea things were so dire for them. She had been so excited to tell them about her pregnancy and show them the new nursery that she hadn't thought of how it might affect them.

"Here, take these to help ease your bills," Iona said. She pulled off her jewelry and handed it to her sisters. "It's not much, but it should help. I wish I could do more."

"Iona, there is something I need to talk to you about," Errita said. She sat up and wiped away her tears. "Something that is far worse than our bad luck."

"What is it?"

"I told you that Theron and I went to the Oracle to find out how we can have a baby," Errita said. "Instead, all she talked about was you – and her words were dire. I didn't think anything of the Oracle's words until I got the news that you were pregnant." Errita draped herself over the arm of the couch dramatically. "Oh, woe! The Oracle's warning is coming to fruition."

Iona sighed. The last time she got news from the Oracle, it tore her away from Amor and her family. Now, the news had her sister sobbing on her couch. "What did the Oracle say?"

Muffled from the cushions and her own sadness, Errita's soft voice said, "She said that if you were to become pregnant, it would be the death of you."

"Just what is that supposed to mean," asked Philomena.

"The Oracle said that your husband only wanted you pregnant because the newborn baby and mother are the sweetest meat he'll ever eat. He only got you pregnant to eat you!"

"No. No, you must be mistaken," Iona said. "That's not true."

Philomena patted her arm. "If the Oracle said it, it must be true. Your husband is a vile serpent. He seduced you with this despicable plan to devour you and the child."

"I can't believe it," Iona said. She pushed away from her sisters. "He loves me. He loves our baby. He was so happy when I told him. He kept telling me our child will be a god."

"He wants to eat the baby," Errita said.

"No! You're wrong!"

"How do you know that? Have you ever seen him," asked Philomena.

Iona looked down. "Well, no. He told me it was too dangerous. He's protecting me. But, he promised I'd know him soon enough."

Errita scoffed. "Of course you'll know him. He'll have to show himself before he devours you and the baby."

"But, he's so kind and gentle," Iona protested. "A monster wouldn't be as nice as he's been, or as loving."

"He's not kind! He tore you from your family. We're not allowed to see you unless he says so. You've not seen Mother since you got married. Would a loving husband keep you from your family?"

"It's for my own protection," Iona said. Her voice sounded weak in her ears.

"You're a prisoner," Philomena insisted. "You even told us you can't leave this house."

"He doesn't let you see him," Errita reminded. "What kind of husband hides from his wife?"

"You aren't allowed to write home," Philomena continued. "We have no way of coming to see you without his permission. It's like you don't exist anymore."

"You don't know anything about him," said Errita. "You can't even trust what he says."

Iona groaned, covering her ears. The more her sisters pointed out how secretive her husband was, the more she feared they were right. She was a prisoner here and her husband hid a lot of vital information from her every day. She felt betrayed, far worse than her betrayal by Amor.

And what of her baby? Iona's hands fluttered down to her stomach as she realized she had to protect the little life inside of her. She grew cold as she thought of her husband only caring about the baby as a snack. She had to protect the baby.

"What am I going to do," she cried.

Over her head, Philomena and Errita shared a smile. Philomena reached into her bag and pulled out a dagger. She held it out for Iona.

"What you should do is wait until he goes to sleep tonight," Philomena said, "and kill him. That way, you'll be free of him and your baby will be safe."

"You can come home," Errita added. "Think of how happy Mother will be to see you."

"What if he's not a monster? What if you're wrong," Iona asked.

"What if we're right," Philomena said. "Do you want to risk it?"

"We'll be a family again," said Errita. "Don't you want to be a family?"

Iona did want to be a family. These rare visits only made her longing ache more. Her sisters would never steer her wrong, would they? And the Oracle couldn't be wrong about her husband. The gods were never wrong. If the Oracle said her baby was in danger, it must be true.

Maybe, she thought, *a peek at my husband will confirm his nature. If he is a monster, I will do what I must to protect my baby. If he isn't, he won't ever have to know I looked.*

"Okay," she said, taking the dagger. "I'll do it tonight."

Her sisters were gleeful as they watched her hide the dagger in her pockets. They changed the conversation in case Zephyrus or Lethia were listening in. Iona feared that the two might have overheard the whole conversation, but there was no turning back. She'd just take a look. That would satisfy her curiosity.

When Philomena and Errita left, they reinforced their plans. Philomena congratulated Errita's cunning with the story of the Oracle, and Errita preened over her own brilliance. When she had gotten the invitation from Iona's sullen messenger that her baby sister was pregnant, Errita knew she had to come up with something and fast. Both sisters felt they knew which of the gods was Iona's husband, and knowing the jealous nature of the gods, if Iona disobeyed him then she'd be disgraced. Philomena believed it to be Apollo because of his connection to the Oracle and the use of a serpent, one of Apollo's sacred animals. Errita was positive it was

Zeus, for who else would have to keep a wife hidden but the king of the gods? It didn't matter who the husband was, he would banish Iona for plotting to kill him, and then the sisters could take her place. With Iona's jewelry in their hands, they dreamed of what other riches would enter their lives when they took Iona's place in the great, glittering mansion.

That night, Iona waited fearfully for her husband to arrive. Under the bed she hid the dagger and a small book of matches. She felt each frantic heartbeat, jumping at every small noise. She couldn't help but think that someone tipped him off of her plan and he would burst through the doors and eat her.

When he did enter the room, he was strangely silent and distant. He blew out the candle that Iona always kept burning for him and slid between the covers. She pretended to be asleep, tensing up when she thought he'd pull her to him as he often did. When he ignored her and turned away, she breathed a sigh of relief. She waited until she heard his breathing become deep and rhythmic.

Slowly, she slid out of bed and got her dagger and matches. As quietly as she could, she lit the candle. Her hands were shaking so badly that she was scared the flame would go out. Taking a deep breath, she took the candle over to the bed, mentally readying herself to see her husband with her own eyes.

Inch by inch, the candle's light revealed her husband to her inquisitive eyes. He was tangled under the covers, lying on his back. He must have turned while she had been busy with the candle. She gulped, moving forward to see him better.

Under the covers, she could see the shape of his long legs. Licking her dry lips, she moved the light up so that it fell across his muscular chest. So far, she saw nothing that made him a monster. No scales or snake-like features were revealed. That made her feel better. Curious, she took in his broad shoulders and strong arms, flung up to cover his face. She blushed as fond memories of being held by those arms came rushing back.

He did have wings. She knew that, but seeing them for the first time was impressive. They were so beautiful and she wondered if he could fly. She had only seen wings that lovely on Amor.

"Wait," she murmured. His face was still in shadow, but she felt the back of her mind start to itch as she took in what she already could see. She reached over and gently moved his arm down from his face. She couldn't stop the gasp that escaped her lips as she stared down at him. She knew that handsome face. She knew that curly brown hair. She felt cold and empty, staring down at him.

"Amor?"

Chapter 20

It took all of Eros' strength to not barge in on his wife and demand an explanation. When he agreed to allow her sisters to visit a second time, he knew better than to trust them. He told Zephyrus to spy on them and report back, but he had no idea the depths that his sisters-in-law would sink to ruin Iona's happiness.

"Her sisters played on her fears," Zephyrus said in greeting when Eros got off the PortMat. "I can't believe Iona would allow them to manipulate her like that."

"What happened?"

"They have her so convinced that you're going to eat her and the baby that she's scared. She has a dagger, Eros. She means to kill you."

"We'll just have to see if she can go through with it," Eros said. He waited until it was well after the time he normally returned home, hoping she would rethink this foolish plan. Lethia greeted him at the door, a slight smirk on her lips. No doubt she knew of Iona's misguided plot, and it amused her.

When he entered the room, he could tell that his wife was up to something. In the past few months, she slept in the nude, as he did. But tonight, she was wrapped in the same virginal nightgown she wore her first night with him. The material covered her from neck to ankles, making sure he could not touch her flesh as he pleased. If that was the game she wanted to play, he could go along with it.

He blew out the candle she left lit and stripped out of his clothes. He knew she was pretending to be asleep, and was doing so badly. She jumped at every little noise and he took great delight in loudly dropping his belt with his dart gun beside the bed. When he curled under the covers, he forced himself to not draw her closer. He knew he had nothing to fear from her and only let her carry out her plan to satisfy his curiosity.

Once she thought he was asleep, he felt her crawl out of bed. He couldn't see what she was doing, but he heard her get something from under the bed. It had to be the dagger Zephyrus warned him about. He turned over slowly to watch her nervously light a candle.

Keeping an arm over his eyes to hide his face, he watched her through lowered lashes as she crept closer. She took her sweet time to bring the light up to his face, and he thought she would chicken out before getting that far.

When she removed his arm from his face and saw him, he heard her gasp. "Amor," she breathed, her voice so sad that it broke his heart. He never wanted her to find out this way.

She backed away and he heard something metallic hit the floor. He knew she was unarmed and hoped that now she'd come back to bed. He could forgive her for this transgression if she returned to him. Instead, she started to look through his stuff. He watched as she picked up his belt and took out the gun. He started to get nervous, wondering if she planned on shooting him with his own darts.

Iona turned the gun over in her hands, slowly tracing his symbol on the handle. She made a choking noise, and he realized she was holding back tears. With the gun still in her hands, she sat on the foot of the bed.

"Why didn't you tell me," she whispered to the gun. "All those stupid hints. Was all this just a game?" She took a deep, shuttering breath and mimicked his words from what felt like a lifetime ago. "When you learn the truth, you'll wonder how you never made the connection."

He spoke those words to her when he caught her talking to his host's mother and staring at his statue. How she hadn't figured it out that he was Eros in that moment was beyond him. Humans, he knew, could be blind to the obvious if it suited them.

He heard her give a startled cry and realized she squeezed the trigger. One glittering golden dart struck her leg. Under his lashes, he watched her reach down to pull it out, only to have it vanish. In that moment, the love serum rushed through her veins, altering her perception.

Eros heard the change come over her almost at once. He spent enough time in amorous lovemaking to know the signs when Iona was aroused. He could hear it now – the small moans in her breathing and sound of her hands tugging on the fabric of her nightgown. When she turned to look at him, the full effects of the serum burst into life. He was engraved in her mind and her heart. Eros knew he had nothing to fear about her ever disobeying him or listening to her viperous sisters.

He closed his eyes as she shifted toward him, the candle light growing brighter when she started to move from the foot of the bed to the top. Her fingers played lightly over the covers, barely skimming his legs as they traveled delightfully upward. He bit his lip as her playful fingers danced where the covers and his skin met. He knew she was standing over him, the light blazing red behind his eyelids.

As her hands lightly skimmed over his taunt skin, he wondered what she planned to do with him. He knew from years of using the darts that a person infected became infatuated with and filled with desire for the first person he or she laid eyes on. What could Iona's most lustful desires be? She always struck him as an innocent, incapable of ever having such thoughts.

Eros nearly jumped as she moved up to touch his lips, tracing them with her fingertips. He held his breath as she touched and traced the lines of his face and neck, lovingly touching the features she only knew in the dark. How often had she wanted to touch him in the light when he pretended to be Amor? Did she lie in bed, wishing she knew what her husband looked like? Would she take advantage of him now that she could see him?

Or, would she, as he always believed, innocently tease him and then stop?

"My Amor, my darling," she breathed. The bed dipped as she climbed on and straddled him. Would it matter that he was 'sleeping'?

She leaned down, careful to hold the candle away from his flesh. Iona planted small, sweet kisses along his cheeks, over his eyelids and on the tip of his nose. It was hard for him to remain still when his beautiful wife wanted him so much.

When she kissed his lips, it was like the first taste of sweet water after years of wandering in the desert. Eros struggled to maintain his ruse of slumber, but finally gave up when her kisses became more urgent and she started to push the covers down. Joyously, he opened his mouth to her attentions, allowing his lustful wife to kiss him deeper. Iona's drugged mind did not register that he would have to be awake to respond to her. All she cared about was the bliss she felt.

Eros enjoyed the amorous attentions of his wife until he felt a painful burning sensation in his shoulder. He flexed his shoulder to alleviate the pain, but only got worse. With a howl, he jumped up and pushed Iona away. As she landed on the floor, he saw that his right wing and shoulder in flames. In her desire, Iona accidentally tipped the candle on to his vulnerable flesh.

"By Hades, woman! Have you lost your mind?"

Iona jumped to her feet, fear and concern etched on her pretty face. "Should I get Lethia? How about a healer? I only know the midwife, but I'm sure she can help. Do you want me to get her?" Her questions came in a frantic rush. The mere thought that she injured him cut through her.

"You've done quite enough already," Eros snapped. He grabbed a cup of water by the bed and doused the flames. When that failed to put all of the fire out, he grabbed the bed linens and beat the flames out, causing more pain to shoot through his body. Finally, the fire was out, but his shoulder and wing were damaged. "You betrayed me, Iona! My own wife is nothing more than a traitorous snake!"

"What are you talking about," Iona asked. The dart's powers fresh in her system clouded her exact memory, making it hard for her to understand how she betrayed him. She was currently upset over how she physically hurt him. Emotional pain was too much for her to consider. All she knew was that she'd never betray such a wonderful and handsome man.

"I told you to never try and see my face," Eros said. "You betrayed my trust. You even planned on killing me!"

The memory of just the past hour came rushing back. "By the love of Hera, you're right," Iona wailed. She scooped up the dagger, holding it poised to stab her breast. "I don't deserve to live after what I've done!"

Eros grabbed the dagger, twisting it out of her hands. "Don't be so melodramatic," he snapped. "That's just the dart talking. Go and get Lethia and tell her to bring some ointment for my shoulder."

Iona ran from the room and returned with Lethia. The older woman looked amused as she put the ointment on Eros' shoulder. Without a word, she left, the air tense between Iona and Eros as he tried to think of what to do with his easily-swayed wife. This was all her sisters' fault. If he could only keep them away, he might be able to salvage this marriage.

"You need to compensate me for this grievous act of treason," Eros said, a plan forming in his mind.

"I'll do anything," Iona pleaded. "Please, husband, forgive my lapse in judgment."

"You are to never speak to your sisters ever again. They will never come here and you will never go to visit them. In fact, I don't want to ever hear their names in this house. They do not exist. None of your family exists from this day on!"

It was a brilliant plan. Without the influence of her family, he could go back to the happy life he had with Iona. He fully expected Iona to comply with his wishes. With the dart so fresh in her system, she should have agreed to anything he said. What he didn't expect was for her to look as if she had been slapped. Her pretty mouth formed words, but no sound came out.

Deep in Iona's being, a new emotion finally peeked through the lusty haze. She realized that, while she would happily spend her life at her husband's feet, she *didn't* have to. When he gave her the order, she wanted to say, "Yes" and do anything to keep him happy. However, this foreign emotion demanded otherwise. It railed against her, robbing her of her voice as it screamed in her mind to resist.

"Not see my family ever again," she croaked. "Never mention them in this house?" Her voice grew stronger as the haze vanished and anger set in. "After what you put me through, you want me to deny my family!"

"What I put you through? I married you. I cherished you. I gave you everything your little heart desired and allowed you freedoms I should have denied you. I knew bringing your sisters here was a bad idea, but I did it to keep you happy! I gave you everything!"

"You lied to me! You let me believe I married a monster! I cried over you, Amor! And that's not even your real name. While I was in your home, playing the happy but deluded bride, you were laughing it up in the arms of my sister!" Iona bent and grabbed the fallen gun. She pointed the empty gun at him. "And what do I find out? I get to find out how I've been played when your stupid gun shoots me in the leg, *Eros*!"

"Put that down," Eros snapped. "It's not loaded." When Iona refused to drop it, he grabbed the gun away. He heard it click a few times as she tried to shoot him. With her disarmed, he said, "I had to keep my real identity a secret. It wasn't safe."

"Oh, this again. You really expect me to believe that Aphrodite is out to kill me? I only have your word for it, and all I remember seeing was you messing with my life. All those suitors, you were the one who got rid of them."

"I was protecting you! Iona, I love you. I couldn't let you marry those men. They wouldn't have made you happy."

"And you do? What lies did you tell Philomena when you slept with her? Is she the only one you were seeing while I wasted my life here waiting for you?"

"What? I never touched your sister! I wouldn't touch that backstabbing little rat if she were the last woman on Space Station *Olympus*."

"That's not what she told me, and who am I to believe? My sister or the man who has been lying to me from day one?"

"You should believe your husband! Your sister is a liar!"

"Don't ever talk about my family like that!"

"Your sisters convinced you to try to kill me. What do you have to say about that?"

"They were worried about me, and they had cause to be," Iona said. "If you had just been honest with me -"

"You were perfectly safe! Have I ever hurt you? No! Have I ever caused you to feel pain or fear? No! I can't say the same about you," Eros snapped.

"You caused me pain with your lies. If you had just told the truth, none of this would have happened! I defended you to my family when I didn't know who you were! You're nothing more than...than...than an arrogant jerk!"

Eros laughed. "I'm a jerk? Oh, that's rich coming from a naïve little backstabber who I *thought* loved me. You, little Iona, are nothing more than a sheep, following blindly any idiocy your evil sisters lead you into."

Eros stormed out of the room with Iona hot on his heels. "You never told me the truth,' she snapped. "Our whole relationship was built on lies. You probably have a girl on every level, Oh Great God of Love!"

"Baa! Baa! Go bleat your woes to your family, you stupid sheep."

They passed Lethia, who kindly opened the front door for

them and waved as their fight took the streets. Iona was too angry at her husband to notice the smug look of satisfaction on the other woman's face.

"Apollo's Oracle was right about you! You are a winged serpent," Iona sneered. Behind her, Lethia closed the door.

"If you think Apollo is so great, why don't you throw yourself on his mercies! That's all you're good for, Iona!" Eros made his way to the PortMat. He needed to get away from Iona. He was too angry to think or wonder why the dart wasn't working on her anymore. This fight should never have happened, but she was being so irrational. All he could think of was getting away from the cause of his pain and crying his misfortune to his mother. Aphrodite would understand him and help his poor burned shoulder.

"Don't walk away from me," Iona snapped. "Eros, get back here!"

"Go back to the house, Iona. I have nothing more to say to a traitor!"

"Pot and kettle, Eros! You betrayed me first!"

"At least I didn't try to kill you," Eros scoffed.

"Yet! How do I know that wasn't your next move? You lied about everything else, how do I know that loving me and wanting our baby wasn't a lie?"

"By Ares, Iona! Shut up!"

Eros turned and pushed Iona back as he slammed the door to the PortMat room shut. He quickly activated the beam, his urge to leave overwhelming. He could hear Iona pounding on the door. No doubt the whole street could hear her and knew that they were fighting. Oh, he could just picture Anteros watching them from his window. And the Fates? Those old hags were most likely cackling and playing with their strings. He was the laughing stock of the whole street and it was all Iona's fault!

The PortMat flared to life and Eros stepped into the light. Behind him, he was almost sure he heard the door open, but it was too late. He was gone, not caring if Iona wanted to apologize. He just didn't care.

Iona forced opened the door, and watched in disbelief as her husband vanished from her sight. In that instant, her anger melted away. He left her. What if he never came back? How could she raise the baby on her own? With her anger gone and her emotions drained, the dart took over again and she only wanted to be Eros. The memory of why they were fighting vanished as she jumped into the light.

Chapter 21

The sunlight that streamed across Iona's face rudely awakened her from the numbing bliss of slumber. Her whole body ached and the light caused her head to pound. She moaned, turning over in the bed, causing the pain to throb through her body even more. She curled up, her hands wrapping protectively around her stomach. A thought passed through her mind before the pain washed over everything. Was her stomach a little flatter than it was supposed to be?

She was still curled up when she heard the door open. She couldn't remember where she was, or why she was in bed. Slowly, she started to remember the fight. Or was it a dream? Being morning, it had to be Lethia coming to get her up for the day. Iona felt horrible and knew she would not be much help. Opening her eyes, she watched the blurry figure of a woman approach the bed. Too late, she realized it wasn't Lethia.

"Oh, are you awake?" The voice was too cheerful to be the sour house matron. Iona winced as that chipper tone cut right into her already aching head. "How are you feeling?"

"Please, softer," Iona begged, her voice scratchy. "It hurts."

"Sorry," the woman said, lowering her voice slightly.

From under the covers, Iona managed to mumble, "I hurt all over. Where am I?"

"You're in my house," the woman said.

"Where?"

The woman gave a twittering laugh. "You're on Level 14, the holy level of Hermes. I'm Casta, proud shepherdess in one of his sacred fields. I am blessed to be the hostess of Lord Pan and Lady Persephone."

Iona made a sound that Casta interpreted as a question. Without pausing, or lowering her voice, she chirped, "Yes! Isn't it just wonderful! I'm well acquainted with them. In fact, Lord Pan has been incredibly curious about you. He visits nearly every day to see how you've been. You're lucky to have the attention of such a wonderful god. I can't wait to tell him you're awake."

Iona blissfully heard the door open and Casta leave the room.

In the silence that followed, Iona imagined that the girl was the kind of person who skipped everywhere, brimming with so much energy that she drained the life of those around her.

Not one to just lay in bed, Iona slowly crawled out from under the covers. The room spun and dipped, causing her to grip the bed to keep from falling. When everything slowed to a near stop, she realized that she could function through the pain. It faded just enough for her to think.

"Wait, what did she say? Level 14!"

Iona couldn't believe it. Levels 4 to 17 were the private living and most holy temples of the gods. The Oracle was in a grand temple on Level 10, the holy level of Apollo. Hermes, Level 14, was well known as a traveler's haven with the most hospitable people, sneakiest thieves and happiest nymphs and satyrs. Of course, that was only if one possessed the money and prestige to travel so far. The only way to live on the levels was to be called by the gods.

The door opened again and Iona was determined to get some answers. Now that she could think, she could finally understand what Perky Casta had to say. However, the person that walked through the door wasn't Casta. It wasn't even human. The creature seemed extremely curly with curly brown hair, curly ram's horns and curly fur covering long goat legs with cloven hooves. Kind brown eyes and a long, curly beard dominated the tan face. It was bare-chested, though the mass of brown body hair could double as clothing. Iona had seen several pictures of satyrs to know she was in the presence of one now.

She cleared her throat. "Uh, you're not Casta, are you?"

The satyr laughed. "Not by a long shot," he said in a merry voice. "I'm a wee bit too male to be her."

"Who are you?"

"I am Pan, son of Hermes and Lord of the Fields. You're in my domain, little lady. I should be asking you who you are."

Feeling a little self-conscious, Iona wasn't sure if she should bow or stand straighter. Deciding that if she bowed, she'd probably never get back up, she chose to stand proudly. "I am Iona Demarchis, daughter of Metasis and Hedlya of Tiryns."

"Iona of Tiryns? That name sounds oddly familiar."

"I don't believe we've ever met, Lord Pan," Iona said. "I would have treasured such an honor."

Pan's smile got wider. "And believe me, I'd remember meeting such a lovely lady."

"Is this really Level 14?"

"It is. Welcome to the official domain of my esteemed father, Hermes. He rarely comes here, though, being the god of thieves, merchants, travelers and messengers. Poor Father, always on the run."

"How did I get here?"

Before Pan could answer, the door opened again. A lovely woman entered the room wearing a spring green chiton, her black hair pulled back in a simple braid. Sprigs of wheat were artfully woven through her hair to form a crown.

"Hi. Casta said she was awake. How is our guest doing?"

"You're not Casta," asked Iona.

The woman laughed. "Oh, no. Not even close. I could never stay that chipper."

"Iona, meet her royal highness and one of my favorite cousins, Persephone, Goddess of the New Spring and Queen of the Underworld," Pan said. "Sephie, this is Iona Demarchis of Tiyrns."

"Oh, that name sounds familiar," Persephone said. Iona knew about the goddess in front of her, though this was not how she imagined her to be. When anyone spoke of Persephone, she was either the bright happy child of Demeter who frolicked in the fields each spring, happy to be with her mother. Or she was spoken of in hushed, pitying tones as the tortured wife of the most feared and hated god in all Space Station *Olympus*; Hades. No temples were built for the dread god of the Underworld, no rituals or prayers performed. If one must invoke his name, it was done through Persephone in the hopes his gentle wife could soften his temper. All the pictures of Persephone were of a sad woman dressed in black as she withered away in the Underworld six months of the year, yearning for the sunlight and waiting to reunite with her mother. This woman, however, was happy. The only reason could be because it was spring and she was free of her husband's dark clutches.

"Um, how did I get here? If this is Hermes' level, is Eros here, too? I have to find him."

Persephone and Pan exchanged a look. The goddess snapped her fingers as she exclaimed, "That's where I heard your name! For a year, maybe more, Aphrodite has been stomping around Olympus, angry that someone named Iona of Tiryns has ruined her great victory. Or that she was trying to replace her. Something like that. With Aphrodite, it's hard to tell."

Iona's heart sank. Lethia and Eros were right. The Goddess of Love was angry with her. Could it really be over something as stupid as the attention she got over a year ago? "Oh, dear," Iona moaned. "As if she didn't hate me before, she's going to really hate me now."

"What do you mean? Did you have a run-in at one of her temples?"

Iona nodded. "Over a year ago, there was a little problem with people in Tiryns calling me Aphrodite-in-the-flesh and shoving gifts into my arms. I couldn't stop them, so I did what I thought was the next best thing. I'd bring the offerings to the temple on their behalf. I thought I was doing something good, until I was told that Aphrodite hated me."

"There you have it," Pan said. "Any woman who gets special attention is automatically hated by Aphrodite. You'd think the Goddess of Love would like it when people found that special someone, but she's a jealous woman. Sometimes, she brings some of those girls who garner mortal favors into her service, but she mostly just makes their lives miserable. Some are killed off or married to whatever horrible monster that catches Aphrodite's fancy."

"That doesn't seem to have happened to you," Persephone said. "Somehow, you escaped, which I fear may have made it worse for you."

"Well, I had help. Eros married me and kept me hidden."

Pan snorted. "And we know that was without Aphrodite's blessing."

"Is that how I got here? Is it because of Aphrodite?"

"Sweet Spring, no," Persephone said. "Only Hermes has jurisdiction here. Maybe Zeus has some rights here, but Hermes will always be the primary god."

"What do you remember before coming here," Pan asked. "I know how you got here, but I don't know the why."

Iona looked down. "I don't know where to begin," she said. They were deities, and she was in trouble with a goddess. If she told them about her fight with Eros, would they deliver her to his angry mother? If she lied, would they believe her?

"Just start from the beginning," Persephone said gently.

Iona took a deep breath to steady her nerves. "The last thing I remember is that Eros and I had a fight. It was rather stupid, really. Mostly my fault, now that I think about it. I followed some bad advice from my sisters, and hurt Eros. Not too badly, mind you," she said, hoping to keep her hosts from getting angry at her, "just a little burn on his shoulder. And it was an accident. But, we were screaming at each other and we said such horrible things. I followed him to the room at the end of the street, a strange room filled with buttons and a console that created a great white light. He made the light appear and vanished into it. I thought I was going to lose him and would have to raise our baby alone. I love him, and that stupid fight didn't change that. I foolishly followed him into the light. I remember the light, and I remember feeling pain, and then darkness."

Pan hummed, pulling on his beard. "That is odd. Eros never came here. I doubt this was his destination choice. Yet, if you followed him, how did you end up here instead of where he was heading? And the PortMat shouldn't cause you any pain. That is most distressing."

"What's a PortMat," asked Iona.

"It's not usual for Eros to even come here," Pan continued. "In fact, the only time anyone connected to him has ever come here has been ... Oh." There was something about what Pan was saying that caused an air of gloom to descend on the room. He and Persephone exchanged another look, a topic that should be discussed passed between them.

Persephone cleared her throat. "I, uh, think I know what happened. If Eros didn't know you were following him, he might have turned off the PortMat when he reached his destination. You would have been connected to the nearest outlet, and the pain you felt was your body being shoved from nothingness to an unscheduled somethingness."

"What does that all mean?"

"Nothing," said Pan. "It's the travel of the gods. Don't ever repeat anything you hear here to anyone."

Iona agreed. She still wasn't sure what they were talking about, and highly doubted anyone below the godly levels would either. All she cared about was that they didn't seem upset with her.

"Iona," Persephone said hesitantly, "you said something

about a baby? How old, and who is taking care of him – or her – while you're here?"

"My baby's not born yet," Iona said softly. Her hands caressed her stomach as she smiled. "I'm only three months along. We just finished the nursery."

Persephone looked down, sadness etched on her pretty face. She muttered, "Oh dear," and looked over at Pan. The normally jovial god's mood became somber.

"What? What's wrong? Are babies not allowed here," asked Iona.

"No, it's not that," Persephone started. She choked back what sounded like a sob, and Pan continued for her.

"Iona, when you travel through the PortMat, it sends you a special and fast way from one point to the next. When you were dumped out, your body had to be recreated from the space you were traveling in to a physical form. A sudden re-emergence like that puts a lot of harmful strain on the body. Not that you're supposed to travel by PortMat if you're pregnant, anyway."

"I understand that. I was in a lot of pain when I woke up today."

"You've been in and out of consciousness for over a week now," Pan said. "When Casta and I found you, you were covered in blood. I don't suppose you or Eros were gravely hurt before you jumped into the light?"

"No. Eros never raised a hand to me. The only wound I received was when I shot myself with his gun, but that didn't bleed at all. And I accidentally burned Eros, but he wasn't bleeding either. I was physically fine when I followed him."

Persephone covered her mouth with her hand. She muttered, "I hoped it would be different. I am so sorry, Iona," and ran from the room.

"Great, Sephie, leave me to tell her," Pan yelled after her. He turned back to Iona, the struggle for words clearly on his face. Finally, he said, "I'm so sorry. The strain from the PortMat being turned off caused a lot of trauma to your body. We had hoped that you weren't pregnant, Iona. Believe me, I wish this hadn't happened."

Iona wanted to ask what happened, why were they both so sad, but she had the sinking feeling she knew. Her hands moved back to her stomach. It was flatter than what she had become accustomed to, the minor little bump of life gone. Tears filled her eyes as a cold emptiness filled her womb.

"My baby," she whispered. "Oh, gods, my baby!"

"I'm so sorry," Pan said softly. "I wish I could make this better."

Iona howled in anguish and fell to the floor, her hands clutching the clothes around her stomach. Her baby was gone, and it was all her fault. She murdered her innocent baby. Pan held her as she cried, whispering his sorrow and support. He told her it wasn't her fault, that things will be all right, but what did he know? Iona knew in her heart if she had just gone back home her baby would be alive. She should have known this was going to happen. She had been foolish.

Sometime during her tears, Persephone reentered the room and offered her support. The two deities held Iona until her grief robbed her of her strength and she fell asleep. Pan lifted her up and placed her back on the bed. He motioned for Persephone to follow him as he left.

"That poor girl," said Persephone, closing the door. "I can't imagine what it must be like to lose a child."

"You'll have to contact Eros and let him know she's here," Pan said. "He has a right to know about the baby."

Persephone shook her head. "I'll talk to Zephyrs, but Eros will be under the watchful eyes of his mother. We can't let Aphrodite find Iona. Not now, not like this."

"Do what you must to protect her," Pan said. "I should get back to Olympus more often. I hadn't known Eros had taken another host. I wish I had been more prepared."

"I can't believe Psyche didn't do anything to stop this," Persephone snapped. "After all her stupid little promises about not wanting the next girl to suffer as she had, she lets it happen all over again. She knew this was going to happen!"

"I don't suppose this time she'll remember this and help out the next girl," Pan said.

"I doubt it," Persephone said. "I'll talk to Zephyrs when I get to Olympus. Mother is expecting me back soon. She insists I spend more time with her on my months away from Hades, but it's so boring just frolicking in the meadows, painting flowers and dancing with nymphs."

"And yet, she has no problem with letting you run around with me," Pan said. "I would have thought old Demeter would be more protective of you."

"Don't take this the wrong way," said Persephone, "but Mother wants anyone to be my husband other than Hades. She'd welcome you with open arms, at first. But we both know she really wanted me to be a child and a virgin forever."

"Well, you know it's never greater than with a satyr."

Persephone rolled her eyes. "That is just horrible, Pan. Don't ever say that again." They heard the jubilant bells of Hermes ringing in the distance, a sign that he arrived in his level. "It looks like it's time for me to go. Stay with Iona, Pan. This has got to be rough on the poor girl."

"I will. Take care, Sephie."

Chapter 22

Aphrodite never felt so mad or so betrayed. She was fuming! Just a few days ago, she thought all was well in her life. True, she still couldn't find that uppity little whore from Tiryns, but that was no matter. Her popularity was growing again and people remembered the real name of Aphrodite. Her coffers were filled with gold and sweet flowers adorned her alters. She felt better and believed all was right with the world.

Then, her son returned and she found out how horribly she had been betrayed. That vile little traitor had been hiding the Tiryns girl. Married her, even! How could he do that to her, his own mother! She who showed him nothing but love! She was the one who handpicked his host body and stroked his head as the change occurred. She gave him everything he ever wanted and still he betrayed her! She could not believe his audacity to fall in love with that little tramp. While she worried herself nearly to the point of wrinkles, he was off playing happy homemaker with that imposter.

Well, he learned his lesson. That little mortal had caused him physical and emotional injury. That should have made Aphrodite happy, giving her an excuse to end the little harlot's life once and for all. But this was her son, her precious baby boy whom she loved above all others, and he was in pain. Her revenge would have to wait until her darling little Eros was better.

"Oh, Aphrodite! A moment of your time!" She turned to see Apollo heading down the marble halls of Olympus to her. She greatly admired the sun god. Though she was married to the disgusting Hephaestus and seducing that simpleton, Ares, she always wanted Apollo. Of all the gods, only he came close to matching her beauty.

"Apollo, always a pleasure," Aphrodite said. "I would love to talk with you, but I am a little busy today. I'm sure you've heard about my poor, darling little Eros."

"Yes, poor Eros. He's the reason I need to talk to you. I know you are caring and love for your son is only exceeded by your grace and beauty. A truly lucky little boy, indeed. However, I am a bit concerned," Apollo said. "I noticed that neither I nor my healers have been called to aid you in your endeavors to help poor, unfortunate Eros."

"I can handle this, Apollo."

He flashed a devastatingly handsome smile. "Ah, I see. Mother knows best. No doubt you heard the reason for his mishap and, in your wisdom, have decided to let his wounds heal at a more mortal pace to give him time to rethink his priorities?"

Truthfully, the idea never occurred to Aphrodite. She merely never called any of the healers because she wanted to keep her humiliation out of the public. Of course Apollo, who had eyes and ears everywhere, would know of her son's disgrace. Though, if he was going to give her a perfectly logical reason for not calling any healers, it would be rude of her to not take it.

"Yes," she said, "that's why I didn't call on you. I want Eros to remember the pain caused by his little human whore when he thinks of betraying me. I'm only doing what is right."

"And this little human wouldn't be his new wife, Iona Demarchis of Tiyrns," Apollo said. Though it was poised as a question, Aphrodite could tell he knew exactly who had harmed her son.

"You knew about her? For how long?"

Apollo smiled, studying his fingernails. "Oh, from the beginning, I believe. I watched as he entered your temple on your command to destroy that upstart, and shot himself in the leg. I watched as he took her on little dates and ruined all those suitors you were gracious enough to send her way. Why, I know that Hephaestus caught them once, and merely let them go without as much as a warning."

"Hephaestus was in on this!" Aphrodite felt as if she were stabbed through the heart. She possessed no love for her legal husband. In fact, she loathed the ugly beast. But she always took it for granted that he had more loyalty to her than this.

"Eros even came to me with tears in his eyes, begging me to order the Oracle to give a very specific prophesy to her father. He wanted it to be divine will that they marry." Apollo sighed dramatically. "And I, being the hopeless romantic that I am, agreed."

"So," Aphrodite hissed, "it was you who pulled the wool over my eyes with that winged serpent nonsense! How could you, Apollo! Everyone knew I was looking high and low to find that deceiver, and you went along with the charade."

"I watched for my own purposes. You'll have a hard time convincing Eros to stay away from Iona. He's infected by his own darts."

"That means nothing," Aphrodite said, waving his warning aside. "Those darts don't always last forever."

"These will," Apollo said. "But, I believe I have a plan that will benefit us both. I know it for a fact that Iona believes that Eros was sleeping with other women while they were wedded. Why not play that up? Give Eros a nursemaid that would be a perfect match for him. You, the mighty Goddess of Love, can help push them towards a new relationship. The dart's powers will weaken if one or both of them falls for another. If Eros won't love the woman you choose, then we'll have to make Iona fall for someone new."

"And what do you get out of this? So far, I only hear how I'm going to win."

"Ah, my part. I want Iona. Oh, don't look so disgusted, Aphrodite, it's not love on my end. You know that I bear your son no kind affections after the many times he's made me a fool. You can pick his new wife, and I want to see the pain in his eyes as his old love adores me before I toss her to the side. And then you can have your great revenge as she wanders saddened and alone. Who knows? She might be so depressed that she jumps into space."

Aphrodite smiled. "Oh, you're just saying that to make me happy."

"I'm serious." Apollo held out his hand. "Do we have a deal?"

"I do," Aphrodite said. She shook his hand. It was only a mortal deal, as neither one said the binding words to keep gods from altering pacts. "Now, what goddess shall we pick to entice my stupid son from that tramp?"

"I was thinking Persephone," Apollo said. "Demeter is still angry over losing her daughter to the dark seductions of Hades, and will gladly welcome another divine suitor. I'm sure she'll agree that Eros is just as good ..." he paused, seeing the look on Aphrodite's face and amended his words, "... an even better match than Hades."

"One problem," said Aphrodite. "Hades has a jealous streak, and would not hesitate to come up to Olympus illegally to destroy my son if he so much as suspected his precious wife was cheating on him. And I do not feel like trying to find Hades another wife. Who would want him? Although," she mused, "there must be something about him that keeps Persephone happy."

"Demeter has other children," Apollo said. "If not Persephone, then why not Despoina? I doubt that poor girl ever leaves the stables. Her only companions are horses and your son Deimos stops by on the rare occasion. She could use some romance, don't you agree?"

"When did Demeter have more kids?"

"She's always had other kids. Since she forgets she has more kids than just Persephone, it's not surprising that everyone else forgets. Despoina is her daughter by Poseidon, along with her twin brother, Areion the horse."

"A horse?"

"Don't ask. I try to not think about it."

Aphrodite tapped her chin as she thought this over. "This Despoina would jump at the chance to marry my darling Eros, wouldn't she? And, if she's as desperate as you say, to be loved, she would easily fall for him. Now, to ensure that Eros returns her affections ..."

"I'll leave that up to you," Apollo said. "Just deliver Iona to me." He waved and left. Aphrodite had a lot to think about. She did like Apollo's plan, but she was sure it wasn't a spur of the moment thing. He had to have been plotting for a while, and with Eros hurt, it was the perfect time to act. Demeter would jump at the chance to align herself with Aphrodite.

Aphrodite made her way to Demeter's chambers. She could only hope that the Goddess of Grain was available. During the spring and summer months, Demeter was exceptionally busy. Between helping with the farms and attending her festivals, she hovered over Persephone. It was possible that Aphrodite would have to wait a few days before she could get Demeter to agree to her plan.

She was in luck, though. Through the door, she could hear Demeter and Persephone fighting. It was about Hades, as all their fights tended to be.

"I will wear what I please, Mother," came Persephone's voice. "You have no right to tear up my new dress!"

"You will wear what I give you to wear," Demeter snapped. "You should only be clothed in colors of spring and beauty. Not that dark trash."

"That dark trash was a surprise for Hades! You tore up part of my anniversary gift to him!"

"Do not say that name in my presence. Never speak of that kidnapper, that despoiler of innocent children."

"He's my husband, Mother. I love him! I will say his name to my heart's content."

"He's a monster, Kore! He stole you from me, brainwashed you against me, and keeps you locked in the dark where you will wither and die. Hearing you spout his falsehoods is like knife though my heart. You're killing me, Kore! You're killing your mother."

"Stop being so dramatic," Persephone snapped. "And stop calling me Kore! I gave up that stupid name when I became the Queen of the Underworld. I'm Persephone!"

"You'll always be my little Kore. Now, put on the dress Mommy bought you. No more talk of that monster, okay."

"I'll talk about him if I want to, Mother! It's only natural for a wife to speak of her husband."

Hesitantly, Aphrodite knocked on the door. The fighting stopped immediately and there were the sounds of a slight scuffle before the door opened. Demeter's eyes widened as she saw Aphrodite.

"Well, what brings you here," the plump goddess asked. "Shouldn't you be in your rooms, pampering your son?"

"I have a proposal for your daughter," Aphrodite said. "May I come in?"

"What do you want with Kore?"

From inside the room, her daughter yelled, "It's Persephone!"

"Actually, my proposal is for your other daughter, Despoina."

Demeter looked confused. "Who?"

"Despoina," Persephone said. She came walking up to the door, straightening the folds of her yellow dress. The color looked horrible on her. "She's my sister." At Demeter's continued look of confusion, Persephone rolled her eyes. "Really Mother! Despoina, the stable-girl. The one you refer to as the 'whelp of Poseidon'."

"Oh, right, that Despoina. Yes, she's my daughter. What about her?"

Aphrodite gave Demeter her most charming smile. "Well, as

you know, my Eros has been cruelly hurt by an ungrateful human girl. I am busy with the demands of the humans below, and need some assistance in nursing my suffering son back to health. I just thought that your single daughter would enjoy the chance to woo and win a divine husband. I hear that the gentle hand that nurses one back to health is a powerful aphrodisiac."

"Why Despoina? Why not Kore? She can use a good husband."

"Mother!"

Aphrodite pulled Demeter to the side and whispered, "I want Eros to fall for someone other than that mortal whore. It can't be Persephone ... I mean, Kore. If her monstrous husband ever suspects she's fallen for another, he will storm Olympus. But, Despoina is single and still counts as a goddess. I'd rather have a divine daughter-in-law than that common little nobody."

Demeter frowned. "But if Kore were to fall in love with Eros, than all my problems are solved."

"I don't need Hades coming up here for my son," Aphrodite snapped. "We can figure out how to help your daughter after we woo my son into the arms of Despoina."

"Why not have it be Eros and Persphone, and Hades can have that tramp?"

Aphrodite paused. She hadn't thought of that. "I promised the girl to Apollo. He's bored with his current playthings."

"What's in it for me?"

"You get a good godly son-in-law and, as the Goddess of Love and Beauty, I'll work on Kore next. I'm sure I can find a suitable match for your lovely daughter."

Demeter smiled. "Deal."

Chapter 23

Slowly, Iona began to recover. Her constant companions were Pan and the ever bubbly Casta, who told her every day that the miscarriage was not her fault. No one knew that she would jump into the PortMat beam after Eros, or that he'd shut the beam off so quickly. They assured her that Eros wouldn't blame her for so tragic an accident. Though kind their words were, it did nothing to lighten the guilt that Iona felt. She grieved silently over the loss of what she knew would be the most perfect baby. But, when the news of Eros' pain reached her ears, she struggled to move past her grief for the time being.

Zephyrus, having found out through Persephone where Iona was staying, visited her when he could sneak away from Olympus. With Eros under Aphrodite's tender care, the protection afforded to Zephyrus was fading and he feared that Apollo would hunt him down. He stayed close to his master's side, leaving only when it was safe. It was he who brought the news of Despoina to Iona. Persephone, on her next trip to Level 14, confirmed that her sister fawned over the handsome god with thoughts of marriage in her head.

"Do you think he likes her," Iona asked fearfully.

"Not a chance," Persephone said. "He is madly, head-over-heels in love with you."

"You're the only person on his mind," Zephyrus added. "He asks about you when we're alone. He only tolerates Despoina in order to get better. It's you that he loves, not her."

Iona smiled slightly. "Thank you. Have you told him about the baby?"

"Not yet. We're waiting until his strength returns."

"It was just a little burn on his shoulder. Why is it taking so long for him to heal," Iona asked.

Zephyrus shrugged. "I have my suspicions. Either Aphrodite is doing something to keep him there, or Despoina is, but his wound isn't healing properly and it's causing him great pain."

Persephone sighed. "As much as I love my sister, I have no illusions that she wouldn't do something sneaky to gain favor with

Mother. Don't forget, Demeter and Aphrodite are in cohoots on this, and so is Apollo."

"I feel as if all of Olympus is against me," Iona said.

"Do not feel as if all is lost," Pan said. "You have us on your side. And I know my Father would be if he knew your situation. And Hephaestus is on your side."

"I heard a rumor that Phobos helped you in the past," Persephone said. "It's unusual for him to be kind to anyone connected to Eros. If that is the case, you have more allies than you know."

"This is all so confusing. I hope I'm not causing problems for you all."

Pan laughed. "Oh, don't worry. Picking sides in squabbles is what we do best."

"You're not causing problems at all," Zephyrus assured her. He looked down for a moment and then said, "Iona, what are you going to do about your sisters?"

"What do you mean?"

Pan cleared his throat. "Well, you told us you broke Eros' rule on the advice of your sisters. They brought a dagger to your house with the intent of having you attack your husband. What kind of person brings a weapon to a friendly meeting?"

"They were just worried," Iona protested. "It was my fault for what happened, not theirs. I betrayed Eros, not them."

"Would you have betrayed him without their pouring poison in your ear," asked Persephone.

"They plotted against you," Zephyrus said. "Iona, I heard them. They are jealous of you and coveted what you possessed. Those deceptive hags may have been sweet to your face, but they were evil behind your back."

"I can't believe that. My sisters love me. They were happy for me."

"You have to at least accept the possibility that they betrayed you," Persephone said. "I know about family and betrayal, Iona. They brought a dagger with them. It was their plan all along to get you to betray your husband."

Iona sighed, rubbing her stomach. "Eros said something like that when we were fighting. I knew he didn't like my sisters, but I didn't think anything of it. I thought it was just ... I mean, I thought from all the time he had been lonely and now he had me, it was just his way of not wanting to share. I never thought there was anything to his distrust." She shook her head as if to clear the dark thoughts. "I still can't believe my sisters would ever betray me like that."

"Why not find proof," Pan suggested. "Go and visit them. Just be careful, though. Aphrodite has her minions looking for you. My poor father has been making announcements for everyone on Space Station *Olympus* to keep an eye out for you."

"My sisters won't betray me," said Iona. "You'll see. This was all just a misunderstanding. They'll help me and together, we'll think of a way to get Eros back."

"I'll keep an eye on you, just in case," Zephyrus said. "I'd hate for you to be hurt because you placed your trust in the wrong hands."

"We'll all look out for you," Persephone said. She jumped and left to get started on the paperwork. As far as any authorities were concerned, she was now Azalia of Eleusis and a devotee of Hecate. Pan cut Iona's hair, offering it up to his father for luck in her travels.

Iona's first stop was to see Philomena. As the eldest, if there had been a plot, it would have been Philomena who orchestrated it. Even as children, Errita always relied on Philomena to create all the games they played. By the time Iona had been born, the two of them were thick as thieves, and she now suspected that her eldest sister would know if there truly had been a betrayal.

Hesitantly, she knocked on the door, pulling her veil more over her head. What would she say to her sister? How could she bring up the betrayal? Iona was frightened that Pan and the others were right.

Iona was surprised when it was Philomena who opened the door and not a servant. Her sister's eyes widened when she saw who was standing at the door.

"I don't give charity to beggars," Philomena sneered. She moved to slam the door when Iona pulled off her veil. "Iona? What are you doing here? What happened to your hair?"

"I needed to see you," Iona said. "Something awful has happened and I didn't know where else to turn."

Philomena peered out of her house, looking around the vast yard. "Did anyone see you coming here? Who else knows you're here?"

"No one knows and I came disguised. Please, Philomena, you have to help me."

Philomena pulled her inside the house, shutting the door firmly. "What happened? Errita and I thought we'd hear from you by now. It's been months!"

Now that she was safe with her sister, Iona felt her strength leaving her. She cried and threw herself into Philomena's arms. "It's awful! I lost the baby! Everything! It's my entire fault!"

"I'm so sorry. I know how much you wanted that baby. What happened? Did he eat it?"

"It was my entire fault. I was so foolish and I wasn't thinking and I should have known better. Philomena, he'll never forgive me."

"Did he leave you because of the baby?"

Iona shook her head. "No, he has no idea. He left before. I lost our baby following him."

Philomena patted her on the back, murmuring that everything would be all right. It took a little urging for Iona to agree to stay with her sister. Though it was Iona's plan all along, she wanted Philomena to believe it was all *her* idea. She didn't plan to stay long. Just until she knew for sure if her sisters plotted against her.

And once she had proof that her sister had not betrayed her, she'd leave.

"Iona, I don't know if you know this, but the devotees of Aphrodite have been looking for you. Ever since we visited you, they've been broadcasting you on the news. There's a reward and everything. What happened?"

Deciding to not give all her secrets away, Iona shrugged. "I don't know," she said. "I'm sure it will blow over soon."

Philomena didn't look convinced, but she said, "Come. Zotikos will be pleased to see you. He's had nothing but bad luck since he became ill. You're sure to brighten his day."

She led Iona to the back room that had become her husband's world. Ever since he mysteriously fell ill, she moved him there to make him more comfortable. The doctors had no idea what was wrong with him. The few times they took him from the house, he seemed to get better, and then relapse once he was back under Philomena's care. The illness was so strange to them.

Zotikos appeared to be wasting away to nearly nothing. His

skin hung in fleshy flaps on his bones, his muscles all gone. He was a sickly gray and the room held the depressing aroma of decay.

When he saw Iona, he struggled to sit up. "Iona? When did you get here?"

"I just arrived. How are you feeling?"

"Horrible. The doctors won't tell me a thing, but I can hear them whispering. They believe I'm going to die and there is nothing they can do about it."

Iona sat on the edge of his bed. "How did this happen? Was there a plague?"

Zotikos shook his head weakly. "I don't know. I just felt ill one day, and haven't gotten well. If it weren't for my sweet Philomena taking care of me, I don't know what would have happened to me. She's been my savior."

Philomena smiled and placed a small kiss on the top of his head. "All for you, my love."

"How long are you staying," Zotikos asked.

Iona shrugged. "No more than a few days. I don't want to impose."

"Iona lost her husband and her baby," Philomena said. "She's all alone."

"You may stay here as long as you like," Zotikos said. "I've never forgiven myself to allowing you to marry that monster. Please, think of my home as yours."

"He wasn't a monster," Iona said. "And you did the right thing. I was happy with my husband."

It was not a relaxing visit for Iona. Philomena put her to work almost at once. She was to help the servants clean the bed linens while Philomena cared for Zotikos. Iona kept her eyes open to any sign of treachery, but she could find none. Her sister never mentioned the cause for Iona's visit after that first night, and all she presented was a caring wife.

At night, Iona would be visited by Zephyrus. His news about Eros' slow recovery worried Iona, both of them knowing a burn should have been healed by now. Zephyrus was waiting to tell his master about the miscarriage.

"Aphrodite has him well guarded," he said on the third night. "It's getting harder and harder for me to see him alone. I think she suspects."

"Her desire to find me hasn't waned," Iona said softly. "I was hoping it would fade. What if someone here decides to go to her temple? The reward has been nearly doubled."

"Don't worry. I have someone keeping an ear open. If anyone betrays you, I'll know about it and can get you out here. Has your sister proven her true colors yet?"

Iona frowned. "No deceit. I still think everyone had the wrong idea about my sisters. Philomena has been so kind to me since I arrived. And she's taking such good care of her husband."

Zephyrus sighed. "Just stay on guard."

By the end of the week, Iona nearly pushed the whole betrayal theory from her mind. It was obvious to her that Zephyrus and the others were just paranoid. Far be it from her to think ill of the gods, but maybe they were not as wise as she assumed. She planned on only staying a day or two more before heading over to Errita's and proving that her sisters were not as evil as Pan, Zephyrus and Persephone tried to lead her to believe.

On night, after sneaking some of her food to the roof garden for the Aneriams, she heard a noise below her. Peering over the edge, she saw Philomena and another man. Thinking the man might be a doctor, she strained to hear what was being said. As their voices drifted up, her blood turned cold.

"Are you positive," the man asked. "One hundred percent positive?"

"Of course I am," Philomena huffed. "I'm her sister. I'd know Iona anywhere."

"The last person who was mistaken was executed on Aphrodite's order. I'd hate for such a thing to happen to you, Philomena, and leave your sick husband all alone."

"Trust me, I have the real Iona Demarchis in my house. Now, let's talk about that reward?"

Iona sat back, still able to hear the treachery below but not able to see her sister. How could she? Philomena was her sister. Wasn't family supposed to stick together in good times and bad?

The sound of a footstep alerted Iona to the presence of another on the roof. She turned, thinking it might be Zephyrus, but was surprised to see Phobos standing behind her. He placed a finger to his lips, and she followed his advice by staying silent. Below her, Philomena's greed knew no end.

"You will receive a reward befitting a god," the man said. "You could ask almost anything of Aphrodite. Perhaps, the health of your husband?"

Philomena snorted. "I have something better in mind. Zotikos will die soon anyway, why waste my one request on him."

"You are a cold woman, Philomena."

"When do you plan on taking her? I want to make sure I'm elsewhere."

"You do not wish your sister to know you betrayed her?"

"I would rather not be subjected to that ninny's tears. You should have seen how she cried at her own wedding. I would hate to see how much she'll overreact for her own funeral."

"We can do it tonight. Why delay this out much longer."

"Not tonight. I just said I didn't want to be around when you take her. Tomorrow, when I go to the market. She'll be home alone and ripe for the picking."

The guard nodded. "If that is your wish."

"Good. Just don't forget my reward," Philomena said. Iona heard them leaving and she was alone in the cold night air.

"Not a blissful family," said Phobos. "Imagine, your own sister selling you to your enemy."

"What is it to you? Aren't you here to drag me off again," asked Iona.

"I am, but I won't. You have until tomorrow night to leave." Phobos smiled, but it was not a friendly one. It reminded Iona of a predator. "You know what you have to do."

Iona did know. She had to stop her sister. Sitting there with Phobos by her side, she thought over everything she knew about her sister. True, Philomena had several faults, but she always assumed that she was loyal to her family. The only major flaw that Iona knew her sister possessed was that of envy. Philomena wanted what others had, envious of anyone's fortune, no matter how small. When Iona was ten, she had received a lovely amethyst necklace that Philomena coveted. It mysteriously broke, but now Iona was sure her sister was responsible.

"Yes," breathed Phobos in her ear, "you're figuring it all out. You know what you have to do."

If Philomena coveted what Iona had, then it should be easy to get her sister to confess to causing her betrayal. Once she heard the confession, she could leave. It would be so easy to leave before Aphrodite's men arrived tomorrow night to take her away.

Next to her, Phobos stood up. "I'll leave you for now. If you're still here when I return tomorrow morning, then you are not the woman I thought you to be. Go, Iona, and make your sister pay for what she's done to you."

Iona got up and walked in the house. She looked back once and wasn't surprised to see that Phobos had vanished. The plan was set and she would soon have her sister's confession. It hurt her to know that the person she looked up all her life would betray her like that.

When she saw Philomena, she made herself tear up and look as miserable as she could. It wasn't hard since the betrayal stung.

"Iona? What's wrong," Philomena asked when she noticed the pathetic figure of her sister standing next to her.

"Philomena, there is something I must tell you. I didn't want to burden you before, but I can't keep it a secret much longer. I know you'll find out eventually."

"What is it? Is it about your husband? Are you finally going to tell me who he is?"

Iona nodded. "That last time you and Errita visited, I was ready to do as you suggested. I had the knife ready and waited until he fell asleep. I had to do it to keep my baby safe," Iona said, sniffling for effect. "And then, I saw him."

"What did you see?"

"Not a monster," Iona said, wiping away a tear. "At first, I thought it was Amor. I was shocked and we started to fight. That was when I found out I was married to a god. I betrayed a god!"

Philomena's eyes lit up. "Who was it?"

"Eros, son of Aphrodite. That's why Aphrodite is looking for me. In our fight, I burned his shoulder. He and Amor are the same person, and I never knew."

Iona looked up at her sister, almost expecting her to mention seeing Amor, but Philomena remained silent. No gasp, no confession. Slightly angry that her gamble wasn't paying off, Iona tried again.

"That wasn't the worst of it," she said. "It was what he told me before he left me."

"What did he say?"

"He said I wasn't his first choice. He only settled on me because his first choice was married."

Philomena leaned closer. "Who was his first choice?"

"You! He said he had been in love with you for a long time and only pursued me because you were happily married." Iona thought Philomena would see through that lie in an instant. Not only was a mortal marriage no obstacle for a god, but Eros had done everything to make sure Iona was his bride. The logic of the situation did not seem to sink in with Philomena as Iona watched her eyes light up with delight.

"Really?" The happiness that crossed her face was out of place with the news. "The son of Aphrodite wanted me?"

Hurriedly, Iona added, "Just before he left me, he said he would wait for you to accept him as a bridegroom. I didn't want to tell you, Philomena, because it hurt me so much. I was going to not tell you, but the guilt of knowing my husband didn't love me was eating me up." The lie was so obvious that Iona was sure her sister had detected it. Iona was never a good liar and she waited for Philomena to declare that she knew it was all deceit.

Instead, Philomena said cautiously, "How would I let him know if I accept him as a bridegroom?"

"What about Zotikos? You're married," Iona said. She couldn't keep the disgust from her voice.

"I know that," Philomena said. "I just want to know. You know, just in case Eros is still interested after Zotikos dies. I'm sure it'll be any day now." There was no mourning in her voice. The coldness of it froze Iona's heart.

Angered, Iona said, "You have to go to the airlock in Tiryns, the same one they brought me to on my wedding day. The eastern airlock, number 135. Sit on the altar and announce why you are there. The light of the gods will lift you up and take you to Olympus."

There was no mistaking the look of greed on Philomena's face. Iona was sure that her sister would sneak out that night to be with Eros. All she had to do was follow in the morning and confront Philomena after she's been humiliated on the altar. No one would be waiting for her, and that should be enough to prove that her sister had wanted her to betray Eros.

Iona went to her room and waited until it was nearly morning to start packing. She put back on her disguise and started to head out. A wailing from the back of the house caught her attention. Thinking something had happened to Zotikos, she ran to the back rooms. She found a gathering of servants in Zotikos' room, all crying.

Her brother-in-law lay on the bed, a large dagger sticking up from his chest. Whoever stabbed him had practiced first, as his face and body was torn open from wounds. The coppery smell of blood filled the room as the room was painted red with it. The sight made Iona sick and she pushed past the servants to empty the meager contents of her stomach in a corner of the hall.

"What happened," Iona cried. "Who could have done such a thing?"

"It's awful," one of the maids said. "It was Lady Philomena! I came in to give Lord Zotikos his bath and I found her on top of him. She was covered with his blood. When I screamed, she ran off."

"We've summoned the authorities," another maid said. "They should be here soon. I just can't imagine Lady Philomena doing such a thing."

Iona panicked. If the authorities were on their way, she'd be discovered. She ran from the house and escaped. She didn't stop running until she was nearly to the lifts. She needed to find Philomena and soon.

"Well, that didn't go well."

Iona turned to see Phobos standing behind her. His bright eyes flashed with a mixture of amusement and regret.

"Did you know that she was going to kill her husband," Iona asked.

Phobos shrugged. "No. And neither did you, so stop worrying. She was really vicious, though."

"How do you know?"

"I watched the whole thing. I was curious as to what your plan was. Frankly, I liked the idea of you sending your sister to the airlock. Very wicked of you. I heard her last conversation with her husband. I guess when you said that Eros only pursued you because she was married, she decided to take out her only obstacle. She told him as much, Iona."

"It was my fault. If I never told her those lies -"

"She still would have killed him," Phobos said. "Trust me, Iona, you did nothing wrong. In fact, I'm impressed with you. I thought you were going to be like the others and just accuse her. Instead, you came up with a brilliant plan to humiliate her. Just because it backfired isn't your fault."

Iona sighed. She looked at him, something finally sinking in her mind. "If my Amor was the real Eros, that makes you the real Phobos, right?"

He smiled. "Right. Now, let's get you to Corinth. That's where your other sister lives."

"But, what about Philomena. She's on her way to Tiryns."

"You'll need someone else on your side, Iona. I can't go with you into Tiryns."

She allowed Phobos to guide her to the lifts. With any luck, they could make it to Errita's before Philomena left the airlock.

PART TWO

Goddess of the Mind

Chapter 24

Zotikos died on the first day of Fall. All over the station, the temperature dropped to simulate the coming winter and the night cycle would last longer. The engineers argued over which levels would receive snow first, and in what order, to mix it up from the year before.

In Olympus, Demeter viewed the day with the solemnity of a funeral. She wore gray to symbolize the bleak nature of the coming winter and her own mourning for her beloved Persephone. With the somber air of death, she escorted her daughter to the PortMat, not fully ready to send her back down to Hades. In attendance this time were two of her other children; Despoina and Arion. Arion, being a horse, was grandly attired with a rich leather and gold saddle where Persephone perched. If he minded carrying his sister, he made no show of it.

"You don't have to do this," Demeter said. "You can always stay here and get a divorce. I'm sure Zeus will gladly pay back any bride price he got from that monster you call husband. No one expects you to stay with him, you know."

"I love him, Mother," Persephone said in a tired voice. It was an old argument, and predictable. Every year, Demeter pleaded with her to change her mind, unable to understand that her marriage was not the punishment many made it out to be. "I will always love him."

"Not if I have any say over that," muttered Demeter.

"What was that, Mother?"

"I said, what if he doesn't love you? I heard that Minthe slut was sniffing around the Underworld again. They used to be lovers, you know, and you are gone six months of the year. Men have needs that they just can't control."

"I know all about Hades and his needs, Mother," Persephone said. She didn't bother to tell Demeter that she and her husband communicated during the spring and summer months. Hades never entered Olympus unless invited by Zeus, and those times were rare, so the married couple kept the flame of love alive through steamy letters and late night calls. Persephone knew that her husband was a healthy and virile man, and he was waiting eagerly for her return. Distance only made their love stronger.

"Well, what are you going to do about it," Demeter demanded, breaking into Persephone's lusty daydream.

"Do about what?"

"Mother asked what you were going to do about Minthe. Or Hecate, who has taken residence in the Underworld. Or any of those half-naked nymphs who think bathing in the rivers of the Underworld makes them dangerous or unique. They'd love to sleep with Hades. It would be something they can brag about," Despoina said. She gave Demeter an angelic smile. "See, Mother. I pay attention to what you say."

Persephone sighed. Because of how much Demeter dotted on Persephone, it made the other children feel abandoned. Despoina made it no secret she hated her sister because, as the only other daughter, she saw what was being denied her. Persephone had a husband and a title, not to mention being included in all of Demeter's feast days and having a section of her temples dedicated to her. Despoina was fairly forgotten.

"Hades is loyal to me," Persephone said. "It won't matter what nymph or minor goddess throws herself at him, he loves only me. He'd deny even Aphrodite for me."

"I'm just saying that men have uncontrollable urges that don't just go dormant for six months. Everyone knows that, Kore. You should know that, too. After all, you can't name a single god who can remain faithful to any woman. They all have been with a woman other than their wives the second their wife turns her back. Actually, the second any of their little flavor of the month isn't looking, every single god has jumped in bed with another person. It's just a fact, Kore."

"Don't call me Kore. And what about Eros? Despite Despoina throwing herself at him, he hasn't once shown any interest in her. He still wants only that mortal girl, even after she burned his shoulder."

Demeter rolled her eyes. "Oh, please. He's not faithful. Not only has he been cuddling with Despoina, despite what you think Kore, he's still married to Psyche. His time with that tramp is nothing more than cheating. He is in no way faithful."

Persephone looked back at her sister and then down at her brother. There would be no help with them. "What about Arion," she asked. Her brother snorted, annoyed at being dragged in the fight.

"He's been with the same mare for years now. I heard they had a foal just a few days ago."

Arion's ear twitched back and Persephone scratched him on the head. Demeter seemed less than amused. "He doesn't count," she said. "He's more beast than god. Damn Poseidon and his affinity for horses. Medusa gets to give birth to a winged horse that is gifted to heroes and what do I get? A plain, ordinary horse."

Arion's ears flattened and he started grinding down on his bit. Persephone gave him a friendly pet. It was obvious Demeter did not spend any time with him after his birth for she did not realize her son did possess the ability to speak. Persephone knew, having spent most of her childhood around him. She was close to most of her brothers, visiting with Plutus, the god of fortune who lived with her in the Underworld.

"What about the Cupids?" Persephone held up a hand, quickly cutting off her mom. "I know we ruled out Eros, but what about his brothers? Anteros has been faithful to his lover and I heard that Himeros had a live-in girlfriend for years."

"For starters, Himeros and his little-in girlfriend were never married and she was mortal. They die out so quickly, it's not worth it to even think of being faithful to them. Secondly, Anteros is only interested in guys, so he doesn't count."

Persephone sighed. "Then what about the mortals? Several of them remain faithful to their wives all their lives."

"We're talking about gods, Kore. Not short-lived insects. Just admit defeat and remember that your husband is a god and most likely has a few mistresses on the side for when you're not around. Or, maybe, when you are around? How can any man be faithful to a single woman anyway?"

"My name is Persephone. Not Kore! I wish you'd stop calling me that!"

"I named you Kore, so that's what I'll call you: Kore." Demeter said. "I hate it that you took that horrid name after you were kidnapped. I will never soil my lips by speaking it."

Persephone shook her head. As far as the faithfulness of the gods went, Demeter was mostly right. The gods and goddesses were not known for the fidelity. It seemed that having more than one lover at a time was a rite of passage and a badge of honor.

"Hades is still loyal to me," Persephone insisted. "Of all the gods in Olympus, I know that Hades will always be faithful to me."

"If you say so," said Demeter in a sing-son voice. She felt she had made her point.

Waiting at the PortMat was Hermes. As per tradition, the god of messengers and travel would escort Persephone down to the Underworld. He alone of all the gods of Olympus knew the truth about the relationship between the King and Queen of the Underworld.

"Ready to go, cousin," asked Hermes as he helped Persephone down from Arion.

"Yes. If we don't hurry, I'm going to be late," Persephone said.

Demeter gave a shrill cry and launched herself at Persephone. Grabbing her daughter, she pulled the girl to her bosom and cried, "Oh! My little baby! I'll just wither away without you!"

"Can't breathe," Persephone gasped, trying to wiggle away from her mother.

"The bleak days of winter will be endless as I worry about my darling daughter in the clutches of that monster. Oh, how I shall sit in the wilting gardens of Olympus waiting for the day my sweet Kore returns to me from the dark hell of the Underworld. You have no idea how this mother's heart breaks every time I must send my baby to the danger that is Hades."

"Really can't breathe!" Persephone pushed against the ample bosom of the Goddess of Wheat and Harvest.

"I only wish to keep my treasured daughter safe from all harm!"

"Demeter, you might want to let her go," said Hermes. "She's turning blue."

Demeter loosened her grip and Persephone gave a gasp of air, moving away from her mother. Hermes pulled her away and patted her on the back.

When she felt better, Persephone turned to her siblings. "It was nice seeing you both again," she said. "Why don't the two of you come down to the Underworld to visit sometime? I'd love to show you around my home and I just know that Plutus would love to see the two of you again. He gets a little lonely down there, especially when I'm gone."

"He's blind," Despoina sneered. "I doubt he even knows

when you're around."

"He likes having visitors. He always asks about all of you,"
Persephone said. "We're family, but we never seem to really talk or
visit with each other."

"I'm going to be too busy," said Despoina. "Unlike you, by
this time next year I plan to be the wife of an accepted god of
Olympus."

Persephone snorted. "If you mean Eros, he's exclusively in
love with his mortal woman. He'll never marry you. I suggest you set
your sights on someone who is available. Or, if all else fails, I hear
that Apollo is looking for another flavor of the week."

"Even being a lover is better than being the slave of Hades,"
Despoina shot back.

"Okay! I hate sappy good-byes," Hermes said, stepping
between the two sisters. "If you two keep up this lovey-dovey 'I'm
going to miss you more' sisterly affection good-byes, I'm going to be
sick." With that, he pulled Persephone on to the PortMat and quickly
activated it. "I swear, I can recite Demeter's good-bye speech by
heart now. How do you put up with it every year?"

Just before the light took her, Persephone heard Demeter say,
"Don't worry Despoina. I have it on Aphrodite's word that Eros will
be yours."

Chapter 25

Down in the populated levels, the air became cooler and the leaves on the mechanical trees turned from green to the vibrant hues of red, golden yellow and orange in a matter of a few hours. The seasons changed on schedule and the cold was not a surprise. On the levels dedicated to Demeter, the inhabitants went into mourning for poor Persephone, who exited Olympus for Hades.

On Level 30, Iona made it to Errita's just as the first chill could be felt. She hoped to find Philomena, that her eldest sister had decided to visit to brag about her good fortune. As yet, the news of Zotikos' death had not reached beyond Thebes. Iona wished to tell Philomena the truth and convince her sister to turn herself in to the authorities. If all else failed, she should be able to find her sister at the airlock.

Iona quickly made her way through the town, keeping the veil low on her head. Around her, the signs of Fall could be seen. Large holographic billboards flashed messages of new thermal blankets and coats to wear when winter arrived. On the sides of shops, view screens showed the news of the changing seasons on different levels. On Level 19, Eleusis, the level most dedicated to Demeter, there was a mock funeral for Persephone. With sweeping camera angles and dramatic reporting, the news of the mock funeral held the top slot. As Iona slipped down the alleyway that lead closest to Errita's house, she saw an important message that Aphrodite was still seeking her as "a person of interest". The photo they used in the broadcast was not flattering.

She knocked on the door and was surprised when Theron answered. Just like Zotikos, Theron had changed so much since her last visit. The accident that Errita told her about must have been worse than she let on. Theron looked haggard and was unshaven, his hair unwashed and his clothes smelled of weeks of not bathing. There were dark circles under his eyes and he leaned heavily on his crutches. Iona believed her sister was caring for Theron, but there was no way Errita would permit her husband to be seen by public like that. Had something happened to Errita?

"Iona! What are you doing here," Theron asked, surprised.

"Did anyone see you coming here?"

"No, I came in disguise. My escort – a friend I'd trust with my life – brought me to the Lifts and got me past the guards," Iona said. "I need to see Errita. It's important."

Theron motioned for her to enter the home. "Are you crazy? Everyone is looking for you. They have your parents under surveillance, in case you head there. What if they have my home under watch? We can be in danger!"

"I'm sorry, but this is really a life or death situation," Iona said. "I have to know if Philomena came through here earlier today. I need to find her."

"Why would you come to Corinth for Philomena? She lives in Thebes."

Iona looked down. "I was there. Philomena left early this morning and I have to find her. Zotikos is dead and ..." She couldn't go on. She couldn't tell her brother-in-law that Philomena killed her husband in cold blood.

Theron's pain flashed across his face. "Oh, Iona, I'm so sorry. Philomena might have come here, but I have not seen her. Errita is in her workshop. You can go ask her if your sister has arrived. I can contact your parents with Zotikos' death, if you wish."

"Thank you Theron."

Iona started to leave, but Theron stopped her. "If you're going to stay for a while, it will be nice to have some company. Errita rarely sees me and no one stops by anymore." He sighed, looking down. "I think she's ashamed of me."

"I'm sure she is not ashamed of you," Iona said. However, if Theron didn't bathe and walked around like that, it was no wonder that Errita was avoiding him. Theron must have seen how Iona was looking at him and realized how he appeared.

"Maybe it's partly my fault," he said. "When Errita first locked herself in her workroom, I stopped caring for how I looked. It was after her last visit with you, and I was just drowning in my own self-pity to notice how she was doing. Go and talk to her while I make myself presentable."

"You could use a bath," Iona admitted.

Theron nodded. "I am embarrassed that you saw me like this."

Iona left for the workroom. It was evident that Errita was

living in there from the small bed in one corner, clothes bunched up at the foot of the bed and dirty dishes still piled by the loom. Errita looked as bad as Theron. Her dark brown hair was greasy and hung down her back in limp strands, her clothes were stained and wrinkled, not at all like the freshly pressed dresses and richly attached gems Iona was used to seeing her sister wear. Errita worked the loom like an automaton, not looking up or noticing that another living creature was in the room.

Iona waited until Errita finished with the section she was working on before saying, "Errita, I just wanted to let you know that I'm visiting."

Errita turned, shocked to see her. "What are you doing here? Don't you know that the priests of Aphrodite are looking for you?"

"I know, but this is important. I won't put you at risk, I promise."

Errita laughed. "Right. You have already put me at risk by being here."

"This is life or death."

"Whose life or death? Mine or yours?"

"Both. I need to know if you've seen Philomena today. She left her home a few hours ahead of me, and I have to find her."

"No, I haven't seen her. Not since our last visit with you. How did that go, by the way? Did you slay the beast?" Errita gave Iona a once-over. "Did you lose weight?"

"Not now," Iona said. "Zotikos is dead, he died this morning. Philomena ... I have to find her. I might have told her something last night, and she might have taken it the wrong way."

Errita turned back to her loom, working on what would be a dress. The clothe was rainbow-colored, blending down together in perfect harmony. Beside the loom was a dressmaker's dummy and a pattern. Clinking another line, Errita said, "What did you say to her?"

"I told her a little bit about my last night with my husband and how I followed your advice. It was horrible, Errita. I lost everything." Iona sat by the dressmaker's dummy. "I went to Philomena in hopes of being with family during my time of need, but I overheard her plotting to sell me out to Aphrodite. In anger, I told her a lie that caused her to kill Zotikos and run away."

Errita scoffed. "What kind of lie could you tell that would

cause Philomena to kill her husband? I swear, Iona, you have gotten such airs since you married your mysterious monster.”

"I'm not putting on airs," Iona protested. “I just can't ignore the fact that Zotikos was murdered after I told Philomena that Eros wanted her as a wife.”

The clinking of the loom stopped. “What did you say?”

Iona burst into tears, huddled over on the stool. “I trusted Philomena and she betrayed me. I thought this would be the perfect revenge, but it went horribly wrong.”

“No, no, no. Go back to what you told Philomena.”

“I was telling her about the fight between my husband and myself after he caught me in my betrayal – the one you and Philomena convinced me to do. I had the dagger ready to destroy the winged serpent, only to find that I was bedding Eros. He left me and I lost the baby!”

“You were married to Eros! Why didn't you tell us this?”

“I didn't know! I never broke the rules. I never peeked. And now he's gone!” Iona lifted the hem of her dress to her eyes. “I just wanted to make Philomena feel bad for my loss, to go to the airlock where Eros took me and be made a fool. I never meant for her to kill Zotikos.”

“And what did you say to her that drove her to leave Zotikos?”

“She killed him!”

Errita sighed. “Fine, be dramatic. What drove Philomena to kill Zotikos?”

“It was the lie. I told her that Eros wanted her for his wife and not me.”

“And that was the lie?”

“Yes! He never said that. Not really.”

Errita laughed. “I can see how that got Philomena to run. I bet she thinks she'll be all high and mighty with her divine husband!”

“I didn't expect it to get this far,” Iona moaned. “We have to go get her from the airlock. We have to convince her to turn herself in.”

“The airlock?”

“Yes. The very airlock in Tiryns where I was left to be the bride for Eros. I told her that he would take her up in the light of the gods if she went there."

"And what will happen to Philomena once she gets there?"

Iona shrugged. "Nothing. Since Eros isn't expecting her, nor do I believe he is even home, nothing will happen."

"Then why are you so worried?"

"Because Zotikos is dead! How can I not be worried? I'm a wanted fugitive and my sister just killed her husband!"

For a few seconds, the only sounds were Iona's sobs and the loom clinking. "He's been incredibly sick, you know," said Errita. "It was bound to happen. Besides, Philomena left him. I doubt she cares."

"What about you? Don't you care," Iona asked. She couldn't believe how cold her sister was being. Had Errita always been this self-centered? "And Zotikos did not die from sickness or old age, he was stabbed!"

Errita shrugged. "Maybe she just got tired of caring for him. I know I'm tired of having to deal with Theron and his constant whining about his leg and how he's no longer the favored son of Apollo and how no one loves him. Blah, blah, blah. Have you seen or smelled him lately? Disgusting."

"I can't believe you two," Iona said. The reality of how cruel her sisters could be shocked Iona out of her misery. "Philomena and you, two peas in a pod. As long as your husbands furthered your own ambitions, you love them. Once they aren't what you wanted, you toss them aside like garbage. Theron has been nothing if not loyal to you, and you talk of him as if he were a lamed horse you plan to put down. Would you kill your own husband, too?"

"And what of you," Errita sneered. "No mortal man was good enough for you. Oh, no, not for the Aphrodite-in-the-flesh! You needed a divine husband. All those suitors you scoffed at and chased away, just so you could be better than all of us. And you –" Errita laughed. "You couldn't even hold on to him!"

"He didn't just dump me! I lost him because of my own stupidity and willingness to follow your advice."

"You still lost him," Errita said. "It sounds to me like he grew tired of you."

"He doesn't want Philomena either! He may not want me, but I know he personally hates Philomena. That was what he told me."

Errita was silent for a moment. Then a smile crossed her

face, the satisfied smile of a woman who just got what she wanted. "Iona, I'm so sorry," she said. "You've been through a lot. Visit as long as you like and do not fear. I won't betray you to Aphrodite. In fact, why don't I call mom and ask her if she's seen Philomena. You look tired. Go to the main house and rest."

"Thank you." Iona left for the main house, but she had the nagging suspicion that she should not leave Errita alone, that she would be betrayed by both her sisters.

Theron washed up and looked more like the handsome brother-in-law she remembered. He smiled when she entered the home.

"How are things with Errita?"

"Not so good," said Iona. "It's like having my eyes opened for the first time. I'm noticing things about my sisters that I had been blind to for so long."

"When you love someone, you are often blind to their faults," Theron said. "I've been made aware of Errita's true self while I was healing. I still love her, and all I want is for life to go back the way it was. I will just always remember now that she has a cruel streak."

"I hope your marriage is a happy one," Iona said. "At least one of us should be happy."

Theron cooked a small lunch while they waited for Errita. Time slowly ticked by and she did not show. Worried, Iona went back to the workshop and found it empty. There was a note on her loom and Iona read it with a dawning horror.

"Theron! She's gone to the airlock on Tiryns," Iona cried, running back to the house. "When I told her that I lied to Philomena, she assumed the wrong thing was the truth."

"What did she assume?"

"That when I said my husband tossed me out and wanted to marry Philomena, that was the lie. I told her that. For some reason known only to the gods, she figured that I was secretly saying my husband wanted her as a wife instead. I never said that! I swear, Theron, I never said anything about him wanting one of my sisters for his wife was true. I told her that was a lie."

"Why is she going to the airlock?"

"I told Philomena that she had to go there to prove that she wanted to be the wife of Eros. It was a lie, a prank. I was just so angry when I learned that Philomena meant to betray me to

Aphrodite's guards that I thought a little pay back was necessary." Iona buried her head in her hands. "I can't believe it's gotten so out of hand. All I wanted was to embarrass Philomena."

Theron sighed. "It'll take me some time to get the right paperwork to travel to Tiryns. I know that Errita has a pass so she can visit your mother whenever she wants."

"I have a pass," Iona said. "I'll go find her. She couldn't have gotten far."

"I'll join you once I get my paperwork in order," Theron said. "Though I don't understand the whole problem. She just goes to an airlock. There are safety precautions so she won't be swept into space."

"I don't know. I just feel like I need to find them. Philomena killed Zotikos, and Errita is running away from you. I have to make this right. I have to talk to them."

"Very well. Get going and I will meet you in Tiryns as soon as I can. How about your parents' house? I'm sure they'll be excited to see you again."

"I just hope all of this ends well, Theron. I have a bad feeling about all of this."

Theron grasped Iona by her arms. "It will be all right. I don't know what madness would have possessed Philomena to kill Zotikos, but Errita has a good head on her shoulders. She will see the error of her ways and the two of you will laugh about this is years to come. I am sure you two will be waiting for me at your parents' home, and we will put this all behind us."

Chapter 26

Iona wrapped the veil around her head before leaving Theron. She could feel the dread growing inside her, fear for her sister gnawing at her stomach. After making sure her disguise was in place, she ran from the house and headed to the Lifts. She did not see Errita on the way and managed to squeeze in the Lifts with a traveling merchant. Once she reached Tiryns, she headed straight to Airlock 135. To her surprise, a crowd was forming by the airlock door and a maintenance man was trying to cut the door open.

"What's going on," Iona asked, pushing her way to the front.

"Some stupid woman has locked herself inside," one of the men said. "We need to get the door opened."

Peering in the airlock, Iona could see Errita sitting on the altar. She must have just gotten there, but where was Philomena?

Iona pounded on the door to get her sister's attention. "Errita! Get out of there!"

Her sister looked back at her and shook her head. "Never! For once, the world will remember me! I'm stepping out of your shadow and I will outshine even Philomena. This is my time!" Her voice was muffled by the heavy door, but Iona heard her clearly, each word like a dagger to her heart.

"What are you talking about? Come out so we can talk. I already told you that nothing is going to happen, so you're wasting your time!" Iona stood on tiptoe to see her sister more clearly, her veil falling back. "And, Errita, you already shine! You're a famous seamstress. You have a talent I could only dream of possessing. And a great husband who loves you very much. Don't throw it all away for this foolishness."

The maintenance man cleared his throat. "Ma'am, there is something false about what you just said. If we don't open this door, and soon, the airlock mechanism will activate and she'll be swept into space. It's automatic."

"What do you mean?"

"Once the door is closed, we only have a certain amount of time before the outer doors open and any trash placed in here is swept out," the man explained. "That's why we need to open the door. That will signal to not activate the mechanism. If we can't ... well ..." He made a whistling noise and motioned with his hand that Errita will fly away.

"Then open the door!"

"We're trying, ma'am. For some reason, Hephaestus only knows why, the door keeps sticking. We've only got –" He looked at his wrist watch and grunted. "– maybe five minutes."

Panic gripped Iona's heart and she pounded on the door harder. "Errita! Errita! You have to get out of there! You're in danger! Open up!"

Errita walked over to the door, but didn't open it. Instead, she smiled cruelly through the little window. "You just don't want me to be the wife of a god, Iona." She sneered. "All my life, it's been 'Philomena this' and 'Iona that'. No one noticed me. Well, not any more. Now I shall be Errita, wife of Eros!"

"You don't understand! You have to get out of there. Please, Errita, please listen to me."

Errita spat on the floor and walked back to the altar. She sat down and crossed her arms defiantly. At the door, the maintenance men worked on the lock, but none of their tools made a scratch. It was clear panic was setting in as one of the men fumbled a torch and nearly burned his foot off, his eyes darting to the doors at the far end of the airlock.

Over the roar of the torch and the noise of the tools came an ominous creak. Metal screeched against metal. It was a sound Iona knew well, having heard it in her nightmares.

"Get the door open! The airlock is opening!"

With a defeated sigh, the maintenance man stepped back, motioning for his crew to do the same. "I'm sorry, ma'am, but once that mechanism starts, we are to step way. To open this door now will place all of us in danger. If we were to actually succeed now, half this level will be swept into space. I'm sorry, ma'am."

"What is that noise," asked Errita as the screeching got louder.

"The airlock," said Iona. "Oh, Zeus have mercy! Errita, the airlock is opening!"

Fear crossed Errita's face. "What about Eros! Why isn't he here to save me! I came because he wanted me! You said he wanted me!"

"I said no such thing! I told you I lied about him wanting Philomena!" Iona grabbed the handle and pulled on it with all her might. The door was locked tight, and she doubted even Hercules could budge it.

Errita ran to the door, pulling on the handle from her end. "Let me out," she screamed. "Let me out!"

The noise stopped and Iona knew what was coming next. Grabbing a screwdriver from one of the men, she stabbed at the window as hard as she could. Over and over again, she brought the pointed end of the screwdriver down. It never made a dent. Not even a scratch.

"Ma'am, please! There is nothing that can be done! There are safety protocols in place to keep the airlock from sweeping all of us into space."

"What about my sister! Why can't you stop it! She'll die!" Iona grabbed on to the door once more. "Please, don't let my sister die! I'm sorry for everything! Please! Don't let her die!"

Iona watched in horror as the airlock doors opened and the air was sucked from the room. Errita's eyes widened and she tried to hold on to the handle, her whole body lifting off the floor. Iona screamed her sister's name as Errita was ripped away from the door and swept into the unforgiving vacuum of space. With a sob, Iona dropped to her knees, her forehead against the metal door. She could hear the airlock doors closing and the entry door finally unlocking.

"That's the second one today," the maintenance man said, picking up his tools. "Don't know what's wrong with girls today. Death by space isn't pleasant. Odd, though. Both women claimed to be the bride of Eros. I guess he wasn't fond of either one."

Looking up, Iona asked though her tears, "The second? Who was the first?" *Oh, please,* she prayed, *please may it not be Philomena. Please may she have decided to go home and see our parents and is still alive. Please, may I have not caused the deaths of both my sisters.*

"Some singer from Thebes. Her husband was found murdered early this morning. It's been all over the news."

Iona felt sick. She got up to leave, putting her veil back on when someone grabbed her arm. At first, she thought it was one of the curious hanger-ons who had just witnessed Errita's death. Someone who might offer a condolence. Instead, the person pulled off Iona's veil.

"I know you," she said, pointing her finger at Iona. "You're that girl that Aphrodite is looking for! There's a reward for you!"

"Can't be her," said the man next to her. "The girl in the newscast has long hair. Hers is short."

"It's her! I know it!" The woman hit the man on the arm. "And she could have cut her hair! It's hair, you idiot! It's not like she has a different face or something."

Cursing under her breath, Iona pushed the woman out of the way and ran. She could hear people behind her, but didn't bother looking back. She ran blindly, not sure where to go. She couldn't go home; Aphrodite had her home under surveillance. Unsure of where she was heading, she nearly screamed as a hand shot out of a wall and clamped around her mouth, pulling her behind the wall. She fought and, as she got away, realized she was behind the walls of Space Station *Olympus*.

"What happened," Iona asked, turning to face her 'savior'. It was the golden-clad Neoma, devoted employee of Hephaestus. While Iona was pleased to see a familiar face, the lovely dark-skinned woman was not happy to see Iona.

"Against his better judgment, Lord Hephaestus wishes to see you," Neoma said sourly. "Follow me."

Iona was led to a long hallway filled with windows out to space. It was much like the hallway on Corinth that Eros had first shown her space. Standing at the windows was Hephaestus, and Iona gave a strangled cry as she saw what he was looking at. There, out in space, floating with a sad grace were her sisters. Their bodies bumped into each other and then drifted apart, lazily drifting on a dark sea of nothingness.

"Oh, sweet Persephone watch over them," Iona whispered. "What have I done?"

Hephaestus looked down at Iona. "This looks really bad," he said. "I mean, like Tartarus bad."

"I never thought this would happen," Iona sobbed. "I just thought they would sit on the altar and be embarrassed as nothing happened. That was all! I swear, I never knew they would die. I just wanted to make Philomena pay for trying to betray me to Aphrodite, and for their deliberate advice that drove Eros away from me."

She looked up at the God of the Forge. The dawning horror

that she was not only in the presence of Aphrodite's husband, but Eros' stepfather finally sinking in. She would surely be shipped up to Olympus for Aphrodite now.

Reading her look, he smiled. The look was grotesque on his face, but fatherly at the same time. "Do not worry about Aphrodite. She never comes down here. This is my domain. What is this about Eros and you, though?"

"We married. Kind of." She thought it over. "Okay, not really. I mean, there was never an official ceremony. The Oracle said I was to be given to a winged serpent, but it turned out to be Eros. He would not tell me it was he, and kept me in the dark as to his identity. My sisters convinced me to break his rules and try to discover his secret, but they had me believing he really was a serpent and would kill me and our baby."

Hephaestus' face lit up. "A baby? You had a baby?"

She shook her head. "Eros and I fought and he left through the ... um ... Port thing? I followed him but was somehow dumped on Pan's doorstep, and I lost the baby."

"You poor child. I take it Eros was wounded before he left you?"

"Yes. I accidentally burned his shoulder. I haven't seen him since." She wiped away her tears. "And now all of this. I just messed everything up. I can't keep a husband, I lost my baby, and I killed my sisters. I don't deserve to ever be with Eros. He deserves a proper wife who is not filled with wickedness."

"Ha! You're perfect for him. You did none of those things on purpose." Hephaestus stroked his beard. "What you need is to be purified."

"Can you do that?"

"No. The problem is, this is a matter of the heart. Normally, you would go to Aphrodite to ask for purification, but that would not be wise. Though, with what happened with your sisters, you might be able to ask Persephone's blessing, but she just got back with Hades and I've learned to not bother her during her first month of being reunited with her husband."

Iona sighed. "What am I to do?"

"Maybe you can ask Apollo. Go to the Oracle and find out how you can be purified. If anyone will know which god to visit, and one that will not sell you to Aphrodite on the spot, it would be him.

After you've been purified, we can figure out a way for you to see Eros again."

"You'd still give me blessings to see him after all of this? After all that I've done?"

He nodded. "Listen, he's been like a son to me. I saw how happy you made him, and his brothers have told me he wants only you. You love him, he loves you. I see no reason why you two should be apart. This will all work out for the best. Of that, you have my blessings."

"It will take me some time to gather the money and paperwork to see the Oracle," Iona said, finally feeling as if a weight had been lifted. "I should find my way to a level where no one knows me."

"Leave the paperwork to me. Neoma will guide you up to the Oracle through the maintenance tunnels, and once you are there, one of my sons will guide you to the Oracle. I'll just have Apollo put it on my tab."

"How can I ever repay you?"

"Be a good wife to Eros," Hephaestus said. "Though, if you ever have a son, I could always use another hand in my workshops."

Chapter 27

Zephyrus paced outside Eros' rooms. Despoina, that despicable witch, decreed that while Eros healed in Olympus, he should have no outside visitors. Except her, that is. She normally locked herself in there, fawning over the wounded god. On the rare occasion when Zephyrus could poke his head into the room, he witnessed her 'tender care'. He was sure that shoving soup in his mouth and prodding his burns was not the right way to help Eros heal.

"Have you seen him," asked Anteros as he walked up. His purple butterfly wings fluttered anxiously.

"Not yet," Zephyrus said with a sigh. "Her royal highness won't let anyone in. She's been in a foul mood ever since she returned from taking Persephone to the PortMat."

Anteros rolled his eyes. "Well, I'm his brother and I demand entrance." He pushed open the door with Zephyrus at his heels, curious to see how this battle turned out.

"What are you doing here," Despoina screeched. "Eros needs his rest. Get out!"

"As family, I have the right to see my brother," Anteros said.

"You've done enough damage for the night. Leave!"

"I'm helping him. He wants me to stay, don't you darling?" She batted her eyes at Eros, who merely gave his younger brother a pleading look.

"Again, I am his brother," Anteros said, pushing Despoina from the room. "I outrank you in this matter."

"Your mother will hear of this," Despoina cried as the door slammed shut in her face. Anteros figured he would have a few minutes to tell Eros his news before Despoina returned with Aphrodite in tow.

Eros sighed. "Oh, thank you Anteros. You have no idea how much I wanted to do just that."

"We're here because of Iona," Anteros said, sitting on the bed. "There are some things you need to know about."

Eros sat up. He winced and grabbed his burnt shoulder, rubbing it slightly to ease the pain. Though time passed, the burn mysteriously remained. "How is she? Does she miss me? Have you told her that I miss her?"

"She misses you," said Zephyrus, "but there are some things we need to tell you."

"As for how she is," Anteros said, "she could be better. I just got a call from Hephaestus. In a few minutes, I'm going to take her to the Oracle."

"She can't go see Apollo! She has no idea what he's like," Eros protested, trying to get out of the bed. "Anteros, keep her away from Apollo. That glittering Casonova has his eyes on my sweet Iona, and I refuse to allow her to just fall into his grubby hands."

"I'll do what I can, but she needs to be purified," Anteros said. "Poor girl feels responsible for four deaths."

"Four? Who died?"

Zephyrus gently pushed Eros back on the bed. "Her sisters died today. Not to mention her brother-in-law."

"How can she feel responsible for them? She's safe at home."

Anteros and Zephyrus looked at each other. After a moment, Anteros said, "She left the sanctuary of your home and, after visiting with Persephone and Pan, she went to confront her sisters. Something got mixed up and her sisters jumped out of an airlock."

"Why would they do that?"

Zephyrus cleared his throat. "She told Philomena that you wanted to marry her instead of Iona. When that backfired, she tried to stop her with Errita's help, but the message got garbled and Errita thought you wanted *her*. So she threw herself out of the airlock in Tiryns believing you were going to save her."

"What possessed Iona to tell either of those treacherous snakes that I'd want them?"

"She wanted to hurt Philomena's pride when her sister sat on the altar and you never showed up," said Anteros. "She didn't know about the airlock mechanism nor did she know Philomena would kill her husband."

"Oh, my poor Iona. She's such a delicate creature," moaned Eros. "She must be so devastated."

"The same thing happened with Errita," said Zephyrus.

Eros sighed. "So, that's all four deaths? Two sisters and two brothers-in-law?"

Zephyrus shook his head. "No. Her two sisters and one

brother-in-law makes only three deaths. I don't know how to tell you about the first."

"Who? Was it Psyche? Did that harpy pass on and blame Iona?"

"No, it was not Psyche, but it was a member of you household. Sort of."

"Well, who was it? Who does my wife feel responsible for? Is it me? Does she believe I am dead?" When no one answered him, Eros snapped, "By Zeus, tell me!"

Zephyrus whispered, "The baby, my lord. She had a miscarriage trying to follow you that night. She was in the PortMat when it was shut off."

"She was near death when Pan found her. I'm so sorry, Eros, but there was no way to save the baby," said Anteros.

Eros visibly wilted at the news. "It's my fault," he whispered. "I shut the machine off. I knew she was angry and followed me, but I never thought she'd follow me into the PortMat beam." His voice choked on his raw pain. "My baby! I killed my baby!"

Zephyrus pulled Eros to him as the God of Love cried. It broke all their hearts to hear the grief as he sobbed. In the back of Anteros' mind, he was slightly relieved to hear that his brother did not blame Iona for the baby's death. That would help her heal the next time they met, and her forgiveness would help heal Eros.

"When I see Iona, I'll tell her how you are doing," Anteros said softly. "After she's been purified, you two can be reunited. You'll be healed and home by then."

"I can't wait to see Iona again," said Eros. "How she must have suffered. She must hate me for what I've done."

"Not to sound stupid," Zephyrus said, "but didn't she also get hit by one of your love darts? Hate for you is not an emotion she should be capable of."

"She got hit, yes, but still managed to argue with me. That's never happened before," Eros said. He frowned and shook his head. "No, wait. My old host had a similar fight with Psyche. It's confusing. Anyone hit with a dart should be so in love that the object of their affection could ask for their life and they'd cheerfully comply. Yet, when I suggested she not see her sisters again, she fought me on that while the dart was fresh in her system. I don't know how that could be."

"We'll figure this out later," Anteros said. "For now, Iona is expecting me."

"Tell her I love her," Eros said. Anteros nodded and left. He passed a fuming Despoina and Aphrodite on his way out, rushing down the hall when they called out to him. He took the PortMat to Apollo's personal level. Half the level was dedicated to schools for doctors, athletes and musicians that only the richest inhabitants of Space Station *Olympus* were allowed to attend, and the other half held the Temple at Delphi, the home of the Oracle. It was the grandest structure on the level and the one that always had the largest crowds.

Anteros looked around for Iona. He finally found her on the fringes of the crowd, her veil pulled low to hide her face. What gave her away was the impassive Golden Girl, a female worker of Hephaestus, standing next to her.

"I can see why my brother is in love with you," Anteros said, tapping her on the shoulder. Iona turned, her veil slipping just enough for him to see the fear in her green eyes. He smiled warmly and gave her a little bow. "Anteros, you brother-in-law and servant."

Iona smiled slightly. "I recognize you. You helped serve my sisters during their first visit to my home. I'm sorry for not recognizing who you were back then."

"Think nothing of it. Hephaestus has asked me to present you to the Oracle." He nodded to Neoma. "Thank you for your work."

Neoma sniffed, touching her golden cap briefly. "Seeing as how she is hot water with gods, I suggest bringing her to the real power behind the Oracle."

"The real power," asked Iona as Neoma walked away.

Anteros nodded. "These Oracles are just for show. They sometimes get it right, when Apollo cares enough to give them the message. But, there is one that he always speaks through. That's whom you'll meet." He fixed her veil. "I'm only doing this so you can be reunited with my brother sooner. I do not trust these Oracles or Apollo. We'll have to be on our guard."

He took her hand and, after a quick scan of the crowd to ensure they were not attracting too much attention, he took away from the Temple. He brought her to the wooded area that split the Temple off from the schools. In the back of the woods, sitting next to a man-made waterfall and surrounded by animatronic deer and chipmunks, was an old shack.

"Apollo's real Oracle lives here," Anteros said. "Only gods are allowed to seek her out, no human is permitted here."

Iona took a step back. "I'm human," she said.

"You're allowed," Anteros said. "There are ... special circumstances. Someday, you'll understand."

He took her hand and led her inside the shack. There was almost no furniture, no kitchen or living areas. Only a large bed in the center of the room with wires coming from the ceiling down onto a figure laying there. Every wall was covered with monitors, showing scenes from various places of Space Station *Olympus*. Some of the images flickered so fast that Iona barely had time to register what she had seen, while others lingered. She gasped as one monitor settled on the image of her parents, crying over two pictures of Errita and Philomena while Theron tried to comfort them.

"Iona, meet the real Oracle," said Anteros. "This poor girl was handpicked by Apollo and lives her whole life in this room. She has never learned to walk or speak with her own voice. This is her life until she dies and Apollo finds himself another baby to raise."

"How sad," muttered Iona.

"Yes, how sad," came a voice from the bed. The wires moved and the figure sat up, her eyes still closed. The woman's head was shaved and the wires connected to her skull, arms and spine. When the woman opened her eyes, Iona felt a shiver race through her. The entity that stared out from that woman was not human.

"Apollo," growled Anteros. He stood in front of Iona, protecting her. "I had hoped it was just a story that you took over the Oracle's body. Whatever happened to merely relaying the message to the woman through wires?"

"Oh, I grew bored of that, little Anteros. Merely speaking through a human lost its charm. Taking over the body is so much more fun," Apollo said. The woman's body levitated off the floor, floating closer to them. "There is no need to tell me why you are here. I see all. I know all."

"Then, you'll help me," asked Iona hopefully.

The Oracle moved closer and Anteros backed up until Iona was pressed against a wall. When the Oracle reached out to touch them, Anteros batted the hand away.

"Oh, I'll help you, but you'll have to do something for me,"

Apollo said. Despite Anteros' attempts, the Oracle managed to get past him and trace a finger down Iona's face.

"Keep your hands off her," Anteros snarled. "She's still Eros' wife!"

"Not legally," said Apollo. "And not for long. As we speak, Aphrodite and Demeter are plotting on a way to have a divine wedding between Eros and Despoina. And poor Iona isn't invited. That is, unless you do as I say."

"Just purify her of her sins," said Anteros.

"Please, Lord Apollo, I must be with Eros. What must I do?"

"Iona," Anteros warned, "let me do the talking. You don't have the experience to bargain with a god. You don't understand what you're getting yourself into."

"I think she does," said Apollo. "Will you accept any price to be purified and reunited with the man you love?"

Iona swallowed and said slowly, "What is it you're asking of me?"

"Serve me for one month. If, for some reason, only Hades knows, you still wish to go back to that slavery you call marriage to that dull, uninspired creature you wish to call husband, I will set you free and declare you purified. However, if you wish to remain since you have come to realize that I am a much more important and viral god, I will train you to be one of my Deliades and allow you to sing my praise and sleep at my feet."

"I can't sing," said Iona. "I garden."

"Fine. You can plant a garden in my honor. Whatever."

"You can't make her your slave," Anteros said. "She's here for purification."

"I can do whatever I want. Hercules had to do seven labors to be purified, I'm only asking for one month."

"I'll do it," said Iona. "I'll work for you for one month, but I want your word that you'll let me go when my month is up, you'll declare me purified, and you will do everything in your control to keep Despoina from marrying Eros in the meantime."

"Yeah, sure, you've got my word."

Anteros laughed. "Oh, no, it won't be that easy. Swear on the River Styx."

"I gave my word."

"Swear it, Apollo, or I take her from here and I'll have Zeus declare her purified."

Apollo laughed, the sound hollow coming from the Oracle's throat. "You don't have the influence over Zeus to get him to declare anything."

"Shows what you know," said Anteros.

Apollo growled. When Anteros turned and started to drag Iona away, he called out, "Fine! I swear on the River Styx that when her month is up, if she chooses to leave, she will be declared purified and have the freedom to walk away."

"And?"

"And I will do all in my power to stop Aphrodite and Demeter from pushing the proposed wedding of Despoina and Eros. Are you happy, Anteros?"

"Ecstatic."

Chapter 28

True to his word, Apollo managed to slow down the wicked plans of Aphrodite and Demeter. Without Depoina's tender mercies, Eros healed faster than most thought possible. He received a cream from Apollo to fix his burns and was soon ready to leave his room and rescue Iona. Anteros left him a note that Iona would be at the Oracle's for the rest of the month, and Eros wanted to be the first thing she saw when her freedom was granted to her. It had been three weeks, and her final day was close at hand.

"Zephyrus, fire up the PortMat," Eros said into his comlink. "I want to get out of here tonight." If Aphrodite tried to stop him, he would just tell her that he felt he'd heal better at home. His burn was nothing more than a pale pink scar and that would soon fade.

"I'll be waiting, boss." Eros felt no fear that his servant would fail. Zephyrus was totally loyal to him ever since he 'saved' Zephyrus from Apollo. Eros felt a pang of guilt over that thought. It was only a matter of time before someone – Apollo or Aphrodite, most likely – let it slip that Apollo only loved Hyacinths because of a love dart. Shot on a stupid dare by Hermes.

Eros poked his head out of his room. Seeing the coast was clear, he crept out of the room. Cautiously, he pressed himself against the wall as he made his way to the PortMat, keeping an eye out for anyone that might spot him. He was one hallway away from the PortMat chamber when he heard, "Leaving us so soon," from behind him. Looking behind him, he felt his blood turn cold as he saw Phobos, Deimos and Enyo standing there.

Phobos and Deimos, twin sons of Aphrodite and Ares, took as much after their father as Eros did their mother. Phobos, God of Fear, wore armor like Ares, his burly hand lovingly stroking on of the various weapons strapped to his side. Deimos, God of Dread, eyed Eros like a bug he was about to squish.

Between them stood Enyo. No one was sure who or what Enyo really was. Some worshiped her as a daughter of Ares, and others as his sister. One thing was certain: she possessed his blood lust and left destruction in her wake. She took great pleasure in causing pain.

"I'm going home," Eros said. "Now that I've healed, there is no reason for me to stay up here."

Enyo took a step closer, her fingers caressing her electric spear. "Going back to that weak little mortal, you mean."

"Eros, son of Aphrodite, most favored above all her children," mocked Deimos, his eyes bright with battle fever. "You're a laughing stock in Olympus. She spurned you, and you're going crawling back to her."

"She didn't spurn me."

"She burned you. Same thing."

"That was an accident!"

Deimos shrugged. "Doesn't matter. You are weak. Instead of taking care of this problem on your own, you came begging Mother for help. Now, just as pathetic, you're going to kneel at the feet of a mortal woman."

"You're a disgrace," sneered Enyo.

"I can't believe Mother would favor a coward like you," spat Phobos.

"How are things between you and what's-her-name? Odette? Odessa? The devotee of Demeter I shot for you," Eros asked, his eyes on Phobos. He knew that this brother had helped Iona on more than one occasion. If any of his siblings would show him mercy, maybe it would be Phobos.

Phobos looked away from the suddenly interested glares of Deimos and Enyo. "She had an annoying laugh so I left her. I think she hung herself." Eros could hear the lie. His brother was still seeing her, though that might come to an end now that his secret was out.

"Yes, well, it's been fun," Eros said. "I must go. We should get together sometime, but not now. I'm sure my home is in shambles without me. Bye!"

He turned and fled, feeling confident that none of his war-crazed siblings would dare shed blood in the hallowed halls of Olympus. Then again, he just outed Phobos and if there was anything the favored of Ares knew, it was exacting a painful and bloody revenge. His only real hope was to make it to the PortMat.

Behind him, he heard a deafening crack and a burning pain laced up his leg. He fell sprawling out on the marble floor, his left leg no longer working. He flipped onto his back, glaring at his brothers. Phobos smiled, waving a gun.

"You're not going anywhere," Enyo sneered. "That would just break Aphrodite's heart."

"And if Mother's heart breaks, it would break Father's heart," said Deimos. "We just can't have that, now can we?"

Eros ignored them, his pain and anger focused on Phobos. "You shot me! Have you completely lost your mind? You shed blood in Olympus!"

"It had to be done. You can't be allowed to leave."

"This will make Mother happy. And Despoina." Deimos stalked over to Eros, who tried to scuttle out of the way. The God of Dread stomped one booted foot down on his brother's chest, stopping him. "She's taken quite a fancy to you, little brother. Did you know that? Despoina's eyes just glow when she talks about how much you need her." With that, he kicked Eros in the ribs.

Eros groaned, curling up in a ball to nurse his cracked ribs. "What does Despoina have to do with anything?"

Enyo laughed. "Oh, didn't you know about Despoina and Deimos? He's been wooing her for two years now, but that uppity harlot never once looked his way. One glance from you baby blues and she's a pile of mush."

"Don't call her a harlot!" Deimos quickly pointed his gun at Enyo. "She's an innocent!"

"She's all yours," Eros groaned. "I'm sure you two will have perfectly psychotic babies together." He tried to get up, but another well-aimed kick from Deimos left him sprawled on the ground and broke a rib.

Deimos scoffed. "Don't be so flippant. You think you're so special, don't you? Just because you're the God of Love, you think you can just take any woman you please and use her? You're nobody! You don't even have a temple! You have to share with Mother!"

"And you have to share one with your father! You don't even have a home on Level 17. You have to share apartments with Ares along his hall in Olympus," Eros spat. Deimos kicked him in the side, and Eros screamed as he was sure something vital burst.

Eros held one hand to his broken ribs, breathing slowly. "You win, okay? I'll go back to my room and keep Mother happy. I won't touch Despoina. I won't even look in her direction, okay? You win, Deimos."

"Not good enough. I don't want *my* Despoina cooing over your wounds. I'm going to make sure you never seduce another woman for as long as you live!"

Eros looked up just as Deimos descended upon him. Feet and fists, knives and the butts of guns all assaulted him as Deimos used everything in his fury to teach Eros a lesson. Enyo joined in and nearly ripped one of Eros' wings out of his body. Eros was only vaguely aware of someone pleading for them to stop, and that, surprisingly, the voice wasn't his.

"That's enough!" Ares' voice boomed through the hall. Mercifully, the beating stopped and Eros opened his one good eye to see Phobos pulling Deimos back. Zephyrus tried to push Enyo back, but the angry goddess stabbed him in the leg. As Zephyrus knelt by Eros, Ares and Apollo came into view.

Ares gave a 'tsk' with his tongue, shaking his head as he studied the beaten god. "Oh, Eros, you don't look so good. I don't think you should be wandering around until you're all better."

"You sent them," Eros accused through clenched teeth. "You told them to do this to me."

"Now, Eros, if you were anything of a fighter, you could have protected yourself. All those years being coddled by your mother has made you soft."

"I hate you, Ares. When I'm well again, I'll make you pay."

Ares laughed. "Please, you can't frighten a flea. Save your pathetic threats for the weaker gods."

Eros moaned as Zephyrus helped him up into a sitting position. His torn wing hung limply at his side and the whole right of him was bathed in blood. "Why would you do this? I'm your son!"

"My son? Don't make me laugh. You only claim that when it's convenient to you. I know all about your simpering to Hephaestus about how you think of him as your real daddy. You're no son of mine," Ares sneered.

"Mother won't be happy to see this," Eros said. "She'll avoid your bed for centuries after she learns you were behind my mauling."

Ares responded by punching Eros in the face. "If you tell her, I'll rip you to such tiny pieces that you'll never be able to take another host again. You're so insignificant that I'm sure we can survive without a God of Love flying around."

Apollo pushed Ares out of the way. "That's enough. Let's see the damage. You don't want him dying on us, do you?"

"You knew, didn't you," Eros whispered. "You knew what he planned. Damn you, Apollo! I settled our debt. I gave you the adoration of the twins."

"You did, and I got tired of them. They were fun for a while, but I have my sights on a different prize. One that will be easier to win with you out of the picture."

Eros' good eye widened. "No! You can't!"

Ares laughed. "Oh, I see he told you of his little plan. That mortal of yours has been Apollo's slave for nearly a month now. Why should she pine for you when she has the attentions of a real god?"

"Iona loves me! She'll never fall for Apollo!"

Apollo grabbed Eros' elbow, twisting it until it popped. The God of Love cried out in pain as Apollo placed his lips by the younger man's ear. "Tell me, Eros, does your little Iona always rake her nails down your back when she climaxes, or is that honor only mine?"

Eros growled and tried to launch himself at Apollo, but his wounds and a well-placed kick from Deimos sent him back into the arms of Zephyrus. He heard his servant murmur that everything will be all right, but a sick feeling settled in his stomach. How would Apollo know anything about Iona's sexual habits if he wasn't bedding her? He wasn't sure which made him feel more nauseous: her willingly submitting to him, or him taking her by force.

"Take him to his room and lock the door," Ares commanded. "Apollo, you might want to set those broken bones and clean him up a bit. Can't have Aphrodite seeing her precious little boy like this. She'll panic and think we were too hard on poor widdle Eros."

"Let's go, brother," Phobos said, motioning for Zephyrus to lift his sibling. "We wouldn't want you to hurt yourself on the way back to your room. It can be so treacherous in these slippery halls."

Deimos laughed, pushing Zephyrus and Eros forward. "I'm sure if you ask nicely, Apollo will tell you how your little mortal woman is doing."

Chapter 29

A week later, Apollo made his way cheerfully back to his temple. He finally put that uppity little Eros down a few pegs and the other minor gods knew their place. Those without temples should not get in the way of those deserving of worship. Just because a few misguided men put on wings and pranced around in his 'honor' did not put Eros on the same level as Apollo.

Entering his temple, he was greeted by his entourage of beautiful women. Many of his special devotees warmed his bed at night, while others were forced to wait for that golden day he took notice of them. He wasn't interested in any of them on this day. He still needed to teach Eros one final lesson, and time was running out. He only had a few more days to make Iona his, and that minx hadn't broken to his will yet.

"Lord Apollo, a gift just arrived for you from Aphrodite." One of his hopeful girls came running up, a sheer little dress in her hands. "Would you like me to model it for you?"

That certainly wasn't the apology that he was expecting from Aphrodite. What should have been a few minute visit stretched on for days. Once she saw what Ares had done to Eros, Aphrodite kept Apollo until all of Eros' scrapes and bruises were healed. Money or offerings would have been a sufficient thank you for his precious time to baby the wounds of her pathetic whelp, not a sheer nighty.

"Lord Apollo, my sister and I miss your bed," said one of the recently unlucky twins. He ignored them, snatching the nighty as he stalked down the halls. He made his way to where Iona was sweeping the floors. If he didn't make her his soon, she'd run back to Eros for sure. And that was a defeat he would not allow!

"You! My bed! Now!" He tossed the sheer garment at her and started toward his room, only to realize she wasn't following him. Turning back, he snapped, "Iona, now! You are my companion for the rest of your stay. Get moving."

"My month is up," Iona said. "It ended two days ago."

Apollo smiled. "So, you decided to stay with me."

"No. I had to wait for you to return to declare me purified."

Angered, he leaned down close to her. "I won't declare a

thing unless you spend the one night in my bed. I'm tired of playing with you, Iona. Any other girl would be delighted to be in your place. Show me some gratitude."

"I'm married."

"So?"

"I love only my husband. Eros is the only man who stirs my blood and awakens my passion. I dream only of him, desire only him, and will continue until my dying day to want only him."

"Oh, well, when you put it that way," Apollo said. "I know all about your little erotic dreams. Were you aware that the Olympian gods can take the form of anyone they choose? Zeus did it with Alcemone and beget Hercules, and she was none the wiser until her real husband returned home."

"What does that have to do with me?"

"That wasn't Eros in your dreams, sweetheart."

Iona's eyes widened as his words sank in. "No! Oh, no! You tricked me!" She turned to leave, but he grabbed her arm, pulling her against his broad chest.

"My bed, tonight." In a swift maneuver, he scooped up the sheer dress and shoved it into her hands. "Wear this and don't be late."

"My time is up!"

"It's up when I say it's up!" With that he left her. Iona wanted to throw the dress to the ground and storm out of the temple. But, without an official declaration that she was cleansed, her soul was still dirty from the deaths she believed she caused. Until then, she was still his prisoner.

That night, she lay in Apollo's bed. He did not care that she was unresponsive, or that she curled up afterward and cried. All that mattered was he had her, knowingly and willingly.

"I liked you better when you thought I was Eros," Apollo commented after listening to her sobs for nearly a half an hour.

"Why do you hate Eros so much? What has he ever done to you?"

"Ever hear of a little nymph named Daphne?" Before Iona could answer, Apollo said, "Besides, what makes you think I hate him?"

"Don't you?"

He laughed. "Of course I do. Always have, always will. He's

just another uppity minor deity who thinks he can stand shoulder to shoulder with us major gods. He has no temple, no real followers. He's nobody!"

"He's the God of Love. How can you hate that? You, who proclaim to love a new woman every day."

"I don't hate love, you silly girl. I hate Eros. Him and only him."

"Why?"

"He has ruined me too many times. The whole Daphne affair –" Apollo's voice cracked and Iona peered up. She was shocked to see tears glistening in his eyes.

"You cared about her, didn't you?"

"I had no choice! Eros got me with one of his damned darts, and her with the anti-love kind. No matter what I said, she would never love me. No matter how hard I tried not to, I was forced to love her. Do you know how heart-wrenching it is to have the woman you are in love with deciding it's better to be a tree than love you back?"

"I'm sorry."

"Not to mention the whole Zephyrus and Hyacinths affair. I didn't even love him, but because of your winged little lover, I had to bury him!" Apollo pulled Iona closer to him. "How much do you wish to bet that loyal little Zephyrus has no idea that he fell in love with Hyacinths because of those damned darts?"

"He's a God of Love," Iona protested. "That's what he does He makes people fall in love."

"He uses those darts on me, watching as I run after these women and men, knowing I must lose them. It hurts, over and over again."

"I'm sorry," Iona said. She meant it. She knew what it was like to lose someone she loved, and she was praying it wasn't forever. A nagging fear started to creep into her subconscious. Apollo knew of Eros' dark side, a side that Iona had never seen. What would happen when she met him again? Would he forgive her for what Apollo made her do, or would he throw her out? She would be doomed to forever wander Space Station *Olympus*, fading away for want of love.

The next day, Apollo called Iona to meet with him. She was dressed in a gown of gold to simulate the sun and draped in gold and jewels. It was a last effort on Apollo's part to convince her to stay. In the room stood Anteros, ready to take her away. Her brother-in-law was not pleased when he found out that Iona had been there for longer than her appointed time.

"It's your day of freedom," said Apollo. "You have a choice; stay here and be a maiden of my temple where I will shower you with gifts and grant you a life as close to divinity as one such as you should ever dream, or go back to Eros and be his little captive wife, hidden away from the world and never allowed to talk to your family again."

Iona knew Apollo was a vengeful god. Her answer would have been clear, but the wording made her pause. It was obvious to her that he expected her to pick him, and if she refused, there would be consequences. How does one turn down a god and not risk his wrath?

"Lord Apollo, I want to thank you for your treatment of me during this month," she said slowly. Her words were picked to show deference to him, and soften the blow. "However, my heart still belongs to Eros. Even if it is just from the darts, I will always long for him."

"You walk out that door, you won't ever come back. I will not be made a fool by some stupid mortal woman."

"No one has ever thought you a fool, Lord Apollo. I wish you all the best in the world."

"Declare her purified and we'll be on our way," Anteros said.

Apollo growled. He declared Iona to be purified and Anteros quickly dragged her from the temple. "There are some things we need to discuss before you see Eros," he said as they walked swiftly away. As they reached the path, Anteros started to tell Iona of Eros' problems, but stopped when he noticed a girl was following them. One of the unlucky twins stood behind them, nervously wringing her hands. When she noticed she had been spotted, she stepped forward.

"Take me with you," she said. "My sister wishes to stay in case Lord Apollo ever looks her way again, but I wish to leave."

"Then leave," said Anteros. "There was nothing holding you to him. You're free to go."

"I have nowhere to go. My sister and I rented a small flat in Oetaea in the Lower Boeotia region on Level 25. One day, we were approached by a devotee of Aphrodite, who told us Lord Apollo found favor in us. We left at once. I fear, we have been gone long enough that our home has been lost." She looked down. "I am homeless."

"What did you do before you were called here," asked Iona.

"My sister and I worked in a shop, but I was taking night courses in nursing. I thought my devotion to the healing arts was what caught his eye. I have not learned anything about healing while here."

"Didn't think you would," Anteros said. "Well, I'm afraid you can't come where we're going."

Iona stepped forward. "I have an idea." She took off some of the grand jewelry and gave it to the girl. "Here, take this to buy passage to Level 32. There, travel to Tiryns and find the home of Metasis and Hedyla Demarchis. I'm their daughter, Iona. Tell them that I plan on coming home after all of this is settled, and that I'm safe and I love them."

The girl took the jewelry. "I'm Chruse. I recognized you, even with your hair cut short. My sister and I were watching your funeral on the news when we were approached." She smiled. "I will give them your message."

Anteros motioned for her to hurry. He waited until she was out of sight before saying, "Eros was hurt a week or so ago. He tried to escape, only to find his path blocked by Phobos, Deimos and Enyo."

"Not Phobos! He's been so nice whenever I met him."

Anteros looked at her. "We are thinking of the same Phobos, right? Son of Ares, God of Fear, one of my brothers?"

"Yes."

"Nice?"

"Yes."

Anteros sighed. "Well, he was not *nice* to Eros. Granted, he wasn't the one that stomped Eros into a puddle of broken bones, but he did nothing to stop the others from attacking. It's a huge scandal in Olympus. Ares had to pay retribution for his sons shedding blood in the halls."

"Will he be all right?"

"Eros will live, but he's in great pain." Anteros slowed his pace, turning to Iona. "About what you said to Apollo back there. Did he really treat you well?"

"Not particularly, but it would be rude of me to say so." She looked down, feeling guilty. "I found out that he had been sneaking into my rooms disguised as Eros. I thought it was really Eros, and that I was having the most wonderful dreams. I swear, Anteros, I would never cheat on my husband! I love Eros too much."

"Eros already knows. Apollo told him. I guess to make my brother mad, but now he's making himself sick with worry for you. I am sorry, Iona. Someone should have warned you about that trick. Normally, Zeus uses it with his lovers, but Apollo must have learned how. You were a victim. Eros won't blame you."

"Apollo doesn't think I truly love Eros," Iona confessed. "He told me all about the darts. I shot myself with one my last night with Eros. What if what I feel is just from the dart?"

"I know you truly love my brother. I know he loves you. You'll see, Iona. It'll all work out."

Iona remained silent. With so many sins against her, what if Eros didn't want her back? Just because she was purified from her sisters' deaths didn't make her truly purified. She fretted all the way to the PortMat station. Anteros signaled for a technician to start the beam.

"Do not worry. Zephyrus is waiting for you on the other side. You've traveled this way before with no problems."

"I only remember once, and that was a disaster."

"This one won't be a disaster. I promise."

Iona took a deep breath and walked into the beam. In an instant, she vanished. Just as Anteros was about to follow her, the beam flickered and wavered before steadying itself.

"What was that," he asked, turning to the technician. The man shrugged, looking over his control panel.

"There doesn't appear to be any disturbance here, Lord Anteros. The beam is still connected to Level 17."

Anteros sighed and entered the beam. He felt the familiar sensation of the ground vanishing under his feet, of falling and being jerked up at the same time. There was a moment of sheer panic as disorientation set in before his vision cleared and he reached his destination. Zephyrus greeted him anxiously, pulling him out of the way and keeping his eyes on the beam.

"Where is Iona," Anteros asked. He swallowed against the wave of nausea that accompanied his transport. "Did she go on ahead? How did she handle the travel?"

"She's not here," Zephyrus said. "I thought she was following you."

"She went first."

"No one came through before you."

"Damn Apollo! Where did he send her?"

Chapter 30

Iona blinked as the light faded away and the nausea set in. She clutched her stomach, breathing deeply to settle herself. Looking around, she discovered she was alone in a small stone house. Zephyrus and Anteros were nowhere in sight. Iona frowned, knowing that neither man would just abandon her. She waited for a few minutes, but the beam never reappeared and no one came to get her.

Walking out of the house, she found herself in the middle of a vast wheat field. In the distance, she saw a large farm house. Further beyond that, there was a hill and what looked like a temple. This area didn't look like any level Iona had been on before, and she wasn't sure if it was a Godly Level or a farming level.

"Well, I guess I start there," Iona said and headed toward the farm house. Maybe Eros was waiting for her at the home or the temple? Though, why would he wait for her so far off and not have his brother or friend escort her?

As Iona headed to the farm house, she contemplated her relationship with Eros. She knew she loved him as Amor, but that had been a physical attraction. She wasn't sure now how deep that love would have ran if their relationship had continued. Would he have ever told her the truth? She had loved him when she thought he was a serpent. As frightened she had been of him, she loved him all the same. And yet, she betrayed him. Could she really count that as love? Knowing him as Eros, she was sure she loved him still.

Fear nagged at her. What if Apollo was right? What if she only loved Eros because of the dart? Would it fade in time and her love of him disappear into a disappointed haze? Could any woman really love a god?

Reaching the home, she realized it was much bigger than she thought. The home stretched across the field and looked like it had its own private temple attached. Iona knocked on the door. Her heart beat so fast in her chest at the thought of finally seeing her husband once again. The door was opened by a dumpy woman with dried stalks of wheat in her hair. Her eyes were red-rimmed and Iona could tell she had been crying.

"Who are you? How did you get here?" The woman gave Iona a once-over, clearly startled to see her.

"I, uh, I'm not sure where here is. I think I'm on the wrong level," Iona said. She wanted to ask about Eros, but there was something about this woman that made her afraid to ask. It could just be the way the woman stared at Iona, as if she were an interloper.

"You are on Level 7, the majestic home of Demeter, Goddess of the Grain."

That made some sense to Iona. The dried stalks of wheat in the woman's hair represented the upcoming winter and the decent of Persephone down into the realm of Hades. If she was on Level 7, then something must have gone wrong. Persephone, her only ally on this level, wasn't around.

Iona quickly pulled out her paperwork. Without being obvious, she peeked at the name as she straightened out the papers. "I think I landed on the wrong level. I, um, I was supposed to be sent to, uh, Hephaestus. I'm Azalia."

"You're a long way from your destination, then." The woman gave Iona a once over. Her dark eyes sparkled coldly. "Maybe I can use you. It's not like Hephaestus has much use for a woman in his shops. And you don't strike me as the kind of girl that would be at home working in a forge. What was your business with Hephaestus?"

"Well, you see..." Iona struggled for words. She didn't want to say the wrong thing and have this woman test her. There was something about her that frightened Iona, something just a little bit off. "I was sent to be a cook. Even the workers of Lord Hephaestus need to eat."

"I see. Azalia the cook. Interesting."

"I really should be going, then. Thank you for your help." Iona turned to leave when the woman reached out and grabbed her arm. Her grip was like iron.

"I could use you here. I'm sure you know that with the winter months, life here is unbelievably dreary until the Hades is forced to return the fair Kore. Lady Demeter could use a good cook to help brighten her spirits. And we always need a new hand around here."

Iona wanted to say no. She opened her mouth to tell the woman that the offer was lovely, but she really needed to be on her way. Before she could, another servant came running up.

"Mi'lady! It's Odessa! Come quickly!"

The woman made a strangled sound that could be a growl. She pushed Iona at the servant. "Very well. Take her to the kitchens. Azalia -" here the woman snorted "- here will be the new cook. Show her what needs to be done and then come back to Odessa's room. I'll fix this once and for all."

Iona found herself being forcefully escorted to the kitchens. Kitchens, it turned out, was a weak word for the room she and the servant entered. It was like a tiny kingdom of fire stoves and ice boxes and pantries of every kind of food. A list of meals hung on one wall and instructions on how to prepare certain dishes lay on a counter. It would take an army to keep this 'kitchen' in well working order. And Iona saw no other cook.

"Who will I be working with," she asked.

The servant laughed. "Just yourself. The other cooks left this morning. Mi'lady has been growing restless and sour as of late, and it always drives the workers away. They'll be back in Spring when her temper is better."

"I noticed she used the name Kore for Persephone."

"We do not use the 'P' name here, Miss. You will call the daughter of Lady Demeter Kore if you value your life." With that, the servant left and Iona sighed. She walked over to the list of meals and noted the times. Interestingly enough, she noted that this mysterious Odessa was to be served nothing but a hearty broth and a hard roll three times a day. Iona would also be cooking meals for Demeter, something that filled her with dread. The last thing she wanted was for a goddess to discover her before she could find her way back to Eros. She wasn't certain if Demeter was friend or foe.

In the following days, Iona fell into a pattern in the house. She woke up, cooked the meals and placed them on a counter for a servant to take away. During her free time, she tried to sneak away and find her way back to the PortMat. Iona never made it far. The lady in charge of the household, the formidable Cere, managed to stop her each and every time. It wasn't that she asked Iona to stay, she commanded it.

"I am expected elsewhere," Iona protested as Cere dragged her back to the house once again.

"You will stay here Azalia. This is where you are meant to be."

"But Lord Hephaestus -"

"Can find another cook!"

After that, the kitchen doors were locked. Iona could not exit for any reason. Servants gathering food were forced to unlock the doors, and enter in pairs in case Iona tried to fight them in a bid for freedom. Officially trapped, she wondered if she would ever see her husband again. Iona's only link to the outside world was watching the news on the view screens. She knew Aphrodite had not stopped her hunt for Iona, and was still using the old photograph of her with long hair. She also saw that Eros was looking for her. It confused Iona as to why both of them would call out for her on the news. Slowly, it dawned on her that all the news she was seeing was only for the gods and goddesses. There was nothing about the average human in the broadcasts, only decrees by the gods. She watched one cast where Phobos and Deimos had to make a public apology for shedding blood in Olympus. That was surely something that would not be seen anywhere on the inhabited levels.

Seeing as she had no choice but to stay, Iona turned her curiosity to the mystery surrounding this Odessa person. She seemed to be a prisoner in the house, and Iona wanted to know why. It was the only thing she could do. Iona couldn't escape.

Iona tested the waters to see how she could get out of the kitchens. Discovering a window she could open, she slowly started exploring the house, hoping to find where this Odessa was being held. She found rooms dedicated to Persephone, each picture labeled Kore. There was one with a picture of a man that Iona assumed was Hades – a tall man with dark eyes and flames surrounding him. Knives and darts stuck out from the picture, as if someone used it for target practice.

Finally, Iona started to explore the basement. There, she found the mysterious Odessa. The poor woman was tied to a bed, her large pregnant belly obvious as her form was nude. Bruises dotted her body and there were three scars down one side of her face. Her skin, if she had been healthy, would have been a lovely dark shade of black. But, with her previous treatment, she was now faded to nearly gray and her tightly curled black hair hung in greasy spirals on the pillow. There was a terrible odor coming from her, something that smelled almost like rotting flesh. When she saw Iona, she started to shiver.

"I'm a friend," Iona said. "I'm a prisoner here, too."

"I have no friends," Odessa moaned. "Demeter destroyed all my allies. She has cut me off from my one true love and plans on taking my daughter."

"Why would a goddess do those things?"

"She is a desperate woman. She has told me that she plans on raising this daughter to be better than Kore. This one won't be seduced by the darkness." Odessa sighed, tugging on her bonds. When she moved, Iona gasped as she saw the gaping wounds forming on the backs of Odessa's legs and buttocks. The skin appeared to be eating itself inward. "I've been here for so long, I've forgotten what the sun feels like. My poor, sweet Phobos must be worried about me."

"Phobos? As in the God of Fear?"

"Yes, but he's not as fearsome as you would think. He's been so kind to me. We were planning on marrying."

Iona smiled, sitting on the bed. "I know him. He's my brother-in-law. I'm Iona, wife of Eros."

"I thought Eros was married to Psyche."

Iona shrugged. "I don't know what happened to her. I only know that I am his wife."

Odessa was silent for a moment. Then she tugged on the bonds and turned as much as she could to Iona. "Can you get a message to Phobos for me? He must be so worried. Before I disappeared, I told him I was pregnant. He promised he would talk to his father about marrying me, to see if there was anything that had to be done to buy me away from Demeter. She must have found out about me wanting to leave."

"If I can get in touch with Phobos, I promise to tell him where you are."

Iona stood to leave, intent on getting a message out as soon as possible. Odessa stopped her, saying, "Has Phobos ever mentioned me to you?"

"No, but we never really had much time to talk. Mostly, when he shows up, I'm on the run." Iona could see how much pain Odessa was in. "Is there anything I can do to help you?"

"No. Demeter will know if you help me. But, talking helps. I can try and forget my predicament." Odessa smiled. "You know, I met Eros once. He arrived one bright Spring day. He had his little gun with him. I nearly laughed at how tiny it was. He said he wanted to know how I felt about Phobos. I told him I loved Phobos with all my heart. He put his gun away and said that was all he needed to hear."

"You don't think he shot you, do you?"

"No. My love for Phobos was genuine. It didn't change after Eros' visit. I think, he was there to shoot me, but he didn't. I don't know why he would have shown up anyway." Odessa looked at Iona. "Maybe the brothers watch out for each other but don't want anyone to know?"

"Maybe. I know Phobos has helped me, despite his insistence that he hates Eros."

Iona and Odessa froze when they heard the basement door open. Scrambling for a hiding place, Iona dove behind a pile of grain bags. Ducking down into the shadows, she watched as Cere and two other women came in to check on Odessa. Iona nearly gasped as she recognized one of the women to be Eileithyia, the same midwife that had helped her not so long ago.

"How is the baby coming along," Cere asked.

Eileithyia placed her hand on Odessa's round stomach. "The baby is coming along fine. Nice and healthy. You have nothing to fear. Though, if I were you, I'd take better care of the mother. If things progress this way, Odessa may die in childbirth."

"It's no matter to me. The baby is all that matters."

"What about me! I deserve to live!" Odessa struggled, but it was no use. A diet of weak broth had taken her strength and the bed sores were slowly eating her alive.

Cere's voice was icy cold as she said, "You are of no consequence. Only the baby matters."

"When can we take the child," asked the last woman. She looked a lot like Ceres but carried herself with more confidence. The low lighting of the basement sparkled off the many gems the woman wore, signifying her as someone of some importance. Iona hated to think that this woman could actually be Demeter. But, what would Persephone's mother be doing trying to harvest a baby from Odessa?

"Tomorrow night, maybe. She is almost ready to pop," said Eileithyia. "I don't approve of this, Demeter. Normally you pick a willing woman to bring forth a new Kore. I do not approve of you keeping a woman tied up."

"I am not worried about your approval, Eileithyia. Just do your job."

Eileithyia finished her inspection and the small group left. Iona waited until she was sure they were long gone before crawling out of her hiding spot. In the bed, Odessa was silently sobbing.

"I'll get help," Iona promised. She had no idea how she could when she was a prisoner as well, but she would do what she could for Odessa. Somehow, she needed to get a message to Phobos. If anyone would know what to do, it would be her brother-in-law.

Though she wasn't caught, Iona had a feeling that her captors knew she escaped for a short time. The little window she used to get out was now nailed shut, preventing her from escaping again. Determined to help, Iona took another long look around the kitchens and her small sleeping area. It took the better part of the day, but she finally found another way to escape. Down in the root cellar, she found a window that had been hidden by boxes on the inside, and overgrown weeds on the outside. It looked so forgotten that she just knew it would be her way out.

Waiting until the cover of darkness, Iona crept down to the cellar. Slowly, she opened the window and wiggled her way out of it. Once outside, she had to get back in the house to save Odessa. That wasn't as hard as she assumed. There were no guards outside the house. When she got back inside, she left the front door unlocked in hopes of being able to just get out that way. If her luck held, she could get Odessa to the little building with the magical light beam. If nothing else, she could figure out how to send Odessa's message to Phobos.

In the darkness of the large house, Iona stayed as close to the walls as she made her way back to the basement. She pressed closer to the wall as she heard someone walking down the hall. Praying she wasn't seen, she waited until she could hear the footsteps pass her. However, they never did and a strong hand grabbed her by the arm, jerking her away from the shadows. Something hard pressed against her chin. She pulled back just far enough to realize someone was pointing a gun at her.

Chapter 31

"Iona?"

Iona looked up past the gun at the wielder. Phobos stared back her, surprise in his bright eyes.

"What are you doing here," Phobos demanded. He released Iona roughly.

"It's a long story. I was supposed to follow Anteros to Eros, but we somehow got separated. I ended up here, and I don't know where here is. When I came to this house to ask for directions, I was...um...'hired' as a cook and they won't let me leave. I've tried, but all ways were blocked."

Phobos' bright eyes narrowed. "The exit is the other way. Why are you sneaking even further into the house?"

"To save Odessa. I met her yesterday, and I'm worried. They're planning on taking the baby, and I don't think she'll survive."

"Where is Odessa? Show me!"

Iona motioned for him to follow her and they made their way to the basement. Phobos was not interested in hiding along the wall, marching straight to where his lady love was being held. When they made it to the small room, Iona stopped. She could hear a baby crying inside, and her heart dropped. She sent a quick prayer to Hera that Odessa was still alive. Iona could not have left her for more than twenty-four hours. Didn't Eileithyia say that it could be a day or so before she gave birth? Wouldn't she have heard commotion if Odessa birthed the baby while she was trying to escape?

Phobos threw open the door and ran inside. Odessa still lay on the bed, but it was obvious that the birth exhausted her life. Her skin was now dull and she stared lifeless at the ceiling. Phobos picked up one cold hand and held it to his cheek, silent tears falling.

"How could this have happened," he whispered. "Of all the goddesses, I would have thought Demeter would know that a baby would need her mom. Why let Odessa die?"

Iona looked down. "Odessa said that Demeter wanted only the baby. I heard them talking, that's how I knew that her life was in danger. The women who were here didn't care about Odessa. I wish I could have gotten to her sooner, but all of my normal outlets were blocked. I'm so sorry, Phobos. I barely knew her, but she seemed like such a nice person."

"She was. I fell in love the moment I saw her. She wasn't scared of me, and we played a game of cat and mouse for months. This was the only time I ever asked Eros' help with a girl. We were so happy." He bent down and kissed Odessa on the cheek. "Then we made the mistake of asking Demeter for her blessing. After that, Odessa vanished. I foolishly believed Demeter when she told me that Odessa was doing important harvest things for her, but when Odessa never contacted me about the baby, I knew something was wrong. She just vanished, and I knew she was pregnant. And with the power of Eros' dart, there was no way she'd just leave like that and Demeter refused to talk to me."

"She loved you," Iona said. "She told me that. She said Eros was sent to use one of his darts, but he never did. Her love was genuine."

Phobos straightened up and turned to the little bassinet with the baby. The little girl stopped crying and was waving her little fists up at Phobos. He reached down and picked his daughter up, cuddling the tiny girl against his chest.

"Demeter took my Odessa from me. I'll be damned if I let her keep my daughter."

The lights suddenly came on and a cold, male voice said, "Then I guess you're damned, Phobos."

The two turned to see a couple standing by the door. The woman Iona noticed earlier with Ceres was standing there, and she knew that it just had to be Demeter. The man next to her was big with bulging muscles and wore a lot of black and leather armor. He also had a lot of weapons strapped to his body.

"Father? What are you doing here?" Phobos held on tighter to the baby and used one hand to grab Iona. He pushed her behind him, protecting her from the two gods.

Ares shook his head. "Oh, really Phobos, you disappoint me. First you fall for a pathetic mortal, and now you're defying everything you are for this whore of Eros'. What has happened to you?"

"Odessa was not pathetic. She had guts, and I admired her for that. She was a fighter! She was mine!"

"And what about Iona?"

Phobos looked back for a moment. "She's not like the others, Father. Eros could have done a lot worse. In fact, he has over the years. But this one...She has backbone. Isn't that worth something?"

"Not when your mother wants to see her head on a plate."

"What about Demeter! She's betrayed us! She let my Odessa die for her selfish desire for another baby when any one of her little sycophants would have gladly handed over their own flesh and blood. She wasn't ever going to tell me about my daughter. I have a right to know and raise my own child!"

Next to Ares, Demeter shrugged. "Why wait for one of my maidens to become pregnant when I had a girl with child already. And what kind of life would you give a baby, Phobos? A life of pain and war, when I can give her the life she truly deserves?"

Phobos backed up a step, pushing Iona closer to the body on the bed. "And what about her hiding Iona? How long has she been here? I know Eros has been searching for her since he fled the clutches of Mother a week or so ago. And Anteros has been searching for longer. With how Mother wants anyone, god or mortal, to be punished for hiding Iona, why would Demeter keep her here?"

"I was keeping her prisoner for Aphrodite. This way, we knew where she was instead of letting her go hiding all over the station," Demeter said. "I was helping Aphrodite."

"Hand over the baby and the girl," Ares demanded. "Phobos, don't make this harder on yourself. You and Deimos have always been my favorites. Don't ruin that now. Just hand the baby to Demeter and give me the girl, and I'll let you leave here alive. Otherwise, boy, do you really think you can protect them and fight me at the same time?"

Phobos looked down at his daughter. "What will happen to Iona if I hand her over?"

"Phobos! Don't!" Iona pleaded.

"I'll take her to Aphrodite. I think your mother has some kind of punishment in mind."

The God of Fear looked back at Iona. She could see that the man who brought terror to the hearts of others had fear in his eyes. Suddenly his eyes hardened and he turned back to his father. "No! I'm going to take her to Mother. I think she's worthy of Eros – By Hades! She's more than worthy of that brat – and I'll vouch for her. You've taken everything else away from me, and I won't let you take this. I demand that Mother test Iona to see if she's worthy of Eros. I'll bet my immortality on her succeeding."

Ares laughed. "Very well, boy. It's your funeral. Just give Demeter the baby and I'll escort the both of you back to Aphrodite."

Phobos took Iona's hand before he walked over to Demeter. He allowed the goddess to take the newborn, hissing low, "I won't forget this." He turned to his father and meekly followed him out to the PortMat. Iona worried that Ares would pull the same trick that had separated her from Anteros, but Phobos seemed to be expecting it. He entered the beam with her, and they were transported to a beautiful temple.

Standing in front of them was the most gorgeous woman Iona ever set her eyes on. Her honey-blonde hair was pulled up in an elaborate braid, small tendrils curled softly around her cheeks. Her gown was sheer pink with golden strands woven in so that it shimmered with each movement. Behind her were women of beauty, but they paled in comparison with this woman. She stared down at Iona and Phobos with cold blue eyes.

The light flared to life again and Ares stepped out. When he saw that neither Phobos nor Iona were on their knees yet, he kicked them down and walked to the woman.

"Welcome back, my love," Aphrodite said. She took Ares' hands and smiled so sweetly at him that Iona's own heart broke. Why couldn't this beautiful creature smile at her like that?

"I brought you a gift," Ares said.

"Yes, thank you. Thank you for finally delivering to me this ugly mortal."

Chapter 32

Aphrodite slowly circled Iona as the girl huddled on the ground. Her beautiful lip curled up in a sensual sneer. "Look at you. Pathetic. How my son ever fell for you is a mystery. What black magic hold do you have over him? What witch helped you? Was it the Graea? Did those three hags bespell my beloved Eros because of their envy over my beauty? Or was it Hecate? You must be in league with that temptress! I just knew she was plotting something."

Iona curled up more onto herself. One part of her wanted to beg for forgiveness to this gorgeous creature that now stared so angrily down at her. The other part struggled to fight back. How did one fight the Goddess of Love and Beauty? Iona was nothing more than a mortal.

Aphrodite kicked out with one tiny foot, forcing Iona to roll over on her back so Aphrodite could finally see her face. "You are ugly," the goddess spat. "Nothing more than a fat girl all hips and breasts. You would be better for some farmer, popping out brats until you are nothing more than a haggard blob of flesh. If my son hadn't pricked himself with his darts, you'd never have caught his eye."

"Funny, but he did and that means he'll love me for all time," Iona said. The pain helped fight off the desire to worship Aphrodite. "And I love him."

Phobos was suddenly up and pushing Iona to the floor. The ground next to her exploded as Ares' gun missed its mark. The God of Fear shoved Iona behind him once more, facing his parents. "Mother, stop!"

"That mortal has insulted me for the last time," Aphrodite cried. "I want her head on a platter! I want to feed her carcass to the vultures. I want even Hades to run screaming from her!"

"She's worthy! She's worthy of Eros," Phobos insisted. "She's able to stand up to you, Mother. How many other mortals can do that? And she hasn't stopped looking for Eros all this time. This is not just some mortal with a fascination. It's real love. And being the Goddess of Love, you should respect that."

Aphrodite's demeanor changed instantly, and Iona could see

Ares roll his eyes and groan. The angry goddess was gone, and in her place was a tearful woman. "How could you side with her, Phobos? Don't you love me anymore? What has this witch done to you?"

"She's done nothing, Mother. I just really think you should rethink your plans. Iona has grit, Mother, and I respect that. I think it would be better to test her rather than just kill her."

"He's willing to wager his own immortality that she'll be proven worthy," Ares said.

Aphrodite wailed and threw herself back into the arms of her maidens. "My son wishes to die for a mortal! How could such a day come to be? She's stealing everything from me! Woe! No one cares enough to stay with me. I am ruined!" Her attendants fanned her and shot angry glares at Phobos and Iona.

"Mother, it's not like that," Phobos protested.

"She is replacing me! I just knew it all along. First they call her Aphrodite-in-the-flesh and then she steals my children! Eros is panting after her, Anteros sneaks around to protect her, and my darling Phobos now thinks she's worthy!" Aphrodite spat the last word. "Ares, do something! Rid me of that wench! Do it before she infects the others!"

Ares raised his gun once more, but Phobos was ready. He launched himself at his father, pushing the gun to the side. The bullet ricocheted off the marble floor close to Aphrodite, who squealed in fright. The two gods of war fought, their blood staining the temple. Finally, Ares got the upper hand and sent Phobos' body sliding across the floor to stop at Iona's feet.

"If you can turn one of my own sons against me, there must be something about you," Ares sneered. "Question is, do I really care enough to find out."

Iona bent over Phobos' body to make sure he was still breathing. Using the motion to cover her actions, she carefully took his gun. This was her first time holding a gun, but how hard could it be? She was not going to go down without a fight.

"As Phobos said, I have grit," Iona said. Without aiming, she brought the gun up and shot. The bullet went wide, missing Ares by several feet.

For a moment, no one moved. Ares stared at her and the gun, and Iona had a feeling she would not be allowed to get a second shot off. Then, the God of War started to laugh. It came out as a chuckle that evolved into a full belly-laugh.

"You do have grit, girl!" He walked over to Aphrodite, who looked scandalized. Bending over his lover, he whispered in her ear. Whatever he said made the goddess smile.

"Yes, that might work," Aphrodite said. She turned back to Iona. "Put that gun down, mortal. It appears that everyone thinks you should be given a chance to win back Eros. Very well, I will grant that wish. If you survive all my tests, you and my son may marry with my blessing. If you fail...well, you won't live for long."

"I can do any task you set before me," Iona said. "There is nothing I wouldn't endure for Eros."

"We will see about that," Aphrodite said. She grabbed Iona, forcing her to drop the gun. Unarmed, Iona found herself being shoved into the arms of one of the attendants. "Take her and Phobos to Apollo. I want my son healed. As for the girl, tell Apollo the nights are his, but she must be ready to take on my tasks in the morning."

Iona shivered. "Please, don't do this. I can't go back to Apollo. Please!"

"Get her out of my sight!"

The attendant dragged Iona back to the PortMat and transported the two of them to the hallowed halls of Olympus. Iona didn't dare to struggle too much, not when she was so alone. Her allies were nowhere near by and the only one who knew she was there was unconscious. She needed Phobos to warn Eros for her.

She was marched down the halls to a door with a bright golden sun painted on it. In moments, she found herself face-to-face with Apollo. He licked his lips, staring down at her. Leaning casually against the door frame, he said, "Look at what came crawling back. How have you been, Iona? Miss me already?"

"Lord Apollo," greeted Iona.

"Oh Great Apollo, shining son of Zeus, bringer of light, I have a message from my lady, Aphrodite," the attendant said. "It is her wish that you take this wretched mortal off her hands during the nights and return her in the days for her tests."

"Well, I don't -" Apollo stopped, staring past Iona at the bloodied mess of Phobos. "What in Hades happened to Phobos? What new enemy has bested the son of Ares?"

When the attendant refused to answer, Iona said, "He fought Ares on my behalf. Lady Aphrodite also wishes you to heal her son."

Apollo looked at Iona with renewed interest. "You're just collecting the gods, aren't you. How many of us do you have under your pretty little thumb?"

"None. I swear."

"Whatever. Fine. I'll do what Aphrodite wants." He took a step back to allow Phobos to be placed inside the room. "I'm sure I can find something to do with Iona until morning."

Never had Iona seen a more narcissistic room. Everywhere she looked were pictures of Apollo, statues to his greatness, and even a little shrine in dedication to himself. On a pile of pillows in one corner lay two beautiful girls, clad in nothing but their long, flowing hair.

"You two, out!" Apollo snapped his fingers and pointed to the door. "I have work to do."

"But Lord Apollo," one girl protested.

"I said out! Out now, or you'll be joining this girl at the mercy of Aphrodite in the morning. And believe me, that is not a place you want to be." The two girls scrambled up and ran from the room, never bothering to look for their clothes.

Apollo turned his attention to Phobos. "This won't take me long. Just a few broken bones and I think some minor internal bleeding. He'll be in pain, but he's a god. He'll live."

Iona sighed in relief. "He's had a hard night."

"I'm sure. But coming to your rescue? That is something I would never have guessed out of him. Had you been Psyche, he would have gladly handed you over to Aphrodite."

"Psyche?"

Apollo grinned. "Yes. Eros' legal wife. I bet you didn't know that, did you? He's still married to this little mousey nobody while he's been romancing you. There wasn't much to her, and I think she's been reduced to nothing more than a bitter woman because of you."

"No. Eros loves me. We are married."

"He's been married to her for nearly a hundred years now. They even had a daughter. Pretty little thing, married off to some lesser son of Zeus'."

"He loves me," Iona repeated. "I'm his wife."

"Not legally, sweetheart." He looked Iona over. "Now, what

to do with you? I'm not really keen on the idea of taking you to bed again. I do have my pride. But, I just can't let you sleep here, all safe and snug as you please."

Iona looked down at Phobos, trying to think of what she could do. "Please, Lord Apollo, have some mercy. Even if you can't spare me, please let Eros know where I am. I'm sure that once I see him again, I can convince him to stop tormenting you. No more falling for doomed lovers. He can see to it that you have that one special person in your life."

Apollo laughed. "Psyche tried to make the same deal. However, as soon as she saw her beloved again, she forgot all about me. I'm not making deals."

"Mercy, Lord Apollo. Get word to Eros, and I will repay you."

"Any price I wish?"

Iona paused. She had already learned this lesson. "Name if first, and we shall see. I will not agree to anything without knowing what I am agreeing to."

Apollo tilted his head to the side as he thought things over. "I'm in no mood for promises that will be broken, Iona. Anything I ask, you will grant me. You understand that?"

"And what is it you want?"

"I want a night with Zephyrus. If I cannot make Eros pay for the whole Hyacinths episode, then I shall satisfy myself by making Zephyrus pay."

"No!" Iona balled her hands into fists by her side. "I cannot just hand over my friend to you. If you must make one hurt for that, I'll take his punishment."

Apollo blinked. "That was not what I expected. You would really take on the torment I planned for Zephyrus just to protect him? You, a mortal woman, could easily die."

"And what kind of person would I be if I handed him over to you?"

"Tempting, very temping. I'll have to think about this." He turned his attention back to Phobos. "Let's see, Despoina was hanging around Eros a lot while he was here. There was even talk that they would wed, blessed by Demeter and Aphrodite. I'm sure none of that pleased Deimos. And now that Eros is gone, she's been so depressed lately. I doubt Deimos can win her little heart back."

He smiled. "An eye for an eye, maybe?"

"What are you talking about?"

Apollo grabbed her arm and dragged her from the room. "Come on. You're about to meet your worst nightmare." The hall he took her to was dedicated to Ares. Iona trembled as she was dragged past statues of the God of War and his sons, all their weapons stained red with paint. At least, she hoped that was paint. It was a hellish place and Iona hated it. Not even in her home of Tiryns, a place that had many temples dedicated to their patron Ares, did such horrors exist. Iona wanted her gardens and green fertile land back.

Apollo knocked on a door and a scary-looking man opened up. His dark hair was wild and he glared at them with black eyes. His eyes burned with an unholy light as he looked Iona up and down. She had the strangest feeling he was contemplating the best place to drive his sword through her flesh.

"Deimos! You look awful! I brought you a gift." Apollo shoved Iona forward. "She's yours for the night, but your mom needs her in the morning. So, don't kill her, and try to not harm her pretty little face."

Deimos gave Iona another once over and slammed his door shut. Apollo rolled his eyes and knocked once more. "Did I mention that this is Iona Demarchis? As in, Eros' little mortal whore that he's been mooning over for months now?"

"I'm not a whore," Iona protested.

"Shut up. Let the big boys talk."

The door opened and Deimos peered out. "That's Iona? She looks like she'll break in half if I sneeze."

"Yeah, this is Iona. I don't have the time for her tonight. I have to fix up your brother."

"Which one?"

"Phobos. The fool got himself beaten bloody for trying to help her. She's got how many of your brothers wrapped around her little fingers? Not just Eros, but Anteros and Phobos. Zeus only knows how many others have fallen prey to her."

Deimos smiled and it sent shivers down Iona's spine. For the first time, she knew what dread felt like. "She won't bewitch me."

"Have fun. Remember, I need her alive in the morning."

"How alive?"

Apollo shrugged. "Your mother has some great scheme set

up, so alive and moving. And don't hurt her face."

"I won't make promises," Deimos said. He grabbed Iona and pulled her into his room, slamming the door shut on Apollo once more. Turning to her, he pulled out a large knife. "I hope you're a screamer. I like screamers."

By the time Apollo came to pick her up the next morning, Iona was barely conscious. Apollo gave a grunt of disgust, staring down at Deimos' handiwork.

"You are one sick puppy, you know that," Apollo said. Iona lay on her stomach, her dress torn down the back. Deimos carved 'Eros sucks' into her flesh. At least he had the foresight to put a healing gel on the wounds. It did nothing to ease the pain, but Apollo could see the beginnings of the cuts scarring over.

"You said leave her alive and don't touch her face. You said nothing about leaving my mark," Deimos said in a bored tone. "She's just fine."

Apollo knelt down and used his godly gifts to finish the healing. Then he slowly pulled Iona up to her feet. "Come on, your first test awaits."

"I suppose if I asked for a day to rest, I would be denied," Iona asked.

"Right."

She sighed, wincing as she moved. "Very well. All I ask then is something that will not touch my back. Please, let me just find a dress like that."

Apollo rolled his eyes and brought her to another room. Lethia was waiting for them and helped Iona find an open-backed dress. If her wounds caused any concern, Lethia kept it to herself.

"Do not let Aphrodite see that you are in pain," Lethia said. "If you stand strong, you can get through this."

"Thank you, Lethia," Iona said.

"Do not thank me yet. Each day will be worse than the last. Just be prepared."

Chapter 33

Aphrodite led Iona to a small room just off the main portion of her personal temple. She pointed to a small wooden stool in the middle of the room. Once Iona was seated, three attendants walked in with large bags of grain. Iona watched as the attendants dumped the grain out in a huge pile at her feet.

"In there you will find wheat, barley, and rye," Aphrodite said. "You have until nightfall to split all the grain into three piles. Succeed, and I will think about letting you see my son. Fail, and I will make sure you never see Eros again. In fact, I just might hand you over to Hades!"

Iona looked at the pile of grain and then up at the dim light. "How am I supposed to sort all of this grain by nightfall? It's impossible."

"Then I suggest you find a way to figure it out. Your time begins now." Aphrodite swept out of the room and slammed the door shut. The dim light overhead flickered, threatening to send the room in complete darkness.

Iona stared at the pile of grain and knew this was hopeless. Her back felt like it was on fire and she could barely see the grain to determine which was which kind. Slowly, she picked through the handful and started the new piles in three corners. She squinted at each grain before carefully putting it in the proper pile. She needed to try, for Eros' sake. Even if she failed, she didn't want to know it was because she sat down and gave up.

"I'm never going to do this," she moaned, holding up a grain to the light. Was it wheat? Or rye? It was too dark to see and there were no windows. How much time had passed?

"Yes, you will." A high, squeaky voice issued from her left. Iona turned but saw no one.

"Hello? Is anyone there?" A movement caught her eye and she saw a line of Aneriams marching from under a crack in the wall toward the pile of grain. A larger one, nearly the size of her hand, meandered toward her.

"Well, hello there," Iona said. She held her hand down for the Aneriam. "I'm sorry, but I don't have food for you. You and your friends can't have the grain. I need it for something. Maybe later, okay?"

"We have come to help you," said the squeaky voice. It took Iona a few seconds to realize that the voice was coming from the large Aneriam in her hand.

"Wait? Did you just talk?"

"Of course," said the Aneriam. "I am Rasmus, Emperor of the Leventi, and you have earned the respect of my people."

"The Leventi?"

"Yes. My people." He motioned to himself and the other Aneriams who were sorting the grain.

"Oh! We've always called you Aneriams."

Rasmus gave a high-pitched huff. "A silly name. Not as dignified as Leventi."

Iona looked back down at the creatures as they worked. "What have I done to gain such respect, Empereror Rasmus? Until now, I never even knew you could talk."

"We know that in every garden you ever attended, you have been kind to my people. You gave us food off your table, a place of shade, and protection. Never have you squished our kind under your feet. For these things, we will help you now."

"How can I ever repay you?"

"When you next get a garden, keep us in mind," said Rasmus. "Do as you have done before and feed my colony that settle there. Shade us from the sun and make sure there is water for us to drink. Be kind to us and we will always remember you."

"I will do that," Iona promised. She gently placed the small creature on the ground and helped them sort the grain. She wasn't as quick as they, who were closer to the ground and could see the differences in the grain better, but she was able to help out. As the last grain was placed in the proper pile and the Aneriams scattered back to the hole in the wall, the door opened and Aphrodite walked in. She eyed the piles with disgust.

"I see you've finished," the goddess said.

"Yes. May I see Eros now?"

Aphrodite looked down at an Aneriam heading to the safety of the wall. She smashed her foot down and twisted it on the crushed corpse for good measure. "You must have had help. I don't know how, but I know you did not do this alone. For that, you will not see my son at all. He is a delicate creature, and you wounded him most grievously."

Iona doubted it was she who truly hurt Eros. After all, Anteros and Phobos had told her that he was beaten when he first tried to leave and find her. She knew he was out there – somewhere – looking for her. Instead of telling Aphrodite that, she hung her head in shame. Getting this goddess angry at her would not solve anything.

Aphrodite grabbed Iona's arm and dragged her back to Apollo's chambers. The sun god barely looked at her as Aphrodite shoved her on to the floor.

"Phobos left here a few hours ago," Apollo said. "Do tell your boyfriend to be more careful when beating his kids. I am not thrilled that I've had to put back together two of your children, Aphrodite."

"After this, you won't have to deal with any of them," Aphrodite said. "Make her suffer." With that, she left. Apollo glanced down at Iona and shook his head.

"I don't have time for you tonight," Apollo said. "Phobos agreed to take you off my hands."

"Thank you, Lord Apollo."

"How's your back?"

Iona shrugged a little. "It still hurts," she said honestly. "I suppose I'll be sleeping on my stomach for the next few nights."

Apollo sighed and leaned back on the wall. He crossed his arms, glaring down at Iona. "Despoina found out that you spent the night in Deimos' rooms. Despite what really happened, she is convinced that you're now trying to woo Deimos. If Deimos were the type, he might think to say thank you for helping him win back the heart of his lady love."

"I take it you're not pleased."

"What do I care about the foolish circles those two go in?" He watched her for a moment longer. "Phobos wants to protect you, you know. Somehow you've impressed him. Frankly, I don't see it. I could bring you to him, or ..." He grinned wickedly.

"Or?"

"Or I could bring you to Ares. We both know that Phobos has gone soft. I'm sure Ares hasn't, and he'll make Deimos seem like a kitten."

Iona scooted back on the floor. "Please, Lord Apollo, no. He'll kill me."

Apollo scoffed and grabbed her arm. "You'll live. Aphrodite will rip him apart if he took away her grand revenge."

"I beg mercy! Please, don't do this! You can't hate Eros so much that you'd be willing to kill me."

He shoved her up against the wall, leaning close. "You have no idea what I can do! Don't flatter yourself, mortal. None of this is with you in mind. You are nothing to us! You are nothing to me! I don't do mercy."

"Please," Iona whispered. "Please, don't send me to Ares. Please, I'm begging you."

Apollo refused to answer her as he dragged her back down the horrid red hallway. The door he stopped in front of was nearly identical to the Deimos' room. Iona felt her heart stop as the door opened and Phobos stood there.

"This is yours," Apollo said. "I don't have to tell you that she needs to be alive in the morning."

"No, you don't." Phobos pulled Iona into his room and slammed the door shut. Through the door, they heard Apollo snap, "Don't any of you know how to shut a door?"

"Thank you," Iona said softly.

"Don't thank me yet," Phobos said. "I have company."

Eager to see if it was Eros, Iona turned toward the main area. Instead, she saw Ares and a woman. Both were dressed in leather armor with their weapons at their sides. Iona's heart sank and she backed up into Phobos.

"I'm sorry," he whispered. "I was hoping they'd be gone by the time you got here."

"So, this is the famous Iona," the woman said. She resembled Ares, but only in female form. "She doesn't look like much. How can she twist so many of your children, Ares? Eros I can understand. That little twit shot himself with his own dart. But Phobos? How did she do it?"

"Leave this matter, Enyo," Phobos warned. "She's under my care until she either proves herself or fails at Mother's tasks."

Ares stood. "She's here for punishment. Deimos told me all about the little incident last night. Turn around girl. I want to see the marks left by my son."

Iona looked back at Phobos before slowly turning around. She made sure the light fell on the scars so they could clearly see her wounds. Ares laughed with delight.

"You can leave now, Father," Phobos said. "This is no concern of yours."

"But it is," Ares said. "Aphrodite won't be pleased to know she had a comfy night. There will be no comforts for her until Aphrodite is finished with her, and even then the only comfort will be death."

"Father," Phobos growled.

"Oh, don't get yourself all worked up," Enyo purred. "We'll only take an hour. That way you can baby her all you want and Aphrodite will be pleased."

Phobos moved to protect Iona, but Ares was expecting it this time. With a cruelty Iona never knew existed, the God of War shot his son. Phobos fell, his hands pressing against the wound on his abdomen.

"Enyo, make sure he doesn't die. I'll take care of the girl."

Iona tried to run for the door. Just as she pushed it open, Ares grabbed her and pulled her back into the room. The walls muffled her screams until there was nothing but silence.

The next morning, Apollo was shocked to see Psyche open the door to Phobos' rooms. "What is going on?"

"Iona and Phobos are both in the Stasis room," she said. "I doubt either will be well enough to do anything today. Ares and Enyo were rather brutal last night."

Cursing under his breath, Apollo ran to the Stasis room. Only two reasons existed for one to be brought to this chamber: either they were there for Transference, or they were beyond his ability were brought there, and that was a rare thing. Inside the room, there were five stasis pods. Only one was occupied. Phobos, fully healed, sat in one corner wearing only a pair of pants and reading from an electronic tablet.

"How is she," Apollo asked.

"Alive. Beyond that, I am not sure. The pod has to fix several broken bones and piece together parts of her skull. She nearly died just on the way to the room," Phobos said. He slammed the tablet down. "There was no call for that! Father and Enyo went too far!"

"I doubt anything can be done," Apollo said. He hated Eros.

He wasn't exceptionally fond of Iona. But no one deserved this. He peered into the pod and nearly gagged at the sight. It would take more than one day to fix that mess.

"I'll go tell Aphrodite," Apollo said.

Chapter 34

By the dawn of the third day, Iona was ready to be released from the Stasis room. It had taken that long for her bones to knit together and her skin to heal. As it was, she now had an ugly scar that ran from the corner of her left eye down to the corner of her mouth. It made her look as if she were smirking. Her hair had to be styled just right to cover the scars on her head where her hair refused to grow. She could see that she no longer resembled the beautiful Aphrodite-in-the-flesh that she once was.

Under Apollo's care, she was given the chance to shower and eat before being sent back out to Aphrodite. The Goddess of Love and Beauty was not amused by having to wait so long before continuing her plan of vengeance.

"I hope you're well rested," Aphrodite sneered. "No more playing around."

Iona nodded, not bothering to point out that she had not been playing around. There would be no sympathy for her.

"By Hephaestus, you look uglier than normal. I don't know why I'm bothering. Eros will take one look at your face and leave you. You're only fit to be the bride of a Cyclops or giant. I suggest you give up now and I will see to it that you marry the least ugly monster I can find."

"I would rather hear the dismissal from Eros' mouth. Until then, what task do you have for me today?"

There was a twittering among the attendants as Aphrodite draped herself over a small couch. "Your task is so simple. In fact, I'm almost embarrassed to give it to you. I must be suffering from all the kindness in my soul to be so lenient to you. Especially after how you just talked to me."

Iona stifled a sigh. The beauty of Aphrodite was starting to fade from Iona's eyes, leaving behind only the dramatic mother of the man she loved. "Forgive my rudeness, oh mighty Aphrodite. I am ever grateful for the opportunity to prove my worthiness of your son. You are too kind."

"It has come to my attention that my sheep need to be sheared. I have a flock of special golden sheep, from which I make my most beautiful dresses. You will go among the flock and shear them and bring me back the wool."

"That's it? Gather some wool?" Iona couldn't help but stare at Aphrodite. There had to be a catch. Aphrodite was not the kind of person to give such a simple task. Maybe the sheep were guarded by a monster? Or their wool was real gold and could not be cut with the shears she was handed?

Aphrodite laid a limp hand against her pale forehead. "I know it's so easy. How embarrassing to give you such a simple task. Why, at this rate, you'll be with my son in no time. I am such a romantic softie."

"When I complete this, will I get to see Eros?"

Aphrodite bolted up from the couch. "See my son? In your condition? Don't be silly. You've not proven your worth yet." She waved Iona away, saying, "Go on with you. I'll tell you when you're worthy enough. Until then, don't worry about it."

Iona looked down at the shears she was handed and left. The way to the golden sheep twisted outside the temple of Aphrodite and down to Level 13 where Hermes kept watch over the herd. As she walked to where the sheep were grazing, she idly ate a few berries from the many fruit-laden bushes. Iona had no way of knowing when she'd eat next.

The area with the sheep was beautiful. The sheep grazed in a clearing almost completely surrounded by thorny bushes. There was a bubbling brook off to one side and shade trees dotted the perimeter. The sheep lazily nibbled at the grass or frolicked under the sun, the light shimmering off the curly golden wool.

"Well, this is just too easy," Iona muttered. There was no guard to be seen, no shepherd watching the flock. Feeling a little uneasy at the deceptive simplicity of the act, Iona made her way to the first sheep. She reached out and barely touched the coarse wool when the sheep bleated and turned toward her. The noise alerted his brethren and they all turned toward Iona. She expected them to run, but they advanced.

"This is not normal!" Iona scrambled back as the first sheep lunged at her. Sharp teeth snapped near her arm and she screamed. Iona got to her feet and started to run, but the sheep, sensing a meal, gave chase. One managed to get the hem of her dress, causing her to fall.

Iona screamed as sharp teeth clamped down on her leg. She turned over, the shears in her hand. If this was how she'd die, then she'd go fighting. She stabbed the nearest sheep through the eye. For a moment, the sheep seemed torn between eating her and their injured companion. She kicked her way free of the herd and limped toward a tree. She could hear tearing noises behind her as the sheep settled for a meal of their own kind.

Quickly climbing up the tree, Iona knew she couldn't sit up there forever. She was losing blood and would eventually have to descend to get help and food. Resting her head on the bark, she muttered, "This is not my day."

"That was a dumb move! Those sheep are meat-eaters! And you just go walking up to them? Are you suicidal?" Looking down the tree, she could see Pan slowly making his way up to her. The cloven hooves made it nearly impossible for him to climb up. He did not look happy. "What possessed you to do that?"

"Aphrodite. This was my task for the day; gather the golden wool. I knew it was too easy. I never thought I'd find carnivorous sheep." Iona pulled her dress up to examine her wound. Balancing on her branch, she managed to tear the hem of her dress and wrap it around the bloody wound.

Pan plopped himself on a branch near hers. "Those sheep are the same breed that the Golden Fleece came from. We breed them here, but only a few gods dare to come near them. You're lucky to have escaped with your life."

Iona leaned back, staring down at the sheep. Finished with their meal, they meandered back around the clearing and returned to their innocent sheep act.

"I take it Aphrodite never warned you," Pan said. His eyes were also locked on the corpse. All that was left was bone and a few clumps of golden wool. Suddenly he looked up. "What's Father doing here?"

Iona looked up to see a man flying down toward them. He set himself on Iona's branch and she could see that there were little flapping wings on his sandals. Even if Pan had not called him Father, she would have recognized Hermes.

"What is going on here? What did those sheep eat?" He paused and looked at Iona. "Who are you?"

"Father, let me introduce Iona Demarchis of Tiryns. She's a

friend," said Pan. "As for the sheep, you can place blame on Aphrodite. She sent Iona down here for some wool and didn't warn her about the sheep or tell her the trick. Poor girl nearly lost her leg down there."

Hermes gently took Iona's leg to study the wound. "That is bad. They took a great chunk from you. I doubt even Apollo can heal all of this. You'll limp for the rest of your life."

Tears stung Iona's eyes. Even if she got to see Eros, would he really want a scarred and crippled wife?

"Hey, it's not that bad. Come on, I'll take you to Apollo. Aphrodite can just wait another day for her wool," Hermes said. Suddenly his smile slipped. "Wait. Iona, was it? As in the mortal girl in love with Eros?"

"That's me." She wiped away at her tears. "All I want is to be with him again. Aphrodite wants me to prove my worthiness. That's why she sent me here. Even if I prove my worthiness, how can he love me when all I'm becoming is scarred?"

"Just your worthiness? That doesn't sound like her. It takes a lot to change Aphrodite's mind, and she's spread it around Olympus that she means for you to die."

"That's just the problem, Father," said Pan. "Iona deserves happiness. She's been through so much. She stayed with me and Sephie for a while, and we'll vouch for her if need be. She fought off one of the golden sheep. I was coming to save her, but she was already up the tree by the time I got here."

Iona looked down. "How did you know I'd be here?"

"Phobos sent me a warning." Pan snorted. "How weird is that? I never get a message from Phobos and suddenly he's sending me a heads up that you'll be here."

Iona smiled. "That was sweet of him. He's really sticking his neck out for me. He bet his immortality that I'll beat Aphrodite at this game."

"Phobos? As in the God of Fear, Phobos?" Hermes looked thunderstruck. He stroked his short beard, studying Iona. "Well, in that case, we'll just have to make sure you can get the wool."

"My shears are down there, and I have no idea how to get close to the sheep and use them," Iona said. "I have no authority to ask for this, but if you can give me a hint on how to gather the wool, I can do it myself."

"What is your reward for getting the golden wool," asked Hermes.

"Someday, I get to see Eros again," Iona said. She winced and stretched out her hurt leg. "However, I have a feeling that it won't be until I'm old and gray, assuming I live that long."

"Did Aphrodite promise this?"

"Yes. Well, in a way. She has been hinting that once I'm worthy, I can finally see him again."

Pan sighed. "Did she swear on the River Styx?"

"No. Why?"

Hermes said, "It's our most solemn vow. It's unbreakable. Any vow made on the River Styx must be kept. So, if you can get her to swear to let you see Eros by a certain point in time, she must comply. Breaking such a vow will have dire consequences."

"Such as?"

Hermes shrugged. "I don't know. No one's ever broken such a vow. Maybe you lose your godhead or something." He shuddered.

"Now, about the sheep," said Pan. "You can't just walk up to them. You've discovered that. But there is a way."

"What way?"

"You wait. They always take a nap in the afternoon sun. Go down then and just gather the wool that clings to the thorny bushes. Trust me, it's easier that way."

"What about shearing them," Iona asked. "Aphrodite clearly said to shear them."

"This is the only way," Hermes said. "You have to wait until they are asleep. Get what you can and run. Besides, the wool is metallic and you'd only ruin your shears."

Iona smiled. "Thank you both. I don't know how I could have done this without your advice. How can I repay you?"

"Those are dangerous words," Pan cautioned. "Never just say them. A less scrupulous god would take you for everything you have. Right Father?"

"Well, you can always do us a favor," said Hermes.

"Father!"

Hermes held up his hand. "It's nothing that will hurt the child. If I recall the rumors, she's a gardener, right? She knows the ways of the fields and flowers."

"I do." Iona looked down. "Well, I used to. I haven't had

much time to garden lately."

"Should you ever have a child that follows in your footsteps, send it here. Pan is the God of the Wild and Fields, and we can always use a gardener to help out."

"Of course," Iona said. "I see nothing wrong with that." She gave a little bow to Hermes, as best as she could on the branch. He smiled and suddenly launched himself in the air. In a few seconds, he was a dot on the horizon.

As Iona and Pan waited until the sheep went to sleep, she told him of all that happened since they had last talked. She told him of Deimos and the damage done to her by Ares and Enyo. She told him about the unlikely friendship with Phobos and her fear of Apollo. Above all, she told him of how much she wanted to see Eros again, but was afraid he'd reject her because of her recent wounds.

"Trust me, Eros won't turn you away," Pan said. "He loves you. I know this. I talk to Zephyrus on occasion and he has let me know that Eros is worried about you. Now that we know you're under Aphrodite's care, he can finally get you."

"He didn't know I was in Olympus?"

"No. Someone, probably Aphrodite, sent word to him that you were seen in some small village near Sparta. He's been searching for you."

When the sheep went to sleep, Iona slowly climbed down the tree. It hurt so much that she was worried she'd pass out. Once on the ground, she moved carefully to gather the wool. To her amazement, the clumps left in the bushes were a bagful. She got what she needed and left.

The Goddess of Love and Beauty was not happy to see Iona. "And you did this all by yourself," she asked.

"I gathered the wool by myself, yes." Iona showed her leg. "As you can see, it was not as easy as I assumed."

"And no one helped you?"

Iona shook her head. "No one helped me gather the wool. I pulled it from the bushes myself." She was not going to admit to receiving advice from Hermes and Pan. If Aphrodite could stretch the truth, she could do the same. As long as she didn't outright lie, all should be okay. And no one gathered the wool for her.

Aphrodite sniffed. "Very well. Since Apollo has yet to return for the day, you are still my servant. My next task is even easier.

Clean my chambers until they shine."

"As you wish, Lady Aphrodite. When will I see my husband?"

"When I say you are worthy."

"When will that be? How many tasks must I complete?"

Aphrodite appeared to think that over. "Well, I think just the one tomorrow and I'll have my answer. That is, assuming you survive."

"After my task tomorrow, you'll let me see Eros?"

"Yes, yes, whatever." Aphrodite waved Iona away.

"Swear it. Swear that you'll let me see Eros if I pass your test tomorrow."

Aphrodite rolled her eyes. "I swear it. Happy? Now get to cleaning my chambers."

"Swear on the River Styx."

Aphrodite narrowed her lovely eyes. All around her, her attendants paused in their fawning. A cold hush fell over the group. "What did you say?"

"I said swear on the River Styx," Iona said. "I want to hear you say it."

"Who told you about that? Who dared to tell you about the River Styx?" Aphrodite grabbed Iona by the front of her dress and shook her. "You weren't alone out there, were you? Who helped you? Who spilled our secrets?"

"I'll only tell you if you swear on the River Styx."

Aphrodite pushed Iona away. "You'll get no such promise from me. Be thankful that I am allowing you to live." With that, the Goddess of Love and Beauty swept from the room. Iona sighed and got to work cleaning the chambers. She should have known that it wouldn't be an easy task. Every time she swept the floors or polished the statues, one of Aphrodite's attendants would waltz in and dirty the room. Mud was tracked in, wine spilled, and sticky foods dumped all over the room. Iona knew that their goal was to make sure she failed in this task.

"Having fun, Iona?" She looked up to see Phobos walking into the chambers. He surveyed the mess with a small shake of his head.

"How are you feeling, Lord Phobos," asked Iona. She winced as her leg started to hurt her again. The pain was unbearable, but she'd suffer all of Hades for Eros.

"Isn't this a torture in Tartarus," asked Phobos as he planted himself on a freshly cleaned couch. "Cleaning a room that will never be cleaned? If not, it should be." He paused, thinking it over. "In fact, I think I'll mention it to Hades the next time I see him."

"I do not see it as torture," lied Iona. "I see it as a task that will bring me another step closer to Eros."

Phobos laughed. "A love you'll never see again. Do you really think that Mother will just allow you to go back to your happy little life? She'll never let you see Eros. In fact, you've lasted longer than most have thought. I'm really surprised."

"After all your talk about how I'm worthy, and you're surprised I'm still around?"

"Worthy is one thing. Mortal is another. I do think you're worthy of Eros. You'll do him a world of good. But I also know my mother. She'll kill you herself if her little tasks don't do it first. This place will be your tomb."

"Then I shall die with the love of Eros in my heart," said Iona. "I've come too far to just give up."

"That's why I like you, Iona. You don't give up." He was silent for a moment, and then he said, "What happened to your leg? I thought the Stasis room healed you."

"This is new. I got it from a golden sheep."

Phobos growled. "Mother did not send you to the golden sheep! By all the tortures in Hades!" He jumped up and stalked toward the door, muttering about how 'it' shouldn't be next. When he got to the door, he turned and looked back at Iona. "You know, he still asks about you. That foolish brother of mine is so deeply in love with you that it torments him. Knowing this will kill him."

Iona stopped in her cleaning. "Please, don't add to his pain. If you must tell him how I'm doing, please, coat your words in honey to lessen the blow. I don't want him worrying too much about me."

"He'll find out anyway," said Phobos. "And if not through me, then through someone who holds even less affection than I. No doubt, Father is ready to tell him every grisly detail of your injuries."

With that, Phobos left and Iona continued cleaning. She was finishing up when she realized something. The whole time Phobos was with her and for a while afterward, no one came in to bother her. She got the task done in time. Whether he meant to or not, he had helped her. She made a silent vow to set some flowers and offerings for him should she survive.

Chapter 35

The next day, Iona was brought before Aphrodite. The Goddess of Love and Beauty radiated anger. Her lips were pulled down in a pouty frown that caused wrinkles to crease her normally flawless face. Her blue eyes flashed with the promise of pain and torment and her skin was flushed red. As Iona was forced to kneel, she noted that the goddess' hands were clenched and shaking. This last task would be the death of her, of that Aphrodite would make sure.

"You've been a thorn in my side for a long time now," Aphrodite snarled. "You've caused me more pain than you are worth. You – you small mortal – thought yourself as my equal, set yourself up as a goddess among the people of Tiryns. And when that no longer slaked your thirst for power, you had the gall to seduce my simple-minded son. Just who do you think you are?"

"I never..." Iona protested, but Aphrodite cut her off.

"My beautiful son betrayed me for you. You, who are nothing! You, who embody all that is foul of the humans. Betrayed for the lowest, most vile creature to ever walk Space Station *Olympus*! You are not worthy of life! And yet, yesterday, you dared with such imprudence to stand before me and utter my son's name with your filthy lips."

Aphrodite started to pace, each step a shaky movement that betrayed her aggravation. She tried to speak, but her words caught in her throat. Finally, the Goddess screamed, "You called yourself his wife!"

One of the attendants pushed Iona lower on the floor. Taking their cue, she called out to Aphrodite. "Oh, Mighty Aphrodite, I am not worthy of being in your presence. I am but a lowly human, nowhere near the magnificence of your divine personage. Forgive me for my impudence, for I never meant to cause one as glorious as you any displeasure."

This caused Aphrodite to pause. The goddess glared down at Iona before turning away. She deposited herself on a pile of silk pillows and laid one dainty hand to her forehead. "You mortals are such fickle liars. You don't mean any of that. You knew what you were doing. You turned my darling Eros against me. He came storming into my chambers last night looking for you." The Goddess stole a glance over at Iona. "Oh, stop looking so hopeful! By now, he's talking to Ares and will stay out of my hair for the day. This task I am about to bestow will be your death. If you fail or receive help of any kind, I will toss you out into the cold embrace of space."

"And should I pass? Swear on the River Styx you will allow me to see Eros."

"Only if you live. Which I doubt. This is a task fit only for a god. Since you like to steal my divine identity, I figured this was a fitting punishment. Do you understand my terms, or shall I speak in slow, plain words?"

"I understand."

"Good. Your task is thus: Go to the mountain on the edge of Olympus Level Two and climb to the top. There, you will find it hollow. Climb down into the hole to where the River Crocus flows from here to Hades and gather for me a jug of water. You will have to get past the ever watchful dragon that guards it and be sure to not let a drop of the water touch you. If it splashes your skin, it is instant death."

Iona gulped. She knew this was designed to kill her, but a river that flowed into the Underworld and a deadly dragon? She was no hero.

"What will I carry the water in," Iona asked. Aphrodite smiled and motioned for one of her attendants to bring forth the jug. Iona could see the cracks on the side and knew that it was meant to leak the water so that she would be drenched.

"You'd best be on your way. You only have until sunset," Aphrodite said. "After that, I will just assume you died and will forever be out of my hair."

Iona picked up the jug and set out. As quickly as she could, she made it to the second sacred level of Olympus and got a ride to the mountain. It took her nearly a half a day just to get to the base of the mountain and tears of frustration pricked at her eyes. Aphrodite thought of everything to see to it that she failed. She would not have enough time to climb the mountain, do her task and get back. This was something not even Hercules could accomplish.

Thinking only of Eros, she climbed up the mountain. It was not as hard as she thought, and not as high, but her wounded leg throbbed and burned. Apollo healed it last night, but the forced journey and kneeling must have done something to bring the pain back. The way down inside the mountain was a bit harder and the path so narrow that she nearly fell into the darkness several times. With her heart pounding loudly and fast in her ears, she made it to the bottom. She could hear the sound of water and followed it.

Suddenly, she screamed as the floor gave way and she slide down the smooth rock to an open chamber.

"I told you Aphrodite was up to something," came Hephaestus' voice. "She really wanted the dragon up and running at full power."

"Well, what are you going to do," came a strong male voice. "This little girl has seen us."

Iona got up and checked to make sure the jug was still relatively together. Hephaestus was standing next to a man with long white hair and rich purple robes. A lightning bolt insignia was clasped at his right shoulder and his blue eyes were the color of a calm day.

"Lord Hephaestus," Iona gasped. She dropped in a quick bow. "I'm sorry for barging in. I didn't know. The floor..."

Hephaestus waved her apology aside. "Think nothing of it, Iona. Are you all right?"

"As well as I can be," she said. She checked to make sure she wasn't bleeding through the bandages on her leg. "Everything appears to be all right."

"What are you doing down here," the other man asked. "What could Aphrodite be thinking to send a mortal in these caves?"

"I am on a task to prove my worthiness. I must bring water from the River Crocus to Aphrodite before sunset. If I do, I may finally see my husband."

The man's blue eyes widened. "This is the mortal girl that Aphrodite has been complaining about? The one that Eros has fallen for?"

Hephaestus nodded. "The one she's been complaining about for over a year now."

"I swear, women hold grudges for the longest period of time. Do you know that Hera is still mad at me for forgetting our anniversary twenty years ago?"

"I think it was because you forgot because you were off

bedding some mortal woman."

The man snorted. "She should be used to it by now. Anyway, about this foolish quest of yours to get water..."

"It's for Aphrodite, and I must do it myself," said Iona.

"It would be easier if you let me do it for you," the man said. "I could turn myself into an eagle and fly down there."

"Oh, no! Please, I have to do it by myself."

"Are you sure?" The man squinted at her. "Not many would turn down the help of Zeus."

Iona's eyes widened and she quickly knelt on the hard ground at his feet. "I didn't know. Forgive my rudeness, Lord Zeus. I didn't recognize you."

"I'll forgive you this once," said Zeus. He helped her up and winked. "Anything for a pretty lady. You obviously had other things on your mind."

"Thank you, Lord Zeus."

"Try to not let the water touch you," Hephaestus said. "That's your only challenge."

Iona looked back at the hulking mechanical form of the dragon. "I was under the impression I would have to sneak past the dragon."

Hephaestus smiled. "Something tells me that the dragon will sleep through this. It's not your fault, Iona, if the dragon never wakes up. That will be on my head."

She quickly bowed to the two gods and went to the back of the chamber. She moved around the sleeping form of the dragon and headed to where the deafening noise of the river beckoned her. The water would be her greatest challenge and she only had a precious few moments to gather it and get back. How could she get the water into the jug and not have it drip on her? Even now, droplets of water flew into the air as the river rushed over rocks and twisted down a bend.

Looking around, Iona noticed an outcropping of rock above the river. It was just high enough to protect her from the water. If she could lean out and lower the jug from there, she could gather the water and remain dry. With no rope, but she did have a belt on her dress. She climbed up to the outcropping and took off her belt. Tying the belt to the jug, she lowered it into the water. Satisfied, she brought the jug up to her.

"Great. Now, how am I supposed to hold it," she muttered, noticing that the water leaked out of the sides and soak into her skin. Thinking it over, Iona took a quick stock of what she had with her. Nothing, basically. A belt, her dress, and a leaky jug that now needed another dip in the river. As she lowered the jug a second time, avoiding the puddle, she got a brilliant idea. Pulling the jug back up, she tore off the bottom of her skirt and quickly wrapped it around the jug. It wasn't perfect, but it did help stop the leaking.

Indecently dressed, she made her way slowly down. Hephaestus and Zeus met her at the chamber and brought her through the PortMat back to Olympus. Thanks to them, she made it back just before the sun set. She completed her task.

Aphrodite was not amused.

"Who helped you," Aphrodite demanded, glaring over at Hephaestus. "You must have received help from someone!"

"No one. I had no one help me. I made the journey alone and got the water by myself."

"You had help coming back," Aphrodite said. "That counts and means you cheated in your task."

"She was going our way," Zeus said. "She already completed the hard parts of the task. And she didn't ask us to bring her back. It was a gift."

Angered, Aphrodite snatched up the jug. "And how did you get the water without getting any on you? And, Zeus, if you helped her with this..."

"I lowered the jug with my belt and tied my skirt around it to keep from getting wet. No one helped me with it. The only advice I got was from you."

"I think it's obvious what she did," said Zeus. "Look at her. The poor girl is practically naked."

"Stop oogling her," Aphrodite snapped. She turned on Hephaestus. "What about the dragon? She was supposed to face a dragon!"

He shrugged. "My mistake. It was asleep."

"I want to see Eros," Iona said. "You promised me."

"You had help," Aphrodite said. "That voids the contract, little mortal."

Aphrodite turned to leave when Zeus called out. "Let her see Eros. We know that the wounds he sustained here in Olympus were not her doing, and she has suffered enough for him. Let her see her husband."

"He's married to Psyche. She can't call him husband."

"Then call me his lover," Iona protested. "I've all that you've asked of me. You, Lady Aphrodite, of all the gods should understand love. I love Eros with all my heart. All I want is to be with Eros. Please, Lady Aphrodite, as the Goddess of Love and Beauty, show compassion on two people who want only to love each other."

"I don't have to understand anything from you," Aphrodite snarled.

Seeing no other recourse, Iona burst out, "You promised on the River Styx!"

"I did no such thing! She's a liar!"

"Today, before you sent me out, I told you to swear on the River Styx that I can see Eros. You said, only if I live. That should count as a promise."

"It wasn't on the River Styx!"

"Enough!" Zeus rubbed his head. "Promises mean a lot to us gods, Aphrodite. It is shameful that you only think that one made on the River Styx is the only one you must honor. She's had a long day. I say, let Iona meet with Eros tomorrow. For the night, she shall be my guest."

Angered, Aphrodite bowed to Zeus' wishes. As she swept past Iona, she hissed, "This isn't over yet."

Chapter 36

Iona awoke the next morning feeling as light as a bird. Today she would finally see Eros again! Happy was too shallow of a word to describe how she felt. Zeus left her some clothes to wear, though she felt it was probably Hera who actually left the clothes. Hephaestus gave her some jewelry to wear. Wearing her gifts, she would see Eros dressed as a queen. Nothing – not even Aphrodite's cruelness – could ruin this day.

Lethia arrived at her door, sour-looking as ever. There was sadness around her eyes and Iona remembered what Zephyrus said about her maid. She was once in love with Eros as well. To serve the woman who replaced her must be torture. She couldn't imagine what Lethia was going through.

"Lady Iona, are you ready?"

"Ready as I'll ever be. I'm so nervous, I feel almost sick."

Lethia nearly smiled. "Try to not be sick on your husband. I'm sure that would ruin his day." She took Iona's arm and led her down the glowing white marble halls.

"Have you seen Eros? Is he doing all right? Has his wounds healed?"

"Lord Eros is doing fine. He recovered well and has been traveling. He arrived back here just yesterday. I'm sure he'll be pleased to have you visit him."

"I've missed him so much," Iona said. "Every day without him has been torture."

Lethia hummed to herself. Turning one corner, they passed by Aphrodite. Iona was surprised to see the normally beautiful goddess looking positively haggard. Her golden hair was in knots and there were bags under her eyes. Her cheeks appeared sunken and her clothes were stained and wrinkled.

"What is wrong with her," Iona asked the moment they were out of earshot of the goddess. What could possibly have happened between last night and today to change Aphrodite so much?

"Lady Aphrodite isn't feeling well. The strain of her sons' betrayals and being ganged up on by the other gods last night has taken their toll. She was outwitted by you, Lady Iona, and that has stung her pride. I'd watch my step around her if I were you."

Iona was silent. She felt that Aphrodite got what she deserved, but she dared not voice that opinion.

Suddenly, Lethia stopped and turned to Iona. "You know, if you were to help out Aphrodite, I'm sure she'd forgive you and welcome you as Eros' wife."

"What about Psyche? I've been told that she's his wife."

"Have you ever met Psyche?"

"No. Isn't that odd? I would have thought that if she was around, I'd have met her by now. Everyone seems to know about her, but I've never seen her. After all, if she's Eros' wife, why hasn't she confronted me?"

Lethia shrugged. "Psyche is dying. Eros doesn't know it, but he's soon to be a widower. She knows about you, but there is nothing she can do. You are going to be his next wife."

"And what can I do to get on Aphrodite's good side?"

Lethia smiled. "I'm so glad you asked me about that. If you were to travel to the Underworld and bring back a bit of Persephone's beauty, it would ease Aphrodite's pains and endure you to her heart."

Iona flinched. "Travel to the Underworld? How can I do that? The only way one gets there is to die."

"Not so. Hercules, Orpheous and Theseus all traveled to the Underworld without dying. And they eventually left. You can do the same. And, Psyche once made the trip as well to do the same thing you will be doing. That was how she won over her mother-in-law."

"Would Psyche tell me how she did it if I asked her?"

"We'll see." Lethia brought Iona to Eros' rooms. Inside she was greeted by Anteros and Zephyrus.

"Iona! I missed you!" Zephyrus scooped up Iona and twirled her around in a strong hug. "How have you fared?"

"I survived. That was all I could do."

The moment Zephyrus put her down, she was swept up by Anteros in another bear hug. "I thought we lost you forever when I realized that you had been sent elsewhere. The moment I heard you were up here, I told Eros."

"It was scary. At first, I thought you meant to send me there, but it became apparent quickly that something went gone wrong. I did all I could to get back."

Anteros let her go, whispering in her ear, "I heard you were injured to the point of being put in the Stasis Chamber. Are you all right?"

"Yes. I healed and then went and got hurt all over again."

"I noticed you were limping."

"I'll be fine. Just a little accident."

"If you two are done, I'd like to see my wife." Eros' voice interrupted them and Iona felt her heart skip a beat. She turned to see her husband entering the room. His soft brown curls looked longer and stubble darkened his chin. He was skinnier and she felt so guilty for not thinking of how much he must have suffered.

"Oh, Eros," she cried and threw herself into his arms. She knew this was where she belonged.

"My beautiful wife. I have missed you so much," he muttered over her hair.

"Every day without you was torment," Iona said before she kissed him. She drank of him like a thirsty woman in the desert. He was her oasis, and she was never going to let him go.

"My lovely Iona," Eros whispered, tracing a finger over her scar. "I heard about the baby. I am so sorry. Can you ever forgive me?"

"Forgive you? It was my fault, my love. I should be asking for your forgiveness."

Eros shook his head. "No. I turned off the PortMat. Your dropping out and losing the baby was my fault. I should have realized that you followed me."

"I should have waited for you at the house instead of jumping in after you," Iona protested. "I had no idea what the light was or what it did. It was foolish of me to follow a god through the device. It was my fault."

"You both are innocent in this. It was a tragedy, but neither of you are to blame," said Anteros. "You forgive each other, right?"

"Yes. As long as she forgives me, I can forgive her," Eros said. Iona nodded and ducked her head as tears threatened to flow.

"I'd forgive you for anything," she whispered. "I love you so much."

Eros smiled and gave Iona another hug before finally letting her go. They sat on a pristine white couch across from their friends. She wanted to know what had happened since they parted, and Eros wanted to make sure she was all right. None of them wanted to believe that Phobos stood up for Iona, despite her insisting that it was true.

"There is a significant matter we need to discuss," said Lethia, entering the room. It wasn't until she walked in did Iona realize that the cold woman left her. Where Lethia had been during the happy reunion was a mystery.

"What important matter," asked Eros. Iona noticed that Lethia's cold gaze was on her and she knew what the woman wanted to address.

"I, uh, I need to know how to get into the Underworld," Iona said. "Eros, my love, can you help me?"

"Why do you want to go there? The Underworld is a dangerous place. And Hades is there. Don't get me wrong, I have nothing against my uncle, but he doesn't like to let go of his subjects easily. Once you enter his domain, you are his."

"Lethia gave me some advice before coming here today about how to soothe your mother's anger. I want to be part of your life, Eros, but I don't want to spend all of my life fighting and hiding from Aphrodite. If I can get on your mother's good side, it will make our lives a lot easier."

"She's made you her enemy," Eros said. "My mother rarely forgives anyone. Even the women she takes into her entourage aren't forgiven."

"What about Psyche? Lethia told me that your first wife did the same thing to get on your mother's good side. She was forgiven, right?"

Eros looked over at Lethia. "She said that, did she?" He sighed and rubbed his temples. "Mother didn't forgive Psyche, per se. She did, however, call a truce that has lasted throughout the marriage. That's the best you can hope for."

"How would going into the Underworld put Iona in Aphrodite's good graces," Anteros asked. He was staring at Lethia with a mixture of anger and realization. Iona had the feeling he knew the answer already.

"She can bring back a box of Persephone's beauty to freshen up Aphrodite. That's what Psyche did."

Eros looked alarmed. He pulled Iona closer to him, protecting her from Lethia's plan. "No! I refuse! Iona, I forbid you to even think of going to the Underworld. Hades is for the dead, not someone so full of life as you."

Anteros and Lethia stared at each other, locked in a silent battle of wills. While Eros vetoed any decision to allow Iona to leave his side, his brother and Lethia fought with looks and slight nods. Finally, Anteros sighed, looking down in defeat.

"Let her go," he said tiredly. "We can make sure she makes it back alive. She is already friends with Persephone, so she has an advantage."

"No! I won't let her go into the Underworld."

"If she doesn't go of her own accord, she will be forced into it," Lethia stated coldly.

Iona blinked. "What?"

"We are here for her," Anteros said. "Zephyrus can get her there safely. Lethia can talk to Psyche to find out all the tricks."

"I'll be careful," Iona promised. "Please, Eros. I have to do this."

"Why? Why would you have to go to the Underworld," Eros whined.

"I don't really know. The moment Lethia mentioned it, I just knew I had to do it."

"I think it's a great idea." Iona and Eros jumped as Phobos entered the rooms. Iona was the only one put at ease to see the God of Fear.

"What do you want, Phobos," Eros asked. "This isn't a reunion for you."

"It should be. I've been on Iona's side for a long time. Without me, she'd be dead by now."

Iona nodded. "He's helped me so much and stood up for me against his father."

Eros sighed. "Fine, whatever. Why do you think this is a good idea, Phobos? It's not like you to help me."

Phobos plopped himself down on a seat, looking out of place in his dark leather armor. Everyone else wore flowing light-colored robes and gowns, and he was a black spot in the room. His bright eyes bore holes in Eros' soul. "It was bound to happen. Do you really think Mother will be pleased with anything less than the most dangerous task ever thought of? She's tried too hard to kill Iona, and your wife has foiled Mother's plans each step of the way. Not even

Father and Enyo could get rid of Iona. She's a fighter, and I believe she can even tame Hades." He grinned. "Though, one small change in plans: I will be the one to escort her. Hades forbid if Father decides to make her trip permanent. Zephyrus will not be equipped to handle that."

"And you will be," asked Zephyrus.

"Naturally." Phobos finally turned his gaze to Iona. "You boys should have seen her stand up to Father. She even took a shot at him! I never said this before, Eros, but I think she'll do you some good. Though, Iona should learn how to handle a gun better."

Eros rubbed his temples. "Okay, you can escort her. Lethia," he stressed the maid's name, "do you have the information on how to get in to and out of the Underworld?"

"I took the liberty of getting that information while you all were hugging and crying," Lethia said with an icy smile. "First, she'll need two drachma coins and bread soaked in honey. A whole loaf, Lady Iona, not just a slice."

"What for?"

"The drachmas are your fare across the River Styx. Charon will need one to take you to Hades, and one to take you out. The bread is to keep Cerebus quiet."

Anteros nodded. "Dog toys and a juicy steak will work just as good, but the bread is tradition. Sometimes, tradition is all we have left."

"Okay, money and bread with honey," said Iona. "What else?"

"Don't stray from your path," Lethia warned. "Charon will set you on the road to the judges. Once you start walking, you cannot deviate for any reason."

"You have such a good heart, Iona, and you'll be tempted to leave the path," said Anteros. "If you take so much as a step off the path, it'll mean your death."

"I won't leave the path," she promised. "Is that all?"

Lethia shook her head. "There is just one more thing," she said. "You will run into the spirits of the dead. Most likely, your sisters will be among them as they were not buried properly. That means, they do not have the passage to get across and will be waiting for you. Do not give in to them, Lady Iona. You did nothing wrong and must remain strong."

Iona's green eyes widened. "But, I killed them. They would not have died if I never tried to embarrass them with that stupid story. How can I face them now? Can't I bring extra drachmas to give to them?"

"No," said Anteros. "Iona, you did nothing wrong."

"I agree," said Phobos. "You really didn't kill them, Iona. All you did was tell a little lie. If they hadn't been so greedy for the riches they believed you possessed, they would not have died. If you give them passage across the Styx, they will only be greeted by a greater torment than just waiting for passage. You'd be doing them a mercy by leaving them there."

"The same thing happened to Psyche," said Lethia. "Her sisters were jealous of the riches she gained while married to Eros, and lusted for the power of a god. Like you, she told her sisters a small lie and they died because of it. Facing them was the hardest thing she had to do, but she did it for Eros. Will you be weaker than she and back down? Give in to your demons, and you will never see Eros again."

"I understand," said Iona.

Phobos shifted in his seat. "I can get why Lethia knows so much about the Underwold, but how do you know so much, Anteros? I don't think you've ever been there."

With all eyes on him, Anteros refused to answer.

Chapter 37

"Are you ready," Phobos asked. Iona nodded, watching the area where the white beam of the gods would soon appear. She made sure the bag over her shoulder was steady. Inside was a loaf of fresh bread soaked in honey, some rubber balls and a few dog treats. Her two drachmas were hidden as earrings so there would be no way she could lose them or tip off the wandering souls that she carried money.

Phobos flipped a few switches and the machine hummed to life. Iona shifted from one foot to the next, waiting for the beam to appear. This was it. She was really going to the Underworld and would face all the minions of Hades for the man she loved. Only a few ever returned from the depths of the Underworld alive, but they were brave, virile men such as Aeneas, Theseus, Hercules and Orpheus. Though all made it back to the living, they paid a price.

As the light appeared, Iona wouldn't help but wonder what price she would have to pay to leave the Underworld?

"The PortMat is ready," Phobos said. "After this, you will be on your own. Are you sure you're ready?"

"I'm as ready as I'll ever be," Iona said.

Phobos took her by her shoulders. "I meant everything I said. You'll do Eros some good. I remember when he married Psyche, and she was this quiet mousey woman who didn't mind being locked behind closed doors. The few times I interacted with her, I could see hatred in her eyes. That doesn't bother me, I don't have much a brotherly relationship with Eros. I don't want one, either. He can stay as Mother's golden boy, and I enjoy my life at my Father's side."

"Your pep talk can use some help."

"I think I may need your help. I've never asked anyone for help before, but I think you may be it. And that feeling makes me believe even more that you will be the best wife to Eros in all the ages."

"What kind of help do you need?"

Phobos looked down and sighed. "Tomorrow, Demeter is planning on presenting her new daughter to the gods. We have to stop it. I refuse to allow her to continue to raise my child as her own.

I have to do something, and I want you to help me. If I succeed, I will need a woman to help raise my daughter."

"I'll do everything I can," Iona promised. She gave her brother-in-law a hug and walked into the beam of light. In the blink of an eye, she found herself at the entrance of the Underworld. Unlike any place she ever seen, it was at first a large empty space of metal floors and walls. A small dome on one wall swiveled toward her and a red light shot out, scanning over her body. Suddenly, the room changed into the most depressing scenery of glittering obsidian rocks, a murky fast-flowing river and pale, colorless shades wandering aimlessly on the shore.

Iona pulled her shoulder bag closer as she ventured into this new world. Pale ghosts mingled around her, both oblivious to her presence and still able to not bump into her. She recognized some as dearly departed neighbors, street venders who vanished, and her betrothed who had the poor grace to die and start this whole predicament. She even spotted a few old pets among the humans.

Fear curled in her heart. This was the first test they warned her about. She knew what was coming, and she was afraid. Keeping her head down, she made her way toward the river. If she could bypass this test and just get on Charon's boat, she would feel so much better. All she needed to do was avoid Philomena and Errita's vengeful ghosts.

From behind Iona came a voice that caused her to freeze. "Well, well, look at what finally decided to show up. Philomena, see who came to visit us?"

Iona slowly turned and found herself facing her sisters. Death had not been kind to them. No longer able to dye her hair or wear fancy wigs, Philomena's hair became its natural dark brown color. It hung in tangled locks over her shoulders. She was dirty and ratty with torn clothes and tarnished jewelry.

Errita fared no better. Her light brown hair now hung in stringy clumps around her face, her clothes were stained with inks and dyes and strings of yarn twisted out of her skin like blood-red snakes. When she smiled, her teeth were yellowed and misshapen.

"Enjoying the view, dear sister," Philomena sneered. "Seeing what your handiwork has wrought?"

"I didn't do this to you," Iona whispered. "You did it to yourselves."

"Did you hear that?" Errita laughed and it sounded like she was gurgling broken glass. "We did this to ourselves. Tell me, Iona, how could we have done this to ourselves?"

"She must think we suddenly got a desire to go playing in airlocks out of the blue," added Philomena. "She actually thinks she's innocent in all of this."

"I am innocent. You went in the airlock out of greed and envy. I didn't make you do anything."

"Yes you did! You made us believe that we would be rewarded by going in there. You," Philomena cried and jabbed one boney finger at Iona, "put the idea in our head. It is your fault."

"You manipulated us. You wanted us to die," added Errita.

"No! I never wanted you to die!" Iona took a step back. "I wanted to embarrass you. That was all! I didn't know the airlock wouldn't open. You were just supposed to look foolish sitting there. That was all, I swear!"

"Liar! You wanted us out of the way," Philomena cried. She and Errita started to circle Iona. "You were always jealous of us, weren't you? You wanted our wealth and power and beauty! Tricking people into worshiping you as Aphrodite wasn't enough! Marrying a god wasn't enough! You wanted to destroy us!"

"No! Not true! I was happy for both of you!"

"You hated us. We had everything you wanted: money, love, and position. You wanted to ruin us!" Their voiced blended together as they circled her faster. Soon, it was like one monster with the features of her sisters.

"You wanted us dead! You came up with the plan to kill us!"

"You watched Errita die. You would have watched me die!"

"No! Not true! You're lying! I never wanted your deaths!" Iona covered her ears and sank to the black rock floor. Her sisters' words taunted her and a small part of her wondered if it couldn't all be true. She always believed she loved her sisters, but did she despise them deep down? After all, she also always believed they loved her, but at the first chance they got, they betrayed her. Not only was it their advice that caused her to betray Eros and lose her baby, but then they both left their husbands to be with *her* husband. Was she really jealous of her sisters all this time, so much so that she'd unconsciously manipulate their murders? Was it revenge for Eros or her own evilness finally showing itself?

Philomena reached down and yanked Iona up by her hair. "You can make things right with us. Give us your drachma so one of us can make it across. You don't really want to make us wait a hundred years, do you?"

"Don't leave us on this shore to become vengeful ghosts," hissed Errita. "You were the reason why we didn't get a proper burial. Make it right, Iona, or we will claw our way back to the living and haunt you!"

"I didn't kill you," Iona protested. "It's not my fault!"

"Give us your bribe for the ferryman," Philomena said. "Give it to me! My body is floating in space because of you!"

"No, give it to me! You stole everything from me, Iona. You watched me die and you did nothing!" Errita pulled at Iona's pockets, trying to find the drachma.

"It wasn't my fault! I didn't know the airlock was going to open." She sobbed. "I tried, Errita, I really did. I told you to open the door and come out. I begged you! You didn't listen to me. Your death is not my fault! Neither of your deaths. I'm innocent in this!"

"You didn't try hard enough! You watched me die! I saw you, Iona. You smiled as I was swept into space."

Iona choked back on a sob. "No. You're lying."

"You owe me the most! Give me your drachma!" Errita pulled out the bread and tossed it aside. Finding no money, she threw the bag to the ground in disgust.

Iona pushed away from her sisters and grabbed her bag before running off. She knew she had two drachmas, and that was enough for her sisters, but she would have no way of making it across the river if she handed them over. She would not wait a hundred years for Charon to ferry her for free. If her choices were to set her sisters free and never see Eros again, or be selfish for her own happiness and leave them on the shore, she was going to be selfish. She was sure she could talk to Persephone about her sisters when she reached the palace.

"I did nothing to you! You did it to yourself. You killed your own husband, Philomena, and you refused to open the door, Errita. I was absolved by Apollo! Your deaths are no longer on my hands! Stay here and rot!"

Before her eyes, her sisters started to change. Philomena's skin hardened to a blue shell, her hair fell out and her teeth elongated into fangs. Iona gasped as her eyes glowed red with blood lust. Errita growled as she shifted too. Her skin turned dark gray and leathery wings exploded from her back. Her hair came alive, withering like a pit of snakes and her hands contorted into claws.

Iona screamed and ran. She could hear the creatures behind her, feel their hot, rancid breath on her neck. She ran blindly through the sea of pale shades. Each time she passed through a shade, she felt like a wind of bone-chilling cold shoot through her soul and steal her breath away. For a moment, she feared if she passed through too many ghosts and never breathe again.

Iona thought she was heading for the river, but the ghosts had her all spun around. With a small scream, she managed to stop before she ran into a wall. She turned and ducked as Philomena clawed at the rocks. Pebbles fell on Iona before she scrambled away from the monsters. Heading back to the river, she could see the ferryman on his way. She had to get on that boat!

Something grabbed Iona's hair, causing her to fall back. She turned and stared in horror at the shade behind her.

"Oh, by Zeus' mercy! Zotikos!"

He looked much like he did when she last saw him. His robes were stained with blood and torn where Philomena stabbed him. The dagger still stuck out of his chest and his hollow eyes stared at her accusingly.

"You killed me," he rasped. "You did this to me."

"Not I," whispered Iona. "Philomena did this to you."

"If you never told her to go to your husband, this would never have happened. You killed me!"

Iona pulled herself free. Now the monsters caught up to her. All three of her nightmares advanced on her as she backed away. They repeated their claims that she murdered them all. A swift look at the river confirmed that Charon now anchored at the shore and was bringing in shades who could pay his fee.

"You want a drachma? Go fetch!" Iona reached into a pocket and found an old button. She threw it as hard as she could and ran to the boat. She could hear the monsters scramble for it.

Iona ran to the boat and jumped inside. Charon turned to her, his skeletal hand held out for his payment. His appearance startled her. He was tall and thin, his skin shrunken to his bones until he was nothing more than a skeleton. His rotting clothes hung in strips off his emancipated body, barely covering him.

"Your fare," he asked in a strange, echoing voice. He clicked his boney fingers against his palm.

Iona took off one of her earrings and placed it in his hand. He bit the coin and nodded. Placing his oar in the water, he pushed off from the shore.

"You're not getting away!" Philomena jumped into the boat, back to her more human form.

"Your fare," said Charon.

"She has it," Philomena declared. She reached out to grab Iona's other earring.

"I have nothing of yours," Iona growled. She pushed her sister out of the boat and grabbed Charon's oar. The moment Philomena surfaced, Iona brought the oar down on the top of her head with a sickening crack. "I used to love you and Errita! I gave you everything you wanted! And you betrayed me! You wanted my husband and you were willing to have me die to get him! I know you sold me out to Aphrodite, Philomena. You two can wait your hundred years. I owe you nothing!"

Charon took his oar back and guided the boat through the dark waters of the River Styx. Iona watched as her sisters glared at her from the shore. Their dead eyes never left the boat as it moved down the river. Even when Iona could no longer see them, she could feel their eyes.

The boat ride was peaceful, despite traveling through the Underworld. The shades in the boat were silent and still, and Iona felt like she could finally think. She checked her bag to see if there was anything left. The bread was gone, but the dog toys and a few treats were still there. At least she will still have her bribe for Cerebus. She passed the first test, and was a step closer to her goal.

Iona watched as the far shore came into view. The rocks looked ordinary enough, but she could already make out the shadow of Cerebus. She reached into the bag and pulled out the treats. They would have to pass under Cerebus to get to the shore. From the stories she's heard, the great three-headed dog would reach down and snap up the souls of the dead. She was ready for him, as long as he didn't eat her.

As they passed under the shadow, Iona could see three pairs of red, glowing eyes. The rumbling growl of Cerebus vibrated through her body, numbing her to the bone. The heads darted down as she threw the treats up in the air. A quick prayer to Hades escaped her lips moments before the heads snapped up the treats. Cerebus retreated back into the darkness and the boat landed safely on the shore. The shades departed and faded from sight.

"This is your path, Iona of Tiryns," said Charon. A path appeared as small lights lit up on either side, winding its way deeper into the Underworld. "Down there are the judges. You must face them, Iona of Tiryns. Do not leave the path."

Iona took a deep breath and started walking. Along the path, she met an old woman. The woman was spinning at a loom and called for Iona to help her. Iona nearly took a step off the path when the warning rang through her head. She remained on the path, ignoring all other calls for help.

Before long, she found herself standing before three tall pulpit of the judges. If she were dead, this would be where her soul would be sorted. Just beyond the judges, she could see the path split into three directions: the Asphodel Meadows where most people went, the Elysian Fields for the good, and Tartarus for those receiving punishment. Off to the left, she saw a sign and lift doors indicating the passage for the privileged heroes who could ascend to the Isle of the Blessed.

Taking a deep breath, Iona stood on the lit square under the pulpits to stand trial and ask for guidance to see Persephone.

Chapter 38

A voice boomed down from the pulpit, startling Iona. "State your name and prepare to be judged!"

"I'm not here for judgment," Iona announced. "I need to see Queen Persephone. My name is Iona Demarchis of Tiryns. She knows me."

There was the sound of ruffling papers. She stood on her tiptoes to try and see the famous judges, having heard so much about them growing up. The pulpit started to lower, bringing the three judges into view. King Minos of Cnossus was a dark-haired man with intense black eyes and a thin, black beard. His robes were equally dark, threaded with silver strands. His brother, King Rhadamanthus of Crete, had dark red hair and burning gray eyes. He was clean shaven and his robes, like his brother's, were woven with gold instead of silver. King Aeacus of Aegina looked out of place among these stern judges. With lovely dark skin and a boyish face, he appeared too happy to be among the dead. His robes were pale gray and embroidered with tiny crystals that sparkled under the torchlight.

"No one just waltzes into the Underworld and sees Queen Persephone," said Minos. "You are not on our list."

"I am not dead, if that's what you mean," Iona said. "I'm here on official business from Lady Aphrodite and must see Queen Persephone."

Rhadamanthus shuffled a few papers on the pulpit, muttering under his breath as he stopped every once in a while to peer closer at a paper. "What is your mission," he asked in a bored tone.

"I am here to ask Queen Persephone for a box of her beauty for Aphrodite."

This got their attention as the three judges gathered around each other and whispered. Every once in a while, one of the judges would look down at her before going back to the private conference. Finally, they sat back. Aeacus said, "We will allow you to go on. You'll need a guide. Do not leave the path. When you reach the palace of King Hades and his dismal queen, do not overstep your bounds, mortal. Do not eat the food of the Underworld, or you will stay here forever."

Iona nodded. "All right. Who will be my guide?"

"Melinoe can guide you to the palace," Minos said. Seeing the fear creep over Iona, he smiled grimly and added, "I see you've heard of our dreary princess. Of course, if you don't agree with our choice, you can turn around now and leave."

"I will do anything to finish this," Iona said. "I accept."

Rhadamanthus waved his hand and the shadows parted. Iona's heart beat faster as a figure walked out. Melinoe was rumored to be the daughter of Persephone, though her father's identity was a little murky. He was either Hades or Zeus disguised as Hades. After meeting Persephone, Ione looked a little into the myths surrounding her new friend. Melinoe was barely a footnote, but an especially dark and foreboding footnote.

Melinoe, the Queen of Ghosts, was a figure of pure horror. The trunk of her body was dark, representing her mother and the gloomy Underworld. However, her limbs slowly lightened so that her fingers were nearly invisible with light. Iona wondered if the coloring also went down to her toes, but was too scared to look. Some said the lightened color represented Zeus, while others said it was because of Persephone's own duel nature. That is, if one talked about Melinoe at all. Much like Hades, respectable people did not utter that name for fear of drawing the attention of that particular deity. Crowding around her, like adoring children, were hundreds of dark shadows; the ghosts of the Underworld.

Melinoe looked over at Iona. For a moment, her body shivered and became like static before wavering back into solidity. Her dark lips curled up in a cruel smile. "Follow me," Melinoe said, her voice as scratchy as static.

Iona followed the Queen of Ghosts as she set off on the path toward Tartarus. The ghosts danced around the both of them, tugging at their dresses and hair for attention. Melinoe reached out on occasion to pet a dark shadow as it darted around her body. Iona tried to not touch any of them for each time they brushed against her skin, her mind was flooded with images of the horrors of each ghost's existence.

As they entered the realm of Tartarus, the screams of the condemned echoed in Iona's ears. All around her were the horrors of hell. Melinoe took delight in pointing out the various torments like a macabre tour guide.

"Over on the left, you can see Tityus," Melinoe said, indicating a giant who was tied down with vultures pecking out his liver. "His crime was against Hera, and his punishment is to be in forever torment. Much like Prometheus, his liver is eaten, only to have it grow back by the next day."

"And, over on the right, we have Salmoneus." Melinoe's voice became hard as she said, "He had the audacity to copy Zeus. Have you ever heard of his story?"

"No, I don't think so," Iona said. "I am not a big fan of ghost stories."

Melinoe's laugh sounded like the swirling of dried leaves in a cemetery. "Ghost stories? That's cute. No, Salmoneus is not a ghost story. He was a king and thought himself above the gods. He wanted his people to worship him like Zeus so he drove his chariot across a brass bridge to emulate the sound of thunder and have sparks fly like lightning. Zeus killed him, of course. You can see his punishment. Frankly, I feel like he got off too light."

Iona looked to find a man lying on an altar. Above him hung a large boulder that looked as if it would fall at any second. The man watched the rock with terror-filled eyes, groaning each time the rock would move.

They passed many other inhabitants of Tartarus: Izion, tied to a flaming wheel for his crime of shedding kindred blood and then attempting to violate Hera; the Danaides, forty-nine sister who slew their bridegrooms on their wedding night, forced to gather water in leaking buckets and fill a cauldron that would never be filled; and Tatalus, who fed the gods the flesh of his own children, was punished to be forever hungry with food and drink just out of his reach. Some of the inhabitants turned in their tasks to watch Iona pass while other ignored her. One of the Danaides called out to her, pleading for help. Iona wanted to help them, every fiber of her being strained to leave the path Melinoe walked and offer assistance, but the knowledge of failing in her task kept her away.

Beyond Tartarus, Melinoe led Iona to a large, dark-stone palace. The five rivers of the Underworld all flowed and blended underneath, creating a castle of imaginable power. Beyond the onyx gates was a beautiful garden filled with dark flowers that Iona had never seen before.

"This is where I leave you. I do not enter the home of my mother," Melinoe said. She turned and left, her eager ghosts floating around her until they all vanished into the darkness.

Iona slowly walked up to the grand doors. No living creature ever walked these hallowed halls and left without paying a price. Iona wondered what price she would pay.

Chapter 39

The doors to the Palace of Hades were carved from the darkest woods known to man and lacquered to a brilliant black sheen. Little images of torment had been lovingly produced in the wood and accented with gold and silver. The door knocker was made of gold with chips of colored gemstones inlaid. It was fitting for the God of the Underworld to show the treasures of his realm and not just the horror.

Hesitantly, Iona used the knocker to announce her presence. After a few minutes, the doors opened to reveal a lovely waif-like woman dressed in a faded green chiton. Dead leaves were wrapped around her head and used as a belt. She looked like a nymph, but the gloom of Hades had sapped her of her Spring beauty.

"What do you want?" Apparently, the gloom of Hades also sapped her of her manners.

"I am here to see Queen Persephone. My name is Iona Demarchis of Tiryns. She knows me."

The woman grunted and shut the door in Iona's face. Iona waited a while, but as the minutes ticked away, she started to wonder if the nymph went to talk to Persephone or just left her there. As she reached up to knock again, the door opened and Persephone was standing there.

The difference between the Goddess of the New Spring and the Queen of the Underworld was apparent. Persephone became paler and a bit thinner down in Hades. Gone were her pretty Spring-colored dresses and wheat stalks woven in her dark hair. Instead, she wore an elegant black dress and was decked out in silver and red-stoned jewelry. She looked older and more mature than she had when Iona last seen her on Level 14.

"Iona? What are you doing here?" Persephone drew her in with a hug. "How did things go with your family? Oh! Oh, my! What happened to your face?"

"It's a long story, I'm afraid. I -" Iona hesitated, placing one hand on the scar on her face. How could one tell the Queen of the Underworld she needed her beauty? Iona felt like she was just there to take and not being a good friend. "I wish I were here just for a visit, but I am also here on a mission. I need a small box of your beauty to bring to Aphrodite."

Persephone looked disappointed. "Is that all? I can't believe she's making you come all the way here for that. Honestly, with all of that woman's thundering about, stating how she's the most beautiful in all Space Station *Olympus*, she has the audacity to send you here for *my* beauty?"

"She, uh, She didn't send me," Iona said. "I sent myself."

"Where did you get the idea to ask me for beauty?"

"Lethia told me that if I got Aphrodite a bit of your beauty, it would help mend the bridge between us. I want to spend the rest of my life with Eros, and to do so, I cannot be fighting with his mother all the time. I know that Eros adores Aphrodite, so I want to at least have a truce between us."

"Lethia? That name sounds familiar. Who is she?"

"She's the stewardess of Eros' home. For a time, she served as my maid and taught me how to run the house in just the right way. At times, I think we might have been friends."

Persephone looked thoughtful. "What does she look like?"

Iona described her and Persephone frowned. "I see," was all the Queen of the Underworld said. Then she smiled and pulled Iona further into the home. "Come! You are just in time to sit for dinner. You must be exhausted and hungry from your journey. My husband will be so delighted to see you."

Iona gulped. "You mean, actually sit with the Lord of the Underworld?"

Persephone laughed and took Iona's arm as she led her through the palace. "Yes. Oh, don't look so scared. He's a sweetheart, really."

"Who's a sweetheart?" Two men entered the hall. One was tall and thin with a stern face, dark hair pulled back in a ponytail and a small, thin goatee. His dark eyes pierced Iona's soul and around his neck was a large key on a chain. The other man was slightly haggard with a blindfold on and a full beard that curled down to his chest. His hair was gray with a few streaks of blond that were too stubborn to change.

"Darling, we have company for supper," Persephone said. "I've told you of Iona?"

"Yes, I have heard of her," Hades said. "Welcome to our

home."

Iona gave him a small smile as she hastily dropped in a curtsy. It was unnerving to know that the God of the Underworld knew about her.

"And, let me introduce you to my brother," said Persephone. "Plutus, God of Wealth." Iona knew of this story. Plutus was the son of Demeter and the demigod, Iasion, and his realm was to distribute riches among humans. However, when he favored the good people, Zeus blinded him so that his gifts would be given without prejudice.

"I am pleased to meet you, Lord Plutus," Iona said.

The blind man smiled. "The same. If I may say, you have a lovely voice, Lady Iona."

Persephone continued to pull Iona into the vast dining room. The long table was filled with foods and drinks befitting a god and goddess. There were only four chairs clustered around one end and Iona felt it was a little lonely. For only six months of the year did Persephone eat in this room. For the other six months, it was just Hades and Plutus.

Hades helped Plutus to his chair and then sat at the head of the table. Iona was about to sit in the chair Persephone indicated was for her when she remembered Lethia's advice.

Do not sit at the table of the King and Queen of the Underworld. To do so would mean you see yourself on par with the gods.

"I, uh, I think I'll sit on the floor," Iona said.

Hades sighed. "I would consider it an honor if you sat at the table. It's remarkably hard to have a conversation with someone who only comes up to my knees."

Iona stammered over how she'd be more comfortable, but Hades would not have it. "I've spent countless eons with people sitting on my floor. Get up and pull up a chair. You have my permission. Whatever you fear, do not worry. I am inviting you to sit at my table and eat my food."

When Iona gave a low "um", Persephone said, "Someone told you to not eat the food, right? That you'd be trapped here?"

"Yes."

"If that were true, then I'd never be allowed to leave. I eat each time I'm here. The food is safe."

Slowly, Iona got up and sat in the chair. It was so strange to be eating with a god. But, if he insisted, she could not say no. That would surely bring down the wrath of Hades. When a plate of food was placed in front of her, she took a small bite, waiting for Hades to jump up and proclaim that she was now and forever will be a denizen of the Underworld. When no one did, Iona relaxed a bit.

"Is this pomegranate," Iona asked, poking the seeds on her plate.

"Yes," said Persephone. "They're my favorite."

Iona looked up, surprised. "I would have thought you'd hate pomegranate."

Persephone laughed. "Oh, no. I'll give you some free advice, Iona. Don't believe everything you're told. I don't hate pomegranate and I love my husband." She patted Hades' hand. He smiled and leaned over to kiss her on the cheek.

"How have you been since you and Persephone parted ways," Plutus asked. "She mentioned you were having some problems with your sisters."

"A lot has happened." Iona sighed, pushing her plate away. "I found out my sisters did betray me. Pan and Zephyrus were right. I went to Philomena first, and she was planning on selling me to Aphrodite. I thought I would embarrass her by telling her that Eros wanted her, but my trick backfired. Both she and Erita locked themselves in an airlock thinking Eros would take them, and ended up dying."

"You poor dear," said Persephone. "I am so sorry."

"After that, I spent a month as a servant in Apollo's temple. He absolved me of their deaths. I was supposed to go to Eros afterward, but I ended up on Level 7 with your mother. I worked as a kitchen servant for a while."

"Since it is winter, I suspect Mother was not so pleasant to be around," Persephone said.

Iona shook her head. "I was a prisoner, and I saw some things that I wish I hadn't. I think that Aphrodite wanting her revenge was the only thing that saved me, ironically enough. Your mother was too busy to just hand me over, and she didn't want to let me leave."

The table was silent for a moment and then Hades said, "What did you see, Lady Iona?"

"There was a woman named Odessa. I'm afraid I only saw

her in her last moments of life. She was pregnant, and from what I overheard and can understand, Demeter wanted the baby to raise. Tomorrow, she's going to present the baby as Kore. Odessa died in childbirth."

Persephone sucked in her breath. "Are you sure about that name? She named the baby Kore?"

"Yes. Phobos and I tried to get the baby out of there, but Ares stopped us. He knew that Phobos was going to try that and made sure the both of us would surrender."

"Phobos? What does he have to do with this?"

"Phobos is the father."

Hades groaned. "Could this get any more tangled? Demeter would plan this for winter to make sure neither of us could be around at the Naming Ceremony. Did you know of Odessa, my love?"

"I knew there was a woman named Odessa, but I thought Mother sent her on a special mission to oversee some farms in Elyusis," Persephone said. "I had no idea she was pregnant."

Iona could feel the weight of unsaid words hanging in the air. She feared she witnessed something not meant for mortals. Would Persephone punish her for this transgression? The feeling of sadness lay over them like a blanket. Hades stroked Persephone's cheek, whispering in her ear.

"I think it's time for you to head back to Olympus," Persephone said. "I'll get you that box."

She left the room, leaving Iona alone with Hades and Plutus. She fidgeted, not sure what to say.

"You said that Demeter is planning on presenting the baby tomorrow," Hades said slowly.

"Yes, Lord Hades."

He tapped the table. "Plutus, do you fancy a trip to Olympus? I'm certain I can find some gems to deliver to Hephaestus or fake an appointment with Apollo to give you an excuse."

"Sounds like fun. I haven't been above ground in a while. I am sure Mother won't mind me meeting my newest sister."

"You also said that Phobos is the father? He's not going to try anything tomorrow, is he? I can't imagine him just allowing someone else to raise his child. Whether or not Phobos has a parental instinct, he guards what is his with zeal."

"He mentioned wanting to stop it," Iona admitted. "This

baby is all he has left of Odessa."

"By the River Acheron, what is Demeter planning?"

"Hades! Language! We have a young lady present," said Plutus.

"We'll worry about Demeter later," said Persephone, walking back into the room. She held a small wooden box in her hands.

Iona stood up and took the box. "Thank you, Lady Persephone. This will help make my life with Eros easier."

"Whatever you do, don't open the box," Persephone cautioned. "Also, you can call me Sephie. All my friends do."

"I will." Iona smiled. "Thank you, Sephie. I won't forget this."

"Your way home is through here." Hades pushed aside a curtain to reveal a private PortMat. He easily activated it and grandly bowed to allow Iona to step into the light.

"Feel free to visit any time." Persephone hugged Iona tightly. "We don't get many visitors down here."

"I promise I will visit when I can," Iona said. "I would love to see you when you are up during the Spring and Summer." With that, she stepped through the light and vanished. Once she was gone, Persephone sighed and sat heavily down in her chair.

"My love, are you all right?"

"She's already picked out my next host," Persephone whispered. "There's a new Kore, and that means there will be a new Persephone. My days are numbered."

Hades wrapped his arms around his lovely wife. "We'll work through this like we always do. We have years until this Kore will be of age, and years before you will go into Stasis sleep to await her. Right now, we must prepare for both the Naming Ceremony and the wedding. I am sure it will mean something to Iona to have us there for her big day."

"It would mean a lot to Iona, but not to... What if she forgets? They all forgot!"

"Maybe this time will be different. She sat at the table. None of the others would dare to do that."

Persephone sighed. "We have it so good. No matter how many hosts we take, I know you'll always love me as I love you. You don't go looking for a new wife each time. You wait for me."

"In that way, I do feel sorry for Eros and Psyche. I always

like them, you know. It's nice to have visitors. Though, can you imagine how miserable it would be to forget me with each new host? Or if I forgot you?"

"It would be torture," Persephone whispered and kissed her husband.

Chapter 40

Iona found herself back on Level 14. It almost felt like home to her. She could see Casta's cabin in the distance and the wooly sheep grazing out in the fields. Winter never touched the godly levels, and the scenery was as cheerful as only eternal Spring could be. Over the bleating of the sheep, Iona could hear the low growling of the golden rams far off in their protected fields. The sound caused her leg to throb.

She found herself turning to walk toward Casta's cabin, but her current mission took precedence. Iona needed to get this box to Aphrodite or her life with Eros would be over. Looking down at the box, Iona realized that her love for Eros was not all physical. In the time before she shot herself with his dart, they spent many nights in each other's arms talking about all manner of topics. That love came before the dart, so what she felt had to be real.

And he loved her. Her scars didn't matter to him. Her wide hips or frizzy hair didn't matter to him. He loved her for who she was, and that was all that mattered. They could now live their lives in the happiness of love.

Looking once more toward Casta's cabin, Iona smiled. After she gave the box to Aphrodite and officially became Eros' wife, she'd return for a visit.

Turning back to the PortMat, Iona frowned. She had no idea how to work this thing. Did she have to be a god for it to activate? Was there a code to keep mortals from mucking with it? Fearful, Iona wondered if she could find Lord Hermes or Pan to help her out.

"No, I came this far on my own," Iona muttered, "and I will finish my journey. I can do this." She gazed at the controls and noticed a small panel. There were forty-three small buttons arranged in rows of seven. Next to each was a number. Could these be the levels? What if she read it wrong and disintegrated herself?

"I wouldn't do that if I were you."

Iona gasped and turned to see Lethia standing behind her. With her was Anteros. While Anteros looked guilty, the predatory look in Lethia's eyes caused a shiver to run up Iona's spine.

"Am I doing this wrong," Iona asked. She was delighted to

see her friends. "Lethia, please help me with this. We can all go and give the box to Aphrodite. I do not know why, but Hades sent me here. Were you two waiting for me?"

"We can't do that, Iona," said Anteros. "I am so sorry."

"Why? Is something wrong?" Iona could see there was something off. Anteros would not meet her gaze and Lethia looked fairly triumphant. "What is going on?"

"Just know that I am so sorry," Anteros said. "I would never hurt you, Iona. You've been my friend. It's just...this has to be done. There is no other way around it."

"What are you talking about?" Iona took a step back, but the PortMat machine prevented her from getting any farther. "What has to be done?"

Lethia took the box and smiled. "You have no idea what you are up against, Iona," she said coldly. "I do. I know all about this. I was once in your place."

"What? What are you talking about?"

Suddenly Anteros lunged forward and grabbed Iona. He kicked her legs out from under her, pulling her to the ground. "This is for your own good, Iona. Believe me, you'll thank me for this someday."

"Keep telling yourself that," Lethia growled. "I never thanked you, and neither will she."

"What is going on? Anteros! Let me go!"

"You think you're going to have some happy life with Eros, don't you," Lethia sneered. "All sunshine and sparkles for the rest of your life. Maybe immortality so that the two of you won't ever grow old?"

"No! I never thought about immortality," protested Iona. "I only want to stay with Eros. That's all."

"It won't be all enjoyment and peace," Lethia warned. She stroked the box lovingly. "We Zyspadaden, we gods, must change our faces every so often. We find a mortal and take that body, gifting them with eternal life for the privilege of being a host. Did you know that? That's why the statues change every so often: to reflect the change in hosts. But we burn up the mortals. Our true form was not meant to be hindered by your pathetic bodies, and we must find new hosts and the cycle starts anew."

"No," Iona whispered. She heard rumors as a child of people

vanishing during ceremonies or devotees being honored and never returning, but it wasn't anything that caused panic. Her mind went back to the old woman in the Temple of Aphrodite while she was visiting Errita. The way the woman gazed at the statue of Eros, and her story of her son being chosen and then returned dead, but she never saw the body. There had been others – other old timers who stared at the statues of gods and goddesses as if their loved ones had returned in the form of rock and stone.

"It's like a switch being thrown, and the gods must re-enact a play. Zeus must always reclaim his throne, Hera always tries at least once to overthrow him, and Poseidon must always fight with Athena for who will name Athens. And Eros will always be forced to re-woo his Psyche."

"What does that mean?"

"I'm Psyche! I was his wife! Once upon a time, Iona Demarchis, I was you," Lethia – Psyche! - declared. "I thought I would be the one to love Eros for the end of time. I thought he loved me. And then I was confronted by the previous Psyche. It's the last step before I was made Psyche. After today, you will be me."

"I don't understand," Iona cried. She struggled against Anteros, but he held her tighter. He kneed her hurt leg, sending pain cycling through her body.

"Think of it as a circle," Anteros said. "When one cycle ends, the next begins. It never truly ends."

"Let me tell you how your life will go, Iona," Psyche spat. "You'll become Eros' wife, and you will be happy. You'll give birth to a daughter who will break your heart. Maybe a few other brats who are not worthy of being named in history, who knows? Then, one day, you'll notice a change in Eros. He'll be distant and not as loving. He'll move away from your touch, start getting irritated with your presence, and spend more time with his brothers. He'll move to another bed chamber and start finding fault with you. And it will hurt you. Your heart will shatter as you can't figure out what you've done. Then, one day, it will happen. He will come home and tell you all about this special devotee who has claimed his interest. He'll train the boy, take him under his wing and shower him with gifts. Then he'll return one day with a new face, a new body. He'll have upgraded to a newer model. And do you know what that means for you?"

"What does it mean," Iona whispered, fearful of the answer.

"He stops loving you. The power of the dart will fade in him, but not in you. The cold shoulder he gives you just before he changes hosts is nothing compared to this. You are no longer the most beautiful woman he's ever seen. He hates you! He calls you his old host's wife, as if that is your name. New face needs a new wife. And it's going to eat you up inside when he comes home, dancing on air and talking about the woman who will replace you. Some pathetic mortal he happens to scratch himself when he sees. He'll be so overcome with his own love formula that *she* is all that matters to him, and you are nothing."

"I'm sorry." Iona felt the hot tears slide down her cheeks. "I'm so sorry."

"That's not the worst part," Psyche continued. "The worst part is when he brings the replacement home. You have to be friends with her! You have to serve her! You have to see her in his bed every night and grow fat with his child!"

"The story does have a happy ending," Anteros protested. "One day, old Psyche and new Psyche meet and trade places. New Psyche can live happily with Eros."

Psyche snorted. "Didn't you hear a word I said, Anteros? It's not happy! She'll be happy for a while, but then he'll do to her what he did to me."

"What happens to old Psyche," Iona asked. "What will become of you?"

"I die," Psyche said. She gave a bitter laugh. "When I leave this host's body and enter yours, this body will die. I have used it up, burned the mortality away. I suppose, in a way, Iona Demarchis of Tiryns will die when you become Psyche. All that will be left of you is me."

"What if I don't want to be Psyche? What if I want to remain Iona?"

Psyche laughed. "You have no choice! Eros needs Psyche. If not you, than it will be another girl. The second you breathe your last, the power of the dart will fade and he'll be free to love another if I am not within you."

Iona struggled to get away, twisting to see Anteros. "That won't happen to me," she declared. "I won't let it turn out like that. I'm going to remain Iona and I will marry Eros. I'll never become someone else just to have him."

"How well I remember those words," Psyche said. "I said them to my predecessor, and she said them to hers. And so on and so forth. The cycle hasn't been broken yet."

"How do you plan on making me Psyche? You said something about hosts?"

Psyche smiled, looking at the box in her hands. "With this. Do you know what the beauty of Persephone really is?"

"No."

"Death. The beauty of the Queen of Hades is the deep sleep of death. When you look at your loved ones before they are buried, that is the beauty of Persephone. So, Iona, you must die first before you can be reborn as a goddess."

Hearing this, Iona screamed and twisted even more in Anteros' grip. He pushed her flat on the floor and straddled her body, forcing her hands down. "Stop struggling, Iona. This will be over shortly and you'll get to be Eros. The more you fight it, the longer it will take!"

"Don't do this, Anteros! Please! I don't want to die! Not like this!"

"This would have been so much easier if you just opened the box like you were supposed to," Psyche snapped. "You have been the most vexing of all my hosts. At every turn, you've done things differently. You were supposed to wander away from the PortMat and open the box. All of this should have happened while you gasped for breath, but no! You couldn't be curious. You had to be different!"

Psyche knelt next to Iona. "Now I know how *she* felt," she whispered, "when she traded places with me. The sheer joy of seeing her replacement die and the sorrow of knowing it meant her own death. I remember what it felt like to close my eyes in one body and open them in another. All those alien memories of lives lived and lost, hundreds of innocent girls who carried the name of Psyche. I was the latest in a long line, and now you will join them. I've forgotten so many of their names, but now I wish I could remember them. I think, at this moment, I always wish that. Whatever became of their bodies?"

"You don't have to do this," Iona pleaded. "You can let me go. I'm not a goddess. I'll die in time. I'm sure he'll love you again."

"That's not how it works. I told you that. You either become Psyche or you die. There is no option three. I've done my job by keeping you alive until this point."

Pysche reached out and traced the scar on Iona's face. "It is a shame. If you hadn't been such a problem, you would have been unscathed. Instead, I guess my next incarnation will have to be less than perfect. Maybe Eros will tire of you faster than the others?"

She opened the box and reached inside. Iona watched horrified as Psyche drew up a handful of dark dirt. As Pysche flung the dirt onto Iona's face, the PortMat flared to life. The dirt coated Iona's face and she started to cough. It was suddenly harder to breathe, and then it was impossible. Black dots danced before her eyes as she struggled to get air into her lungs. Her back arched as she clawed the ground, unaware that Anteros had gotten off her. Her last vision was of four people standing over her; Psyche, Anteros, Hades and Persephone.

Psyche waited until Iona became still before closing the box. She didn't bother to look at her audience. She knew what she'd see in Anteros' eyes; she's seen it several times before when he'd help her take care of her new host's body. The sadness and guilt always hurt because it was for *her* and not Psyche.

"I was not expecting you two to show up," Psyche said, finally looking at Hades and Persephone. "A bit early? The wedding isn't for another couple of days. I still need to transfer myself."

"Well, I was planning on sending Plutus to see about this Naming Ceremony Demeter is having, but imagine my surprise when I got a message from Zeus to come on up early. I must have forgotten to reset my PortMat," Hades said. He looked down at Iona and nudged her with the toe of his boot. "She needs to get to a Transference Pod."

"I have one ready," Anteros said. He looked at Psyche for the first time since they started this. "Any last requests?"

"Yes. Bury this body under her birth name. No one will remember Lethia of Crete, but she deserves a real funeral. There is no one left to mourn her."

With that, Psyche closed her eyes as she felt herself prepare to move between bodies. There was the pain of her host's body dying and then darkness.

Chapter 41

Eros pushed open the doors to the Transference Chamber when they didn't open fast enough, panting with the effort. Sweat glistened on his body as he rushed into the room, his eyes fastened on the pod at the far end. Next to the pod stood Zeus wearing a lab coat and checking facts on a clipboard.

"How is she," he asked. "Will she be alright?"

"She'll be fine," Zeus said, checking the readings. "So far, everything is working. She was brought up in time."

Eros placed his hands on the glass of the pod. In the pod next to it there was another body. Just as beautiful with long dark hair. As the first occupant made a full-body jerking motion, the monitors hooked up to the second pod registered a slowing heartbeat. The more life signs in the first pod registered, the more they stopped in the second. Eros watched as Psyche fought her way back to life.

"How long until we can get her out of there," Eros asked. Being away from his love was torture. He had been so sure she'd be by his side when she returned from her little trip to the Underworld. Instead, he was told that she was in the Transference Chamber, and would be there for a few days. She missed the Naming Ceremony for Demeter's daughter Kore, and the hoopla over Demeter screaming at Hades. She missed the fight between Ares and Phobos, who tried to take baby Kore. Eros never thought his brother would be in league with Hades. Olympus would be talking about that match for ages to come. He couldn't wait to tell his wife about it.

Zeus shrugged. "It depends on her. Normally they wake up by now, but she's been twitching a bit and not opening her eyes." At the sudden loud and constant beep coming from the second pod, Zeus sighed. He turned the pod off. "Well, looks like it's done. If she doesn't wake up soon, we'll have to start all over again."

"It will work," Eros whispered. It had to. Psyche's old host was dead. That meant that this woman was all he had left. He knew in his heart that it would work. Every sign pointed in that direction. He had wounded himself with his own dart, his mother hated her, she completed the three tasks and traveled to see Hades. Everything that was ordained for the host of Psyche, she completed. She would be his wife.

The chamber radiated with a bright golden glow. All around the host lit up as Psyche took on her natural form to take over her new host. Eros' breath caught in his throat as he could behold his people's true form just over the flesh-and-blood body they often occupied. The Zyspadaden couldn't survive without a host body, and humans were most compatible with their needs.

The energy filled Psyche's body, causing her to twitch more. She jerked violently, her hands reaching up to claw at the oxygen mask over her face. Zeus cursed and quickly pushed the button to drain the pod before the mask could be ripped off. Psyche opened her eyes as she pulled the mask off, gasping for real air. The pod opened with a hiss and Psyche tumbled out on to the floor, wet and weak. Eros watched entranced as his wife learned how to live again. She looked up at him through wet strands of red hair.

Though she still looked like Iona, Eros knew she was more. Same body, but different soul. He never knew Iona had been missing anything, she was so perfect in his eyes. But now, filled with the essence of Psyche – becoming Psyche – she was so much more. He could see what was missing now, the spark that drew him closer to his wife. Now, she was beyond perfect.

"How do you feel," he asked, helping her up.

"Tired and weak," she said. She clung to him, getting his clothes wet from the stasis fluid. He didn't care. He was just happy to be holding her again.

"Are you up for a wedding, my darling Psyche?"

Psyche smiled, and it looked so beautiful despite her host's scared face. The extra lift to her lip was simply charming. "I thought you'd never ask," she said. "Give me a few minutes to get my bearings, and I will marry you."

Zeus clapped his hands. "Wonderful! I'll send someone to get you a pair of clothes, Psyche. Eros, my boy, we must announce this great news at once. All of Olympus must know! You will marry in style!"

Eros kissed Psyche before letting her go. A small envoy of servants entered the room, their arms filled with dresses and flowers and jewels. Eros hurried to the throne room of Olympus as Zeus called for all the gods to assemble. He could see many friendly faces, and a few he wished didn't show up for his big day.

"Father, how nice of you to make it," Eros said. He eyed the dark clad figure of Ares as the God of War stood with Enyo, Phobos, and Deimos.

"When Zeus calls, we all answer," Ares said, folding his beefy arms.

"My friends and family," Zeus announced, "I am pleased that today there will be a wedding! Just this moment, a new Psyche has emerged and she will wed Eros, God of Love."

"She is not a goddess," Aphrodite interrupted. "Iona of Tiryns is a mortal and cannot marry a god. I won't allow it! What happened to the old Psyche? She was just fine to be married to my son. Or what about Despoina? She's a goddess! I would approve of her!"

"Iona Demarchis of Tiryns is no more. She is now Psyche, Goddess of the Mind. I have witness the transference with my own eyes. Long live Psyche!"

With that, Zeus flung his arms wide with dramatic flourish and the doors to the throne room opened. The Graces entered first, throwing lilies on the ground and dancing across the floor in a twirl of multi-colored silks. Next came in Zephyrus and Anteros. Between them was a veiled figure, dressed in pale lilac and draped with strands of silver and amethyst. Every movement caused the dress and veil to shimmer under the lights. Overhead, cheerful Cupids and doves flew, some holding sheer scarves so their looping patterns would hide and then reveal the bride.

Psyche stopped once she was standing in front of Eros. He took off her veil and kissed her soft lips. She moaned low, melting in his arms. Zeus cleared his throat and the couple approached him to start the wedding ceremony.

"Are there any who object to the marriage of Eros and Psyche," Zeus asked as the ceremony drew to a close. Eros turned to look around the room. No one dared to object, not even Aphrodite. The bride was a goddess now, no longer the mortal woman she objected.

Eros felt as it time stopped as he gazed into the eyes of his wife. He barely heard Zeus proclaim them married and give his blessings on their union. The only thing he was aware of was when Zeus told him he could kiss Psyche to seal the deal.

The room exploded in cheers as he pulled Psyche closer and

kissed her deeply. His tongue danced with hers in a promise of how his body would meet hers that night. The tiny moan of satisfaction that issued from her was all the encouragement he needed.

"I present to you, Eros, God of Love, and Psyche, Goddess of the Mind," Zeus boomed. Eros turned toward the room, raising his and Psyche's hands. At last, he was with the woman he loved and nothing would ever change that. She would be the one to stay with him for all time.

Aphrodite walked up to Psyche, her back stiff and her eyes cold. She was the picture of beautiful anger, a woman forced to admit she was wrong. "I guess this means a truce," Aphrodite said stiffly.

"At least until the next time," Psyche said.

"The next time, I won't make it so easy on your little chosen host," Aphrodite swore. "No more little games where she can wiggle out of it. I'll just kill her."

"Not my problem. Someone will survive to be my host. No matter how much you try, someone will always get through. It's fate. There will always be a Psyche for Eros."

With icy smiles and the promise of triumph the next they met, the two shook hands on their temporary peace. All around them, the gods and goddesses partied, unaware of the drama unfolding and would be played out again in the not-so-distant future.

Aphrodite walked off and Psyche smiled. She won this round. With a laugh, Psyche turned to the other gods and goddesses, mingling with her own. It was a good life.

Epilogue

Hedyla Demarchis of Tiryns knelt by the graves of her three daughters. Two had committed suicide the previous year by jumping out of an airlock. Her third daughter simply vanished. Though a stranger came to the house saying Iona promised to return, the next news they received was that Iona died, but there was never a body. Hedyla could believe her last daughter came to some foul play. All of the station had been looking for her on behalf of Aphrodite. Then, just before she got the news of her daughter's passing, the announcements and warrants stopped. Hedyla knew in her heart that Aphrodite found Iona.

"Old woman, are you done yet?" The gatekeeper tapped Hedyla on her shoulder. "I want to get going. I heard the Temple of Aphrodite was going to unveil a new statue of Eros and Psyche today."

Hedyla struggled to get up. The year had not been kind to her. Not just her daughters were gone, but her husband's health was failing and her only living son-in-law remarried and moved to another level. She felt so much older than she was. She finally stood, the gatekeeper never once offering to help, and hobbled toward the exit.

"Another new statue," she asked. "Didn't they just update the Eros statues a few years ago? If that long?"

The gatekeeper shrugged. "I don't know and I don't care. My sister is a devotee at the temple, so I better be there. The last time I missed something like this, she didn't talk to me for a month."

"Mind if I walk with you," Hedyla asked. "My youngest daughter used to love to go to the Temple of Aphrodite. She would make daily trips."

"Is she a devotee?"

"Hardly. They once called her Aphrodite-in-the-flesh. My Iona was beautiful, but cursed. She never got married. Her sisters died horrible deaths last year. I guess my whole family was cursed."

The gatekeeper looked at her and then back at the graves she had been visiting. "Iona Demarchis?" He scratched his chin. "I remember that. Everyone was looking for her. The last time she was spotted was working at the Temple of Delphi. Maybe she became an oracle?"

Hedyla shook her head. "If she was, she would have contacted me by now. She never showed up for her sisters' funerals. Or her brother-in-law's wedding. I don't know what to think."

They walked to the temple, Hedyla's heart heavy with unanswered questions. She only came because it was so dear to Iona. She could almost hear her daughter's laughter in the walls and see her, just briefly, dancing between the columns. She was sure Iona never did that in life, but it was just the dreams of an old woman.

"Greetings, faithful followers." A priestess of Aphrodite spoke to the crowd. She moved to stand by a covered statue. "As you know, today is a special day. Today, we will reveal the new statues dedicated to the most favored son of our great goddess and his humble wife. The old statues will be taken down and destroyed. We have been blessed to receive the first of the new restorations."

With that, she took off the covering. Everyone gasped as they looked at the beauty of the marble statues. Even in cold stone, the warmth and love of the two deities could be seen. Soon, the murmurings began as everyone got a good look at them.

"How extraordinary. I don't think I've ever seen a goddess statue less than perfect," one man muttered.

"I agree," said a woman. "I think the scars on her face only enhance her beauty."

Hedyla covered her mouth and felt the tears flow down her cheeks. All around her, people talked about the statues as if they had a connection to them, as if they knew what it meant. The gatekeeper said how moving an experience this was, but that wasn't why Hedyla was crying. She finally had an answer to her prayers.

In cold, unmovable stone, her daughter's likeness smiled warmly at the handsome youth by her side. Scars that Hedyla had never seen marred her face, causing her smile to quirk up slightly on one side. Trapped forever in love, it was the best comfort an old mother could ever wish for.

Character Pronunciation

All the character descriptions given are for the traditional Ancient Greek myths, unless they are an original character.

Amor – Ah/More
Son of Penia, this is the name of Eros' last host and the name he uses while wooing Iona.

Aneriams/Levanti – Ann/Ear/E/Ams // Lee/Van/Tea
Little blue ant-like creatures that can be found around real flowers, their origins are unknown and possibly have been among the first aboard the Space Station.

Anteros – Ann/Tear/Os
Son of Aphrodite and Ares, God of Requited Love but he also is the avenger of those scorned by love, he has butterfly wings, in one myth, Eros refused to grow up until Anteros was born so they could be friends forever, part of the Erotos (Eros, Anteros, Himeros, and Pothos).

Aphrodite – Ah/Froh/Die/Tea
Daughter of Zeus and Dione (though some sources say she is the product of a disemboweled Uranus), Goddess of Love, Beauty, Pleasure, and Procreation, wife of Hephaestus but a lover of Ares, Poseidon, Hermes, and bunch of others, mother of many children, among them are Eros, Phobos, Deimos, Pothos, Anteros, Himeros, and the Graces.

Apollo – Ah/Paul/Oh
Son of Leto and Zeus, twin brother of Artemis (not appearing in this book), God of the Sun, Light, Music, Archery, Medicine, Prophecy, and Knowledge.

Ares – Air/eees
Son of Zeus and Hera, God of War (though the more blood lust part of it), lover of Aphrodite and father of Phobos and Deimos, and the Erotos (Eros and Anteros).

Deimos – Dee/Mohs
Son of Ares and Aphrodite, God of Dread and Terror, twin brother of Phobos.

Demeter – Deh/ME/Ter
Daughter of Cronus and Rhea, one myth states she started hating Hades while in the stomach of her father because he, as the eldest, did not save them, Goddess of Agriculture, Fertility, and Harvest, mother of Persephone, Despoina, Arion, and Plutus.

Despoina – Dez/Poy/Nah
Daughter of Demeter and Poseidon, known as "Mistress of the Horses", twin sister of Arion (a talking horse), also known as another name for Persephone according to some of the Mysteries (secret rituals) surrounding Demeter.

Eros – Ear/Os
Son of Aphrodite and Ares (though some myths have him much older and an original God of Love before being replaced by Aphrodite), God of Sexual Desire, Attraction, and Love, best known today as Cupid, husband of Psyche, part of the Erotos (Eros, Anteros, Himeros, and Pothos), father of Hedone.

Errita – Er/Ee/Tah
Middle daughter of Hedyla and Metasis Demarchis of Tyrins, married to Theron, a very successful weaver, she is jealous of anyone's success and wants only to "crawl out of the shadows" of her sisters.

Eileithyia – Eel/E/Thigh/Ya
Daughter of Zeus and Hera, Goddess of Childbirth, she shares this with Hera.

Hades – Hay/Dees
Eldest son of Cronus and Rhea, brother to Zeus, Demeter, Poseidon, Hera, and Hestia, God of the Dead and Underworld, sometimes mixed in with Plutus, God of Wealth (Plutus and Hades became Pluto in Roman mythology), because of this, he is technically also a fertility god, husband of Persephone.

Hedyla – Hed/eh/La
Parentage unknown, wife of Metasis Demarchis, mother of Philomena, Errita, and Iona, she once worked in a temple of Hera before meeting her husband.

Hepheastus – HE/Fess/Tus
Son of Zeus and Hera (though, some sources say Hera alone), brother of Ares, God of Fire, Metalworking, Forges, and Scuptures, husband of Aphrodite, known as the only ugly god among the beautifully perfect immortals.

Hermes – Her/Mees
Son of Zeus and Maia (one of the Pleiades), God of Trade, Thieves, Travelers, Sports/Athletes, and Crossroads, father of Pan, known to be a trickster god.

Hyacinths – HI/ah/Sinths
Parentage unknown, some myths have him as a prince, lover of Zypherus the West Wind but also beloved by Apollo, while he was playing with a disc with Apollo, Zyphrus grew jealous and caused the disc to accidently kill Hyacinths, from his name we get the flower hyacinth/iris.

Iona Demarchis –
Eye/Own/Ah Dee/March/Is
Youngest daughter of Hedyla and Metasis Demarchis of Tyrins, betrothed to Kelmis before he died, mistaken as Aphrodite. She earns the ire of Aphrodite but becomes the wife of Eros. Mother of Hedone and other children. Iona is probably the second ugliest god due to some scars and near-fatal mauling's that happened while she was still a mortal.

Kelmis – Kale/Miss

Parentage unknown, he was the business partner of Metasis Demarchis and betrothed to his youngest daughter, Iona. Before Iona reached marriageable age, Kelmis died of a heart attack.

Kore – KOh/Ray
Daughter of Demeter and Zeus, another name for Persephone, her name means "Maiden" and is often used to refer to her pre-Hades.

Lethia – Leh/The/Ah
The name Psyche uses while working for Iona, it's the name of her last host.

Melinoe – Mel/In/Oh/A
Daughter of Persephone (father rumored to either be Zeus or Hades), Goddess of Ghosts, Night, and Madness.

Metasis – Met/ah/Sis
Parentage unknown, husband of Hedyla, father of Philomena, Errita, and Iona, he has a very prosperous wool-dying business in Tyrins, his partner and friend, Kelmis, was betrothed to his youngest daughter, Iona, but Kelmis died before they could be married.

Odessa – Oh/Day/Sah

Parentage unkown, a devotee of Demeter, she is beloved by Phobos. Odessa becomes pregnant and is kidnapped by Demeter. She dies in childbirth and Demeter raises her daughter as Kore.

Pan – Pahn
Son of Hermes (many different mothers depending on the myth, including Aphrodite, Driope, and Hecate), God of the Wild, Shepherds, Flocks, and some association with Sexuality, from his name we get Panic.

Persephone –
Per/Sef/Phone/A
Daughter of Zeus and Demeter, wife of Hades, Goddess of the New Spring/Vegetation and Queen of the Underworld, if one wants a favor of Hades, they often sent prayers through Persephone to sweeten up her husband, mother of Melinoe (father might be Hades or Zeus).

Philomena –
Fill/Oh/Mean/Ah
Eldest daughter of Hedyla and Metasis Demarchis, sister of Errita and Iona, wife of Zotikos, she is a singer and performer. A very vain and envious girl, she grew up expecting the best and not wanting to share with her sisters.

Phobos – Foh/Bohs
Son of Aphrodite and Ares, God of Fear, twin brother of Deimos, while Deimos isn't mentioned in mythology, Phobos is mentioned briefly in *Seven Against Thebes* by Aeschylus.

Psyche – Syk/Key
A human princess who was too beautiful and angered Aphrodite, she eventually becomes the Goddess of the Soul/Mind, this story is the basic premise of famous fairy tales like *Beauty and the Beast*, mother of Hedone.

Theron – They/Ron
Parentage unkown, rumored to be the son of Apollo, a star athlete, married to Errita. After his wife's death, he remarries and moves to Eleusis, a level that is very devoted to Demeter. He becomes a farmer and leaves his athletic stardom behind.

Zeus – Zoos
Youngest child of Cronus and Rhea, King of the Gods, God of the Skies,

Thunder/Lightning, Hospitality, Honor and Order, well-known for his playboy ways, has many children with many women, notably: Persephone (Demeter), Apollo and Artemis (Leto), Hermes (Maia), Athena (Metis), Dionysus (Semele), and Ares, Eileithyia, Hebe and Hephaestus (Hera).

Zotikos Arcius – Zoh/The/Kos Are/Key/Us Parentage unknown, husband of Philomena, he is murdered when Philomena believes a god wants her for a wife.

Zyphyrus – ZI/Fir/Us Parantage unknown, one of the four major winds (Boreaus/North, Notus/South, Zephyrus/West, and Eurus/East), lover of Hyacinths (and accidently killed him), some myths have him as the lover/husband of serveral women, including Iris, Goddess of the Rainbow, and Chloris, Goddess of Flowers.

About the Author

S. L. Wideman is a woman born to write. Her first venture into the wonderful world of the written word was a masterpiece penned in crayon. Following her love of writing, S. L. Wideman used to create short plays for her day camp and one play for the neighborhood kids to perform. There may or may not still be video evidence somewhere. It wasn't until she discovered Nano Wrimo in 2009 did she manage to really push for her dreams of being a writer.

Currently, she is a full-time student at NOVA in Springfield, VA, studying Health Information Management and Coding. She lives in Stafford, VA and is close to her father and sister.

Upcoming Books

Coming in 2015
<u>Verucca Victorious</u>

When she woke up in a strange place with a new name, it wasn't anything new. Verucca was a character. She existed only to fulfill the will of the Author and further a Story. But this time was different. Waking, she finds that she is not the ugly stepmother, evil witch, or abusive parent. She's successful with a handsome fiancé. As she tries to figure out what the Story could be, she sees only a Happily Ever After in her future. She's a bit of a hard taskmaster, so maybe it's a Christmas Carol kind of story, where she learns her lesson at the end. After all, she does have her very own Bob Crotchet. Or, because she's not the most beautiful woman in the world, maybe it's a Make Over story, where her fiancé will realize he loved her all along. Shallow, but she'll take it.

Then, things start to go wrong. Verucca realizes she is not the heroine, that this is not her Happily Ever After. She's supposed to just sit back and let the Author take control and tell the Story. She's supposed to allow herself to be regulated to the ugly woman and let the real – and beautiful – heroine shine.

Not this time! Verucca wants her Happily Ever After, and she's willing to fight the will of the Author to get it!

Coming in 2016
<u>Kore, Space Station *Olympus* novel, book 2</u>

Eighteen years have passed since the birth of Kore, daughter of Demeter. She's ready to take her rightful place as Goddess of the New Spring. At her coming out party, she meets the most fascinating man, one who captures her heart with one glance of his sad, dark eyes. He gifts her with a small necklace with a ruby pomegranate charm. This man is Hades, Lord of the Underworld. A man she was raised to fear.

For eighteen years, Hades waited for Kore to come to age. Persephone has gone into a Stasis Pod, waiting for her next host. He knows his time is limited to convince Kore to become the next Persephone. Demeter tries to thwart him at every step, determined to stop the natural order of things, to bring eternal Summer to Space Station Olympus. Without a wife, Hades knows he'll live in eternal torment until the next Kore is picked.

Joined by an unlikely group of allies, Hades woos Kore away from the safety of her mother and into the depths of the Underworld. When Demeter finds out, she makes the entire Station suffer in grief with her. Can Hades convince Kore to be his wife before all life on Space Station Olympus dies?